A Girl with a Bad Reputation

DAVE GIOIA

ISBN 979-8-9929327-1-3 (softcover)
ISBN 979-8-9929327-0-6 (ebook)
Library of Congress Control Number: 2024906352

Printed in the United States of America.

DEDICATION

To a girl I knew in the Sixties and every girl who has one

CONTENTS

CHAPTER 1

Megan

Colleen and Megan sit side by side on the top step of the staircase, listening to the boisterous crowd of Colleen's parents' friends in the living room. This is the first of her parents' famous "Jim and Mary Hanrahan cocktail parties" that Megan has experienced, and Colleen can see that she's impressed. Colleen knows Megan's parents and has been to her house many times and she knows that nothing like this has ever happened or will ever happen there.

She glances at Megan and sees her staring wide-eyed, with her lips slightly parted and scratching her knee absent-mindedly, at the three people who are standing in the entrance to the crowded living room, off the vestibule by the front door, which is all that can be seen of the party from where they're sitting. Colleen recognizes two of them from past parties, a married couple—he's a lawyer, like her parents, and she's a woman who obviously loves spending his money, on her hair and clothes and jewelry—but not the man they're talking with. Like all the guests, they have drinks in their hands and are talking loudly and gesturing animatedly. Like most of the guests, the couple is smoking, puffing away when it's their turn to listen.

"They sure make a lot of noise," Megan says, sounding awe-struck.

"Yeah," Colleen says, "They're drunk. My parents' parties are always like this."

Although she can't see him, Colleen can hear her father's voice, now and then rising above the others; a brash, bellowing, bullying voice that, when you hear it, seems to match perfectly his slightly scowling expression and ruddy cheeks and height and broad shoulders and chest; a voice that commands attention. She's seen him in action in court, defending high profile local clients who've run afoul of the law, which is his specialty, and she's seen the effect that voice can have on the members of a jury. She knows how it feels to have that voice used as a blunt instrument on her when she runs afoul of him, especially when he has a few drinks in him, and she understands why he rarely loses in court.

As usual, when she hears her father's voice above the others, she hears her mother's voice rising to meet his and coax it back down in that gently chiding, cajoling, soothing tone of voice she uses, which works well when they're in public, but not always so well at home, when other people aren't around.

Her mother is a good lawyer too. Her specialty is family law and her voice and temperament and stature are every bit as important to her success as her father's are to his. Her mother's a tall, slender attractive blonde, a few inches shorter than Colleen's father, and her default facial expression is one of sereneness, her pale blue eyes seeming fixed on the middle distance and her mouth slightly upturned at the corners in what looks like an understanding smile. Her mother has the ability to remain calm and composed even in the most potentially explosive situations at home, which happen often when her father is in his cups and is probably why he married her and respects her, despite the horrible way he treats her sometimes. Her mother acts as a counterweight to her father's top-heavy personality. She's his gyroscope, keeping him balanced and upright and Colleen wonders sometimes what would happen to her father if her mother ever left him, which she threatens to do sometimes when they argue. Her father is barely in control of his personal life as it is and the idea of what he would be like without her mother around is scary to contemplate.

"C'mon," Colleen says, getting up and heading down the hall toward her bedroom.

She and Megan sit on the bed crossed-legged, facing each other, and kill time waiting for Megan's mother to arrive to pick her up, paging through the latest issues of *Seventeen* and *Teen* and listening to Leslie Gore's album *I'll Cry If I Want To.* Everyone seems to be wild about the Beatles and The Rolling Stones and The Beach Boys, but Leslie Gore is Colleen's favorite artist. There are a lot of songs about teenage angst on the radio—that's pretty much what rock 'n roll is all about, isn't it?—but they strike Colleen as pandering. Leslie's songs ring true to her. Leslie seems to be singing from personal experience and there's something about her voice, hard-edged, yet sensitive and vulnerable, that Colleen relates to and identifies with.

She was surprised to read that Leslie was only sixteen when she recorded this album, and also that her real name is Leslie Sue Goldstein and that her father is a wealthy manufacturer of children's clothes and swimwear. Colleen assumed that with a name like Gore and that voice of hers, Leslie was Irish and that her father was a drinker, just like her father. Anyway, Leslie sounds as if she's already had a hard life and when Colleen sees her on TV shows like *Hullabaloo,* she seems so sincere, even though she's lip-syncing the lyrics, and her hurt expression looks genuine. Colleen would like to meet Leslie in person someday and has the feeling they'd have a lot to talk about. She knows Megan doesn't share her appreciation of Leslie and sees her roll her eyes when Leslie sings the chorus of "It's My Party" again.

"God," Megan says, "she's such a whiner."

"Wanna smoke?" Colleen asks.

Megan looks up and glances nervously at the closed bedroom door. "What if your folks catch us?"

"They won't."

"What if they smell the smoke?"

Colleen smirks. "Are you kidding? The house is filled with smoke. Anyway, we'll blow it out the window." She climbs off the bed, opens the closet door and retrieves the pack of cigarettes and lighter she keeps hidden in a sock stuffed into the toe of a pair of sneakers. She takes out two cigarettes, puts the pack back, walks to the window and raises it. Megan joins her and Colleen hands her a cigarette, lights it, then her own, takes a deep drag and blows smoke rings, one after another, like the Camel billboard in Times Square and almost as well. She watches them float out into the darkness and disappear.

"Wow!" Megan says, "You're good!"

She is, and not just at blowing smoke rings, which is why she has a bad reputation at fourteen. She knows what boys want and is willing to give it to them—on her own terms. She enjoys the feeling of power over them giving them what they want gives her. She prefers to think of the act of performing oral sex as "fellatio" and not the crass slang terms people use for it, like "giving a blowjob" or "head" or "cocksucking." She's read about it and knows it's a practice that dates back thousands of years in many cultures and probably has been around ever since there have been boys and girls and men and women.

Boys are so stupid—clueless! They act so smug when she's giving them what they want, as if they've conquered her somehow, when really, it's she who's conquered them. She knows they consider her a slut and talk trash about her and act with their friends as if they wouldn't be caught dead with her, but they call her up and ask her out and she knows the only reason they're calling is because they've heard the rumors and hope they're true. They're not at all interested in pleasing her, although they do like fondling her breasts, which are big for her age, so big they give her backaches—her mother has suggested breast reduction surgery when she's a few years older—and they do finger her when she places their hand between her legs, but no one's gone down on her yet, which is what she wants. She won't ask them to do it. She's waiting to see who will, without having to be asked. Based on her experience with boys so far, she's resigned to a long wait.

"Anya says there's this new kid, Henry, who hangs out with her brother and Ronnie," Megan says. "His dad's in the Army and his family's from the Bronx. She says he's cute and plays the guitar."

"Yeah?" Colleen says. About Henry playing the guitar, she wants to say who doesn't? Ever since the Beatles arrived on the scene, it seems every boy does. She hasn't gotten together with Anya in a while. It's not that New Windsor is all that far away. It's just that their schedules seem to conflict lately. She'll have to give her a call.

"He's a freshman at Saint Pat's. His family was living in Virginia and moved here recently and he transferred."

Colleen eyes the leaves of the big elms lining the sidewalk. Silhouetted as they are by the light from the streetlights, the leaves look like swirling schools of small black fish, frozen in place. She rankles at the mention of Saint Patrick's, the all-boys Catholic high school. The school admits only about a hundred and twenty boys, thirty per class and there are only four classes, freshman through senior. While the vast majority of kids in the city and surrounding area attend Newburgh Free Academy, Saint Pat's is where the sons of the elite, the well-to-do business owners and doctors and lawyers in town go, and they don't necessarily have to be Catholic to attend, although it's preferred.

Her parents have been pressuring her to attend Mount Saint Mary Academy next year, the all-girls Catholic high school. She's done a pretty good job so far of thwarting that idea. She knows kids who attend Saint Pat's and the Mount and they all have this "ivory tower" air of superiority about them that rubs her the wrong way. The idea of being cooped up with that crowd every day seems unbearable and the only way she'll go is kicking and screaming. She does have a reluctant ally in her mother, who knows Colleen will share their little secret with her father if it comes to that. She knocks off the lit end of her cigarette, balls up the butt and flicks it out in a high arc. "Want another?"

"Sure," Megan says.

Colleen goes to the closet and gets two more cigarettes. She leans on the windowsill next to Megan, hands her one and lights them both. She draws on her cigarette and inhales the smoke deeply.

It's not the fault of the kids that attend Saint Pat's and the Mount that they act the way they do. It's their parents' fault. They're the ones who taught their kids to act that way. And it's not just *their* parents who've made a complete mess of the city.

She's read the books her father has about the history of Newburgh and it's a long, rich and distinguished one.

Henry Hudson stopped here on his exploration of the river and thought it would be a good place to settle, which German Lutherans first did in the early Eighteenth Century and then were joined by English and Scots.

Newburgh was, for a time, the headquarters of the Continental Army during the American Revolution, which is why Washington's headquarters appears on the city's seal. There was a movement at the time to make Washington king and he received the famous "Newburgh letter" here, urging him to accept the proposal and, the story goes, his rebuke was so vigorous that in honor of his refusal, what had been called King's Highway was renamed Liberty Street, which is now in steady decline along with the entire waterfront area of the city.

Given Newburgh's location on the Hudson River, midway between New York City and Albany, it became a transportation hub and an industrial center in the Nineteenth century and the city grew and business boomed. Everything from felt hats and baking powder and soap to steam boilers and automobiles was manufactured here.

The city was home to the first Edison power plant and was the first American city to be electrified. Newburgh played an important role in the development of television. RCA chose to test market televisions here. Six hundred sets were sold and the people who bought them were among the first to enjoy the new medium.

This place had everything going for it, Colleen thinks, as she blows a line of smoke rings and watches them drift out, looking like ghostly zeros. The stupid white racists who live here managed to fuck it up.

She remembers what it was like when she was a kid, shopping with her parents on Water Street at Schoonmaker's Department Store at Christmastime. The streetlights were decorated with holly wreathes and red ribbon and the buildings were ablaze with lights. The scene was amazing, marvelous, magical, like being on a movie set, and the place was filled with families, all white, doing their holiday shopping.

Then they built the Newburgh-Beacon bridge across the Hudson and the New York State Thruway to the west, both bypassing the city, and commercial river traffic was replaced by hauling goods by truck. Businesses began relocating their manufacturing operations down South, where labor costs were lower and, in return, poor Blacks from down South began arriving in Newburgh. She's heard the stories about how these people were told that if they wanted to collect their welfare checks, they'd have to get on a bus that would take them up North. She's not sure if the stories are true but, in the end, it doesn't really matter. The poor Blacks came and the White flight to the suburbs began, and the city went into steep decline.

Looking out the window of their big house on the hill on Townsend Avenue, at the elm-lined street and the big houses across it, you'd never know that the city of old is gone, that only remnants of it now remain and that the complexion of its citizens is changing and with it its culture. They seem a dark mysterious people to her, and she knows her parents consider them marauders at the gate. Her parents seem content for the time being, living in this White upper middle-class enclave, but she has the feeling that it's only a matter of time before that changes too. For her part, she doesn't want to live walled off, which is part of the reason why she doesn't want to attend Mount Saint Mary's. It might be a changing city but it's her city and she wants to understand who these new people are.

"Colleen," she hears her mother say from the bedroom doorway. She flicks her cigarette away and turns to face her. She sees that serene expression on her mother's face, but she can tell by the look in her eyes that she's irritated about catching her smoking and by the sound of her mother's voice that she's tipsy.

"You know you're not supposed to be smoking in the house," her mother says.

"Yeah, well, everybody else is," Colleen says and sees her mother turn her gaze toward Megan and raise her eyebrows slightly. Colleen knows her parents consider Megan's family beneath them. Her mother probably didn't even invite Megan's mom in and has her waiting on the front porch.

"Your mother's here to pick you up, Megan."

"Okay, Missus Hanrahan, I'll be right there."

Colleen's mother gives Colleen a final disapproving look and turns and leaves, leaving the door ajar. Megan picks up her bag and stuffs her math textbook into it and looks worriedly at Colleen.

"Are you in trouble?" Megan asks.

Colleen smirks and shakes her head. "She won't remember in the morning."

"See ya Monday," Megan says, "and thanks for the help."

"Yeah."

* * *

Colleen lies in bed, listening to the murmur of voices, growing thinner as people leave, and the sound of people walking down the porch steps and the front path, still chatting and laughing and calling out their good-byes, to car doors shutting and car engines starting and cars driving away. It's all so familiar to her.

She thinks about having spent her Saturday evening helping Megan prepare for Monday's math test. She could have gone out on a date instead but chose not to because Megan's her friend and she wants to help her try to better herself. Her mother's condescending expression when she looked at Megan lingers in her mind. Who is her mother to think she's better than Megan and her family? Her mother is Boston Irish and comes from a working-class family in Southie! All right, so she went to college and law school and became an attorney but that doesn't make her better than anyone.

Her father's wanting her to attend the Mount is part of his plan to have her follow in his footsteps into the law. He thinks she'll receive a better education there than at NFA and have a better chance of being accepted at better colleges and universities. Maybe, maybe not, but she's an honors student at North Junior and getting what she considers a first-rate education and has every reason to believe the same will be true at NFA. The irony is that her father attended NFA and he's done just fine, thank you. Based on the conversations she's had with friends and acquaintances attending the Mount, there doesn't seem to be any real advantage to going there, unless you consider being segregated from boys and having to wear a uniform and study religion and be brow-beaten by Dominican Sisters an advantage.

At last, the only sounds she hears coming from downstairs are her parents' voices as they clean up and the loud clink of bottles, lots of them, being tossed in the trash. She tries to imagine herself elsewhere, being lulled to sleep by more pleasant sounds; on the Coast of New England, listening to the sound of the waves breaking against the shore and a fog horn in the distance; in the farmland of the Midwest, listening to the mournful sound of a train's whistle as it rumbles by in the night; high atop New York City, in a big comfy bed in a nice hotel room, listening to the hum and honking of traffic far below. How nice it would be to be lulled to sleep by sounds like those.

As it is, the sound she's most accustomed to hearing as she falls asleep each night is her father's footsteps as he emerges from his office at the end of the hall and walks past her bedroom, down the stairs and into the kitchen, the clink of another empty whisky bottle being tossed in the trash, the slam of the door of the always well-stocked cabinet where he keeps his liquor supply. She follows his footsteps back to his office and pictures him there, pouring himself another drink, putting the bottle down within easy reach, picking up the glass and taking a long sip of booze before carrying on with whatever the hell he's doing.

She can't even stand the smell of the stuff. She took a sip from her father's glass once, at his urging, at one of their cocktail parties. She forced it down and it made her retch, much to everyone's amusement. Did he dislike it as much when he was a kid? Probably. Her grandfather is a drinker and her Uncle Mick is too, so it must run in the family. Will she acquire a taste for booze? She doesn't know. She hopes not, anyway, at least not the way they did, although she has the feeling that her mother wasn't born to drink the way her father was, that she learned to, to keep pace with him and win him. Some prize he turned out to be.

It doesn't matter. In the end it's all the same. Her parents are so alike when they're drunk. The ugly aspects of their personalities come roaring to the surface and all pretense of civility disappears. In their dinner table conversations of what's become of the city and where it's headed, the poor Blacks from the Deep South are no longer referred to as such, but as "niggers plain and simple, the way they truly view them, and she's called a "nigger lover" for trying to defend them as people, as fellow human beings.

Her parents' friends seem to find the caricatures her parents become when they drink at their cocktail parties amusing, but she doesn't. They aren't at all amusing when you have to live with them, day in and day out. She's come to see her role in the family as being the person who tries to keep things on an even keel and prevent the family from running aground on the rocks of inebriation. She uses logic and reason as delicately and persuasively as she can, but she's learned that where drunks are concerned, logic and reason don't apply or do in a crazy sort of way that only drunks understand, and trying to understand it can be maddeningly impossible sometimes. She gave up trying to talk reasonably with her father about not wanting to attend the Mount. As far as he's concerned, she's "a spiteful ingrate who enjoys biting the hand that feeds her." End of discussion.

She feels herself drifting off and her Uncle Mick comes to mind. He and her aunt Mary, a sweet person and an obese diabetic, and her cousins Moira and Micky live down the hill and around the corner on 3rd Street, across from Downing Park, the largest of the three parks in Newburgh. It was designed in the late Nineteenth Century by Frederick Law Olmstead and Calvert Vaux and named after their mentor, Andrew Jackson Downing, a Newburgh native who died in a steamboat accident on the Hudson River. The park was once the jewel in the city's crown but it's no longer a safe place to be after dark. The neighborhood surrounding it is filled mostly with modest single-family homes and was once a nice place to live and raise a family. Not anymore. As close as Uncle Mick and his family live to her family, they might as well be living on the moon. While her family's house is grand, her uncle Mick's house is small and cramped, a shotgun shack in comparison.

Her uncle is a drunk like her father, but slight, meek and soft-spoken, the antithesis of her father. He's a blue-collar worker for Parks and Recreation and seems to be perpetually on workers compensation, ostensibly because of a bad heart but she knows it's because he's unable to get out of bed in the morning and report to work because of his drinking the night before. Still, he's a loyal member of the clan and acts like an obedient serf in the presence of her father, all but tugging his forelock.

She and Moira keep each other abreast of the happenings in their families. They recognized each other early on as kindred spirits and formed a friendship that has withstood all the crazy twists and turns the family has thrown at them.

Micky is a junior at Saint Pat's and already a heavy drinker like his father. He's the stick in the spokes of her family's belief that a parochial school education is the ticket to a well-paying white-collar job. Micky's planning to enlist in the Army after graduation and seems eager to be sent off to fight in Vietnam, unlike everyone else his age she knows, who are planning to go to college to avoid the draft. Micky seems to her to have something to prove, although she can't put her finger on what. He just seems lost to the point where the only thing left for him to do is put himself in harm's way. If he does go to Vietnam, she has the strong feeling he won't come back alive.

Now she can't sleep and gets out of bed, takes another cigarette out of the pack in the sneaker in the closet and walks to the window, opens it and lights the cigarette, drawing deeply on it. She doesn't blow smoke rings. Instead, she blows out the smoke in a huff, trying to expel with it all the feelings of frustration and disappointment and anger she harbors toward her family.

She imagines George Washington leaning on the windowsill beside her, having a smoke with her. She's never read anything about Washington that would lead her to believe he smoked but she can imagine him here beside her now with a cigarette in his hand, gazing out with slightly narrowed eyes at the houses across the street and the city beyond, silently understanding and commiserating. She imagines him putting a steadying hand on her shoulder, as if to say that what she's witnessing now is nothing new, that the country was born of conflict and struggle and this too it shall endure. She'd like to believe him.

* * *

As usual, the corner store is crowded with kids at lunchtime. Most are from North Junior but the four boys standing by the pinball machine with Coke cans in their hands are from NFA. Colleen's seen them here before, although she doesn't know them and has never spoken to them. They've never paid any attention to her before but they are now, trying to be discreet when they glance over at her and not doing a very good job of it. She recognizes the knowing looks they exchange between them. They've heard the rumors. This is what she enjoys about this little game.

These boys look to be at least a couple of years older than she, sophomores or juniors in high school. You'd think they'd have more sense than to be messing around with an eighth grader. You'd think they'd be more mature but they're not. When it comes to sex, they're just like the rest of them—little boys.

She can see how nervous they are and how awkward they feel. The biggest problem in their lives now is figuring out how to talk to her about what they want. Every now and then she fixes her gaze on them and enjoys watching them squirm. They try to keep their eyes on hers but can't and turn away and she knows why. They know she knows what they're after, but as much as they want it, they're too embarrassed and ashamed to come right out and ask for it. It's like sticking a pin in a worm and watching it wriggle. And the best part of the game is that she doesn't have to do anything. She can either choose to give them what they want or not. It's entirely her decision. She's the one who's controlling the situation. She has power over them and all she has to do to exercise it is sit here and do nothing.

She looks around the table at her friends' faces. She knows they know what's going on and are purposely ignoring it. Her friends have been through this with her before and know that the thing to do is mind their own business and let her handle the situation.

Jeanine grimaces and shifts in her seat again. "My cramps are killing me."

Kathy reaches into her purse. "I've got Tylenol."

"Not strong enough," Jeanine says, massaging her lower abdomen. "I take this prescription stuff. They still hurt like hell."

"Mine get really bad sometimes too," Megan says. "I use a heating pad. It helps a little."

Colleen glances at the boys by the pinball machine and, predictably, sees they're looking at her and quickly turn their heads away, all but one of the boys, the taller Irish-looking one with the pug nose and ruddy cheeks and wreath of curly auburn hair. He holds her gaze for a moment, and she sees the flicker of a smile before he turns his head away too.

Listening to her friends talking about menstruation and knowing what the boys by the pinball machine want makes her shake her head. This is the side of girls that boys are truly clueless about, the messy side, the menstrual cycle with its attendant tenderness and moodiness and, for girls like Jeanine, painful cramping and bleeding. It scares boys to death, and she knows they consider girls who are menstruating to be unclean and the idea of having anything to do with them sexually disgusting. The reality of the situation, of course, is that by menstruating, girls are preparing themselves to be fertile, readying themselves to receive sperm and produce babies and ensure the continuance of the human race. As far as she's concerned, menstruating girls are God's gift to humanity and it's just like boys to refer to girls who are in this divine state as being "on the rag." Who's disgusting?

She knows she's fortunate where menstruation is concerned. She doesn't experience painful cramping the way Jeanine does, in fact, doesn't experience much pain at all. She looked forward to beginning her period. She discovered when she finally began using tampons that she enjoyed the feeling of having one inside her, nestled there secretly, so much so that she took to putting one in when she wasn't menstruating, just to enjoy the feel of it, as she is now. She hasn't shared this little secret with anyone.

She knows her mother knows she's sexually active, just by the way her mother looks at her from the living room when she appears at the bottom of the stairs, ready to leave on a date. Recently her mother commented that Colleen might have a problem with being "over-sexed" whatever that means. As far as she's concerned, her sexuality is perfectly natural and normal and maybe she's just a bit more interested in sex and open and honest about it than most girls. What's so bad about liking sex, anyway? It feels good, whether someone else is doing the touching or she's touching herself. This game she's playing with the boys by the pinball machine, all girls play it, in their own way and to one extent or another. It's the nature of girls to toy with boys.

"Hey!" she hears a boy call from behind her as she and her friends walk back toward North Junior. She sees her friends glance at her and each other as she slows and watches them continue on without looking back. They know what to do. Soon enough the boy is walking beside her and she looks up at him and sees it's the Irish-looking one, as she knew it would be. She shows him just the hint of a smile. "Hey," she says.

"You're Colleen Hanrahan, right?"

She can hear it in his voice: *the* Colleen Hanrahan. He seems like a nice enough boy, and it would be nice to think he's interested in her for more than that but she'd be surprised if he were. She's yet to meet a boy who is. "Yeah," she says.

"Kevin," he says.

Of course, he'd have a name like Kevin. Just look at him! Parents are so unoriginal when it comes to naming their kids. Look at hers. It couldn't be more Irish. She studies his eyes and sees he's blushing and seems to be tongue-tied, which strikes her as funny. Here he is, older than she and in high school and she's making him feel embarrassed and nervous and unsure of himself. He glances over his shoulder at his friends. She does too and sees them waiting at the corner. He looks at her and she sees he's trying to muster the courage to ask her out.

"My friend's throwing a party Saturday at his house," he finally manages to say. "His parents won't be there. Should be fun. Wanna go?"

"Where?"

"Chadwick Lake."

"Sure," she says and sees him smile and look relieved. He should be. She let him off easy.

"Gimme your phone number and address," he says.

She fishes a pen and a scrap of paper out of her bag and writes down her number and address and hands it to him.

"Around eight?" he asks.

"Sure."

"Great!" he says. "See ya Saturday!"

She watches him walk back toward his friends and sees the spring in his step. She knows just how he feels right now and how he'll sound as he shares the news with his friends, like a conquering hero. What a fool. Boys are such easy prey.

CHAPTER 2

Valerie

Colleen sits at her vanity and gazes at herself in the mirror as she combs her shoulder-length strawberry blonde hair. She's finally gotten it to the point where it's glowing, so she puts the hair brush down, picks up a blue barrette and puts it on her head to hold her hair back. She sits back and inspects herself. She knows she's not model material, but she's attractive in her own Irish American way and knows how to make herself look her best. She leans forward for a final close inspection of her makeup; eyelashes blackened with mascara and nicely separated; pale blue eyes outlined with black eyeliner; eyelids glowing with smoothed pearl blue eye shadow and lips glistening with pink lip gloss. It's the perfect counterbalance to her pale complexion.

She walks to the full-length mirror hanging on her bedroom door and inspects the overall effect of her hair, makeup and outfit, a medium blue cotton V-neck sweater over a white oxford button down shirt and neatly ironed and creased blue jeans with burgundy penny loafers. It's her favorite look: "preppy." It conveys the idea to boys that she's intelligent and comes from a good family and aspires to go places and accomplish things in life and that she's deemed to spend a bit of her precious time with them, for which they should be appreciative and grateful and enjoy it while they can, because they'll almost certainly soon be forgotten.

She takes a cigarette and the lighter out of the sock in the sneaker in the closet, walks to the window, opens it and leans on the windowsill. She lights the cigarette, inhales and blows a line of smoke rings out into the evening air. She eyes the street at the bottom of the hill. Will it be a pony car or muscle car? That's the question on her mind. A Camaro, Mustang or Cougar or something more powerful, like a 442, Roadrunner or GTO? Well, she'll see soon enough. She'd be surprised if he arrives in the family's station wagon, or some beat up junker and hopes he doesn't.

She knew she could count on her mother to persuade her father to let her go to the party with an older boy. Her mother's been her advocate ever since she discovered her with Sheldon Goldstein in that compromising situation in her parents' bedroom at one of their cocktail parties last year. She'd arrived home from seeing a movie. The party was in full swing with her father the center of attention, as usual. She headed upstairs and was walking down the hall toward her bedroom and heard lowered voices coming from her parents' bedroom. She recognized her mother's voice but not the man's. The door to her parents' bedroom was ajar and she slowed and looked in and saw her mother and Sheldon, one of her parents' friends she knew from parties past, reflected in her mother's vanity mirror. Their bodies were pressed together, and they were gazing into each other's eyes and fondling each other. Sheldon had his hand on her mother's breast and her mother had hers on his crotch. It was like passing the scene of a car crash. Colleen was shocked but couldn't look away. She saw her mother glance at her as she moved away, and they didn't say a word to each other about the incident afterwards and haven't since. They've been unspoken allies, supporting each other and keeping each other's secrets.

She hears a car turn the corner at the bottom of the hill and peers through the leaves of the elms to try to make it out. It doesn't sound anything like what she'd been imagining and is disappointed to see a beat up turquoise and white hard top Nash Metropolitan, a bathtub of a car, pull up to the curb in front of the house. She grabs her bag, bounds down the stairs, stops at the front door and rummages in her bag to make sure she has everything she needs: cigarettes, lighter, new pack of tissues and a pack of Tic Tacs. As usual, her mother is sitting on the couch in the living room, with her back to her, reading.

"Home by midnight, and no drinking," she hears her mother say without turning to look at her.

"Yeah. Bye," she says. She walks down the front steps and is curious to see if she can mentally check off the first item in her "date evaluation list": *Happy to see me.* She sees Kevin as she approaches, sitting behind the wheel of the idling car, staring straight ahead. She stops by the passenger side door, bends down and looks at him through the open window. "Hi," she says and sees him glance at her and force a smile.

"Hi," he mumbles.

She opens the door, gets in and pulls the door shut. So much for items one and two: *Opens the car door for me.* He puts the car in gear and off they go, She sits, holding her bag in her lap, watching the houses on her street go by and then the houses on the neighboring streets as they head toward North Plank Road. "Your car?" she finally asks.

"Is now. It was rusting away in my uncle's apple orchard in Marlboro. He said if I could get it out of there, I could have it."

"Good mechanic?" He glances at her.

"Yeah."

"That what you wanna do?" He shrugs.

"My friend Izzy owns Newburgh Collision on Lake Street. He wants me to work with him when I graduate."

"*With* or *for.*" He glances at her.

"*With.* He wants me to be his partner."

"Think you will?" He shrugs again.

"I'm thinking about chemical engineering."

"That what your dad does?"

"Yeah. He works at DuPont. I can always get a job there."

"My dad's a lawyer."

"I figured he was either that or a doctor. Your house is almost as big as the ones in Balmville."

"He does pretty well."

"That what you're gonna do?"

"Maybe. If I do, it won't be defending rich scumbags like my dad does."

"Somebody has to."

"I guess…."

"So, who would you defend?"

"People who really need it…poor people." Predictably, she sees his eyes open wide.

"What, niggers? You're not a nigger lover, are you?"

She studies his profile. Racism has so many faces and as good looking as Kevin is, his is just as ugly as the rest of them she's seen.

"Pretty soon there'll be more of them than us here," he says. "They're like a plague! They breed like fucking rabbits!"

"That what your parents think?" He glances at her and smirks. "That's what *everybody* thinks. They might not say it, but they do."

She stares out the windshield at the passing buildings and imagines a time when they'll all be occupied by Blacks. Will it ever happen? Maybe, maybe not. If it does, it won't be any different than when the poor Irish, her great grandparents among them, came to America in waves, settled in the cities, "bred like rabbits" and quickly overtook the population of the English, Germans and Dutch, the then ruling class. She doesn't even know Kevin's family name but guesses it's Flynn or Kelly or Ryan, something like that. Not so long ago he would have been considered the nigger and here he is saying the same racist bullshit about Blacks that the people who once considered his people a plague would have said about him. It's too ironic for words. Well, technically, she can check off item three in her list now: *Enjoys talking with me.* It isn't a very intelligent or interesting conversation, but at least he's talking, which is more than she can say for most of the boys she's gone out with, who answered her questions with grunts and barely managed to mumble more than a few words in an entire evening.

It's been a long time since she's been to Chadwick Lake, not that it's all that far from her house. She was a kid and a friend had her birthday party there. She remembers it as being large and learned from her father that it was created by damming Quassaick Creek in the 1920s and that its purpose was to provide water for the Town of Newburgh, which now gets its water supplied by New York City's Delaware Aqueduct. She didn't think much at the time about the fact that Newburgh gets its water from a city sixty miles to the south but now it strikes her as odd. She's seen pictures of the type of aqueducts the Romans built and there's nothing like that on either side of the river. It's probably a big pipe in the ground. And what's Delaware got to do with it? She'll have to ask her father about it. It's the one good thing she'll say about him: he's knowledgeable about all sorts of things and especially local history.

She also remembers the area around the lake as being sparsely populated and the houses being at a distance from one another and separated by dense stands of trees. As they turn off North Plank Road and drive toward Kevin's friend's house, things look pretty much the way she remembers. Some of the houses have gotten a new coat of paint but nothing seems to have changed much.

They park on the side of the road at the end of a long line of cars and she can hear Mitch Ryder and the Detroit Wheels' "Jenny Take a Ride" blasting from the stereo inside the house. She sees people sitting on the front porch and the front steps and standing in small groups in the front yard. She recognizes the boys who were with Kevin in the corner store, standing with some other boys. Everyone seems to have a can of beer in one hand and almost everyone a cigarette in the other. Kevin's friends call out his name and slap him on the back as they make their way through the crowd and up the steps and into the house. They glance at her and she can tell they're wondering who and how old she is but Kevin doesn't seem at all interested in introducing her to them. In fact, he seems embarrassed to be here with her—so much for item four in her list: *Is proud to be with me*—and she feels offended and humiliated and angry with herself for having allowed herself to be put in this situation. She wants to ask him to take her home but can't muster the courage.

She follows him through the crowded living room to the kitchen and up to a group of people, standing by the refrigerator. Two people in particular—a tall stocky boy and a tough-looking blonde who she figures is the boy's girlfriend—seem to be the hosts of the party. They just have that "in charge" look about them. They're both dressed plainly in tee shirts and jeans and sneakers. As she and Kevin approach, the boy smiles at her but his girlfriend doesn't and stares at her with an expression of barely concealed contempt.

"Kevin!" the tall stocky boy says and opens the refrigerator, reaches in, takes out two cans of beer and hands Kevin and her one.

She waits to see if Kevin will introduce her or even acknowledge her presence. Even if he does, item four will remain unchecked. Given the way she feels now, she can't see a way that he could redeem himself.

"This is Colleen," Kevin says.

"Ritchie," the tall stocky boy says and nods toward his girlfriend. "Darlene," he says.

"Nice to meet you," Colleen says. Ritchie seems nice enough but not Darlene, who strikes her as being used to throwing her weight around. Darlene seems to have already formed an opinion about her and not a good one. Has she heard the rumors? Colleen wouldn't be surprised. Kevin naturally would have shared what he'd heard with Ritchie, who naturally would have shared it with Darlene. Colleen takes a sip of beer and tries not to make eye contact with Darlene as she listens to the conversation pick up where, she assumes, it left off, talking about a friend of theirs, a boy named Stevie, who decided to enlist in the Army right after graduating from NFA and is in Vietnam. According to Stevie, Saigon is a wild place, a real party town and every time they meet the gooks in battle, they kick their asses and there's nothing to worry about. Based on what her father's shared with her about the history of what's going on there, she's not so sure Stevie's right, but isn't about to voice her opinion. Far from it. Her entire being is now focused on trying not to say or do anything to draw attention to herself, in particular Darlene's. Colleen can see out of the corners of her eyes that Darlene is staring at her with narrowed eyes and now there's a lull in the conversation. Colleen can't help glancing at her.

"C'mon," Darlene says, nodding toward the door to the backyard.

The menace in Darlene's voice and her expression is clear and Colleen feels a jolt. She glances at Kevin to see if he's going to come to her aid, but he and Ritchie are looking at each other and chatting and sipping their beers, as if none of this is happening.

She follows Darlene to the door and out into the backyard and away from people and Darlene stops and turns and glares at her. She takes a pack of cigarettes and lighter from the pocket of her jeans and Colleen takes hers from her bag and they stand facing each other in silence. They light their cigarettes and smoke. Darlene looks her slowly up and down and isn't bothering to try to conceal her contempt now.

"Preppy bullshit," Darlene says. "Who're you kidding? I've heard about you."

Colleen has the feeling things are about to get physical. Her legs feel rubbery, she feels a knot in her stomach and she's certain Darlene can see she's trembling, but she tries hard not to let it show. "Like what?" Darlene raises her eyebrows and looks at her in disbelief.

"Like what? Like you're a cocksucking slut, that's like what."

Colleen doesn't know what to say or if she should say anything, but she knows what it must feel like to be a mouse facing a snake in a cage.

"It's one thing to take care of your own boyfriend," Darlene says, "but *not* other people's boyfriends. Know what I mean?"

Colleen nods.

"So, if I hear about you and Ritchie, I'll mess that pretty face of yours up so bad you won't be able to give anybody a blowjob because your jaws will be wired shut. Understand?"

Colleen nods again.

"Good," Darlene says with a smirk.

Colleen watches Darlene flick her cigarette away and walk past her toward the house. She feels tears welling in her eyes and tries hard to fight them back. She doesn't want to cry, doesn't want to give Darlene the satisfaction. "Hey," she hears a girl nearby say with concern in her voice and quickly wipes her eyes with the back of her finger. She glances over her shoulder and sees the girl walking toward her with a can of beer in one hand and a cigarette in the other. The girl is slender and has short dark brown hair. She's wearing black horn-rimmed glasses, a Barnard College sweatshirt, black jeans and black Keds high top sneakers. The look couldn't be more "beatnik."

"You okay?" the girl asks. "What was that all about?"

"Nothing," Colleen says, and the girl puts a hand on her arm, leans closer and studies her eyes.

"You sure you're okay?"

"Yeah, I'm fine," Colleen says, and the girl looks toward the house and back at her.

"She's a pushy bitch, Darlene. Always has a hair across her ass. I try to steer clear of her. She's nothin' but trouble."

Colleen can tell by the girl's accent that she's not from around here. She sounds like she's from New York City.

"I'm Valerie," the girl says with a smile, "Sansone."

"Colleen Hanrahan."

"You a freshman?"

"I go to North Junior."

"Ah! What grade?"

"Eighth. You?"

"Sophomore. You goin' to NFA next year?"

Colleen nods.

"Good! We'll see each other!"

"Are you from New York City?" Colleen asks.

"Yeah," Valerie says, "Bensonhurst, Brooklyn. My family moved here last year. I'm still not used to it. This place is kinda dead, know what I mean?"

"Yeah. Whydja move here?" Colleen asks and smiles to herself. She never says things like "whydja" and "wouldja" and did because Valerie's accent is as infectious as is it comical. When Valerie said she was from Bensonhurst, it sounded like "Benzinhoist."

"My dad got a job at West Point. No way we were gonna live in Highland Falls. Talk about sleepy!" Valerie says, rolling her eyes.

Now Colleen smiles openly. She likes Valerie and feels relaxed and easy with her. Valerie seems like a person she can talk with about things, anything. Valerie looks her up and down, purses her lips and cocks her head.

"Preppy's a good look for you. Plannin' to go to college?"

"Yeah."

"Know whatcha wanna major in?"

"Law. My dad's an attorney. He handles a lot of the high-profile cases around here." Mention of this piques Valerie's curiosity.

"James Hanrahan?" Valerie asks with raised eyebrows.

"Yeah."

"*The* James Hanrahan who's always in the paper?"

Colleen nods and feels herself flush.

"Wow! He's a real celebrity around here! I don't know how he manages to get his clients off. They're all guilty as hell!"

"You haven't seen him in action."

"I guess," Valerie says. She jiggles her almost empty can and takes a step toward the house. "I'm gettin' another. Want one?"

"Here, finish mine," Colleens says, handing Valerie hers, "I only took a sip. I don't really like beer." Valerie sets her can down on the lawn beside her for them to use as an ashtray takes of sip from Colleen's.

"You here with someone?" Valerie asks.

"Kevin," Colleen says. She's embarrassed that she doesn't know his last name and hopes Valerie doesn't ask. She doesn't want her think she's just a stupid kid.

"Flynn?" Valerie asks.

"I guess," Colleen says, relieved that it doesn't seem important to Valerie that she doesn't know.

"Tall, pug nose, real Irish-lookin'?"

Colleen nods.

"Yeah, that's him. Don't know him very well. He hangs with a different crowd. Howdja meet?"

Colleen makes a mental note to try not to mimic Valerie's accent but knows it isn't going to be easy. "He and his friends were in the corner store where we eat lunch."

"Huh."

"How about you?"

"Mike Doyle," Valerie says and scans the people in the backyard. "He's here somewhere."

"No way!" Colleen says. "His sister Megan's my best friend."

"Yeah? Well, we're just friends. We're on the debate team."

"Planning to go to Barnard?"

"Yeah."

"I hear it's a really good school. One of the Seven Sisters, right? Sister school of Columbia?"

"Yeah," Valerie says and shakes her head. "Why they don't just make it one big university is beyond me. My brother's a freshman at Columbia. He loves it. I wanna teach English Lit after college, but first I'm gonna join the Peace Corps."

Colleen knows about the Peace Corps, established by President Kennedy in 1961 for the purpose of helping people outside the United States better understand US culture and vice versa. She's thought about joining. The idea of putting many thousands of miles between herself and Newburgh and doing something that promotes understanding in the world in the process is an appealing one. "I've thought about joining," she says.

"You should! It's a great experience. There's just so much ignorance in the world, you know? It would be nice to try to change that, even in a small way."

Colleen recognizes the sentiment. It's why she wants to defend poor people and as far as ignorance in the world is concerned, you only have to consider people like Kevin and Darlene and her friends in the kitchen. She imagines the conversation going on in the kitchen right now is as unlike the one she's having with Valerie as night and day.

Colleen listens, rapt, as Valerie tells her about the Peace Corps and where it is she might be sent and what it would be like living in a foreign country for two years. She tells her about what life was like growing up in Bensonhurst, being a subway ride away from Manhattan, going to the Guggenheim and The Museum of Modern Art and seeing movies at Radio City Music Hall, with its enormous screen, and the Rockettes at Christmastime, and, in the summer, going to Coney Island and riding the Staten Island Ferry over and back on hot muggy nights just to enjoy the cool breeze. It makes Colleen's experience growing up in Newburgh seem uneventful and culturally impoverished.

They talk about books they've read that they enjoyed, and Colleen isn't surprised to hear that among Valerie's favorites are *The Chronicles of Narnia* and everything by Jane Austen. Valerie asks her if she's read anything by Jack Kerouac, an author Colleen's heard of. Colleen shakes her head and Valerie urges her to read *On The Road*, which she says is pretty racy.

They talk about the type of music they like and Colleen tells Valerie that her favorite artist is Leslie Gore, which Valerie finds interesting. Colleen's not surprised to hear that Valerie's favorites are Bob Dylan, Joan Baez and Judy Collins and songs written by this new artist, Joni Mitchell, who's Canadian. Valerie tells her she's also into modern jazz, which Colleen's unfamiliar with and doesn't really get when she hears it, and that Miles Davis's *Kind of Blue* is her favorite jazz album. She urges Colleen to pick up a copy and listen to it and says she's sure she'll get into it. Colleen's impressed when Valerie tells her that she's seen Miles Davis and lots of other jazz artists perform at The Village Gate in Greenwich Village. She's taken aback when Valerie mentions, matter-of-factly, that she likes to smoke marijuana and get high when she goes to concerts or listens to music in her room, that it heightens her enjoyment of the music.

Colleen's never even seen marijuana, let alone smoked it. The little she knows about it she's heard from kids at school, although they don't seem that knowledgeable about it either, and her parents, during dinner table discussions about how the Blacks are ruining the city. According to her parents, marijuana use is common and widespread among Blacks, as alcohol use is. Blacks smoke it to get high and forget the reality of day-to-day life, which is that they have nothing and, so, nothing to look forward to, which, according to her parents, they'd rather do than pull themselves up by their bootstraps, as every other ethnic group has done in the country. Colleen's not so sure about all that, but she does know that it's a favorite drug of musicians, Black and White, and that it's illegal and you can go to jail if you're caught with it on you. "Aren't you afraid of being arrested?" she asks and sees Valerie shrug.

"Nah," Valerie says.

Valerie tells her that lots of kids in Bensonhurst smoke pot, that marijuana used to grow wild in Brooklyn and Queens and that New York City tried to eradicate it in the 1950s, but that there are still wild plants to be found and she knows where to find them. She can also get it anytime she wants when she goes to visit her brother at Columbia. Marijuana use is widespread there, as it is at just about every college and university in the country now. Valerie smiles at her impishly and leans closer.

"Maybe we'll get high sometime," Valerie says in a lowered voice.

Colleen's not sure what to think about this. She has no idea what being high is like, but she has the feeling it's pleasurable and that it would be fun to get high with Valerie. Maybe they will.

Standing here in the backyard, talking with Valerie, Colleen's forgotten about the party and lost track of time, and she's never felt more comfortable being with anyone than she does now with her.

"Hey," she hears Kevin say and turns to see him approaching with a can of beer in his hand. She recognizes the slur and the expression on his face. It's how her father sounds and looks when he's drunk. She notices that Kevin doesn't even look at Valerie.

"C'mon," Kevin says, taking her by the arm.

"Where," Colleen asks.

"For a walk," he says and leads her toward the woods.

Colleen looks back over her shoulder at Valerie and sees her look of concerned surprise. "Be right back!" Colleen says. Valerie half-waves and turns back toward the house.

Kevin isn't so much leading Colleen as pulling her now and she tries to slow him down. "Where are we going?" she asks but he doesn't answer, and she feels his grip tighten. Resigned, she allows herself to be pulled along. She feels she really doesn't have a choice.

In the dusk she can make out a path through the trees, bordering the backyard. They follow it and arrive at a shed. He pulls her around behind it and lets go of her. She has a pretty good idea what happens next and isn't surprised to see him lean back against the shed and unbutton and unzip his jeans. She knew it was going to happen, sooner or later, if not here now then probably in the car later. This is why he brought her, after all, so, better to get it over with and be done with it. She stands in front of him and looks at his face. Even in the darkness she can make out in his drunken expression his eagerness to experience the pleasure she's about to give him. She can see that he hasn't the slightest concern for her, that to him she's just a mouth. "Give me your jacket," she says.

He hands her his beer and struggles out of his jacket, unsteady on his feet. He hands it to her and takes the can back. She tosses the jacket on the ground, drops her bag and kneels in front of him. She pushes his hand away from the back of her head and wraps her around his penis. It's flaccid and she knows it's because he's drunk and that if she doesn't get him hard, she might be here on her knees a long time. The quickest way, she knows, is to take him in her mouth, which she does and begins pumping. She feels his penis getting harder and knows that it's as much because of the feeling of being in her mouth as it is the sight of her bobbing head. She's certain he's gazing down at her and is thrilled by what he sees.

This is the part she finds disturbing, the kneeling. She's a Catholic, albeit a skeptical one, and she can't help associating kneeling with worshipping and receiving the Eucharist at the altar rail, during Holy Communion. She can't reconcile the two situations, one sacred and the other profane and both involving being on her knees. She tries to get boys to lie on their backs to avoid having to kneel in front of them but most of them, like Kevin, prefer to stand.

She feels Kevin's hands pressing against the back of her head and bats them away. She doesn't allow boys to do that. She doesn't want them to think they're somehow in control of the situation or have any power over her. She's the one who's in control. She's the one exercising power over them, even if she's the one on her knees.

She does what she did the first time she knelt in front of a boy and has every time since, imagines he's Jesus. He was the Son of God, but he was also a man, so he had a penis. If anyone would understand and forgive her for being the way she is and doing what she's doing, Jesus would. Didn't he defend that whore? She imagines Jesus gazing down at her with that understanding and compassionate expression of his. Jesus's love for her is perfect and perfect love is all-forgiving.

She feels Kevin's hips begin to buck and knows he's about to come and as her mouth fills with semen, she imagines it's Jesus's and that it's the Eucharist she's receiving. If it were, she'd swallow it, but it isn't, so she does what she always does and spits it out on the ground. She hears Kevin make an animal-sounding grunt as he zips up his fly and she fishes in her bag for a tissue to wipe her mouth. She watches him disappear around the shed as she wipes. She's about to take out the Tic Tacs and put several in her mouth to take the taste of the semen away when she sees one of Kevin's friends appear and lean back against the shed, unzipping his jeans. She's angry with herself for not having seen this coming and her instinct is to get up and leave, but she hesitates and thinks about the situation.

If she did leave, it would leave his friend here and the others she's now certain are waiting their turn with the impression that Kevin is somehow special when he's not. He's just a stupid drunk boy, like this one and the rest of them. She's never done more than one boy at a time and the idea of doing so now makes her uneasy. She knows if she does, she will have crossed a line reputationally, reached a new level of promiscuity that can only be described as scandalous and that her reputation, already bad, will be even worse. On the other hand, even if she did leave now the story the boys will circulate to save face is that she took them all on behind the shed at the party. It seems to her she's damned if she does and damned if she doesn't. She's here on her knees anyway and there's always the possibility that if she denies this boy, he might get angry and get physical. He is drunk, after all.

She services him as she did Kevin, having to get him hard and batting his hands away from the back of her head and spitting his semen on the ground. When she's done with him, she doesn't reach in her bag for a tissue, but just waits on her knees, without looking up, for the next boy to appear and does the same to him and to the next three. When the last boy leaves, she spits for a good minute, wipes her mouth and puts a handful of Tic Tacs in her mouth. She stands and slings her bag over her shoulder and walks along the path to the backyard and through the crowd of people, not looking at any of them, toward Kevin's car.

"Hey!" she hears Valerie call from behind her but keeps walking with her eyes straight ahead and when she reaches Kevin's car, she gets in and sits with her bag in her lap, staring out the windshield at the darkness.

She doesn't know how long she's been sitting here, but people are getting in cars and leaving now. Kevin finally arrives and leans down. He stares at her through the open driver's side window.

"Where's my jacket?" he asks.

He's clearly pissed off. "Where you left it," she says flatly without looking at him.

"Shit!"

She watches him walk around the front of the car and disappear into the darkness behind the house. He reappears a few minutes later, gets in without looking at her, starts the car and they drive in silence all the way to her house. As he pulls up to the curb in front, she thinks about how ridiculous items five and six in her list now seem: *Asks to see me again* and *Gives me a sweet good night kiss.* She gets out, shuts the door without looking back and hears the car pull away as she walks up the front steps.

Passing the entrance to the living room, she sees her mother, still sitting on the couch reading. "How was it?" she hears her mother ask without interest as she heads up the stairs. "Okay," she says. At the top of the stairs, she sees the crack of light at the bottom of the closed door to her father's office at the end of the hall. She knows just how he looks in there, sitting at his desk with the collar of his white dress shirt unbuttoned and the sleeves rolled up, crafting the defense of one of his scumbag clients with a glass of booze close at hand and an almost empty bottle beside it.

She looks at herself in the bathroom mirror as she vigorously brushes her teeth, trying to remove the taste and the stinging shame of the evening. The eyes she sees staring at her in the mirror seem pale, lifeless, like a zombie's, a person without a conscience or a soul. She spits out the toothpaste and rinses her mouth again and again with water, as if she could ever wash the taste away. It was her decision and she wouldn't have done anything differently. Still, thinking about it disgusts her and she's most disgusted with herself.

She climbs into bed, takes the small transistor radio from her nightstand and turns it on. It's tuned to WABC in New York City. She turns off the light, puts the radio under her pillow, lays her head on it and adjusts the volume so that it's just loud enough for her to hear. She listens numbly to a segment of top 40 hits that say nothing to her—"A Hard Day's Night," "Hang On Sloopy," "There I've Said It Again," "Silence Is Golden." At the end of the segment, she listens to Scott Muni, with that gravelly voice of his, read the same advertising copy she now knows by heart. Fortunately, she doesn't need any help clearing up acne. Her skin may be the color of boiled potatoes but at least it's blemish-free. She's about to turn off the radio when he mentions that the next song will be Leslie Gore's new release, "You Don't Own Me." It sends a thrill through her body, which she's felt disconnected from all evening. She listens without paying attention as Muni reads more advertising copy. All she can think about is the title of this new song and how perfect it is. Finally, the talking is over and the song begins, and from the first melancholy-sounding downbeat she knows that this song is going to speak to her as no other song has before, and she knows she's right the moment she hears the resentment and defiance in Leslie's voice.

"You don't own me
I'm not just one of your many toys
You don't own me
don't say I can't go with other boys"

Okay, it's about a girl and her typically stupid, possessive and controlling boyfriend, but Colleen has the same feeling about this song that she did about "It's My Party" when she first heard it, that this teenage angst-ridden boy/girl relationship business is only a device Leslie's using, a simple scenario any teenager can understand and relate to, so that she can get across her real message, which isn't so much in the words and lyrics as the sound of her voice; the message being life is cruel and unjust and unfair and it will knock you down at every opportunity and you shouldn't be surprised when it does and you'd better learn how to take it and get back up on your feet and get ready for more, like an inflatable clown punching bag, which is just what she felt like kneeling there behind the shed, servicing boy after boy.

She hears her father's footsteps passing in the hall as the music swells and the chorus begins. She sees him in her mind's eye, carrying the empty bottle down the stairs and into the kitchen, and hears the "clink" as it hits the other empty bottles in the trash and then the "slam" of the liquor cabinet door.

> "Oh, I don't tell you what to
> say I don't tell you what to do
> so please let me be myself
> that's all I ask of you "

In fact, until she's eighteen, her father does own her, legally, the way slaves used to be owned. She might not do back-breaking chores all day or have to sleep with him whenever he feels like it, but he has the ultimate say about what happens in her life and can make it a living hell when he wants to and there's *nothing* she can do about it, short of running away from home, which she isn't about to do. He's the one man in her life who does have real power over her and as much as she tells herself that, despite his browbeating and bullying and berating and oafish behavior when he's drunk, she loves him because he's her father, the truth is that she loathes and despises him and, yes, hates him for being the loutish, albeit clean-shaven and well-dressed, brute with slicked back hair that he is and she guesses her mother feels the same way about him, which is why she's having an affair with Sheldon Goldstein.

"I'm young and I love to be young
I'm free and I love to be free
to live my life the way I want
to say and do whatever I please

You don't own me"

She listens to his footsteps, passing in the hall, back toward his office, and as the song fades, she turns off the radio, places it on the nightstand, curls up under the covers on her side with her knees tucked up and hands under her chin and cries until she can't anymore and just lies there, trying to turn off her brain and fall sleep.

CHAPTER 3

Megan's Family

Jeanine shrugs. "Maybe she's sick."

Maybe, although Colleen can't remember the last time Megan stayed home from school sick. She sips her coffee, draws on her cigarette and glances at the two boys sitting at the counter. They've been glancing over their shoulders at her and exchanging knowing looks. She doesn't know them personally, although they go to North Junior and are regulars at the corner store. She's used to boys looking at her this way, but something's different in their expressions and she can't put her finger on what.

Kathy glances at her wristwatch. "Let's go or we'll be late."

* * *

Colleen sits in homeroom, listening to the drone of the principal's crackly voice coming out of the loudspeaker on the front wall during morning announcements. Megan finally arrives and Colleen watches her make her way to her desk two rows over. She sees Megan glance at her as she sits down, and it seems to Colleen that she's avoiding making eye contact. She figures Megan must have heard about what happened at the party, probably from her brother. The two boys in the coffee shop must have heard something too. Word gets around fast in this town.

The principal finally finishes and now it's the teacher's turn to address the class. Colleen listens as she watches Megan hunch forward with her head down and her arms arranged on the desk so that they shield what she's doing. Colleen knows she's writing a note. She watches Megan fold it and hold it cupped in her hand until the teacher turns to write on the board and when he does, she quickly hands it to the girl sitting between them, who quickly hands it to Colleen. She unfolds and reads it:

Is it true?

She folds the note, tucks it in her bag and doesn't look at Megan again the rest of the period, or as they leave home room, or when they pass each other in the hall at room change, or when they meet on the front steps of the school at lunch, as they always do. Out of the corners of her eyes she sees Megan arrive at her side and they walk toward the corner store, Colleen a little faster than usual and Megan trying to keep up. When they're across the street from the school, they stop and light their cigarettes without making eye contact and then walk on.

"So, is it?" Megan finally asks.

"What?" Colleen asks, still not looking at her.

"What happened at the party?"

The anger Colleen's felt seething inside her all morning erupts and she stops abruptly, startling Megan, who stops. Colleen can see by Megan's sheepish expression that she knows she's pissed her off and isn't so sure now that passing her the note was such a good idea. Colleen's father is famous for his temper and as much as she hates his, she's glad she inherited it and knows how to use it when she's finally had enough of a situation. She fixes her eyes on Megan's. "What did you hear?" Megan shrugs, looks away and down at the sidewalk, shifts her weight nervously, looks back at Colleen and squints her right eye.

"That you blew a bunch of guys."

Colleen narrows her eyes and sees Megan's uncertainty about what's going to happen next. She wouldn't be surprised if Megan was afraid she's about to get slapped. "What if it were?" Colleen asks. "Would you stop being my friend?" She sees that Megan is totally unprepared for this question and enjoys watching her squirm as she tries to think of what to say. She can tell Megan's worried now that she's put their friendship at risk and feels that she's the one being judged now.

Colleen feels sorry for her, the way she does all amateurs who think they know how to negotiate their way around her, only to find they've gotten themselves in over their heads. It's another trait she's inherited from her father—the art of setting and springing traps to catch hapless prey. She imagines it's a skill passed down from her ancestors in Ireland, who developed and used it to put food on the table, and that it's been refined through the generations until it no longer has anything to do with using one's hands and everything to do with using one's head. Her father is expert at using his to ensnare and discredit witnesses with their own testimony and, while he's more practiced at it than she is, she feels she's every bit as skillful.

"No," Megan finally says.

"Then it doesn't matter," Colleen snaps. "It's *my* reputation, not yours." She walks on and Megan follows her, looking like a puppy on a leash. "Why were you late?" Colleen demands.

"My brother's car wouldn't start," Megan says sheepishly, sounding and looking ashamed.

Colleen shakes her head. It's one calamity after another with the Doyles, mostly having to do with things breaking down. If it's not her brother's junker car, it's the water heater or the furnace or the stove or the washer or dryer. The source of all the problems is Megan's father and the fact that he's a drunk like her father, except he's a blue-collar drunk, like her Uncle Mick, and doesn't earn very much, so when things break down, they're either patched together and gotten running again or replaced with another piece of junk that's about to break down. She feels sorry for Megan. "Why don't you just take the bus?"

"It usually starts," Megan says defensively. "You're still coming over Wednesday, right?"

Colleen's not surprised that Megan now sounds worried she won't because she pissed her off. It serves her right for overstepping her bounds. "Yeah," Colleen says reassuringly.

She knows people view her as cold and unfeeling and that's fine with her. It's just how she wants to be viewed. She's not seeking anyone's approval. She wants people to seek hers, which Megan is now doing and even the stupid boys at the party were doing, whether or not it occurred to them, hoping she'd deem to give them what they wanted.

She's actually pretty generous. She doesn't have to help Megan with her studies but does because they've known each other forever and Megan struggles with academics and Colleen wants her to do well in school and go on to college and escape the situation she's dealing with at home and make something of herself.

The only thing about tutoring Megan she doesn't like is that it happens every other week at Megan's, a ramshackle house on a dead end street on the outskirts of town. Megan's father, who grew up with her father, gives her the creeps. He's just a big blob of a man—a slob, really—always sitting on the couch in a stained tee shirt, watching TV with that stupid grin on his face and a can of beer in his hand. She tries not to make eye contact with him and gets through the living room to Megan's room as fast as she can, but she sees the way he looks at her, even when Megan's mother is there. How that woman puts up with him she doesn't know and what a living hell her life must be. Well, as they say, we all have our cross to bear.

* * *

Colleen's always struck by how dark it is on Megan's street. It's a short street that runs uphill and ends at the woods and all the houses look as ramshackle as Megan's and as dark, with here and there a porch light on and light in a window. All the families who live here must be in the same dire financial straits as the Doyles, the husbands earning barely enough to put a roof over their families' heads. Living here strikes her as being one step up from living in cardboard boxes.

Her mother brings the car to a stop at the side of the road in front of Megan's house and Colleen notices Megan's mother's car isn't in the driveway. She gets out and shuts the door and her mother opens the passenger door window, leans down and looks up at her with a look of concern, as she always does when she drops her off at Megan's. "I'll call you," Colleen says and her mother nods, closes the window and slowly pulls away.

She looks at the dark house, slings her bag over her shoulder and walks up the front path, mostly dirt with a few cinder blocks set in the ground at cocked angles, more obstacles to be avoided than help. She glances uneasily at the taillights of her mother's car, heading down the street, and knocks on the front door. A few moments later the door opens and Megan's father is standing there, his large flabby body filling the doorway. As usual, he's in a soiled tee shirt and has a can of beer in his hand and is grinning at her with that leering expression of his.

"C'mon in," he says and steps back, waving her into the house.

She sees he's watching *The Munsters*. The lights in the living room seem to be the only ones on in the house and she's pretty sure they're alone. She stands awkwardly in the living room and looks around. "Help yourself to a drink," she hears him say behind her. "There's soda in the fridge."

"No thanks," she says and turns and sees him settling back down on the couch. "Where's Megan?" she asks.

He looks up at her and grins. "Getting' her hand stitched up. She cut it pretty bad. Broke a glass when she was doin' the dishes."

What the hell is he grinning for? she wonders. Her antennae are out and tingling and she has a bad feeling about the situation. "When will she be back?" He shrugs and looks at the TV.

"Hour or so, I guess."

The thought crosses her mind to call her mother and have her come pick her up, but that would be unfair to Megan. It isn't her fault she cut herself and she needs help studying for her math test. The best thing to do would be to wait for Megan in her room, but she hesitates. It's not that she's worried about being impolite. She just doesn't want to give Megan's father any reason at all to think she's afraid of him or that she wants him to follow her into the bedroom.

She sits at the opposite end of the couch, puts her bag on the floor, crosses her arms on her chest and stares at the TV. *The Munsters!* Just the type of entertainment an idiot like Megan's dad would enjoy. She glances at the few pieces of bad artwork hanging on the walls in the living room and the crucifix and picture of Jesus in the nook on the wall by the dining room table.

It's funny how people turn out. Megan's father and her father grew up together in the same neighborhood. They were childhood buddies and went to school together all the way through NFA. Then their paths in life diverged. Her father went on to college and Megan's father got a low-paying job as a maintenance worker with the city and as the difference in their income levels and social status increased, they saw less and less of each other until now they see each other rarely, usually only on Saint Patrick's Day when the old crowd from the neighborhood gets together at the tavern they used to frequent, to get drunk and reminisce. They still do see each other, though, so they're still connected, albeit loosely, and it's just a feeling she has, but that fact is worrying her for some reason.

She listens to his chuckling and sees the mechanical way he brings the can of beer to his mouth and drinks and brings it down to the armrest again and wonders how anyone could have been attracted to him? She'll bet he hasn't changed much since Megan's mother first met him, other than to get fatter.

Finally, the shows ends and the theme music plays and she hears him say off-handedly, "Heard about the party." She feels a shock shoot through her body, her back stiffens and she glances at him. He's still staring at the TV with that dopey grin and expression of his and she looks back at the TV and now her mind is racing. Why did he mention it? What are the implications of his knowing? A long moment passes and she hears him say, "Be a shame if your dad found out." She feels herself panicking. He wouldn't tell her father, would he? "Jim's got a real temper," she hears him add pointedly, "I don't have to tell *you.*"

Her father is notorious for his temper. He's been known to pick fights with fellow members at the Powelton Club when he's been drinking. He bloodied the nose of a prosecutor he particularly dislikes when the man said, during an argument about her father's practice, that he ought to be more concerned about his own questionable character than he is with defending every questionable character in the county. They had to call the cops to restrain her father and an ambulance to take the man to the hospital. For some reason the man didn't press charges.

She remembers the first time her father's anger was directed full force at her. She was around six and had done something at school, she can't remember what and it couldn't have been all that bad, but her mother told her, "Just wait till your father gets home," and when he did arrive home, her parents had a brief conference in the kitchen and the next thing she knew she was on her back in the hall with her father on top of her, screaming and banging her head against the floor Her mother had to drag him off her to keep him from seriously injuring or even killing her, he was that out of control.

She looks at Megan's father and sees him looking at her with that same dopey grin and expression, only now his eyebrows are raised. She sees him move his feet a little farther apart and sway his legs back and forth. He might be an idiot, but he still has that Irish cunning. So, now the only question is, is it worth it? Would he really tell her father? The ironic thing is that Megan's father might end up getting beaten bloody, if he did. Whether or not he would, she can only imagine what her father would do to her. She's older now, but his temper hasn't changed and having his reputation besmirched by his daughter's scandalous behavior? Well, he's likely to do anything.

She stares at the TV. "And that'll be the end of it, right?" she asks and out of the corners of her eyes sees him nod. She takes a deep breath, gets up, kneels in front of him, unzips his fly, takes his penis out of his boxer shorts, puts it in her mouth and pumps until it's hard. She's always kept her distance from him, but now, being this physically close to him, his body odor makes her wonder when the last time he bathed or showered was, or if he even does. She feels his hand on her breast and bats it away and then on the back of her head and bats it away again and hears him grunt like an animal as he comes. She stands and gets a tissue from her bag and spits the semen—a surprisingly small amount for such a blob of a man, or maybe not so surprising—into it.

She walks toward the bathroom and sees him finish zipping up his pants as the front door opens. She glances at Megan's mom, who's standing in the doorway, staring at them with her bag hanging from her crooked arm and her keys dangling from her hand. Colleen can tell by her expression that she's put two and two together. How could she not? There's her husband with his hand on his zipper and here she is with a wadded tissue in her hand headed toward the bathroom. She knows Megan's mother won't say a word about what's happened, though. She's like the appliances in the house—worn out and on the verge of breaking down.

CHAPTER 4

Henry

Colleen watches Anya's older brother, Casmir, play the bass pedals on the rank organ with his feet and the top keyboard with one hand and the bottom one with the other. She knows it's difficult, but Casmir makes it look effortless, which is understandable. His father owns Kaczmarek's music store and teaches piano and organ and began teaching Casmir when he was a baby, sitting in his lap on the bench. Until Casmir had grown to the point where his feet could reach the pedals, they concentrated on the keys. After that, it was full immersion in the rank organ. Casmir grew up playing Classical music and his approach to Rock music is pretty much the same. It strikes her that this is the way The Beach Boys' "In My Room" would sound at a roller-skating rink. Ronnie and Henry on guitars complete the trio. Ronnie's clearly a better guitar player than Henry, which is why Henry's playing rhythm and Ronnie lead. She's not crazy about The Beach Boys and considers this song to be particularly wimpy, even as an instrumental. She's not even listening to it, really. Her attention is focused on Henry's hands and her eyes are riveted on them as he fingers the chords and strums. They're so expressive and she's fascinated by them and knows Anya's noticed, which is why Anya keeps glancing at her with that grin and knowing look.

The boys finish the song and decide to take a break. They all make their way slowly out of the living room, through the kitchen and into the backyard. They arrange themselves around the picnic table on the patio. Henry takes a pack of cigarettes out of his shirt pocket and a cigarette from the pack and offers Ronnie one. Ronnie takes one and Henry lights it and then his. Colleen fishes the pack out of her bag, takes out a cigarette and lights it. They sit and smoke and no one says anything. Casmir and Anya don't smoke, having been raised by strict non-smoking parents, but they're tolerant of smokers and in deference to them, the smokers take note of the direction of the wind and aim their exhaled smoke so it blows away from them. Everyone else is looking at nothing in particular—around at the yard and up at the clouds—and Colleen is pretending to do the same, but she's looking at Henry's hands out of the corners of her eyes, the one holding his cigarette, the other palm down on the table with his fingers spread slightly. What is it about his hands? No one has said anything yet, so she decides to break the ice. "Did you grow up in the Bronx?" she asks Henry He looks at her and smiles and shakes his head.

"My parents did. We stay with my mom's parents between assignments."

"How often is that?" she asks.

"Every two or three years."

"Wow! You move a lot!" Henry shrugs.

"That's Army life. You get used to it."

"Is your dad an officer?" Henry nods.

"Major."

"At West Point?"

He shakes his head. "He's at Walter Reade."

She knows it's a famous Army hospital in Washington, D.C. and hopes to hear that Henry's dad is a doctor or just there for tests but judging from his expression and those of the others she knows he's a patient.

"He had a massive brain tumor," Henry says. "They performed radical surgery but couldn't remove it all. They give him another year or so to live."

She finds herself wishing it were *her* father. She knows she should feel ashamed for wishing that but doesn't. "That's awful," she says, "I'm so sorry." She watches him shrug and draw on his cigarette and look off into the distance She studies him; his dark brown hair worn long over his ears, his tan skin much darker than hers, his dark brown eyes and long eyelashes, his sensitive mouth, his tortoise shell glasses and black turtleneck sweater, which give him an "artist-intellectual" look. He's cute, all right, and those hands—Ana looks impishly at her.

"Henry's Japanese," Anya says, smiling.

Colleen sees the others smile and shake their heads, obviously in on the joke. Even if you didn't know his last name is Chiaromonte, any intelligent person would know by looking at him that he's not Japanese and would also probably guess he's of Italian descent or descended from some other Mediterranean people. "Were you born there?" she asks.

"Yokohama," Henry says.

"How long were you there?"

"Two years. We arrived in San Francisco on my second birthday."

"So, you don't remember anything, huh?"

"Not really. There were two Japanese women who came to the house every day to help my mom with housework and they looked after me. The Japanese adore children and, apparently, these two women adored me, so I'm sure that affected me, somehow or another."

She bets it did. She's beginning to view Henry as a puzzle and this piece about the two adoring Japanese women seems an important one. "So, what's the joke about being Japanese?"

"We were stationed at Fort Rucker, Alabama, when I was younger and there wasn't any housing available on post when we arrived, so we stayed in a rented house for a year in this little town nearby, Ozark. The kids there had a hard time understanding why I didn't look Japanese, since I was born in Japan." Henry smiles and shakes his head. "It's different down South. I went to Emma P. Flowers Elementary School, just up the street from where we lived. It was 'White's only.' I didn't have any Black friends in Ozark, but I did when we moved on post and every morning the White kids would get on one bus and the Black kids another and off we'd go to different schools."

"That must have been weird," she says.

"It was. The whole situation in the South is weird. They're still fighting the Civil War. Not that there isn't prejudice and racism in the North. It just has a different face."

She knows it does, and her father is a perfect example. She remembers overhearing the comment he made to her mother when her uncle Mick won the World Series betting pool at work last year. The prize was fifty dollars and her father said his brother was "nigger rich" and wouldn't save a penny of it, that he'd spend it all as fast as he could, buying drinks for his buddies at the tavern.

She feels a little self-conscious about asking Henry all these questions while the others have been listening quietly and she wants to ask him more questions about himself, lots more, but decides not to, at least, not now. She sits silently and, well, half-listens as the conversation moves on to a discussion of new albums released by the boys' favorite groups.

Henry, she learns, is a big Beatles fan and likes The Rolling Stones and The Animals. The boys talk about how they can't wait to get their own cars and how much easier life will be when that happens. Henry's only been at Saint Pat's a few weeks and Casmir and Ronnie, who both go there, share stories about the differing personalities of the Christian Brothers who teach there. They sound to Colleen like quite a cast of characters and, according to Casmir and Ronnie, all come from tough neighborhoods in New York City and probably joined the order to escape the streets and the draft. She's most interested when she hears that, again, according to Casmir and Ronnie, despite the Brothers' vow of celibacy, rumor has it they fool around on the weekends, when they're not wearing their cassocks. She knows all about rumors and wonders if this one is true. She wouldn't be surprised, if it was.

Through it all, she watches Henry's face and the movement of his hands and fingers as discreetly as she can, as he takes a cigarette from his pack and lights it and holds it in between puffs, or gently scratches his forearm, or pushes his glasses back up on his nose. What is it about him she finds so intriguing? It's the same thing she found so intriguing about Valerie. They're not from around here. They're from a different world—in Henry's case, having lived in so many places, different worlds—and don't have the "small town" mentality kids who've grown up around here do. Henry and Valerie have seen and done things that she can only imagine and just being around them is exciting. She definitely wants to spend more time with Henry. Making that happen is now her top priority.

The thought occurs to her that he might have heard the rumors about her, and she's surprised that it didn't occur to her until now. She's been so caught up in watching him and talking with him and listening to him. He hasn't said or done anything that would lead her to believe he has, but she's not sure. She doesn't think Casmir and Ronnie have heard the rumors, hanging, as they do, with the St. Pat's crowd. She knows Anya has, though, because Anya told her. Anya also told her about her concern that if her parents, who are devout Catholics and very conservative, were to learn about her bad reputation, they might not let Anya see her anymore, which she said she doesn't want to have happen, so Colleen knows she wouldn't say a word about it to Henry. Still, He might have heard.

Thinking about it fascinates her. If Henry has heard the rumors and this is the way he treats her, like it doesn't matter to him, looking her in the eye and engaging her in conversation, then that's pretty remarkable. If he hasn't, then it still feels wonderful. Wouldn't it be great, though? A boy who's able to treat her with courtesy and respect, despite all the bad things he's heard about her. She's tried to imagine it in the past but, until now, doubted it was possible. She never thought she would think this but now she finds herself hoping he has heard the rumors. It seems crazy, but she does.

* * *

Henry puts the speaker back in its holder and noses the car into the line of cars that are slowly making their way out of Middle Hope Drive-In. Just as Colleen had hoped, when they were leaving Anya and Casmir's, Henry asked if she'd like to get together sometime and she said she would and gave him her number, which she was going to do anyway and was delighted that he gave her a reason to. He called a few days later and asked her out on a date to see *Doctor Strangelove,* which she'd heard about, but hadn't been planning to go see, but Henry said he knew she'd enjoy it, and she said, "Sure!" which she would have to anything he suggested they do.

He picked her up at her house in his family's blue Chevy Malibu station wagon and got out of the car when he saw her coming down the front steps. He walked around the car and opened the door for her. He looked genuinely happy to see her and they chatted all the way to the drive-in.

They laughed their way through the movie, and he never once gave any indication that he had anything on his mind other than watching it. He put his arm around her when the movie began and she put her hand lightly on his thigh and waited to see if he would take it in his and move it to between his legs and pull her head down to his lap, which was what usually happened on dates at the drive-in, but he didn't, which she somehow knew he wouldn't, although she wanted him to, which was a new feeling.

It was at the beginning of the scene in which General T.J. "King" Kong, played by Slim Pickens, sits on the H-bomb, trying to fix the damaged bomb bay doors, so they could drop the bomb on the target. Henry moved slightly and her hand brushed against the bulge in his jeans and she watched General Kong fall out of the bomb bay riding the bomb, whooping and waving his cowboy hat. She wanted to unzip Henry's pants then and there, but she didn't, which was another new feeling.

She's still savoring it as they head back to Newburgh on 9W, to have a bite to eat at Henry's favorite place, Phil & Neal Restaurant, a pizza shop on the corner of Broadway and Fullerton Avenue she's passed many times but has never set foot in. They chat about the movie on the way and both agree that Peter Sellers is hysterically funny but must be out-of-his-mind neurotic as a person, and they agree that the Cold War standoff between the United States and The Soviet Union is stupid, like two bullies staring each other down. She shares with him that she feels like those SAC bombers in *Fail Safe*, another movie they've each seen, flying beneath the radar to bomb Moscow, only her mission isn't one of mass destruction but just to destroy all the people who try to prevent her from being who she is, which, she admits upon reflection, is probably the same thing, and he smiles and nods and she feels the relief and happiness of being understood, as she did, talking with Valerie.

Phil and Neal look up from their pizza making as they enter. They smile and wave and greet Henry by name in their thick Italian accents. They obviously like him and consider him a regular now and it strikes her as telling that she's lived in this town all her life and isn't greeted like that by shopkeepers. They seat themselves at a table and she looks around and sees that the only other people in the restaurant are an elderly couple, sitting at a table in the corner, eating spaghetti.

She sees Henry looking at the TV, mounted on the wall above and behind her. She noticed when they entered that *American Bandstand* was playing with the volume barely audible and she glances over her shoulder and sees Dusty Springfield, with her coiffed big hair, like Leslie Gore's, and whom she likes almost as much. Dusty's standing in a cone of light, lip-synching "Wishin' and Hopin'." It doesn't matter that the sound is turned down. Colleen knows the lyrics by heart:

"Wishin' and hopin'and thinkin' and prayin'
Plannin' and dreamin' each night of his charms
That won't get you into his arms"

It sure won't, she thinks. She has other plans in mind. She turns back and looks at Henry, who's still looking up at the TV. "How old's your brother?"

Henry looks at her, settles back and crosses his legs. "Nineteen."

"In college?"

He nods. "Virginia Military Institute."

"So, he wants to be an officer, like your dad, huh?"

He nods again. "He's wanted to follow in our dad's footsteps as long as I can remember."

"How about you?"

He shakes his head.

"So, what do you want to do?" She knows that most of the boys who go to Saint Pat's go on to be professionals of one sort or another, doctors or lawyers or engineers, either that or they take over their father's business in town.

He shrugs. "I dunno. Something involving writing."

She's not surprised to hear this. She can easily see him as a writer and his photograph on the back cover of a novel. "What type of stuff do you write?"

"Short stories, plays."

"Can I read them sometime?"

"Sure."

"What're they about?"

He shrugs. "Life."

She can tell by his expression and shrug, both kind of weary, that he writes about serious stuff, which isn't surprising, given what's going on with his dad. "It must be hard, knowing your dad doesn't have that long to live."

He shrugs again. "That's life."

She wants to share with him what she thought when he told her about his dad, that she wished it was her father who didn't have long to live, but she hesitates and doesn't. It's not that she thinks he wouldn't understand. She knows he would. She's just not sure she wants to go there right now. "How long has he been sick?"

"A couple of years."

She sees either Phil or Neal—she doesn't know who's who yet—arrive at the table and place their slices of pizza in front of them. "Enjoy!" she hears him say as he walks away. She and Henry know the pizza is still too hot to eat and let it sit there and cool and she keeps her eyes on his.

"My mom got word through the grapevine that he was acting strange in Korea," Henry says. "He was there on a one-year hardship tour. My mom and I picked him up at Kennedy. We waited on the tarmac and watched everyone get off the plane and were beginning to think he wasn't on the flight when there he was, the last person out, standing in the doorway, looking around as if he didn't know where he was. I guess he didn't. Anyway, we could see he wasn't himself and his behavior just kept getting more bizarre. He finally collapsed at work one day in his office at Fort Eustis, Virginia, his last assignment. They drove him to Walter Reade. He's been there ever since."

"How long ago was that?"

"A year."

She watches him pick up a slice of pizza, blow on it and take a careful bite. It must be like living in a nightmare. It makes what she's going through with her father seem like nothing at all and herself a real whiner. What does she really have to complain about? She's been living in an upper middle class cocoon with all her needs met and nothing to worry about, and as far as her father is concerned, she knows her way around him and how to stay off his radar screen, and all she has to do is bide her time until she turns eighteen and then she can do whatever she damn well pleases. Henry, on the other hand, is facing his father's certain death and will have to deal with that when it happens. she hasn't met his mother, but she can only imagine how all this is affecting her. It almost makes her feel like an ingrate.

They finish eating, Henry pays and they leave, Henry waving to Phil and Neal and they waving back, calling, "Ciao!" and telling him to come back soon. Henry opens the car door for her, they both get in and off they go. They haven't gone far when she says, "I'm going to my cousin's house," and gives him directions as they drive along. "There," she says, pointing to her cousin's family's narrow house on a street lined with them. He slows and stops the car. "Want to come in?" she asks hopefully and sees he's trying to figure out why they're here at her cousin's house instead of hers. She leans over and kisses him and places her hand lightly on the lump in his jeans, giving it a gentle squeeze, then leans back just far enough to see his eyes searching hers and his grin.

"Sure," he says.

She told Moira she'd be bringing someone back to her house, as she has many times before, not that she had to. The basement door is right inside the front door and anyone letting herself or himself in would go unnoticed. Her Uncle Mick will be sitting on the couch in the living room, drunk and staring at the TV screen, if not passed out. Her aunt Mary will be mending clothes in the small room in the back of the house and even if her aunt did hear the front door open, she'd assume it was one of the kids, arriving home, and pay it no mind. Still, they enter the house as quietly as they can and Colleen opens the basement door, turns on the light and they tiptoe down the stairs. If Moira's here with a boy, Colleen knows she'll be in the storage space on the left, so she leads Henry by the hand to the one on the right and opens the door and pulls him in after her.

She sees by his expression that he knows this isn't the first time she's brought a boy here and is pleased that he doesn't look judgmental, just curious about what she has planned. She takes the quilted packing blanket from the shelf and spreads it on the cement floor, then turns and wraps her arms around his neck and kisses him. She feels his arms around her waist, holding her tightly. She parts her lips slightly and slowly puts her tongue in his mouth and feels his tongue meet hers. She pulls him down slowly onto the blanket, kissing him as they lie down next to each other. She can feel by the way he's kissing and holding her that he's different than any boy she's been with before. For one thing, he's kissing her like he really wants to and is enjoying it, not like it's something he feels he must do to get what he really wants, as the others have, if they've kissed her at all. In fact, he seems to be enjoying kissing her as much as she's enjoying kissing him. For another, he's still holding her tightly around her waist and isn't manhandling her breasts, as the others would have been by now. Is he hoping to get a blowjob? Maybe, maybe not. If he is, he's sure going about it the right way, treating her gently and respectfully. What girl wouldn't be happy to reward a boy like him with one for being so nice?

At last, she feels his hand on her breast, and she's delighted by the way he's fondling and caressing it. She arches her back and presses herself harder against him, encouraging him to do more. She feels him unbuttoning her blouse as they kiss and gently pulling it out of her jeans and opening it, exposing her bra. The other boys she's let get this far have all been so clumsy when it comes to her bra. She prefers the type with the clasp in front because it's more convenient, but they all assume the clasp is in back and fumble around trying to find it. One boy was so flummoxed and became so frustrated that he tried to yank her bra over her head and nearly choked her. She took to undoing it herself to spare herself the bother of waiting for them to figure it out. It's not the case with Henry. She's impressed with how adroitly he undoes the clasp with just a twist of his thumb and forefinger.

As her bra parts she's surprised to find she feels self-conscious about her large breasts. Does he think they're too big in relation to her slight build, that she looks freakish? She can see by the way he's admiring them and the rest of her that he doesn't. She watches him bring his lips to her nipple, closes her eyes and enjoys the feeling of him kissing and licking and sucking it as no one has before and it feels wonderful.

She hears footsteps and giggling on the stairs and feels Henry pulling his head away and sees him in the dim light, looking at her uncertainly. "It's okay," she whispers, "it's just my cousin." They wait a moment, listening to the sound of Moira and whichever boy she's with, settling down in the storage space next to theirs, and then the murmur of their voices and more giggling. "It's okay," she whispers and reaches out and puts her hand lightly on the back of his head and brings his lips back down to her nipple and feels him sucking again as he fondles and caresses her other breast. It feels more than wonderful. It feels fantastic and she wants him to know. She runs her fingers through the hair on the back of his neck. "No one's ever touched me this way," she whispers and sees him look up at her with that curious expression of his.

"Why's that?" he asks.

She shrugs and searches his eyes and sees him smile slightly.

"Because they think you're a slut?"

She feels her body thrill. So, he has heard the rumors, and yet he's treating her so tenderly. She shrugs again.

"Are you?" he asks.

"No," she whispers. "I guess I act like one, though."

"Why's that?"

"I dunno."

He shrugs. "What you do with other people is your business. When you're with me, it's our business."

She feels grateful tears welling in her eyes and wraps her arms around him and kisses him hard and doesn't ever want to stop kissing him or let him go. That feeling gives way to her desire for him to please her the way she's let a few boys in the past, always before giving them a blowjob. She learned pretty quickly that once she's blown them, the last thing on their mind is pleasing her. She knows it's not like that with Henry, that he'll enjoy pleasing her as much as she'll enjoy being pleased.

She stands and takes a security candle out of the pack on the shelf and lies back down beside him and hands it to him. She sees him look at it with that curious expression of his again and then at her. "Put it inside me," she whispers. He smiles and slowly shakes his head and puts the candle down. He unbuttons and unzips her jeans and she wriggles as he pulls them and her underpants off. She watches him place her clothes aside and put his hands on her knees and spread her legs and she's surprised and delighted when he doesn't pick up the candle but instead brings his face between her legs and feels his lips on her clit, kissing it and then his tongue licking it and then his mouth sucking it. So, she thinks, this is it, it's finally happening.

Her cheeks and neck feel hot. She closes her eyes and smiles and enjoys the feeling of him gently massaging her clit and then two of his fingers entering her and moving slowly and carefully inside her, reaching all the way up to her pelvic bone. She feels his other hand on her breast and his lips on hers again now, kissing her sweetly and fondling her as he massages her. The pleasure she's experiencing is beyond anything she has before. What she's been doing with boys seems childish now. How can she possibly go back to doing that after experiencing this? There's just no way.

She feels him bring the two fingers inside her to just a few inches inside her opening and he's massaging her there and pressing a bit harder and it's producing an entirely new sensation. She's heard talk among girls about there being this magical pleasure spot in the vagina, called a "G-Spot." Some girls believe it exists, and some don't and those that do have different ideas about where it's located. Now she knows it does and just where hers is. She's touched herself in this same spot and it's felt good, but not like this, and she knows it's because it's Henry who's touching it and she feels like a fish on a hook that's been only too willing and happy to be caught.

The pleasure she feels between her legs increases, surpassing what she's experienced when she's masturbated, and she opens her eyes a bit and sees Henry gazing down at her, smiling. He looks perfectly happy doing nothing more than giving her pleasure and she can tell be the way he's massaging her more quickly now and pressing harder that he wants her to come. No other boy has cared at all about how she feels, let alone about pleasing her or making her come and she wants to, just for Henry, because she knows it will please him as much as it will her.

She closes her eyes again, tilts her head back and moves her hips in time with the strokes of his fingers, slowly lifting her hips off the blanket and pressing herself harder and harder against his fingers. Her legs begin shaking and her body trembling and then thrusting against his fingers and she's panting and biting her lip to keep from making noise and the feeling between her legs explodes as she climaxes. Still trembling, she slowly lowers herself to the blanket and lies there with her eyes closed, panting and feeling her body glowing.

Finally, she opens her eyes and sees Henry gazing down at her and smiling. She must have been quite a sight, out of control, like an animal. The idea of letting a boy see her looking like that was out of the question before, but she was happy to show this intimate side of herself to Henry. She watches him pull off his jeans and underpants and sees his penis is stiff and circumcised and makes the idea of having the candle inside her also seem childish now. He lowers himself down on her and brings his face close to hers. "It's okay," she whispers, "I'm on the pill." He kisses her gently and she feels him entering her and it's the first time anyone's ever been inside her.

How many times has she wondered when this moment would finally arrive and what it would be like and with whom? Her hope had been that it would happen soon and her fantasy was that she would meet a handsome man in his twenties, someone experienced, who worked at the hotel where she and her parents were staying while on vacation, and that they would go to his apartment and he would undress her in the bedroom and lay her on the bed and kiss her all over and then make glorious love to her. That's one version. In the other, he'd be nice until he got her in the bedroom and then he'd get rough, ripping off her clothes and forcing her to have sex with him against her will, which, of course, was just what she wanted him to do, so it wasn't really rape, just pretend rape, and she would play along, struggling as he held her wrists tightly, pinned to the bed, and had his way with her.

She used to worry about the first time being painful, as any girl whose hymen is still intact does. Hers was the first time she let a boy put the safety candle in her and she has no one to blame but herself for what happened. She chose to experiment with Collin, a not so bright younger boy who lives a few houses down from Moira. For a time, last summer, it seemed that whenever Colleen walked down the hill to visit Moira, Collin would be sitting on Moira's front steps, gazing at her adoringly, like she was a goddess descending from the heavens. She knew he'd do whatever she told him to and keep his mouth shut about it. She took him to the storage space and told him what to do and he tried his best to follow her instructions and ease the candle in above her hymen, but got carried away and the next thing she knew she felt excruciating pain between her legs and the world went white. She hit him so hard he bounced off the wall and when she inspected herself, she saw her hymen was torn and there was blood trickling down the inside of both thighs.

No, she wasn't worried about pain and Henry feels wonderful inside her, filling her up. What she's waiting to see is whether he'll keep his eyes on hers. It seems like such a small thing but, to her thinking, it's the most important thing. Having someone inside you who either can't or won't look in your eyes is just fucking, but if he looks at you, as Henry is now, gazing down at her serenely as they slowly rock back and forth, then that's making love. She runs her fingers through the hair on the back of his head and smiles up at him sweetly. "Let me know when you're gonna come," she whispers.

"Why? It's okay isn't it?"

"I want you in my mouth." She can see he likes this idea by the way he turns the corner of his mouth up slightly. Does he understand that, despite everything he's heard about her, it won't be the same as it was with the other boys, that those were just blowjobs, as impersonal and mechanical as it sounds; that having him come in her mouth and swallowing it will be, for her, a first and the perfect ending to a wonderful experience and that, having done so, she'll feel redeemed of her bad reputation and absolved of all her past sins? Maybe, maybe not. She thinks he does, though.

She sees him close his eyes and part his lips slightly and feels his body tense and hears his breathing quicken. He begins pumping faster and harder and she knows he's about to come. She quickly scoots out from under him and scrambles forward as he leans back. She lies down on her stomach in front of him and takes him in her mouth and sucks and swallows his semen as it spurts out of him. She doesn't imagine she's receiving the Eucharist. Just Henry's gift. She slowly pulls her head back, letting him free, and looks up at him. She sees him gazing down at her, the way she imagined Jesus was when she was giving the other boys blowjobs, and she feels cleansed, innocent and pure.

* * *

Valerie sucks on her straw and looks sympathetically at Colleen as she listens intently to her account of how her relationship with Henry has been going or, rather, not going. Colleen's frustrated that Henry doesn't seem to want to do anything more than date her occasionally and when she's finished her story, Valerie shrugs.

"Sounds like he just doesn't want a steady girlfriend," Valerie says. "Not every boy does, you know?"

Colleen searches Valerie's eyes a moment, hoping to see even a hint of encouragement appear in them but doesn't. "Yeah," she says glumly and sucks on her straw. She knows Valerie's right and it's maddening. She's certain her adoration of Henry and desire to do anything for him couldn't be more obvious to him, yet each time he drops her off after a date, while she knows he's enjoyed being with her, she has the feeling it was just another date to him and nothing special.

She even stopped seeing other boys, which he knows she has, to show him how strong and deep her feelings for him are. He seems perfectly content with their relationship continuing just as it is and his attitude about it seems to be what it is about pretty much everything, she's come to learn, and even more so since his father died: non-committal. He seems removed and above it all and she wants desperately to bring him down to earth and somehow open his eyes and make him see her for the loving, perfect person for him she is and make her his own.

She's come to believe he is the way he is because he's an Army brat, having lived all over the place and not really calling anyplace home. Even <u>he</u> said that he feels like he's "just passing through which, in fact, he is, since a year from now, when he graduates, he'll go off to college somewhere. Having grown up like a nomad is another piece of the puzzle, like the two Japanese women who doted on him for the first two years of his life. His relationship with his mom is still another.

Colleen finally met his mom and likes her and knows his mom likes her too. She's enjoyed the few times she's sat at their dining room table with them, drinking coffee and smoking and listening to them talk, which they can do for hours on end. His mom's a real storyteller and Colleen enjoys listening to her reminisce about the family history and her childhood, growing up in Yonkers during the good times, before the market crash, and then how the family moved to the Bronx, where she met Henry's dad, and how they married and he enlisted in the Army and was recruited by the O.S.S. because he spoke Italian, and worked with the partisans in Italy and how, when he came home, he tried to make a go of it in her father's construction business but, after a year of experiencing family politics, asked her one day what she thought about his going back into the Army and she said, "Let's go!" and she felt like it was the beginning of a great adventure.

Colleen glimpsed another piece of the puzzle the first time she and Henry saw each other after his dad died. They were sitting in the Vail's Gate Diner and she remembers listening to "Don't You Care one of the songs he'd selected, coming out of the little speaker at their table, and she listened as he talked about his dad, saying that he was really out of the picture in his life for the last few years, having been in Korea and then not himself when he came home, and then at Walter Reade, and then at their house in New Windsor in pretty much a vegetative state. That person was a far cry from the man he remembers from his childhood, who loved movies and musicals and was extremely talented, with a great singing voice and always bursting into song, and skillful with his hands, able to build or fix just about anything. Henry said his dad was the type of man people naturally liked, charming and always smiling. It was sad watching someone so vital waste away.

Henry told her how he arrived home from Saint Pat's one day to find his dad downstairs in the family room, lying on the couch, having wet his pants, shaking and staring vacantly at the ceiling, obviously having a seizure. Henry called his mom at work and she called the police and he and his mother followed the ambulance to the V.A. hospital in Manhattan, where his dad was placed in a bed in the terminal ward, and when they were finally permitted to see him, they found that he was the only patient there, lying in bed in a coma, looking greenish in the fluorescent light and surrounded by beeping machines, with tubes running into and out of him.

They drove back to New Windsor, and it was only a few hours later that his mom woke him and told him his dad had died and to get dressed and off they went back down to the city for the wake, which lasted a week, and the burial at the National Cemetery on Long Island. It's a piece of the puzzle that fits beside the dream he told her he had a few weeks after his father's death.

In the dream, Henry was sitting at the kitchen table in his grandparents' house in the Bronx in the early morning, before anyone else in the house was up. The sky was just beginning to lighten and the light was eerie. He saw a shadowy figure through the kitchen doorway, coming down the stairs, not walking, but floating. It didn't look like his dad, but Henry knew it was, and when the figure turned at the landing and looked at him, he saw his father's face and that most of his head was gone. Henry woke, sat up in bed and stared at the spiderweb pattern of frost on the window pane, illuminated by the street light, and it took him a long time to get back to sleep, even though it was the middle of the night.

She wondered then as she does now if his father's illness and death is the reason he's unwilling or unable to commit to a relationship with anyone, if it's caused him to wall himself off emotionally. It's been an awful experience for him, and she wouldn't blame him for not wanting to expose himself to the possibility of any type of pain and loss again. She wants to tell him that she wouldn't disappoint or hurt him, that he can trust her not to play with his emotions, and that if he commits to her, she'll always be faithful to him and always be there for him, but she doesn't. She has the feeling that if she did, he'd feel pressured and wouldn't want to see her anymore and that's the last thing she wants to happen.

If he only knew the degree of self-discipline she's been exercising not to make him feel pressured. She's surprised by it herself. Whenever she looks at the Princess phone, she finally convinced her parents to have installed in her bedroom, she wants to pick it up and call him. Sometimes she picks up the receiver and puts it to her ear, just to hear the dial tone, and sometimes she dials his number, all but the "8" at the end, and keeps her finger on the "8" button, enjoying the thrill of wanting desperately to press it, but not letting herself do it.

There was that one time when she did press it. She hadn't seen him in a while, had been thinking constantly about making love with him and arrived home from school feeling horny, even though she was beginning her period. She sat on her bed, staring at the phone, trying to decide whether to pick it up and call him or just masturbate. She finally gave in and picked up the receiver and dialed his number, not even knowing if he was home, and he answered. She asked if she could come see him and he said she could. She got in her mother's car and drove to his house. He opened the front door and she took him by the hand and led him to his bedroom without saying a word. They watched each other as they pulled off their clothes and climbed on his bed and made glorious love for an hour.

That was a special day and she smiles as she remembers it. Two things happened that were wonderful and new: first, when he spread her legs and saw that she had a tampon in her, he smiled up at her took it out, put his face between her legs and carried on as he usually did, enjoying giving her pleasure; second, he massaged her anus as he was kissing and licking and sucking her clit and put his finger just inside it and then a finger on her G-spot and massaged them both. That was a truly amazing sensation and the first time she'd ever experienced multiple orgasms. Why wouldn't she want him all to herself? It's only natural that she would.

She knows from Anya, who gets news about Henry from her brother and Ronnie, that Henry sees other girls but that none of them is really his girlfriend. She tries not to think about him being with other girls but can't help imagining him doing what he does with her with them, which she knows he does and when she does think about it, she tries to console herself by thinking that he doesn't enjoy it as much with them as he does with her, but she knows she's being foolish. It silly of her, really, not to go out with other boys, when he's going out with other girls, but she can't and her relationship with Henry has taught her that love isn't always fair and can be cruel.

She realizes that she's been lost in thought, staring out the window, and that Valerie's been studying her with a look of concern.

"Well, don't lose sleep over it." Valerie says.

In fact, she is losing sleep over it and every other aspect of her relationship with Henry, but she's not going to share that with Valerie, as close as the two of them have become, now that Colleen's at NFA, much closer than she is with Megan. She values Valerie's friendship and feels grateful that she treats her as an equal, even though Valerie's two years older. She doesn't want to give her any reason whatsoever to think that she's just a foolish love-struck kid, although that's how she feels.

"Hey!" Valerie says, "Miles Davis is playin' at the Village Gate next month. Wanna go?"

Colleen has listened many times now to *Kind of Blue,* which Valerie gave her as a birthday present, and with each listening, she's become more familiar with the music and has found herself liking it more and now when she listens to the album, she recognizes her own different moods and feelings expressed by the different songs. It would be great to hear the music live. "Sure! When?"

"March Nineteenth. It's a Saturday. We'll take the bus into the city Saturday mornin' and stay at my grandmother's. You'll meet Sandy. It'll be fun."

Colleen smiles to herself, hearing Valerie pronounce "bus" "buzz" as she always does, just as she always pronounces "Bensonhurst" "Benzinhoist." "I'm looking forward to it," she says and is. She's curious about Sandy.

When Valerie first mentioned her, she said she was her best friend and that they'd grown up and been through a lot together. There was something about her expression and the way she said it, both filled with meaning, that Colleen found curious and intriguing. She's never pressed Valerie for details about her relationship with Sandy, both out of respect and, it must be said, the fear of crossing a boundary that Valerie might not want her to cross. This much she does know. Every weekend that Valerie can, she's on the bus, traveling back to Bensonhurst, and Colleen knows without having to ask that it's to spend it with Sandy. "I'll okay it with my parents, but I don't see any problem."

"Good. Lemme know ASAP so I can get tickets. They go fast."

CHAPTER 5

Valerie and Sandy

Colleen's been answering Valerie's question, "How's things goin' with Henry?" for what seems a long time now, since shortly after they left Newburgh, heading south toward New York City on Route 17, and here they are arriving at the Short Line stop in Suffern and she's finally run out of things to say. Valerie looks at her and shrugs.

"You can't make someone love you," Valerie says.

Colleen looks out the window at the dingy gray winter landscape passing by. She knows Valerie's right and she feels like a fool for continuing to try, but she can't help herself. "What's Bensonhurst like?" she asks, to change the subject.

"Nice, you know? It's so close to Manhattan, but it's really like a small town. Everybody knows everybody."

"Are there Blacks there?" Judging from Valerie's expression, Martians would have a better chance of living in Bensonhurst.

"Nah. Mostly Italians and some Jews. My family's been there since the turn of the century. My grandparents on both sides are Sicilian. You'd be surprised the number of famous people come from there."

"Yeah? Like whom?"

"The Three Stooges."

"No kidding?"

"Yeah, Moe and Curly Horowitz and their older brother Shemp and Larry Fine. All from Bensonhurst."

"Who else."

"Barbra Streisand and Elliot Gould."

"Wow!"

"Yeah. Her name used to be 'Bar-bar-a' but she dropped the middle 'a' when she was singin' at gay clubs in the Village. Who knows why? Gould's mother sold artificial flowers to beauty shops and his father worked in the garment business. That's Bensonhurst."

Colleen takes notice of Valerie's use of the word "gay" to mean "homosexual." She hears it used this way more and more now and it rankles her. Since she was little, she's always understood the word to mean "happy in a carefree and lighthearted way. That's what she was taught and every time she's encountered the word in print, that's what it's meant, but now she feels the word is being appropriated to describe illegal sexual behavior that's considered a mental disorder by the psychiatric community. It's not that she has anything against homosexuals, but she can't help feeling resentful that the word is being sullied and no one seems to want to come to its defense.

"Sandy Koufax," Valerie says.

"Yeah?"

"My hero from Bensonhurst is Abe Burrows."

"Who's he?"

"A writer. He wrote *Guys and Dolls.*"

"Are all the famous people from there Jewish?"

"Nah," Valerie says and reflects a moment. "Well, most of them, I guess. Vic Damone's from Bensonhurst. He's Italian American. His real name's Vito Farinola. Of course, there're the mobsters. Most of them are Italian American and famous in their own way, although I'm sure you've never heard of them. Maybe we'll take a walk over to Dyker Heights. The houses there are really beautiful. It's kind of an exclusive community. Old Man Benson bought the land when it was just farmland and developed it. He didn't want Italian immigrants livin' there. He did a good job of keepin' 'em out for a long time, but now it's all Italian Americans. Things change."

Colleen is reminded of what's happening in Newburgh and now she's certain that one day, and perhaps much sooner than later, there'll be Black families living in those houses along North Plank Road and probably everywhere else in the city. You can't stop change and you just have to deal with the changes and make the best of them.

She thinks of the Freedom Riders, the Black and White men and women who risked their lives in the early '60s, traveling in the South to test anti-discrimination laws, who had their bus bombed and were beaten by the Ku Klux Klan and were thrown in jail and, in the case of three of them, were murdered.

She thinks of how events unfolded so quickly in 1963, first with Medgar Evers being gunned down in his driveway just hours after President Kennedy's speech on television in support of the civil rights legislation making its way through Congress, and then the four little black girls being killed in the church bombing in Birmingham, and then the march on Washington and Martin Luther King, Jr.'s "I have a dream" speech, and then the assassination of President Kennedy, and it seems so discouraging and sad to her, to think that it took all that for Congress to finally pass the Civil Rights Act and then the Voting Rights Act in 1964, that that's what had to happen for Black people to enjoy the same constitutional rights as citizens as Whites. And there's still a long way to go, so it's good that people like Martin Luther King, Jr. and Bobby Kennedy are around to carry on the fight. She's heard that Kennedy might run for President, which she thinks would be a good thing. She'd vote for him, if she could.

And then she thinks of the Italian-Americans in Bensonhurst, not being allowed to live in these big fancy houses, and it seems pretty small in comparison but she knows she's wrong, that discrimination is discrimination and they probably felt the same way, looking at those houses and not being able to live in them, as Blacks in the South did, looking at "White's Only" signs on restaurants and restrooms and drinking fountains and not being able to use them. Thinking about it makes her weary.

"You'll have to come for The Feast," Valerie says excitedly.

"What's that?"

"The Feast of Saint Rosalia. It's at the end of the summer. It's a big party. They close off 18th Avenue."

"Who's she?"

"The patron saint of Palermo, in Sicily. I'm tellin' you, *lots* of Sicilians in Bensonhurst! We've got the best pizza in New York!"

Colleen gets her first glimpse of the Manhattan skyline off in the distance and watches it grow larger as they approach the Lincoln Tunnel on the Jersey side of the Hudson. As the bus makes the sweeping turn down toward the entrance to the tunnel, there it is—Manhattan!—rising into the sky and she stares at it in wonderment. In all deference to Boston, which, she learned on a trip there with her parents to visit her mother's family, once fancied itself the "Hub of the Universe," she knows that New York City is the capitol of the world, the place people at all points of the compass look to for direction and come to, like pilgrims to a shrine, for business and culture and entertainment.

She always has the same feeling when she visits New York City that big things are happening here—all the time. The first time she visited the city with her parents when she was little and gazed at the skyline from the West Side Highway, she imagined New Yorkers to be a race of giants, living and working and playing in the clouds and only descending to the streets far below when necessary, to hurry from one skyscraper to another. It was childish, but she still thinks of them that way.

This is the first time she's taken the bus to the city and traveling through the dark Lincoln Tunnel strikes her as theatrical, as if the house lights have been brought down at the beginning of a play to prepare her for what comes next, whatever that might be, and as they exit the tunnel into the bright sunlight, she looks up and sees the buildings rising into the sky, towering overhead. It's an awesome sight and she feels exhilarated and dwarfed, all at once. She's always wondered what living here would be like and whether she could make it. She's not sure but she thinks she can and now she wants to try someday. It feels like her kind of town.

They ride the subway from Port Authority to Brooklyn and walk down the stairs from the elevated station onto the busy intersection at 18th Avenue and Bay Parkway. Valerie points out businesses owned by families in the neighborhood as they walk along, among them the pizza shop where her brother Vincent—he hates being called "Vinnie she says, as much as she hates being called "Val"—works part-time to earn spending money. They turn down a tree-lined side street, with rows of well-kept single-family homes facing each other.

"What's your grandmother's name?" Colleen asks and sees Valerie giving the house they're passing a careful inspection.

"Regina Girafalco," Valerie says and looks from the house down at the sidewalk. "My mom's mother. My dad's parents live a few blocks over. I've always been closest to Regina. I don't know, maybe it's because we lived on the same street and I was always in her kitchen. You would have liked my grandfather Amedeo. He was such a lovely man, such a gentleman, old school, ya know? He died a couple of years ago. Hardening of the arteries," she says, shaking her head. "He wasn't himself at the end. He'd wander out of the house in his underwear and my grandmother would call the cops and they'd go find him and bring him home. It was so sad."

"I'm so sorry for you," Colleen says and Henry's dad comes to mind.

They arrive at Valerie's grandmother's house, in the middle of the block, and Colleen follows Valerie down the side path to the side door and into the kitchen, where she sees Regina, a short, plump gray-haired woman in a floral print house dress, sitting at the far end of the table, knitting a beige sweater for someone as she watches a soap opera on the TV set on a counter by the window. Regina's glasses look like they're about to fall off the end of her nose and she has a cigarette dangling from her lips with an ash on the end of it that also looks like it's about to fall off into her knitting. She looks up and smiles at them as they enter.

"Hi, Nonna!" Valerie says.

"Hi, Dolly!" Regina says, smiling broadly. She puts down her knitting and her cigarette in the ashtray, hoists herself up, walks around the table with some difficulty and gives Valerie a big hug, patting her on the back.

Valerie steps back. "This is Colleen."

"Nice to meet you!" Regina says, opening her arms to Colleen. "Nice to meet you too, Missus Girofalco," Colleen, says, trying her best to roll the "r" as she heard Valerie do when she pronounced the name. She steps forward and receives the same big hug and pat on the back. Regina steps back and looks at her appreciatively and reaches out and pinches her cheek.

"Ma che brava che sei! Call me Regina."

Regina looks Colleen and then Valerie up and down and shakes her head disapprovingly.

"Look at you two! You're both skinnymalinks! You need to eat!"

Colleen sees Valerie roll her eyes. Colleen's never heard the word and has no idea what it means, other than skinny something.

Valerie shrugs. "She picked it up from my grandmother, who got it from a neighbor. I know. It's weird. I hope you like to eat," Valerie says. "It never ends with her."

"Can I help with anything?" Colleen asks.

"Sit! Sit!" Regina says, waving her toward the table and pulling back a chair for her.

Colleen listens to Valerie and Regina chat and watches Valerie as she collects plates and utensils and napkins and puts them at their places, then takes a Saran wrapped platter filled with meats and cheeses from the refrigerator and puts it on the table, then opens a drawer and takes a large round loaf of bread from it and a bread knife from another drawer and puts them on the table.

"Fresh from the bakery," Regina says proudly.

"When isn't it?" Valerie asks.

Valerie takes a bottle of olive oil from the counter, puts it on the table and sits next to Colleen. Colleen leans over and whispers to Valerie, "What did your grandmother say to me in Italian?"

"How brave you are. It's a compliment, like 'Good for you!'"

Regina settles into her chair across from them, picks up her knitting and looks at them both with raised eyebrows.

"So?" Regina asks. "Don't just sit there. Eat!"

Valerie slices the loaf of bread and places two pieces on Colleen's plate.

"Ever had prosciutto and provolone?" Valerie asks.

"No," Colleen says.

"It's delicious. Drizzle some olive oil on it. You'll love it."

Colleen places slices of provolone and prosciutto on a piece of bread, drizzles some olive oil on it and places another slice of bread on top and brings it to her mouth and takes a bite. The crust is just crunchy enough and the bread is more flavorful than any she's tasted before, with a hint of what she thinks is rosemary and a buttery consistency. No sooner does she begin chewing than it melts in her mouth. The taste puts the baloney and Swiss and tuna fish with mayo on white bread sandwiches she's been eating all her life to shame. "Hmm…this is delicious."

"I knew you'd like it," Valerie says with a grin. "The house looks good," she says to Regina.

Colleen assumes Valerie's referring to Regina's house and looks around at the kitchen, thinking maybe it's been repainted recently, or maybe the exterior. Valerie notices her inspecting the kitchen.

"My family's house," Valerie says. "We passed it on the way. We're rentin' it out."

"I watch those people like a hawk," Regina says.

"You don't have to worry, Nonna. They're nice people."

"Ahhh," Regina says with a dismissive wave of her hand, as if to say, "They might seem like nice people, but you never know," which is why she keeps an eye on them. "So, how's school, Dolly?"

Valerie finishes chewing, swallows and wipes her mouth with her napkin. "Good."

Regina looks proudly at Colleen. "Such a good student, my granddaughter."

Valerie rolls her eyes. "Colleen's an honors student too, Nonna."

Regina raises her eyebrows. "You are? Good for you!"

"How's Sandy?" Valerie asks.

"Good, good. She brought me groceries with the bread this morning. We had cawfee."

Colleen smiles at Regina's pronunciation of "coffee just as she does whenever she hears Valerie say "buzz."

"She miss me?" Valerie asks.

"Aiyee!" Regina says, gesturing with another dismissive wave of her hand.

Colleen takes the gesture to mean, "You have no idea!" When she was vacationing with her parents in Italy, she saw a lot of this shaking of the back of the hand at someone, with the fingertips together, that ends up looking like the person is throwing salt over his or her shoulder. It struck her as funny and theatrical and unlike the way the people in Ireland, where they spent the next week of the vacation, related to each other. The Irish were friendly enough and quick to smile but more reserved and wary than the Italians. Her father strikes her as being as un-Italian as it gets. His favorite gesture when he wants to add emphasis is to point his finger at her, like the barrel of a gun.

"I missed her too, a *lot*," Valerie says. "Can't wait to see her."

Colleen has the feeling, judging from Valerie's sad expression and the longing in her voice, that she and Sandy are inseparable. As long as she's known Megan and as good friends as they are, she knows she doesn't feel about her the way Valerie obviously does about Sandy. Well, Valerie said they've known each other all their lives and grew up on the same street together, so it stands to reason they'd be close.

Colleen follows Valerie up the stairs, both carrying their overnight bags, and they pass a bedroom in the upstairs hall that even at a glance shows all the telltale signs of being a boy's room. She knows from the Columbia pennant above the desk that it's Vincent's. "So, your brother lives here?" she asks, following Valerie into her bedroom, just down and across the hall.

"Yeah," Valerie says, and puts Colleen's bag on the floor at the foot of the bed.

"When you said he was at Columbia," Colleen says, "I thought he was living in a dorm there."

"He is, but he stays here on the weekends, and sometimes durin' the week too. He gets more studyin' done here, plus he works at the pizza parlor. Columbia's awfully expensive, almost as expensive as Harvard. Even with student aid, my dad could barely afford to send him there. That's why he took the job at West Point and moved us all the way up to hicksville. It pays better."

Colleen is stung by Valerie's comment. She'd be the first to agree that Newburgh is no New York City, but it's her hometown, it's where she grew up and it means as much to her as Bensonhurst does to Valerie. "It's not exactly hicksville. It was an important city and has a lot of history." Colleen sees Valerie's surprise as it dawns on her that she found her comment offensive.

"Hey, I'm sorry," Valerie says. She puts her arms around Colleen and gives her a hug. "I didn't mean to offend you."

"I know," Colleen says.

Valerie steps back, takes her hands and looks at her contritely. When it comes to not letting her feelings show, Colleen is masterful and the fact that she forgot herself for a moment and let Valerie see that she was hurt is unfortunate and regrettable. Whenever that happens, she usually feels exposed and vulnerable, but she doesn't with Valerie. For the first time in their relationship, Colleen feels she has the upper hand, if only momentarily. Part of her wants to forgive Valerie, but part of her wants to take her sweet time doing it, so that when she does forgive her, it will be truly appreciated.

"Besides," Valerie says, "if we hadn't moved to Newburgh, we never would have met. Right?" She chucks Colleen's chin with a knuckle and searches her eyes for a sign of forgiveness but doesn't see any.

"Jeez, I'm really sorry!" Valerie says contritely.

"It's okay," Colleen finally says. "Forget it." Valerie grins.

"Remind me never to badmouth Newburgh again. Okay? C'mon, let's go see Sandy."

They walk across the street and a few houses down. The houses all look to Colleen to be the same basic design: two floors and a basement and attic with a peaked roof. She figures they were all built at the same time by the same developer and modified by the families over time. One house has a gable on the side, so the attic has probably been made into a bedroom. As they walk down the side path of Sandy's house to the kitchen door, Colleen sees they've added a sunroom on the back and, when they enter the kitchen, that's where they find Sandy's mom—Colleen assumes that's who she is—standing at an ironing board, ironing a shirt with a laundry basket full of clothes by her side. Colleen's first impression is that she looks like an Italian-America version of Lucille Ball. Her dark brown hair is pinned up and she has a blue scarf around her head, knotted at her forehead. The collar of her white blouse is turned up and she's wearing light blue Capri pants and light blue mules. Just like Regina, Sandy's mom is watching a soap opera and has a cigarette dangling from her lips. She looks at them, smiles and puts the iron on the plate, takes the cigarette out of her mouth and puts it in the ashtray.

"Hi, honey!" Sandy's mom says, beaming at Valerie.

She walks around the ironing board and up to Valerie and they wrap their arms around each other and hug, swaying from side to side. They step back and hold hands and stand looking in each other's eyes and something about the way they're looking at each other strikes Colleen as very interesting. She can't put her finger on what it is but, it's definitely not the way a best friend's mom looks at her daughter's best friend and vice versa. It's more the way two people who love and respect each other and have an understanding between them about something important and personal and private do. Sandy's mom strokes Valerie's cheek tenderly with her fingertips. "She missed you, honey."

"I missed her too," Valerie says and nods toward Colleen. "This is Colleen."

"Nice to meet you," Sandy's mom says, holding out her hand. "I'm Connie."

Colleen takes it. "Nice to meet you, Connie."

"I know Regina fed you," Connie says. "Would you like anything, Colleen? Somethin' to drink? A soda?"

"I'm fine, thank you," Colleen says and sees Connie look at Valerie tenderly again.

"She *really* missed you this time," Connie says softly, "a *lot*."

"I know. Nonna told me."

Connie shakes her head slowly and strokes Valerie's cheek again. "It would've been so much better if they'd just let you stay with Regina and finish school here," she says sadly. "Your father can be so unreasonable sometimes. He's always been like that, since he was a kid."

Valerie shrugs. "Tell me about it. He's a typical Sicilian when it comes to women, possessive and overly protective. I mean, I love him, but I don't know how Ma's managed to stay with him all these years. A guy like that would drive me crazy."

Connie smiles, places a hand on Valerie's arm and nods toward the staircase. "Go on," she says. "She's dying to see you." She looks at Colleen. "Make yourself at home. Help yourself to whatever you like."

"Thanks," Colleen says and follows Valerie. From the bottom of the stairs, she can hears Sandy, blowing out her breath in a steady rhythm, the way people do when they exercise. She wonders what Sandy's doing. Sit-ups? Push-ups? Knee squats? It sounds more strenuous than that.

She stops behind Valerie at the open doorway to Sandy's bedroom and looks in over her shoulder. She sees Sandy, lying on her back on a weightlifting bench, holding a bar with several large weights on either end that's resting on her chest. She sees by the way Sandy strains to push the bar up and lock her arms that it's really heavy and probably weighs more than she and Valerie do combined.

"Hey," Colleen hears Valerie say and can tell by the sound of her voice that she's grinning at Sandy. She sees Sandy carefully rest the bar on its holder and sit up. She looks at Valerie the way someone who's felt alone and lost and miserable because the love of her life has gone away looks when she sees her standing in front of her again.

"Hey, baby!" Sandy says gleefully, beaming at Valerie and opening her arms wide.

The three of them are frozen for a moment and it feels to Colleen that time has stopped. There's Sandy, sitting on the bench, beaming at Valerie with her arms held wide open, and here's Valerie, standing in front of her in the doorway with her hands on her hips and her feet planted, grinning at Sandy, Colleen knows.

She studies Sandy and she's an impressive sight. Her light brown hair is pulled back tightly in a ponytail and she's wearing a gray tee shirt with ARMY printed in black on it and gray exercise shorts and white athletic socks. Her body looks firm and toned, and her face is beautiful. She has a high forehead and full wing-like eyebrows; her cheeks are chiseled and her nose is long and sharp; her mouth is small and her lips full and she has a square jaw and a slight cleft in her chin. Colleen notices a small tattoo on Sandy's right arm that looks like the head of a Greek or Roman soldier wearing a helmet.

Suddenly, Valerie springs from the doorway and is across the room in two bounding steps. She jumps into Sandy's arms and Sandy falls backward with Valerie on top of her and the two of them embrace and kiss and, Colleen can see, not on the cheek and they're not pecking each other on the lips. Their mouths are locked together, and they look as if they want nothing more than to stay in each other's arms, kissing this way forever.

As fascinated as she is by what she's witnessing, it's embarrassing standing here in the doorway, watching them, even though they don't seem to mind in the least that she's here. Still, she feels like an intruder in their moment of intimacy and averts her eyes and busies herself looking around the inside of Sandy's bedroom—at the stack of exercise magazines by the bench; at the hospital folds on the grey wool blanket covering her tightly made bed; at the ARMY pennant on the wall above the headboard; at the famous "We Can Do It!" poster on the wall, the one with the iconic illustration of the woman factory worker, wearing a red bandana and blue work shirt with her sleeves rolled up, flexing her muscle; at the woman in military uniform in the "THIS IS MY WAR TOO!" WAAC recruitment poster; at the poster of the Triumph Blue Pearl motorcycle; at the framed picture on Sandy's nightstand of herself and Valerie when they were kids, standing side by side with their arms over each other's shoulder, Sandy looking at Valerie and smiling and Valerie looking at the camera with a big grin on her face.

Have they always felt this way toward each other? Whatever the case, what Colleen observed going on between Connie and Valerie in the kitchen makes sense now and it's obvious that Regina knows how they feel about each other too. It's probably common knowledge in both their families and if Regina and Connie are any indication, far from thinking anything's wrong with it, they're happy for them.

Colleen's never experienced anything like this before and she feels foolish for having been taken completely by surprise. She thought she could read people better than she did Valerie. She could see Valerie had little interest in boys, beyond being friends, but she never anticipated this and now she feels stuck, not knowing whether to stay here, looking around Sandy's room, or go quietly downstairs to get a soda and let them enjoy their reunion in private.

She hears the two of them giggling and looks at them and sees they've stopped kissing and are gazing lovingly into each other's eyes and stroking each other's cheek, acting just like a boy and a girl in love, only they're girls. If they were a boy and a girl, however, it's clear to Colleen that Sandy would be the girl and Valerie the boy, which is confusing, since Sandy's bigger and so buff. It's the way Sandy looks so adoringly at Valerie and acts so submissively with her and seems ready to do anything and everything to please her that makes Colleen thinks so. "Would you like to be alone?" she asks delicately. They both look at her.

"Sorry," Valerie says, "we're being rude. We haven't seen each other in a while. C'mere," she says and waves Colleen over as she and Sandy untangle themselves and sit up.

"Nice to meet you," Sandy says, holding out a hand to Colleen. "Heard a lot about you."

Colleen takes it, they shake and she sits on the floor in front of them and crosses her legs. "Yeah?" Colleen asks. "All good, I hope."

"Any friend of Val's is a friend of mine."

Colleen's surprised and looks at Valerie. "I thought you hated to be called that."

"I do," Valerie says, shrugging, "by anyone else."

"So, everyone knows, huh?" Colleen asks. They both nod. "Other people?"

"The whole neighborhood," Valerie says.

"Isn't it kind of risky? It's illegal, and people talk."

"We take care of our own here," Sandy says.

Valerie narrows her eyes a bit. "You've got more problems with your reputation in Newburgh."

Colleen feels stung again by Valerie's comment, but she doesn't react the same way this time. She walked right into it and knows Valerie's right. She deserved what she got and is beginning to feel she doesn't have to keep up her defenses with these two, that she can be herself and share what she thinks and how she feels without fear of being misunderstood or judged. They're remarkable people. It must take a lot of courage to feel the way they do about each other and not try to hide it. She wishes she were as brave. She sees Sandy looking at her like she's been curious about something and dying to ask her. "What?" Colleen asks.

"What's it like?" Sandy asks.

"What?"

"Givin' blowjobs," Valerie says. "She's been wonderin'. When we were kids, there was this older girl in the neighborhood, Donna Cenci, who had the same reputation. They called her 'the pump.' She wasn't very bright or all that good lookin', so you could understand why she did it. It made sense. Not like you, you know?"

Colleen's beginning to understand that if she's going to be friends with Valerie and Sandy or, rather, if they're going to have her as a friend, then she's going to have to learn to stop taking things personally and be open and honest about herself, and that if she can do that, she'll be a better and stronger person. She knows it'll be a painful process, but it'll be worth it. "I used to think it gave me power over boys. I guess I still do, but I've begun to think it's not worth the bother."

"Huh," Sandy says. "Then why do you do it?"

Colleen looks at them as she considers what to say, beyond what she just told them. She suspects the answer is deeply rooted in her psychology and has to do with her relationship with her father. "I wish I knew," she finally says. "Anyway, I don't anymore, not with just anyone. To be honest, it's humiliating."

"She knows," Valerie says, giving Sandy a nudge, "she just doesn't want to admit it to herself."

Colleen feels her cheeks and neck flush and stares at Valerie, trying not to let her anger and resentment show. "Admit what?"

Valerie shrugs. "How should I know? I said *you* know."

Colleen feels she's making a complete ass of herself, being so defensive, so insecure and intent on protecting herself. From what? She couldn't feel more foolish. Valerie looks knowingly at her and grins.

"I bet it's different with Henry," Valerie says. Colleen hesitates a moment. "It is."

"See? So, there you go." Valerie says, looking tenderly at Sandy and stroking her cheek. "The most important thing is bein' with the right person. That's all that matters."

Colleen long ago came to the same conclusion, which is why she stopped going out with other boys and sits around waiting for Henry to call. The problem is she knows he doesn't feel the same way about her and always in the back of her mind is the nagging suspicion that he could take her or leave her. It's even more humiliating than giving blowjobs. She wants to change the subject. "I can't believe your parents accepted the fact that you're lesbian just like that. They weren't concerned or upset or angry with you? You're all Catholics. They didn't think it was a sin? I just can't believe it? It doesn't seem real. It's like a fairy tale."

Sandy and Valerie look at each other and Colleen sees the memory of something dark and painful in their eyes. Valerie looks at her while

Sandy gazes at the side of Valerie's face, her ear, her hair, her neck, her arm, her wrist and places her hand lightly on it.

"Are you kiddin'?" Valerie asks. "They were *plenty* upset. We went through hell. They did everything they could to keep us apart."

Colleen sees Sandy smile slightly at the mention of this.

"I can't go over to her house and she can't come over to my house," Valerie says in a singsong voice, "her parents send her away to camp for the summer, way out on the Island, and I don't hear from her." Valerie frowns at Sandy, who looks guiltily at her, shrugs and looks at Colleen.

"I'm not much of a writer," Sandy says apologetically.

Valerie rolls her eyes. "Yeah, so my parents decide the thing we've been missing all our lives is seein' the Grand Canyon, so off we go in our old Chevy Bel Air and it's a nightmare. I'm carsick the whole way there. I'm a city girl. I'm not used to ridin' in cars. So, we're stoppin' all the time so I can throw up by the side of the road and if I'm not throwin' up, I'm dry heavin'. We finally get there, and we can't afford to stay in the park, so we're holed up in some fleabag hotel that seems a hundred miles away and the air conditioner's broken and we're sweatin' like pigs and I'm thinkin' of her," Valerie says, nodding toward Sandy, who places her fingers around Valerie's wrist and gently strokes it, "constantly. I mean, *all* the time. What's she doin'? How's she feelin'? Is she havin' a good time? Does she miss me? I know she does, but I'm worried sick about it. So, we get home and she's not home from camp yet and I can't take it anymore. I go across the street and walk into Regina's kitchen and she's sittin' there watchin' *The Edge of Night*, knittin', with her readin' glasses on the end of her nose and a Chesterfield stuck to her lower lip, with an ash on it about an inch long, ready to fall off into the sweater she's knittin'—all our sweaters have ashes knitted into them—and I took a steak knife out of the drawer and sat across from her and put my arm wrist-up on the table and the knife blade on my wrist and looked her in the eyes."

Having seen Regina when they first arrived, looking just as Valerie described her, and having sat at the kitchen table with them, Colleen can see the scene clearly in her mind's eye; the two of them sitting across from each other, Regina shocked and staring at the knife blade on Valerie's wrist and Valerie with her eyes fixed on Regina's. "What happened?" Colleen asks, wide-eyed.

"I told her if things didn't change, I was gonna slit my wrists."

Colleen glances at Sandy's hand, lightly stroking Valerie's wrist, and then looks back at Valerie.

"Poor Regina," Valerie says, "I scared her to death. I hated to do it, but I had to. I knew if anyone could talk sense to our parents, she could. She got them together and they talked. Things were different after that."

"Would you have done it?" Colleen asks and sees Valerie's eyes glaze.

Valerie's still looking at her, but Colleen sees she's not really focused on her. Valerie's staring right through her at something far off in the distance.

"Yeah," Valerie finally says, "I was ready to."

Colleen sees Valerie focus on her again.

"It wasn't easy for our parents to accept the fact that we're lesbians and it didn't happen overnight, it took time, but whenever I felt we were still getting grief for being who we are, all I had to say to Regina was, 'Don't make me get the knife'."

Sandy smiles and shakes her head at the mention of this. "We joke about it now," she says, "but it was no joke then, believe me." She looks tenderly at Valerie. "I was so afraid of losing you."

"Have you always felt this way about each other?" Colleen asks.

Valerie looks at Sandy and they search each other's eyes. "I don't know," Valerie says and looks at Colleen, "probably, it sort of developed over time. I always looked up to her," Valerie says, looking at Sandy. "I was such a scrawny kid and she was bigger than all the other girls in the neighborhood."

"Most of the boys too," Sandy adds proudly.

"Yeah. She always looked out for me and stuck up for me. She was like my guardian angel. So, when she wasn't doing so well in school—sixth grade, right?"

Sandy nods.

"Yeah, sixth, I offered to help her with her homework. I'd go over to her house and we'd sit at her desk in her bedroom and I'd tutor her and at first we sat with a space between us, but you know how it is when you study together, sometimes you have to sit close together, like when you're doing a math problem, so I was showing her how to order rational numbers and we were sitting really close together and I feel her put her arm around my shoulders." Valerie glances at Sandy and Sandy looks at her sheepishly with her eyebrows raised and shrugs. "I couldn't believe it. I didn't know what to think, or do, but it felt nice, you know? Friendly, but more than friendly. So then whenever we'd work on math problems she'd do that, sit real close with her arm around my shoulders and her cheek almost touchin' mine, so close I could feel the heat from her skin, and I don't know where I got the nerve to do it, but this one time I pressed my cheek against hers and felt her pressin' back and her arm tightenin' around my shoulders and we looked at each other and she kissed me and we ended up on the bed making out! I finally felt complete, like a whole person for the first time. That's when I knew."

"I already knew," Sandy says, smiling shyly.

Valerie looks at her and raises her eyebrows. "Yeah? You could've fooled me. All I can say is thank God for math!"

Colleen thinks of the many times she and Megan have sat together the same way, side by side at her desk with their heads close together, doing math problems, and how nothing like that has ever happened and how they've never felt anything more than friendship between them. What would Megan's reaction be if Colleen pressed her cheek against hers? She knows just what Megan would do. She can see her in her mind's eye, recoiling and looking at her as if she were crazy. Colleen would react the same way if Megan did it to her. You can't make the way Valerie and Sandy feel about each other just happen. They had to have been born this way. Maybe they didn't know it until they met each other and if they'd never met, they would have found out with someone else eventually, but they had to have been born this way. So why is it considered taboo and why is it illegal? Why punish people because of their sexual orientation? It doesn't make sense to her and it doesn't seem fair or right, just as Blacks being treated like second-class citizens because of their skin color doesn't. There's so much injustice in the world and she feels her conviction deepen to become a lawyer and defend the people who most need defending.

* * *

Colleen watches Valerie in the mirror as she applies makeup, preparing herself to go hear Miles Davis at the Village Gate. Knowing what she now does about her and Sandy, she can't help wondering if Valerie likes wearing makeup or wears it just to disguise the fact that she's lesbian. Not that she doesn't look and act feminine. She does and she's pretty, but Colleen can't help wondering. She'd ask Valerie but doesn't want to risk offending her. Valerie may be lesbian, but she's a young woman and why wouldn't she want to look her best?

She studies herself in the mirror and now her own made-up face and hair and preppy outfit seem like a disguise. Is this really who she is or just who she wants people to think she is? Now that she thinks about it, aren't all clothes a kind of costume we put on to play a role? The boys at Saint Pat's in their sport coats and dress trousers and the girls at the Mount in their plaid pleated skirts and white blouses and her father in his dark suit? The models in *Seventeen* and *Mademoiselle?* They're all wearing costumes too.

She watches Valerie remove the studs from her ears and replace them with dangling earrings about an inch long, turning her head this way and that to study their effect. Satisfied with it, she ties a fuchsia and black silk scarf around her neck and arranges the knot to the side. Colleen studies herself in the mirror again, looking herself up and down. If this isn't who she really is, then who is she? "Penny for your thoughts," she hears Valerie say and looks at her in the mirror and sees her looking back at her with a curious expression and her hand on her cocked hip. "Just thinking," Colleen says.

"About?"

"Disguises." Valerie turns and faces her and narrows her eyes slightly.

"You wonderin' if I wear makeup to disguise the fact that I'm lesbian?"

Colleen feels herself flush. "Yeah."

"You should've just asked me. Why didn't you?"

"I…I didn't want to offend you."

Valerie smiles and takes Colleen's chin in her hand. "That's sweet," she says.

Colleen looks from Valerie's eyes to her lips and watches them come closer. She's never been kissed on the lips by a girl, but knows that's what Valerie intends to do. She closes her eyes and feels Valerie's lips on hers. It feels like a friendly kiss, but it's a lingering one. She remembers how she thought she'd react if Megan were to suddenly kiss her like this. Maybe she would react that way, if it were Megan, but she doesn't feel that way with Valerie and presses her lips against hers and feels Valerie's hand on the small of her back, drawing her closer. She's aroused and feels her nipples getting hard and wishes Valerie would touch them. It's a crazy and confusing situation. She knows Valerie loves Sandy and is just being affectionate in a friendly way but imagines what it would be like to lie on the bed with her, embracing and kissing passionately the way Valerie and Sandy were earlier. Would it stop there? Would they want it to? Colleen feels Valerie pull her head back and opens her eyes and sees her looking at her, surprised and bemused.

"Don't worry," Valerie says, "it's not catchy. Anyway, the answer is I like to. Not all lesbians are butch."

Colleen sees her cock her head toward the mirror and study her eyes and face and hair. Valerie reaches out and smooths the hair at her temple with her fingertips.

"You're really pretty, you know?" Valerie says. "Anyone ever tell you that?"

"Just Henry." She sees Valerie shake her head slowly.

"Why am I not surprised?" Valerie says and puts a hand on Colleen's arm. "Listen, I know you love him, but don't get your hopes up."

"I try not to, but I can't help it."

"He's just passin' through. He's not goin' to commit. That's who he is. I just don't want to you to get hurt."

"He's the only boy who treats me with respect," Colleen says forlornly. Valerie sighs and strokes her cheek with her fingertips.

"Yeah, he would be."

Colleen knows she looks and sounds pitiful, and that Valerie knows exactly how she feels—desperate and willing to do anything to win Henry's love. Things worked out well for Valerie, but she knows and feels in her gut they're not going to for her where Henry is concerned. Maybe the experience will make her a stronger person but maybe it will leave her feeling bitter about love and reluctant or even unable to love again. Well, she just has to go through it and deal with whatever happens.

"C'mon," Valerie says, "let's get Sandy."

Colleen sits at the kitchen table at Sandy's, chatting with Valerie and Connie while they wait for Sandy to make her appearance. When she does, in a black turtle neck sweater and tight-fitting above the knee black skirt and black flats, Colleen stares at her wide-eyed. Sandy looks powerfully beautiful, like an Amazon. She's also wearing makeup and lipstick and has silver hoops dangling from her earlobes and the overall effect, given the fact that she's tall and has such a fit body, is stunning. She looks like the girl any red-blooded American boy would die to live next door to. If they only knew! Appearances can be so deceiving. Colleen and Valerie look at each other and Valerie raises her eyebrows. "What?" Colleen asks.

"She's somethin', isn't she? There's only one problem," Valerie says wryly. "Every guy who sees her wants to get in her pants."

Hearing Valerie say this in front of Connie flusters Colleen. She feels embarrassed for Valerie and glances at Connie and sees her gazing at Sandy, lovingly and admiringly.

"I'd hate to be the poor bastard who tries," Connie says.

Bleecker Street in Greenwich Village is on the cool side this evening, feeling more like the end of winter than the beginning of spring. The sidewalks are crowded with mostly White high school and college age kids who are all dressed pretty much the same, in blue jeans and sneakers and loafers and sweatshirts and sweaters, either worn or draped around their shoulders. Collee, Valerie and Sandy walk toward the Village Gate and pass vendors, selling Sabbrett hot dogs and Nedick orange drink and all kinds of trinkets, jewelry, watches and the like. Colleen sees the brightly lit Village Gate sign in the distance on the corner and can read "Miles Davis Quintet" in the white area on it.

"C'mon," she hears Valerie say at the entrance to an alley and follows her and Sandy down it. She can tell the two of them have stopped here before. They reach the end of the alley and step into a recess at the back entrance to one of the buildings, where they can't be seen from the street. She watches Valerie open her bag and take out her pack of cigarettes and select one she's marked with red lipstick on the tip of the filter. Colleen told Valerie she's never smoked pot and was willing to try it and now the moment has arrived. She feels nervous anticipation, eager to find out how it feels, but not knowing what to expect. Valerie lights the cigarette and inhales deeply and hands it to Colleen.

"Hold the smoke in as long as you can," Valeries says, still holding her breath.

Colleen inhales tentatively and draws the smoke into her lungs. She manages to keep it there a few moments until it begins burning and she coughs it out and hears Valerie and Sandy giggling. She holds the cigarette out to Sandy, who shakes her head and takes it and hands it to Valerie, who inhales deeply again and hands it to Colleen.

Colleen doesn't feel anything yet, at least not that she can notice. She inhales the smoke a little deeper this time and hands the cigarette back to Valerie. She manages to hold the smoke in longer without coughing and blows the smoke out in a thin stream. She takes the cigarette from Valerie again, inhales as deeply as she can this time and hands it back. As she holds the smoke in, she imagines she can see it swirling around in her lungs and now she feels like her head is expanding and the world is closing in, that she and Valerie and Sandy are standing in a bubble and nothing outside of it matters at all.

She's aware of another feeling now, a tingling between her legs that intensifies with each passing moment until she's feeling horny as hell and squirms discreetly. How she wishes Henry was here!

She can still hear the sounds coming from Bleecker Street at the end of the alley, but they seem far off in the distant now, an indistinct rumble punctuated by the occasional honk of a car horn. She takes the cigarette from Valerie, inhales as deeply as she can again and hands it back. As she holds in the smoke, now she feels like she doesn't want to move from this spot. It's a new and pleasant sensation, being perfectly content just being where she is and not needing or wanting to go anywhere else. She remembers that they're on their way to see Miles Davis at The Village Gate—it seems odd to her that she'd forgotten—and she feels uneasy about it, like she's not sure she can move her feet to take a step, let alone walk all the way there, which seems to be a great distance now. She's afraid she won't be able to make it and feels the need of a reassuring hug.

How long has she been staring at the light over the door across the alley? It seems like forever and she realizes she's been completely ignoring Valerie and Sandy. She looks at them and sees they're grinning at her. Sandy reaches out, puts her arms around her, draws her to her and hugs her. How did Sandy know that's what she needed? Did she read her mind? It's seems uncanny. Colleen puts her arms around Sandy's waist and hugs her back and she knows now how Valerie feels when she's in Sandy's arms and why she loves her. Colleen feels safe and protected, like nothing in the world could harm her. Sandy takes Colleen's arm and wraps hers around it and leads her toward the Village Gate. Colleen doesn't even bother to look where she's going. She just allows Sandy to lead her there while she looks around at the people, studies the faces of the passersby, listens to the snippets of their conversations and it feels like she's experiencing life from inside a kaleidoscope.

Inside the club, they follow the host, making their way carefully around tables filled with customers. Colleen has the feeling everyone in the club knows she's high and is watching her every move. She knows she's probably just imagining it, being paranoid, which Valerie told her happens to people sometimes when they smoke pot, but that's what it feels like.

They arrive at a small round table just below the drum kit on the right side of the low stage and squeeze themselves into their seats. They order expensive Cokes, which they have to as a minimum. She listens to Valerie explain that the people who'll be playing with Miles Davis this evening aren't the ones who played on *Kind Of Blue,* that Davis's music has changed through the years and so has the personnel in his group and the musicians who'll be playing with him this evening are Wayne Shorter on saxophone, who's also a talented composer, Herbie Hancock on piano, Ron Carter on bass and this young guy, Tony Williams, on drums, who's created a lot of buzz in the jazz community because of his musicianship and especially his polyrhythmic playing.

"The guy's a monster," Valerie says. "I've never seen him live. This should be somethin'."

Colleen eyes the microphones arranged around the drum set, which is so close she can reach out and touch the ride cymbal. It'll be something, all right. She'll probably be blown out of her seat. She looks around at the customers. "Why are there so few Blacks here? Seems kind of strange."

"Modern jazz isn't for blacks," Valerie says with a smirk, "it's for White intellectuals. They've got the money. It makes them feel hip listenin' to it and thinkin' they understand it. The Blacks are at the Apollo, listenin' to James Brown and the Famous Flames."

"So, what are we doing here?" Colleen asks.

Valerie grins. "Good question. Tryin' to be hip, I guess, like everyone else."

"I like James Brown," Sandy says. "We should go see him sometime."

"Yeah, we should," Valerie says. "You can dance in the aisle." She looks at Colleen and grins. "You should see this girl dance to James Brown records. She can shake it like a real jungle bunny."

Colleen doesn't take offense at the racial slur. She knows Valerie's as concerned about discrimination and as passionate about civil rights as she is and just said it the way friends can say things among themselves freely, without fear of being misunderstood or judged. She looks at Sandy and imagines her moving that body of hers in the aisle at the Apollo Theater with James Brown and the Famous Flames on the stage playing *I Feel Good (I've Got You)*. That would be something to see!

"Ladies and Gentlemen," Colleen hears a deep voice announce from the P.A., "The Village Gate is proud to present The Miles Davis Quintet!" Everyone begins clapping and she does to and looks around and sees a line of Black men, all dressed in dark suits, making their way slowly from the back of the club to the steps at the far side of the stage. She recognizes Miles Davis, last in line, carrying his trumpet and the only one wearing dark glasses. For the first time she experiences the thrill of being in the presence of a celebrity.

The men take the stage. Tony Williams seats himself at the drums and picks up his drumsticks and she can see the beads of sweat, glistening on his temple, as he looks at Miles, waiting for the sign to begin. Williams looks young, not much older than she. He can't be more than seventeen or eighteen and here he is playing with Miles Davis. She knows he's good but he must be *really* good.

She looks at Miles and sees him point the bell of his trumpet at the microphone. He nods slightly and they begin playing a song she doesn't recognize. It sounds uncertain at first, as if it doesn't know which direction to head in, but then it takes off and the melody makes her think of a giant playing hopscotch. Miles launches into what sounds to her a very angry solo and Tony Williams seems to be urging him on, his hands moving with blistering speed, his drumsticks a blur, the veins bulging in his neck, the sweat flying from his forehead, some of it landing on their table and glistening in the light from the stage. She's transfixed by the sight and sound of Williams and stares at his face as he plays. He's grimacing but whether it's from pleasure or pain she can't tell. Probably a bit of both, she figures.

She thinks of her own half-hearted attempt to learn to play the piano and what she thought was Casmir's masterful musicianship and they seem nothing compared to what she's seeing and hearing now. It doesn't seem possible that someone's hands can move so quickly and deftly. Just when she thinks she knows where the beat is and tries to anticipate where it will land next, she guesses wrong. He's all over the place and always in the right place, just one step ahead of her and everyone else, driving the music forward.

She looks at Miles, bent backward with his trumpet pointed accusingly at the microphone, soloing even more insistently and angrily now, forcing the notes out of his trumpet in ever-rising bursts with each flurry of his fingers on the valves. Valerie has it all wrong. This isn't Black music *for* White intellectuals. It's Black music aimed *at* White intellectuals.

She looks around at the people in the darkened club, all staring reverently toward the stage, watching and listening to Miles play, unable to see his eyes as he studies them through his dark glasses. It seems to her they're completely missing the point, at least the White listeners. Here Miles is, giving voice through his music to all the anger and bitterness and resentment felt by Blacks in America, from the first slaves who arrived in chains to those living in the South who are still treated like slaves in so many ways, and there are the Whites, listening raptly to the music and digging it, but they don't seem to be getting the message. It seems to her they could as easily be listening to Beethoven's Fifth in Carnegie Hall and that the ultimate joke is that they've paid for the privilege to sit here and be musically tongue-lashed by Miles Davis. Maybe it's just the pot, she thinks, fanciful thinking, but maybe not.

She sips her Coke and glances at Sandy and sees she's listening politely, but disinterestedly to the music, which makes sense to her. Sandy strikes her as a simple straightforward type of person who'd much rather be dancing to James Brown at the Apollo right now than trying to make sense of this jazz stuff and while the blizzard of notes being bestowed on them by Miles sounds to Colleen like a thinly disguised political statement about the Black experience in America, she has the feeling it's all noise to Sandy and that the only reason she's here is to look after Valerie, the way she'll be looking after everyone else in the country when she joins the Army, regardless of their race, creed or color.

Valerie's a different story. She's listening intently to the music and Colleen can tell she gets what it's all about. Undoubtedly, it's her awareness of her own people's struggle to be accepted by the descendants of the first settlers in Bensonhurst that connects her to the music, and the fact that she's lesbian, "different" *and* a member of a minority. If Blacks began appearing in Valerie's community the way they have in Newburgh, Colleen knows she would be tolerant of them and accept them. Would Valerie's parents or Regina? Would Connie? You never know where people really stand on the issue until something happens that forces them to show their hand. It's easy enough to say you're for racial equality and want Blacks to enjoy the same civil rights as everyone else, but do you really want them living next door to you? Are you willing to travel to the Deep South like the Freedom Riders and walk arm in arm with Blacks toward a line of baton-wielding police in riot gear, holding attack dogs on leashes? Colleen doubts that she, herself, has the courage to do it. The reality of the situation is that, except for a small group of activists, where the vast majority of White Americans is concerned, the answer is no. Maybe that's what Miles is so angry about—the hypocrisy of it all. We're all perfectly happy to sit here and listen to him scold us musically about our apathy, believing that by paying to listen to it we're absolved of the sin.

She studies Miles as he finishes his solo and Wayne Shorter begins his, sounding very melodic and not at all angry. Miles turns his back to the audience and takes a step toward the back of the stage. He stands there hunched over, blowing the saliva out of his trumpet through the spit valve. It feels like an insult and she wonders if it strikes anyone else the same way.

She knows a bit about his history from Valerie, that his name is Miles Dewey Davis the Third, that he was born in Illinois to an affluent family, that his father's a dentist and that he learned to ride horses on his family's ranch in Arkansas. On the face of it, he's no different than any other person who grew up in a family of means in this country, except that he's Black. Has he experienced discrimination firsthand? He must have and knows the sting of it. Is the fact that he's Black the reason he became a heroin addict? Who knows? Lots of people do, people of all colors. Anyway, he managed to kick it and here he is, apparently healthy and more famous than ever, but he sure seems to have a chip on his shoulder. What must he be thinking as he stands there, with his shoulders hunched, and his head bowed and his back to the audience? She'd love to know. Finally, the song ends and she claps along with the others. "What's that song called?" she asks Valerie, loudly enough to be heard over the applause.

"'Seven Steps to Heaven'."

Huh, Colleen thinks. It certainly <u>was</u> a spirited musical journey, but she never would have guessed that heaven was the destination. Thinking about it, though, heaven is just a concept and different people have different ideas about what it means, and maybe the idea of being accepted by Whites in this country and treated as equals and welcomed as neighbors represents a kind of heaven on earth to Black people in America and their journey to get there is a long and hard one, filled with anger and bitterness and resentment, so maybe it makes sense after all.

She listens to a number of songs she's never heard before, each changing the mood and atmosphere in the room, or so it seems to her. She recognizes the beginning of *So What,* with its questioning bass notes and piano chords, and feels herself coming down a little from the pot high, less edgy and more relaxed. She understands now why Valerie likes to get high when she listens to music, and particularly live music. It makes hearing it such a pleasurable experience. She can feel each note resonating inside her body, as if her body is itself an instrument. So why is pot illegal if it makes you feel so good? It doesn't make any sense.

She smiles when she hears the lazy, swinging opening to "All Blues," her favorite song on *Kind of Blue.* The first time she heard it, it sounded like a lullaby and she pictured a mother with her baby girl, cradled in her arms, swaying as she hummed it to her. She has the same mental image now and wonders, as she always does when listening to this song, if her mother ever acted that way with her when she was a baby. Maybe, but she still can't picture it. Her mother's much too detached and distant. Did she even want to have a baby, or did she have one because her father wanted children, because she felt that's what was expected of her? Colleen gets the feeling from her mother that if she'd never had her, it would have been fine with her. It's not a nice way to feel about your mother but that's how she feels—alone and unloved.

She claps along with the others as Miles and the rest of the Quintet leave the stage and slowly make their way toward the back of the club, shaking hands and chatting with people at the tables as they pass by. Colleen sees Valerie grin at her as they stand to leave.

"Whadja think?" Valerie asks.

"Great!"

"When're we gonna see James Brown?" Sandy asks.

"Next time he's at the Apollo. Wanna come?" Valerie asks Colleen.

"Sure. I like James Brown. Ever been to the Apollo?"

Valerie and Sandy shake their heads.

"Think it's safe?"

Sandy looks at Valerie and shrugs. "Natalie and Joey saw the Supremes there," Sandy says. "There were other White kids there too. The place has a bad rep, that's all."

Well, Colleen thinks, if Sandy goes, she'll go. She's never been to Harlem. All she's heard about it is that it's where the Blacks live and is filled with drug dealers and prostitutes and is a dangerous place for Whites. She knows there must be more to the story. It's not walled off. Cars and buses and taxis and trains go through it. The people who live there are part of the city. She has the feeling Harlem's bad reputation has been manufactured as much by Whites to keep Blacks in as by Blacks to keep Whites out. It can't be all that bad a place. Still, she'll feel much better about going, knowing that she'll be with Sandy. Colleen's never met a person like her before. Sandy doesn't say much, but when she does speak you listen, carefully, and she has this air of quiet watchfulness about her. She's like a lounging cat that only appears relaxed and is ready to pounce at any moment. Valerie's right. Sandy will make a great soldier.

They make their way slowly toward the back of the club and Colleen can see Herbie Hancock and Tony Williams, standing in the middle of a group of people, chatting. Where Miles and the others have gone she doesn't know. Probably backstage. "I'll be right back," she says. "I have to pee."

* * *

Colleen sits on the toilet, smiling with her eyes closed, enjoying how pleasurable peeing feels being high, and, as the stream slows to a trickle, she hears the ladies' room door open and the shuffling of feet. "How long ya known?" she hears a young woman ask with concern. She doesn't sound like a New Yorker. More like from the Midwest. "A couple weeks," Colleen hears the young woman's friend say, so softly she can barely hear her, but the friend has the same accent and there's worry in her voice. Colleen leans forward and turns her ear toward the stall door.

"Does he know?" the young woman asks and there's a long silence. "Ya haven't told him?" she asks, sounding really surprised and her question is followed by more silence. "It's his, right?"

"Of course, it's his," her friend snaps. "I don't sleep with every Tom, Dick and Harry."

"Just askin'. Are ya gonna tell him?"

"I dunno. I'm not sure I want him to know."

"Why?"

"He might get angry. He might break it off. I don't want to lose him. Anyway, it's not like it's his fault, ya know? I'm the one who told him he didn't have to wear a condom. I thought it was okay."

"You're gonna get rid of it, right?"

"Of course, I'm gonna get rid of it!" the friend shoots back, clearly irritated by the stupidity of the question.

"He should pay for it, dontcha think?"

"I dunno know what to think," Colleen hears the friend say and she can hear the panic in her voice. She's aware that she's been sitting here in the stall for some time now, too long, listening to their conversation. What she should have done was make some noise to let them know she was here or leave as soon as they entered, but she hesitated and leaving now seems out of the question. There'd be no disguising the fact that she's been eavesdropping on them all this time and especially given what they've been discussing, she can only imagine what their reaction would be. They'd have every right to be furious with her.

"So watcha gonna do?" the young woman asks. "Think your parents will help?"

"Are you kidding? My mother would have a heart attack and my father would disown me."

"Know anyone around here?"

"This girl in the dorm says there's a guy in Pennsylvania who'll do it cheap."

"Yeah, with a coat hanger probably."

"She used him."

Colleen hears the ladies' room door open. "Colleen?" she hears Valerie ask with concern, "You all right?" "Yeah," Colleen says, "be right there!" She hears the door close again. She finishes up, arranges her clothes, opens the stall door, steps out and glances at the two young women, standing together in the corner, leaning against the wall with their arms crossed, glowering at her. "Sorry," she says, hurrying to the door without looking at them and hears the friend with the problem hiss, "You little shit!"

Colleen feels mortified and hurries down the narrow hallway with her head down. She bumps into someone walking toward her and steps back. She looks up embarrassedly to see Miles Davis standing there, looking at her through his dark glasses, and she's surprised that he's not much taller than she is. She sees the hint of a smile appear.

"Wuz happenin'?" Miles asks in a barely audible growl.

"Excuse me," she says, feeling even more mortified now. She hurries around him without looking back.

* * *

Colleen sways in her seat beside Valerie, as the subway back to Brooklyn lurches from side to side. She stares at the screaming headline of the newspaper the old man wearing a fedora sitting across from her is reading: "SUPERTANKER CATASTROPHE!" They heard about it earlier on TV at Valerie's. The Torrey Canyon, a supertanker, carrying 120,000 tons of crude oil, ran aground off the coast of Cornwall in England

and is spilling oil. The fear is that it's going to cause an environmental disaster. It's the first accident involving a supertanker and now everyone's speculating about just how safe the ships are. If it can happen to this one, who's to say it can't happen to others.

It's a catastrophe, all right, a big one, but then, so is what's happening to the young woman with the problem in the ladies' room at The Village Gate. It might seem small in comparison, but to the young woman it must seem like the biggest catastrophe that's ever happened. And it's not the first time it's happened. Who knows how many times it's happened in the past and how many girls and woman are experiencing the same thing right now? She imagines the train, clacking through the dark tunnel toward Brooklyn, is the one unwanted sperm, squiggling its way up her own fallopian tube, that's going to make it through and fertilize an egg and cause a catastrophe in her life just as big as the *Torrey Canyon.* "I feel bad for her," Colleen says.

"Reminds me of Nadine," Valerie says to Sandy.

"Yeah. That was awful," Sandy says.

"What happened to her?" Colleen asks.

"She got knocked up when she was fifteen," Valerie says. "Only a few of us knew about it. She was terrified that her parents would find out and wanted to get rid of it as soon as she could, before she started showin'. Someone told her about this woman, supposedly a midwife, in Jersey, who could help her. She stole enough money from her parents to go see her. What she got for her money were a couple of sharpened plastic tubes and the woman told her to insert them in her cervix and blow air into it."

This sounds bizarre to Colleen and she makes a face. "Huh?" "They were long enough. Anyway, that was supposed to cause an abortion."

"So, what happened?"

"She punctured a vein. By the time her parents found her in bed, she'd pretty much bled to death. The family doctor came, but it was too late. She was able to tell them what happened, though. That's the only way we found out about it. Her mother sat us all down and told us. She wanted to scare the shit out of us."

"It didn't work," Sandy says.

"Yeah," Valerie says. "So, a year later our friend Rosie gets knocked up and her family uses the same doctor as Nadine's family, and by then, I guess, the doctor had had enough of young women dying due to botched abortions and his attitude about things changed. He told them about this doctor in Texas who's performin' abortions, and that women and girls are comin' to him from all over the country, that his practice is impeccable and takes really good care of patients. Nadine went with her mother, and they did take good care of her. He's a courageous man. He could go to jail for what he's doin'."

"It shouldn't be illegal," Colleen says.

"If men got pregnant, it wouldn't be," Sandy says.

"It didn't use to be," Valerie says. "Abortion used to be legal, if it happened before what was called 'quickenin'.'"

"What's that?" Colleen asks.

"When a woman first feels the fetus move. Herbalists and midwives used to perform them all the time, but the medical community in the mid Eighteen Hundreds viewed them as quacks and wanted to get rid of 'em. And then later in the century, Victorian society viewed women seekin' abortions as selfish and immoral, so the medical community and the Church got together to condemn abortions and laws began being passed makin' it illegal. And now here we are. That girl in the ladies' room is only one of the latest victims of paternalistic society."

The anger in Valerie's voice brings to Colleen's mind the question of how Valerie and Sandy really feel about men, being lesbians, which she's been wondering about. "Do you hate men?" she asks.

"Not at all," Valerie says. "I hate the fact that women let men run their lives. It's time we stood up for ourselves, dontcha think? I mean, how many more of us have to die? Enough is enough."

Colleen knows Valerie's right and that she, herself, is as guilty as everyone else of allowing it to happen, and that taking her anger and frustration with her father out on boys is misplaced, and cowardly. What she should do is stand up to him and confront him and she wishes she had the courage to do it, but it's so much easier just waiting until she turns eighteen and is far away from him at college and doesn't have to deal with him anymore. It occurs to her that if she's going to be a lawyer, maybe she should get involved in politics, run for office and get elected and help repeal existing law that denies women the right to make decisions about their own bodies and fight for new legislation that secures their right to do so. Thinking about it, the plight of women doesn't seem all that different than the plight of Blacks. They both have the foot of an oppressive White male-dominated society on the backs of their necks. If she were a member of the State Legislature or, even better, Congress, she'd be better able to effect change that would help them both. Huh, she thinks, why not?

"I'm starvin'!" Valerie says as they walk down the stairs to 86th Street.

"So am I," Colleen says. In fact, she's been craving something to eat ever since she got high and wanted to stop and get a hot dog when they left The Village Gate, but no one else seemed hungry and she didn't want to hold up Valerie and Sandy.

"I'm always hungry," Sandy says.

"My brother's workin'," Valerie says, "but I think Franco's there too, otherwise we'd eat free."

CHAPTER 6

Vincent and Byron

Through the plate glass window, Colleen sees the pizza parlor is nearly empty. There's a man sitting alone at a table, eating a slice, with another waiting on the white paper plate in front of him. His blue uniform makes her think he's a transit worker, maybe a bus driver or subway conductor. At another table there's a young teenage boy and girl, sitting across from each other under a "See Sicily!" travel poster, with a pizza between them and each eating a slice.

She sees a young man and a middle-aged man, both wearing white aprons and leaning against the back counter in the kitchen with their arms crossed, chatting. The young man is thin and resembles Valerie somewhat and she figures he's Vincent. The middle-aged man is stocky and has dark wavy hair and an olive complexion and she figures he's Franco.

As she and Valerie and Sandy enter, she gets a better look at Vincent. With his black frame glasses and black hair combed back, he looks like an Italian American Buddy Holly, only not as nerdy and more handsome. He and Franco both turn their heads and look at the three of them and Vincent, Colleen sees, is looking directly at her with a scrutinizing expression, while Franco is smiling at Valerie and Sandy.

"Hi, Franco!" Valerie says.

"Ciao!" Franco says with a wave.

"How's the baby?"

"Goodah! Goodah!" he says with a thick accent and pats his stomach. "Anuddah inah dee oven!"

"Wow! Already? Tell Fran I said hi."

"I willah!" Franco says with another wave.

"Unbelievable," Valerie says in a lowered voice as they sit at a table. "That girl is a baby factory."

"His daughter?" Colleen asks.

"Yeah. That's all she ever wanted to do, get married and be a housewife and have babies. It's *so* Sicilian. They breed like rabbits."

Again, Colleen doesn't take offense and, anyway, Valerie's talking about her own people, and she's entitled to her opinion. It's interesting that it's exactly what people once said about the Irish and still say about Blacks. Who will it be next, she wonders? Puerto Ricans seem to be next on the list.

"There's nothin' wrong with havin' kids," Sandy says. "Where would we be without 'em?"

Colleen sees Sandy looking patiently at Valerie and she can tell by the way Sandy said this and her expression that what she meant was that she and Valerie aren't going to have any, so someone has to. "Was she born there?" Colleen asks.

"Yeah," Valerie says. "She was four or five when they got here."

So, Colleen thinks, here's the other side of the story. The last thing the young woman at The Village Gate wants is to have a baby and this Fran wants nothing more than to have as many as she can. Colleen wonders what Fran thinks about women's rights and abortion. It would be interesting to ask her. You'd think she'd think it's a bunch of bullshit but then, you never know. Colleen looks up and sees Vincent standing by the table, looking down at her and then at Valerie.

"How was it?" Vincent asks.

"Great! This is Colleen."

"Vincent," he says with a slight nod but without smiling. "Nice to meet you."

"Same here," Colleen says. The way he's scrutinizing her is making her uncomfortable and she shifts nervously in her seat. Did Valerie tell him about her reputation in Newburgh? It's one thing to tell Sandy, that's understandable, but her brother? Would she do that? Colleen doesn't think so but can't think of another reason why he would be looking at her so critically. They've only just met. Vincent finally looks at Valerie.

"The usual?" he asks. "Yeah."

He glances at Colleen. "Coke?"

"Yeah, thanks." Colleen watches him over her shoulder as he walks away and looks back at Valerie and Sandy. "I feel shitty about what happened in the ladies' room."

Valerie shrugs. "You just spaced out."

Colleen's heard this expression before and knows intuitively what it means, but she'd never experienced it until now. She didn't mean to be eavesdropping, it's just that their conversation fascinated her, the way the light over the rear door of the building in the alley did. So, now she knows what being high on pot is like. You're spellbound by the mundane and, despite the occasional tinge of paranoia, find most everything mildly amusing and some things, quite inexplicably, hysterically funny. She must not be high anymore because she finds Vincent's reaction to her disturbing and she knows she's not just being paranoid. She's been curious about Sandy's tee shirt and the pennant and posters in her room and has been wanting to ask her about them. Henry's father and brother come to mind. "Was your dad in the Army?"

"Nah," Sandy says. "He worked in the Navy Yard as a pipe fitter durin' the war."

"Someone in your family in the Army?"

Sandy shakes her head.

"That's all she's ever wanted to be," Valerie says and looks at Sandy admiringly, "a soldier. She'll be a good one too."

Colleen's intrigued. A girl who grew up wanting to be a soldier, not a teacher or nurse, like a lot of girls.

"I'm gonna join the WACs," Sandy says, "when I finish college."

"What made you want to be a soldier?"

Sandy shrugs. "Probably all those World War II movies I watched when I was a kid."

"But the soldiers are all men."

"Didn't used to be that way," Sandy says. "There's a long history of women warriors. Goes back thousands of years."

"See her tattoo?" Valerie asks.

"Yeah," Colleen says, "who is it?" Sandy pushes up the right sleeve of her sweater and turns her arm toward Colleen.

"Pallas Athene," Sandy says, "the branch insignia. She's the patron of Athens and the goddess of just warfare, among other things, like wisdom and courage and strength and strategy."

"But you can't fight."

"Not yet," Sandy says, pushing her sleeve down. "Maybe someday. I'll be ready."

Colleen studies Sandy's face and sees her resolve and remembers the way she looked when she first saw her, lying on her back on the bench, lifting weights. Colleen's certain she will be.

"She gets to go to Alabama," Valerie says, rolling her eyes.

"Fort MacClellan, WAC headquarters," Sandy says. "I'm gonna go to OCS."

"What's that?" Colleen asks.

"Officer Candidate School. I don't just wanna serve. I wanna lead."

Colleen can picture Sandy as a soldier in uniform and just as easily see her calmly studying an enemy through her binoculars, prepared to engage it on her terms, at a time and place of her choosing.

She considers the path Sandy has chosen to follow, which will take her to Fort MacClellan and from there, likely, to some other distant posting, perhaps overseas, and Valerie's plan to join the Peace Corps after graduating from college, which will take her far away from Sandy for at least two years. She thinks of the scene she witnessed earlier in Sandy's bedroom when they were reunited. How will they ever endure being separated that long?

"When's the last time you saw each other?" Colleen asks.

"Month ago," Valerie says.

"How are you going to do it?"

"What?" Valerie asks.

"Be separated from each other for so long?" Valerie and Sandy look at each other and then at her. She can tell they've asked themselves this question many times and haven't yet arrived at a satisfactory answer.

"We'll manage," Sandy says.

It seems to Colleen that Sandy's more convinced of it than Valerie, or maybe just more resigned to the fact that a long separation is inevitable.

How great it must be to have a partner in life like Sandy, so calm and strong and unshakable. Will she ever find someone like that? Does everyone eventually? She'd like to think so, but she knows not necessarily. Valerie is one lucky girl.

Vincent returns with a tray and places a large pizza with extra cheese topped with sausage and pepperoni in the middle of the table and a paper plate and napkin and bottle of Coke and plastic cup filled with ice in front of each of them.

Valerie and Sandy busy themselves pouring their cokes and putting slices on their plates and Vincent, Colleen sees, rather than returning to the kitchen, is now standing with a hand on the back of Sandy's chair and holding the tray by his side, looking down at her with that same scrutinizing expression. What is it with him? She hates the fact that he's making her feel self-conscious. She's hungry and wants to eat, but he seems to expect her to say something, and she has no idea what he wants to talk about. She picks up the bottle, watches the Coke pour into her cup, puts the bottle on the table, takes a sip and looks up at him. "How do you like Columbia?"

"There's a lotta shit goin' on," he says.

"Yeah? Like what?"

"Like most of the students at Columbia are pampered middle class White kids who suddenly think the university should sever its ties to the defense industry. They feel the administration is insensitive to them, especially Grayson Kirk, the president. They seem to forget or never bothered to read the literature in the first place, that Columbia's a research institution and has long-standing ties to the defense industry. So now there are groups like SDS."

"What's that?"

"Students for a Democratic Society, advocating for a campus-wide strike to shut down the school. That's the situation with the White kids. The Blacks hate Kirk just as much, but they have their own gripes. They feel they're being treated like second-class citizens and they resent the fact that Columbia owns a lot of real estate in Harlem. Columbia owns real estate all over the city, but the Black students think the university's insensitive to its neighbors and the main issue is the Morningside Heights Gymnasium the university's building on city-owned land that abuts apartment buildings in Harlem. The administration added a community center to the plans, as a gesture of good will, but the problem is the neighbors' entrance will be down the hill at the back of the building and the Blacks see this as having to use a back door to get in, like having to sit in the back of the bus. The atmosphere on campus is so tense you could cut it with a knife. It's gonna explode."

Colleen takes a cooled slice of pizza and puts it on her plate. What a character Vincent is! First, he's tight-lipped and then she asks him a simple question about Columbia, fully expecting to hear him say something like, "It's okay," or "It's great," but instead he gives her a detailed account of the political situation at the college! She feels a bit more relaxed with him now as a result. She has the feeling his initial scrutiny of her wasn't personal but that he's just an intense person and scrutinizes everyone and everything. "So, you think it's all bullshit?"

"Definitely. Everyone has their own agenda."

"What's yours?" she asks and takes a bite.

"I want to go into business and make a ton of money. Everybody's complaining about how Columbia's just a factory, turning out technicians and managers and executives to fill positions at big industrial companies that support the DOD. They think having major players in real estate and finance and law on our board is a bad thing. Those people are the *reason* I'm at Columbia."

Having listened to Vincent's lengthy account of the current situation at Columbia, Colleen's struck by the fact that Vincent doesn't have the same Bensonhurst accent as Valerie and Sandy and she wonders how that happened and why? She understands why Henry doesn't have a discernable accent. After all, he lived all over the place and never in one place long enough to acquire one, but Vincent and Valerie grew up in the same family and the same place. It's curious.

"He's gonna rule the world one day," Valerie says, rolling her eyes, "wait 'n see."

"What?" Vincent asks. "You think the Peace Corps is somehow above it all? It's just part of the government's propaganda machine. Having people making nice with the natives in Third World countries serves the government's purpose, the same way having the military fight Communists in Viet Nam does. It's all the same, all inter-connected."

"They developed the A-bomb at Columbia," Sandy says. "It ended the war with Japan. Killed a lot of people, but it saved a lot more lives."

Valerie glances uneasily at Sandy and then looks at Vincent. "Yeah, well, I thought Columbia was supposed to be all about gettin' a classical education."

"It is," Vincent says. "Studying the core curriculum, you learn about what made Western Civilization so dominant and powerful—the arts and the sciences. It's about preparing you to live in the real world, not some dream world."

"Yeah? Look where it's gotten us," Valerie says "enough nuclear bombs to destroy everyone on the planet."

"I wouldn't worry about the Soviets," Vincent says. "They're coming from the same place we are. We think alike."

"If not the Soviets, then whom?" Colleen asks.

"The Chinese. They're different, the way the Japanese are. They value life differently and there are so damn many of them."

The Chinese? Colleen thinks. Why worry about them? The picture she's formed in her mind of the Chinese is of a dirt poor people who not so long ago wore their hair in pigtails, men and women alike, and dressed in funny-looking clothes and wore funny-looking shoes with curled up pointy toes, and now they all wear quilted jackets and are being ruled by Mao Tse-tung, a dictator with big hair who's shaped like a bowling pin, always wears the same drab uniform and looks only slightly less ridiculous than his shorter, goofier counterpart in North Korea, Kim Il-sung.

"Wait and see," Vincent says. "If we stay in Viet Nam, we'll end up fighting the Chinese, the same way we did in Korea."

That's right, Colleen thinks. The Chinese did fight against us in Korea, so it's not as if they're afraid to confront us, but the country seems so backward. She can't imagine China ever really being a serious threat to the United States, the way the Soviet Union is. Still, there must be a reason why Vincent's worried about them. He seems knowledgeable and certain of what he's talking about. He's probably studied the Chinese at Columbia.

"All right, already," Valerie says, having heard enough. "Let's change the subject."

Vincent shrugs. "You can keep your head in the sand if you want. When it happens, don't say I didn't tell you."

Colleen watches him over her shoulder walk toward the kitchen and turns and looks at Valerie. "Is he always this intense?"

"He's got an opinion about everything. Drives me crazy sometimes."

"Did you tell him about me?"

Valerie frowns. "Of course not. Why?"

"The way he was looking at me when we came in."

Valerie waves dismissively. "He's like that with everyone he meets for the first time, very cautious, until he gets to know you, then you can't shut him up."

"Anyone mind if I have the last slice?" Sandy asks.

"Eat!" Valerie says and grins at Colleen. "That's my baby. She eats like a horse and never gains a pound."

* * *

Colleen takes her toiletry kit and bathrobe out of her bag and puts them. Valerie walks in, holding a folded white towel and washcloth and puts them on the bed. "Here you go."

"Staying at Sandy's?"

"Yeah. That okay?"

Colleen nods. "I figured you were."

Valerie smiles, puts her arms around her and gives her a hug and Colleen hugs her back. She can tell Valerie feels guilty about leaving her alone for the night. It really is all right with her. She can imagine what it must be like to feel about each other the way Valerie and Sandy do and be separated for long periods of time. They naturally want to make the most of every moment they have together.

Valerie pulls her head back and smiles and Colleen looks from her eyes to her lips and watches them come towards hers. She closes her eyes and feels Valerie's lips pressing against hers and she presses back. It's the same friendly, lingering kiss as before and again she feels herself getting aroused and her nipples hardening and wishing they would do more together than just kiss. She wants to open her mouth and slide her tongue into Valerie's but feels that it would be crossing the line. She can't resist the temptation to part her lips slightly and brush Valerie's lips with her tongue, though, and thrills when she feels Valerie do the same. She hasn't even begun to think about why she's gone from finding the idea of doing this with a girl unthinkable and repulsive to actually doing it and enjoying it in the space of a day. It's just too much to think about now, anyway. She feels Valerie's lips leave hers and opens her eyes and sees her grinning at her and searching her eyes. Valerie smiles and gestures toward the bed.

"Clean sheets," Valerie says. "Sweet dreams."

"Thanks. You too."

* * *

Colleen spits out the toothpaste in the stream of running water and watches the bluish blob elongate into little strands that swirl in the sink and disappear down the drain. She's reminded again of the young woman in the ladies' room at The Village Gate, whose problem isn't going to be washed down the drain so easily, and she can only imagine what's in store for her. Will she visit the doctor in Pennsylvania? Will she be treated well or will she be given sharpened plastic tubes, as Valerie and Sandy's friend was, and told to go home and blow air into her cervix? It seems crazy to Colleen that women are treated this way. Sandy's right. If men got pregnant, abortion would be legal. She rinses her toothbrush, puts it in the clear plastic toiletry case on the counter, wraps her bathrobe around her and ties it tightly.

Stepping out of the bathroom into the hall, she sees the light on in Vincent's room and the door wide open and thinks why not say hi, if only to let him know she's here? She finds him standing by his desk with his back to her, removing his wristwatch, and she leans against the doorway. "Hey," she says. Vincent puts the watch on the desk and looks over his shoulder at her.

"Got everything you need?" he asks.

"Yeah, thanks," she says, and he shakes his head.

"It's just like my sister to leave you here."

She shrugs. "It's okay. I figured she'd spend the night at Sandy's. It's great your family is so understanding." He turns and leans against the desk, crosses his arms and legs and cocks his head.

"They didn't understand. They were forced to accept it. It was either that or risk losing their daughter. People don't like 'different' any more than they like change and they only accept it after putting up a fight. It's human nature. That's what's happening at Columbia. The trustees are a bunch of men who either don't understand how society's changing or do, but don't want to accept it. They'll put up a fight, all right. We'll see who wins."

"How do you feel about it?"

"I don't want my education to suffer as a result of what's happening, or my career prospects hurt by it."

"I mean about Valerie." Colleen sees that this comment took Vincent completely by surprise. He's so self-absorbed! Does he have a girlfriend, she wonders? If he does, what must she be like? What type of girl could put up with him?

"The same as I always have. Her sexuality is her business and everyone else should butt out of her life."

"So, you don't like staying in the dorm, huh?"

"I get more done here."

"Too noisy?"

"Too everything. As I say, there's a lot of shit going on. It's all one big distraction."

"Serious about your studies, huh?"

"I'm not at Columbia for the fun of it. My dad's paying good money to send me there. I owe it to him to take it seriously."

"You like to have fun, though, right?"

"Sure."

"What do you do for fun?"

"Go to movies, plays, museums. There's no end of stuff to do in New York."

"Girlfriend?" She sees his expression soften for the first time and the hint of a smile.

"Yeah."

"What's her name?"

"Yvonne."

"What's she like?"

"Smart, pretty."

"In college?"

"Barnard."

"I'd like to see it."

"Valerie can take you."

"Columbia, I mean. I'd like to see Barnard too sometime."

"Sure."

"When are you going back? Our bus doesn't leave tomorrow until late afternoon."

He raises his eyebrows. "What's Valerie got planned?"

She shrugs. "She mentioned something about maybe taking a walk over to Dyker Heights, to see the houses. I dunno. I've seen plenty of big houses."

"I usually go back Sunday evening, but I can go earlier. Just let me know."

"Yeah, I will. Can I ask you something?"

"Sure. What's that?"

"Why don't you sound like Valerie and Sandy. You know, the accent."

He looks at her a moment and cocks his head slightly. "I learned early on that people are judgmental," he says, "often unfairly, and I saw the effect of being unfairly judged has on people. I've always wanted to accomplish things in life. I didn't always know what, but I knew I wanted to. I didn't want to be unfairly judged or defined by the way I sound, so I forced myself not to sound like everyone else. I took heat from my friends when I was younger for what they perceived to be me putting on airs, thinking I was better than them." He shrugs. "It was a price I was willing to pay."

"Got it," she says. "Thanks. Good night."

"Sleep tight," he says and turns toward the desk.

* * *

Colleen's exhausted but still buzzing and not tired enough to sleep yet. She scans the spines of the books on Valerie's bookshelf. *On the Road* by Jack Kerouac catches her eye, in between *Dharma Bums* and *Howl* by Allen Ginsberg. She knows a bit about Kerouac and Ginsberg and

William Burroughs, whose book *Naked Lunch* she also sees on the shelf. She knows Burroughs is the son of the founder of the business machines company and was a drug addict and shot his common law wife at a party in Mexico City playing a game of "William Tell." She's always wondered how that could have happened. It just seems so incredible. It must have been the drugs. She knows that drugs were an important part of the Beat Generation and fueled the writing and as she looks at the collection of books by the most important writers of the movement, it seems curious to her that she's never read any of them and that they've never been assigned or discussed in her English classes. It's as if they're a dirty secret no one wants to talk about.

She takes *On the Road* from the shelf and climbs into bed under the covers. She sits with her knees up and looks at the picture of Jack Kerouac on the back cover. He looks to her a little like Lee Harvey Oswald. It's his sensitive eyes and mouth. She scans the synopsis under the photo and reads that *On The Road* is the story of Salvatore Paradise, a young writer who's recovering from physical sickness and the draining emotional experience of separation from his wife and his troubled friendship with Dean Moriarity, a fast-talking, fast-moving reform school kid and wannabe writer from out West, who Salvatore meets in New York City and who inspires him to leave his aunt's house, where he's staying, and hit the road to see America, and that the result is a non-stop adventure fueled by booze and drugs and filled with philosophizing con-men and the women who love them and are mistreated by them.

She reads that Kerouac is considered one of the most important writers of the Beat movement, which railed against the crushing conformity of post-World War II life in America, and that it was heavily influenced by Zen and Western radical political thought and drugs and jazz, and that Kerouac died in 1957 at the age of 46, done in by alcohol. She does the calculation. Were he alive today, she figures Kerouac would be around her parents' age. It strikes her as curious that the same generation that produced her father and mother, who, like most everyone else their age she knows, couldn't be more conformist in their thinking and the way they live their lives, could also have produced Kerouac and the other Beat writers. Maybe it's always that way with society. Maybe there's always a small group of people who are unhappy with the status quo and want things to change, or just want to live their lives differently and feel compelled to tell others about it. Maybe every generation has its Kerouac.

She turns the book over and opens to the first page and reads the opening line:

"I first met Dean not long after my wife and I split up."

She can already tell that this book is unlike any other she's ever read. Those books are all about some character, a hero or heroine, real or imagined, but someone other than the author. This book is going to be all about the author, even though he calls himself Salvatore Paradise, and it's not going to be about the passing scenery or the places he travels to, but what's going on in his and other people's heads while they're getting there and after they arrive.

She reads how Sal comes to know about Dean, through letters Dean has written to his friend Chad King and which Chad has passed to Sal, in which Dean asks Chad to tell him about Neitzsche, whoever he is, "and all the wonderful things that Chad knew and how Sal goes to meet Dean and his new wife Mary Lou, a "beautiful little sharp chick," in their cold water flat in East Harlem. When Colleen reads the way Dean talks to Mary Lou:

> "Now darling, here we are in New York and although I haven't quite told you everything I was thinking about when we crossed Missouri and especially at the point when we crossed the Booneville reformatory which reminded me of my jail problem, it is absolutely necessary now to postpone all those leftover things concerning our personal love-things and at once begin thinking of certain worklife plans..."

She knows she doesn't like him and doesn't trust him, and that he's just using Mary Lou the way he probably uses everyone to get what he wants, and that he's going to dump her at some point, and the prospect of spending the entire book traveling around with this guy, watching him use people and listening to him talk this way, doesn't seem very appealing, but she reads on, struggling to keep her eyes open, through the meeting of Dean and Carlo Marx, and the description of Dean racing cars around in the parking lot where he worked, and of Sal and Carlo seeing Dean off on a bus that "said Chicago and roared off into the night," and when she reads, "And this was really the way my whole road experience began, and the things that were to come are too fantastic not to tell," she closes the book, puts it on the nightstand, turns off the light, curls up under the covers and thinks that maybe she shouldn't give up on the book so easily. Maybe she should tough it out and see where it takes her. After all, it is an important book, or at least that's what they say.

Her head is filled with the cadence of Kerouac's prose and, yes, it does seem like jazz, going all over the place to make its point, but it's not like Miles Davis's music at all. There's longing in both, but where Miles's music is angry and insistent, Kerouac's voice is sad and searching. She imagines that's the difference between feeling like a Black outsider and a White one in America.

She wonders what Yvonne must be like. Having gotten to know Vincent a little, she's eager to meet her to see what type of woman he finds attractive. He's just so intense. Maybe Yvonne's the complete opposite; bright and bubbly and smiling all the time. She thinks about what Vincent shared with her about wanting to accomplish things in life and forcing himself not to sound like everyone else. She thinks it kind of sums up his personality. "Driven" is the word that comes to mind.

She remembers the scene she witnessed in Sandy's bedroom. She'll never forget it and there's no denying that what she saw shocked her, but the word that comes to mind now is "sweet." It is sweet the way those two love each other. She wishes her relationship with Henry were like that.

Kissing Valerie comes to mind and she's still not ready to think about why she let Valerie kiss her like that and kissed her back and enjoyed it and wanted to do more. She's not lesbian, so where is it coming from? Enough. Sleep.

She's standing in a sea of pigtailed Chinese people in quilted jackets. Everyone's gazing up at a giant poster of Groucho Marx, who's dressed just like Mao Tse-tung. "Seven Steps to Heaven" is blaring from loudspeakers, flanking the poster, and each person is holding up a copy of *On the Road.*

* * *

Colleen and Vincent walk along West 114th Street—"Frat Row" he calls it—Vincent carrying her overnight bag. Valerie and Sandy were fine with her visiting Columbia with Vincent. In fact, Colleen had the feeling they were relieved and happy that she'd found something else to do, because it would give them more time to themselves, which she understood and is fine with. She wouldn't be surprised if they spend the day in Sandy's bed. Anyway, she'll meet Valerie at Port Authority later this afternoon to catch the bus back to Newburgh. She's been checking out the façades of the buildings. "So, you don't belong to one, huh?" she asks Vincent.

"I'm not into Greek. It's a bunch of bullshit, all about getting drunk and making noise. It's a big reason I stay at my grandmother's whenever I can. My dorm's a street over and these jerks can be really loud, especially on weekends."

She follows him into a nondescript building, with corkboards filled with mimeographed notices and posters lining the walls inside the entrance, and up two flights of stairs and down the hall. She hears a song playing in one of the rooms up ahead. The music has a loping thumping beat and beefy horns and heavy bass and a busy guitar. The singer is definitely a Black man and he's complaining to his girlfriend about not being able to keep her mouth shut. "You just a blabber-mouth baby, and spreadin' gossip is your game," she hears him sing and he really sounds ticked off. He reminds her of James Brown, but his voice is deeper, throatier and sexier.

Vincent stops at the open doorway to the room the music is coming from and she stops behind him. "Hey, Bryon," she hears him say. The music lowers and she hears Bryon say, "Wuz happenin'?" just as Miles Davis did, only not in a low growl, but in a higher-pitched voice and she can tell by the sound of it that he's Black. She shakes her head. This is exactly what Vincent was talking about, kind of.

Byron appears in the doorway, his hands stuck in the pockets of his blue jeans. He's about Vincent's height and wearing black Keds, unlike

Vincent, who's wearing the same black leather shoes with narrow toes and pegged black slacks he was yesterday. Byron's gold wire rim glasses make him look studious and professorial. He has on a gray Columbia sweatshirt and she can see, from the shirt collar, a white button down shirt. His skin is a deep rich brown and she finds herself thinking it's the same color as a Hershey Bar and hates herself for thinking that.

For a moment she despairs that anything will ever really change between Blacks and Whites in America. If she's so concerned about racism and yet can't help thinking racist thoughts, how are the minds of the people who discriminate against them ever going to change? It just doesn't seem humanly possible. She forces herself not to think about it and studies his face. He's handsome with sparkling brown eyes and softly rounded features and full lips. She likes the fact that his hair is bushy, but not too bushy, and neatly trimmed. He looks at her and smiles and Vincent turns to introduce them.

"This is Colleen," Vincent says. "She's a friend of Valerie's. Wants to see the campus."

"Nice to meet you," Byron says, smiling and holding out his hand.

"Same here," she says, taking it and glancing at their clasped hands.

It's the first time she's held a Black person's hand and felt a Black person's skin against her own and she can feel the difference. The skin of Byron's palm and fingers is a bit smoother and tauter than what she's used to feeling and she's struck by the contrast of colors—her skin milky white and his chocolate brown—and likes the way they complement each other.

"Feel like goin' for a walk?" Vincent asks Byron.

"Sure. I could use some fresh air," Byron says.

Vincent puts her overnight bag in his room and the three of them leave the dorm. She listens as Vincent and Byron tell her about Columbia as they walk toward the campus proper. Vincent calls Columbia "The glory of Morningside Heights a bit sarcastically, and says that it's the oldest institution of higher learning in the State of New York and the fifth oldest in the country, that it was founded in 1784 and was originally called King's College, and that the campus was first located downtown at 49th Street and Madison Avenue and moved to Morningside Heights a century later.

She hears about famous alumni—Teddy Roosevelt and Franklin Roosevelt, Dwight Eisenhower, Richard Rogers and Oscar Hammerstein, Upton Sinclair and J.D. Salinger, Art Garfunkel. She's surprised to hear Jack Kerouac's name mentioned. She never would have guessed and based on even the little she's read of *On The Road,* she has a hard time imagining him as an undergraduate at Columbia and isn't surprised to hear that he dropped out.

She hears from Vincent about some of the long-standing traditions at the university, like Orgo Night, when, the day before the Organic Chemistry exam, at precisely the stroke of midnight, the marching band occupies Butler Library and plays, to distract students from studying, and then moves on and plays at other residences on campus and ends up at the residential quadrangle at Barnard College, where the girls throw trash and water balloons and, Byron interjects, grinning, underwear at them from the windows. It all sounds goofy to her and great fun, which is what she's always imagined being at college is all about, when you're not cramming for exams.

She notices the bed sheet banners hanging here and there beneath windows, one with just a peace sign on it, another demanding "U.S. OUT OF VIETNAM! another with "ROTC" in a circle with a slanted bar through it, another with "GYM" in the same circle with the same slanted bar through it. She sees a small sign taped to the inside of a window that says "SHL = RIGHTS" and asks Vincent about it and he explains that it's the newly formed Student Homophile League. She's surprised and impressed that there are people on campus who are so open about their homosexuality. It *is* a college campus, and you'd *expect* people to be more open-minded and tolerant here but, still, it's against the law and she knows it takes courage.

They climb the granite steps, making their way around the students sitting on them, to the upper terrace and Vincent points out Butler Library and Low Memorial Library and she sees small groups of students sitting here and there on the grass. In some groups, White and Black kids sit together, in others, only White kids or Black kids. She senses the tension in the air that Vincent was telling her about. She can't put her finger on why, but it's there, she can feel it. Maybe it's that everyone looks so serious and there's a lot of furtive glancing around going on.

They stand at the top of the fenced in construction site, where the gymnasium is being built, and look down the sloping dirt lot at the idle bulldozers that will continue, bright and early tomorrow morning, busily grading and smoothing the ground. In the distance, across the street at the far end of the lot, she sees a row of drab apartment buildings, staring accusatorily back at her. Taking in the scene, the conflict between the residents and the university and their competing interests couldn't be more apparent.

Behind her is an institution that doesn't just symbolize everything that being White in America stands for but embodies it—in its grand steps and classical architecture, with its pillared entranceways and statue of Alma Mater on the steps of Low Memorial Library, sitting on her throne, draped in her academic robe and wearing a crown of laurels. Columbia, she thinks, is an institution established to instill in the descendants of the European settlers the knowledge and wisdom of the Greeks and Romans, who long ago conquered and ruled and civilized them, and its purpose is to perpetuate Western culture, a great culture, to be sure, but a culture that laid claim to Africa and enslaved and exported its people to the New World, where they lived and worked and died like animals for the benefit of their masters.

Before her is Harlem, whose namesake city Haarlem she knows about, having studied and written a paper about the Netherlands. Haarlem, she learned, was a city of toll collectors and beer brewers and flax spinners, and if people here ever did associate this section of New York with the city in the Netherlands, she figures that ended long ago. This place is viewed by Whites as the holding pen for the modern day descendants of those original African slaves, who were sold into slavery by their own kind, some of whom were royalty but most of whom were just average people and all of whom were considered chattel, and were separated when they arrived and sold on the block, like cattle, to the highest bidder. She can almost feel the weight of Columbia behind her and Harlem before her, pressing against her and squeezing the breath out of her. It's like being stuck between two worlds, one she's familiar with and comfortable in and the other completely foreign to her, and if what they say about Harlem is to be believed, inhospitable and even hostile to her and her kind.

She thinks of the defensive walls the people of Haarlem built around their city to keep invaders out and it seems to her that this gymnasium the university is building will serve pretty much the same purpose, and, if nothing else, will hide the buildings on the other side of the lot from view. They might be out of sight, but she knows that won't solve anything. The neighbors in Harlem are a problem for Columbia, just like the young woman's in the ladies' room at the Village Gate. It isn't going to go away on its own or without pain.

They walk back to the steps to have lunch. She's worked up an appetite from all the walking they've done and buys a Sabrett hot dog smothered with onions and mustard, a bag of chips and a can of Coke. Whenever she's been in New York City with her parents, this is what she's had and whenever she thinks of the city, it's the deliciously fond memory that always comes to mind. She sits between Vincent and Byron on the steps, spreads her napkin on her lap, unwraps the foil around her hot dog, takes a bite and chews slowly, savoring it.

"What time's her train?" Byron asks Vincent.

"Four-twenty," Vincent says and looks at Colleen. "Your bus leaves at five-thirty, right?

She nods, savoring another mouthful of hot dog.

"We'll have plenty of time to get to Port Authority," Vincent says and looks at Byron. "You wanna come with us?"

"Sure," Byron says, "got nothin' better to do."

She finishes chewing, swallows, washes the food down with a sip of Coke and looks at Byron. "Where are you from?"

"Washington, D.C."

"Your family lived there a long time?" He nods.

"We're originally from Prince George's County, in Maryland."

The word "originally" sticks in her mind. She knows that's not where his family is really from originally but rather somewhere in Africa and she'd like to ask him if he knows anything about his African roots, but is reluctant to, because he probably doesn't. She doesn't know for how many generations his family has been in America or if he's descended from slaves, but if he is, asking about his ancestry might be a sore point. It might embarrass him, make him uncomfortable, or even upset him.

This is a new experience for her. She's never talked with a Black person about his or her family's experience in the U.S., but Byron seems like such a nice, open easy-going guy, and she figures she'd better take the opportunity to begin learning how to, so she can learn from Blacks about what they think and feel about their past and how they think it's affected them as people and made them who they are. If she's going to defend them, she thinks, she needs to understand them. She takes a deep breath and lets it out slowly and as quietly as possible. "Know much about your family's history?" she asks, as delicately as she can, and sees him nod slowly.

"Oh, I know plenty about my family's history."

She notes the bitterness.

"My ancestor arrived on a slave ship, off the coast of South Carolina, sometime in the mid Sixteen Hundreds. He was sold into chattel slavery and worked on a tobacco plantation. The story goes he was African royalty."

She notes the dismissiveness and the indifferent shrug.

"Who knows? It doesn't matter. All that matters is that he was a slave, as were his children and their children—generations of them. As time went by, the 'African blood' became more and more diluted until today, there are Blacks who pass for White. The fact that I look the way I do," he says and shrugs again. "Who knows why?"

She sees an opportunity to lighten the mood and grins. "I think you're handsome."

"Whoa!" Vincent says, smiling at Byron and raising his eyebrows. "Watch out, 'Lover Boy!'"

Byron smiles and looks at Colleen. "Thanks. I think you're pretty cute."

She smiles and feels herself blush and knows he can see it. She thinks he's blushing too, but it's hard to tell. "Thanks. Do you know anything about where your family's from in Africa?"

"We think West Africa someplace, where Ghana is now, but we're not really sure. It's almost impossible to trace."

She thinks of what she knows of her own family's history. She knows her father's family is from Donegal and her mother's from Galway and the oldest birth records date back to the 1860s. Just as with Byron's family, her family's history earlier than that is murky and a lot of it based on conjecture and speculation. So, when all is said and done, she really doesn't know much more about her family than Byron does about his. "What's your dad do?" she asks.

"He's a lawyer."

"So's my father! What type of law does he practice?"

"Corporate."

"My father's a criminal trial attorney, a good one too. He handles most of the high-profile cases where we live. He's in the paper all the time," she says and rolls her eyes. "He's like a celebrity."

Byron smiles. "My dad's work is unglamorous. He makes a great living, though. He takes on civil rights cases and works pro bono. It's his way of giving back."

The idea of her father defending anyone for free is unimaginable to her. "That's what I want to do," she says, "be a civil rights lawyer!"

"Ah," Byron says, "following in your dad's footsteps, huh?"

She frowns. "Well, as far as being a lawyer is concerned, anyway."

"Not on good terms with your dad?"

"Let's just say that I respect the fact that he's good at what he does and leave it at that."

"Ever been to Martha's Vineyard?" Byron asks.

"No. I hear it's pretty, though. My mom's family lives in Boston and I've visited them, but that's it."

"It's beautiful. We vacation there every summer, in Oak Bluffs. Have for years. A lot of Black families stay in Oak Bluffs. It's kind of become the Black place to stay."

"Because they want to or have to?" she asks.

"Want to. Massachusetts is a very Liberal state and most of the people are very open-minded and tolerant and anti-segregation. At least, the better educated people are."

She thinks of her mother's family. Her mother's parents never made it past high school and are openly bigoted and racist. Anyone who's not a member of the tribe, and certainly anyone who isn't White, is viewed as unwelcome and a threat. Her aunt and uncle, who both graduated from college and still live in Southie, are just as openly bigoted and racist as her grandparents. "Well, I dunno," she says, "I can tell you that if you walked into South Boston, you'd be taking your life in your hands."

"Listen," Byron says, "I know there's racism in the North, even in Massachusetts. There's racism everywhere and it'll never go away, at least not in my lifetime. I don't dwell on it. I have a sister who does and friends who do and I see what it does to them. It poisons them. It turns them into the same type of people they hate so much." He smiles playfully. "Maybe you can come visit sometime."

"Where?"

"Oak Bluffs, during the summer."

Vincent looks at Byron and smiles and shakes his head. "You are one smooth operator, man."

She studies Byron's expression. It looks playful and he sounded playful when he suggested it, but he seems sincere about the offer. She'd like to take him up on it, but could she? Would her parents let her visit him and stay with his family? She doesn't think so, but maybe she can figure out a way to make it happen. She'll think about it. There's plenty of time between now and summer vacation.

Now Byron's looking at her expectantly, waiting for her answer, and she's having second thoughts about accepting his offer. Should she? She's almost certain that if she does, she'll receive an invitation at some point, and what would happen if she actually was able to go? She has the feeling things would almost certainly get physical and does she want that with him, a Black? She feels guilty for thinking like a racist again. "Sure," she finally says, "that would be nice." She watches his smile broaden and sees the delight in his eyes.

"Great!" he says, "maybe this summer."

"Yeah, we'll see. I'm not so sure my parents will let me." He looks at her knowingly.

"I'm sure you can make it happen."

"I'll try my best."

* * *

The three of them stand on the sidewalk on 8th Avenue, by one of the tunnels that now take people to and from Penn Station, waiting for

Yvonne to appear. The tunnels are the only access because Penn Station is in the process of being demolished and is surrounded by fencing. Colleen and Bryon listen to Vincent describe the once magnificent building and bemoan the fact that the growing outcry over the planned demolition—from the architectural community, preservationists, the press and, finally, the public—since it was announced by the Pennsylvania Railroad, the building's owner, failed to stay the wrecking balls and now people traveling by train to and from New York City, the financial and cultural capital of the country—no, the world!—are forced to negotiate a network of tunnels, like subway riders. It couldn't be more undignified.

Vincent reminisces about the grandeur of the place, having once been inside it with his family to take the train to Florida for a vacation, they being car-eschewing city dwellers. He recalls the Corinthian columns on the façade of the building's main entrance, which were modeled, he learned later, after the Brandenburg Gate in Berlin; the caryatids arranged around the base of the clock towers in the building's cavernous interior public waiting space; the vaulted glass ceiling, high overhead, supported by iron beams that he says reminded him of the Eiffel Tower, which he'd seen in photographs but has yet to visit, although he hopes to one day.

"It sucks," he says. "I've seen a picture of the architectural model of what they're planning to build here, an office building that looks like an anonymous Communist Bloc slab. I read in a review of the design, in a *Times* article, that 'a city gets what it wants, is willing to pay for, and ultimately deserves.' I couldn't agree more. This is what we've come to. Moses wants to build an expressway through Lower Manhattan. I won't be surprised if that happens too."

"Moses?" she asks, thinking what's the guy with the tablet have to do with it?

"Robert Moses," Vincent says disgustedly, "the city's urban planner and the head of God knows how many Authorities. He considers himself 'New York's Architect.' The guy's never seen an expressway or housing development built on what used to be a low-income neighborhood he hasn't liked. You can thank him for the Dodgers leaving town. He's a power-hungry Jew who no one seems able to stop. I read he converted to Catholicism. I'm sure he did because he thought being a Christian would somehow work to his political advantage."

She's surprised and dismayed by Vincent's anti-Semitic remarks about this man Robert Moses. It's just another form of racism and she's disappointed that a person like Vincent, who's intelligent and thoughtful and who she thought was above this type of thinking, has turned out to be just like everyone else, including herself. She wonders if anyone's above it. She's beginning to think not, that it's so deeply ingrained in people and society and the culture that it's impossible to escape and she finds this thought troubling and worrisome. She hears Byron pshaw and looks at him and sees him staring off at nothing in particular with a look of disgust.

"The Jews," he says.

"What about them?" she asks and can see that whatever it is, it's a real bone of contention with him.

"Don't get me wrong. I abhor what the Nazis did to them as much as anyone, but I guarantee you that if they'd been Black people, the world wouldn't have given a damn what happened to them."

She's astonished to hear this. "You don't really believe that, do you?" He looks at her and raises his eyebrows.

"No? There were probably as many Africans who died during the Middle Passage as Jews who died in the camps. Nobody gave a damn about them. The Jews were persecuted for—what?—ten years in Nazi Germany? For hundreds of years in this country, nobody gave a damn that Blacks were slaves and were treated like animals. To this day, there are plenty of people who consider Blacks to be subhuman, an inferior race."

Her immediate reaction is to want to dispute the facts of what he said, but she has the feeling he knows what he's talking about and he's certainly right about Blacks having been slaves for hundreds of years and no one having cared about them, not many people, anyway. She wants to defend White people and say that not everyone's racist, but here she's just heard Vincent call Robert Moses a "power-hungry Jew" and she, herself, is guilty of thinking racist thoughts and she finds herself frustrated and not knowing what to say.

"Hey!" she hears and turns to see an attractive young Black woman with an Afro, striding toward them from the tunnel entrance. She's wearing blue jeans and a Barnard College sweatshirt, has a big brown leather bag slung over her shoulder and is carrying a suitcase. She has bright eyes and a big smile and walks up to Vincent, puts down her suitcase and throws her arms around him and he puts his around hers and they kiss. So, Vincent's girlfriend is Black! He's okay with Blacks like Yvonne and Byron, who are attending college and whose families have money—she assumes Yvonne's family is like Byron's—but not with Jews like this supposedly power-hungry Robert Moses. Now she's more confused than ever.

Colleen glances at Byron and sees he's been looking at her all this time and smiling, obviously amused by her surprise at learning that Yvonne is Black. She's embarrassed and feels herself blush and knows her cheeks and neck are now pink. It doesn't seem fair that she can't hide her embarrassment because of her skin color but Byron can his. It's the first time in her life she's felt at a disadvantage because of the color of *her* skin, and it gives her a better appreciation for how Blacks must feel.

* * *

The four of them wait in the Short Line departure area in Port Authority for Valerie and Sandy to arrive, Colleen sitting next to Byron with Vincent and Yvonne sitting on the other side of him. "So, what do you want to do, when you graduate?" Colleen asks Byron.

He shrugs. "I dunno. Haven't decided yet. My dad wants me to go into law, but I'm not sure that's what I want to do professionally. I've been toying with the idea of becoming a psychiatrist."

"Really? That's interesting. Why?"

He shrugs again. "I can read people pretty well, and everyone has psychological problems of one sort or another, some more than others and some problems worse than others. Most people just live with them and don't try to deal with them and work them out. Seems like it would be really interesting work."

"Yeah, I guess it would be. I'm sure you'd be good at it." Colleen wonders what Byron has seen in her and what he thinks about it. "So, what do you see in me?"

He smiles and cocks his head. "Really want to know?"

"Yeah."

He furrows his brow and purses his lips and stares thoughtfully at the wall for a moment. "I see an intelligent White teenage girl, who admires and respects her dad, but has issues with him and probably has for a long time. I'm guessing that one of those issues is the way he views Blacks. I see someone who's concerned about civil rights and racial inequality but thinks maybe she is just to spite him. I see someone who's trying hard, a little too hard, maybe, to appear not to have a racist bone in her body, but who realizes she's just like everybody else and feels uncomfortable and a little threatened when Blacks become more than symbols of a cause." He looks at her and smiles. "How am I doing so far?"

She's been mesmerized by Byron's analysis of her and listened to it staring at his face, and then his full lips, and now his bright brown eyes. It seems uncanny to her how well he's read her. "Pretty good," she says softly. "What else do you see?" She sees he doesn't bother to stare at the wall and reflect now but continues looking at her eyes and smiling and she welcomes him doing so.

"I see a girl who wants in the worst way to come visit me in Oak Bluffs next summer, is already thinking about how to make that happen and will do anything and everything she can to make it happen, because she knows we won't just be sunbathing at the beach. Isn't that right, baby?"

Hearing Byron call her "baby so smoothly and silkily, thrills Colleen. "Yeah, it is," she says softly. She's reminded of the song Byron was playing when she and Vincent arrived and the singer's sexy voice.

Byron chucks Colleen under her chin. "That's my girl," he says.

"What was that song you were playing in your room?"

"Otis Rush…"Keep It To Myself"…Chicago blues."

"I like his voice."

He cocks his head again and smiles. "Yeah? Why?"

She glances down at the lump in his jeans and wants to put her hand on it and give it a gentle squeeze. "He sounds so sexy, like you."

"Yeah," Byron says, brushing her cheek with his fingertips, "I think you're sexy too, baby."

She keeps her eyes on his eyes as he leans forward and then looks at his lips as they come closer. She closes her eyes and feels his lips pressing against hers and she presses back and it feels wonderful, like she's kissing a pillow, so wonderful that when he draws back his head and gazes at her, smiling, she looks at him questioningly, as if to say, "Why did you take your lips away?" She puts her hand on the back of his head and draws his lips back to hers.

"Hey," she hears Valerie say. She starts and sits back and looks up at her, feeling flustered. She sees Valerie and Sandy standing there, both grinning down at her, and doesn't have the slightest idea what to say. As it happens, she doesn't have to say anything, because she can tell by the way they're looking at her that they understand perfectly well what's going on and are amused by it.

* * *

The six of them stand by the door leading to the bus, Vincent and Yvonne off to one side, chatting, and Valerie and Sandy off to the other, more hanging onto each for dear life than hugging, and Colleen and Byron at a safe distance from the others, where they can't be overheard, if they speak in lowered voices. He has his arms around her waist and is looking down at her with those bright brown eyes and that sweet smile of his and she's gazing up at him. He gives her a squeeze.

"I really enjoyed meeting you," he says.

"Same here."

"Summer's a long way off, baby. Maybe you can come visit sooner."

"Yeah...maybe...we'll see."

"You know," he says suggestively, "when you stay at *Valerie's*."

"Yeah."

"Give me your number. I'll call you."

She fishes in her bag for a pen and scrap of paper to write her number on, finds them, writes down her number and hands the scrap of paper to him. Byron looks at it and smiles. He folds it, puts it in the pocket of his jeans and takes her in his arms again. She watches those marvelous lips as he brings them closer to hers and closes her eyes. She feels them pressing against hers and she presses back and enjoys that same wonderful feeling of kissing a pillow, but there's more to his kiss this time. She feels his tongue brushing her lips and she opens her mouth and feels his tongue entering her mouth and puts hers in his and they press closer together, their tongues swirling around each other. "C'mon!" she hears Valerie say, "We're gonna miss the bus!"

* * *

They ride in silence as the bus makes its way slowly in rush hour traffic through the Lincoln Tunnel toward the Jersey side of the Hudson. Colleen gazes out the window at the people in the cars and trucks and buses headed toward Manhattan and reflects on everything that's happened on her visit. A lot has and the most important thing, to her thinking, was meeting Byron and the feelings she now has for him.

They're not the same feelings she has for Henry, that's for sure, and Byron's feelings for her seem completely different than Henry's. She loves and admires Henry and longs for him to feel the same way about her. She's only just met Byron and while she's attracted to him and likes him and thinks he's sweet and sexy, she's also a little afraid of him and, yes, it's because he's Black and she's unsure whether she wants to become involved with him beyond friendship because of the possible repercussions.

Her father would go ballistic if he learned that she was romantically or, God forbid, sexually involved with a Black. Who knows what he might do, possibly disown her. And who knows what else might happen because of the two of them being seen together, walking hand in hand, or embracing and kissing in public. Sure, this isn't the Deep South, but not everyone's so tolerant here in the North.

"You really like him," she hears Valerie say and can tell she's grinning by the sound of her voice. Colleen looks at her and sees that she is and her knowing expression. "Yeah, I do," she says. "He's nice."

Valerie nods. "He is, *very* nice. He also has a thing for cute White girls and a reputation for usin' 'em up pretty quickly. Just so you know."

"Huh, I wouldn't have figured. He seems really sweet and thoughtful."

"He is. That's his thing and he does it really well."

"Yvonne seems nice. Does your family know about her?"

Valerie shakes her head. "Vincent doesn't want to tell them. He knows how they'd react to that news."

Colleen considers whether she should ask the question Valerie's comment has brought to mind and, if she does, how to ask it delicately.

There doesn't seem to be a delicate way to ask it, though, so she just does: "So, they're okay with you and Sandy, but they wouldn't be with Vincent having a Black girlfriend?" Valerie seems surprised she even asked.

"Are you kidding? No, and for obvious reasons."

Well, Colleen thinks, the only "obvious" reason is the color of Yvonne's skin; the same reason getting involved with Byron makes her feel uneasy. She's struck again by how powerful a force racism is, that it can cloud and control the thinking of otherwise intelligent people. She's sure it springs from the deeply rooted fear of the "other" that developed in human nature early on, but you'd think people would have risen above it by now. Now she's more despairing than ever that relations between Whites and Blacks in America will improve anytime soon and that her efforts to try to change things for the better will make any difference.

CHAPTER 7

Byron

Walking down Frat Row with Byron is a different experience than the one Colleen had with Vincent a month ago, aside from the fact that Byron is also politely carrying her overnight bag. She was curious then about Columbia and looking forward to seeing it and was filled with excitement and anticipation. Now her curiosity is about what spending the night with Byron in the dorm will be like—Vincent's at his grandmother's, as usual, so they'll have the room to themselves—and, yes, she's filled with excitement and anticipation, but more than anything apprehension.

She's thinking now more than ever about what Valerie told her about Byron on the bus ride back to Newburgh, that he has a thing for cute White girls and uses them up pretty quickly. She asked Valerie on the bus ride down this afternoon if she knew anything more about his reputation and Valerie said she didn't, but what she'd heard was enough and told Colleen to be careful. Valerie didn't say as much, but Colleen could tell she was uneasy with the idea of allowing herself to be used as cover, so that she could spend the weekend with Byron, and her uneasiness got Colleen thinking and she hasn't stopped. The contrast between Byron's reputation and the way he's treated her ever since she arrived—courteously and respectfully—is stark and she's confused.

As he said he would, Byron called her a week after she returned from her trip to the city. They chatted for an hour or so and had a nice conversation and he sounded very sweet, just as he had when she was with him, with the exception of that one moment, when he said what he did about the Jews, which she was willing to overlook, since his anger wasn't directed at her, specifically, but at all Whites.

He invited her to his friends' party off campus later in the month and told her that Valerie and Sandy and Vincent and Yvonne were planning to go, and that maybe she could stay with him for the weekend and they could go to the party and have fun in the city, and she said sure, that sounded nice, and as soon as she placed the receiver back in the cradle after the call, she began questioning whether she'd made the right decision and wondering what would happen and, really, she hasn't stopped since.

He was waiting at Port Authority when she arrived and seemed really happy to see her again. He gave her a big hug and one of those "pillow" kisses she remembered enjoying so much and did again. She and Valerie hugged and said they'd see each other at the party tomorrow evening, and Valerie headed to Bensonhurst and Colleen and Byron to Columbia. They had a nice conversation on the subway ride uptown and continued it when they stopped at a pizza parlor in the neighborhood for a bite to eat.

He brought up the idea again of her coming to visit him in Oak Bluffs this summer and she said she'd still like to and was still thinking about how to make it happen, and that they'd have to wait and see if she could, but assured him that she'd try her best and he smiled and nodded and said very smoothly and sweetly, with a wink, "I know you will, baby. That's why you're my girl." It was the first time she thought she glimpsed the person behind the reputation, but she wasn't sure, because the way he said it and looked at her when he did made her feel special, like she was the only girl in his life and that she had his undivided attention, and she knows that's not true, but wants to believe it and now she's more confused than ever.

Byron leads her by the hand into the dorm and up the stairs and they meet a few friends of his in passing on the staircase and in the hall, on the way to his room. She notices the way they look at her and then him and sees the same knowing expression on their faces as Valerie's, when she first told her about Byron's reputation—the same but even more so, and Colleen figures it's because, unlike Valerie, they've actually seen him in action.

She follows him into the room, stands in the middle of it and looks around, taking it in. She'd only gotten a glimpse of it through the doorway the last time she was here. She can tell Vincent's side of the room because it looks like no one uses it. There are no pictures on the walls by the bed or on the desk, no personal items to be seen anywhere. Byron's side of the room, however, looks very much lived in and personalized. There are *Playboy* centerfolds on the walls next to his bed and above his desk—all photographs of White women—and she sees a framed picture on the desk of, what she assumes, is his family.

She walks to it, picks it up and studies it. In it, Byron and his sister—a pretty girl, wearing her hair pulled back, whose skin is much lighter and features much sharper than Byron's and who looks to be about her own age—stand flanking their parents. Byron's dad is a handsome bespectacled man with short hair and his mom, who Byron's sister clearly resembles more than her dad, is an attractive woman with well-coiffed hair, sparkling eyes and a gleaming smile. Except for Byron's sister, they're all dressed in polo shirts of different, bright solid colors and smiling at the camera. Byron's sister is wearing a gray tee shirt with "BLACK POWER!" and an upraised fist under it printed in black on the front and stares defiantly at the camera with her arms crossed. Colleen assumes from what she can see of the gingerbread house behind them and the New England-looking coastline, and the houses across the water in the distance that the picture was taken on one of their vacations on Martha's Vineyard. "Oak Bluffs?" she asks.

"Hm-hmm," Byron says, walking over to her.

His voice sounded silkier than ever, and she starts when she feels his arm around her waist but, forces herself to maintain her composure. "Your sister's pretty," she says as casually as she can. "What's her name?"

"Jasmine."

"What're your parents' names?"

"Edgar and Janice."

She starts again when she feels his hand on her breast. "Relax, baby," she hears him say, soothingly, next to her ear. She doesn't know why she suddenly feels so uncomfortable about what's happening. After all, she agreed to spend the weekend with him in his dorm room. What did she expect would happen? Maybe it's the way he seems to think he can do whatever he wants with her.

Now she's certain what Valerie said about him is true and she's wondering what it is he does to White girls, once they fall under his spell. Whatever it is, she knows she's about to find out and feels like she's headed toward being just another one of his conquests. She steps away and turns around and looks at him. "Going a little fast, aren't you?"

He smiles. "Why waste time, baby? Don't be so uptight."

She watches him walk to the closet and return with a bottle and places it on the desk. He opens one of the desk drawers, takes out two shot glasses and places them on the desk next to the bottle. She sees by the label that its Hennessy VSOP cognac and watches him pull out the stopper and fill each of the shot glasses with honey-colored liquid. He hands her a glass and picks up his.

"This'll relax you and get you in the mood," he says, clinking her glass.

"I don't really like the taste of alcohol."

He raises his eyebrows. "Ever tried cognac?"

"No."

He smiles. "Then you don't know if you like it, do you, baby?"

"No, I guess not," she says and sees him lower his eyebrows and fix his eyes on her.

"So, try it and see. Cheers," he says and takes a sip.

She sees him watching her over the rim of his glass. "Yeah, cheers," she says and brings the glass to her lips. Even before tasting it, she can smell the alcohol and it tickles the insides of her nostrils. She takes a tentative sip and holds the liquid in her mouth a moment before swallowing. It doesn't taste bad at all. It's sweet and has a bite to it. She swallows and feels the liquid stinging her throat as it goes down. She can see by his expression that he's pleased with himself for having made her do as she was told, and she bristles at the idea that he or any other man, other than her father, would think he could control her. Byron's sweet, all right, but deceptively so, and she decides to confront him about his reputation. She takes another longer sip of cognac, keeping her eyes on his as she swallows. "So, I hear you have a thing for cute White girls and go through them pretty quickly." He cocks his head.

"Yeah? Who told you that?"

"A little birdie," she says and takes another long sip, liking the taste more and more, and now also her feeling of lightheadedness.

"I bet she did."

She watches him pick up the bottle, refill their glasses, and put the bottle back on the desk. He takes her by the hand and leads her over to the bed and sits beside her. They both take long sips, looking at each other's eyes over the rims of their glasses. "Is it true?" she asks.

He purses his lips and narrows his eyes a bit and looks at her thoughtfully. "Let's just say there are a lot of White girls who believe what they've heard about Black males being well-endowed and fantastic lovers." He grins. "I just happen to be both and I enjoy satisfying their curiosity."

She studies his eyes as she considers what he's just said. She's heard the same things said about Black males but, hasn't thought much about it and hasn't been curious about finding out if there's any truth to the racist stereotype—until now. There probably are a lot of White girls who are really curious, though, and maybe the "goes through them pretty quickly" part of his reputation isn't really his doing. Maybe once they've gotten what they want and satisfied their curiosity, they're done. "Huh," she says.

"I wouldn't want to be in a relationship with most of them anyway. They're naïve and gullible, not very interesting or intellectually stimulating, and most not very good sexual partners. Too uptight, as most White people seem to be."

This is the second time he's mentioned White people being "too uptight first her and now all whites, and she takes offense at his sweeping generalization, itself a racist stereotype, and finds it surprising, coming from him, but she masks her feelings and watches him sip his cognac and takes another long sip of hers and notices her glass is almost empty again. He glances at it and looks at her and raises his eyebrows.

"Another?" he asks.

"Sure," she says and sees he's pleased with himself and smiles. She watches him stand and walk to the desk, take the bottle and return and sit next to her. He refills her glass and then his, this time hers to just below the rim, and sets the bottle down on the floor next to him, where it's handy. She takes a long sip and now she's beginning to experience a completely new sensation. She feels expansive and uninhibited, kind of the way she did when she smoked pot, but different and not at all horny. Still, the same way in that she feels like she'd do whatever he wants and would let him do whatever he wants to her.

Her father comes to mind again. She realizes now that she's never really understood him until this moment, feeling tipsy. Her father feels this way every day and for the better part of it. He's spent most of his life feeling this way—expansive and uninhibited. Is it any wonder he is the way he is? Not caring about anyone but himself? Being perfectly happy and content to be alone in his self-induced state of dizzy numbness? Feeling immune from the pain of criticism from prosecutors and the newspaper-reading public about his courtroom bullying and the fact that he works so hard to win acquittal for his obviously corrupt and guilty as hell clients? No, it isn't. She understands him now. She doesn't forgive him for the way he's treated her and her mother or for what he's done to them as a family, but she does now understand.

She takes another long sip and swallows it slowly and savors the sharp sweet taste and feels the sting in her throat as it goes down. It's just like smoking. There's the burning sensation in her throat as she swallows the cognac and then the little rush of pleasure she feels when the alcohol is absorbed into her bloodstream. Pleasure mixed with pain. That's the way life is. You don't get to enjoy pleasure without feeling pain. You just have to take the bad with the good.

She takes another long sip and sees her glass is almost empty again. She looks at him and sees he's smiling at her with slightly hooded eyes, and she watches him lean over and pick up the bottle and refill her glass, knowing that she wants him to without her having to ask, then set the bottle back on the floor. She feels emboldened now by the alcohol, enough to speak her mind and ask him the question she's been asking herself. "So, am I just another curious white girl?"

He shakes his head slowly. "No, baby. You're different. You're plenty curious, all right, and I'm going to satisfy that, but you're different. I have special plans in mind for you."

She keeps her eyes on his as he leans forward and closes them just before she feels his lips pressing against hers and she presses back. She feels his hand on her breast again and keeps her eyes closed and puts her hand on his thigh and continues pressing back against his lips as he fondles her and brushes her nipples. It feels good and her nipples are hard now and she's tingling between her legs, but she feels uneasy about what's about to happen. How is she different and what "special plans"? She feels him take his lips away and opens her eyes and looks at him and waits to see what happens next. He moves his hand from her breast to her cheek and slowly strokes it with his fingertips.

"I'm going to educate you," he says.

"Yeah?" she asks softly, "About what?"

"How it feels to be Black."

"How?"

"You'll see. You have a big guilty conscience about the way Blacks have been treated in this country, don't you, baby?"

She does, but no more so than most White people, she thinks, who think the mistreatment of Blacks is wrong. Still, the answer is yes but she's reluctant to admit it. She knows it's a leading question, just like the ones her father's famous for asking in court, knowing full well that he's going to be challenged by the prosecutor and that the judge will sustain the prosecutor's objection. She knows that all Byron's questions will be leading ones. She wants to object, but there's no judge to appeal to for a ruling and the subtle change that's occurred in Byron, his now slightly less friendly expression and slightly more serious tone of voice, makes her think that she shouldn't. "Yeah, I guess I do," she says softly and can see now by his cool look and slight nod at her answer that she's not going to like where he's leading her. He nods toward the middle of the room.

"Stand up and face me and get undressed."

She didn't like the sound of that at all, stern and almost like a command, ordering her to stand and undress for him. Nobody's ever ordered her to do anything, except her father and she hates him for it. She doesn't hate Byron, though. She's not sure how she feels about him at the moment, but she doesn't hate him. She looks at his eyes and slowly raises her glass to her lips, takes another long sip and thinks about what's happening as she savors the sharp sweet taste of the cognac and feels the sting of it in her throat as she swallows it.

Maybe this is some type of sex game he plays, like the game of "doctor and patient" she used to play with Moira when they were kids and curious about their own bodies and the bodies of others and what it felt like to be touched and to touch others. Maybe that's it. The pretend visit to the doctor to be examined lent what they were doing together a kind of legitimacy and eased their minds about the naughtiness of it. There's nothing at all naughty about the game Byron seems to be playing, if it is a game. It's a mind game, whose purpose is to assert his control over her, his superiority, to put her in her place and keep her there. Well, she thinks, we'll see if I can beat him at his own game.

Byron nods again toward the middle of the room and Colleen takes another long sip and puts the glass down on the floor. She stands and takes a step and turns and faces him. She watches him lean back on his elbows and smile, getting ready to enjoy the show. Yeah, that must be it, she thinks, a sexy game of pretend. He's the Black "Massah" and I'm the cute White "slave girl."

She slowly undresses and tosses her clothes to the side in a pile and stands looking down at him, waiting to see what happens next. She's arrived at a new place now, because of the amount she's had to drink. She's still apprehensive but no longer feels afraid. In fact, she feels emboldened and eager to play along, to learn what these "special plans" he has in mind for her are.

"Hm-hmm," he says, looking her slowly up and down. "You are really something, baby...honey-color hair, creamy white skin, pretty face, nice big tits, nice rosy hard nipples, nice small waist.... And just look at that pussy! Hm-hmm." He holds up a finger and twirls it. "Turn around, baby. Show me that gorgeous ass of yours."

She turns her back to him and looks over her shoulder and watches him admire her ass. He nods toward the floor in front of him.

"C'mere and kneel in front of me, baby."

She steps forward and slowly lowers herself to her knees and sits back on her heels with her back straight. She eyes the bulge in his jeans. It's big, all right, really big and long. She glances up at him and sees he's noticed her looking at his crotch and that it pleases him that she did and he smiles. That must have been what she was supposed to do next, notice the size of his penis.

He cocks his head. "Like what you see, baby?"

She nods.

"Want me to take it out so you can get a real good look at it?"

Now she's really aroused and squirms and sees him notice and look pleased again. So that's what his "special plans" are, a game of "master and slave" to get them both worked up into a heightened state of arousal. Well, it's working for her and she's getting into it and beginning to really enjoy it. "Yeah," she says, "I do."

She keeps her eyes on his crotch as he unbuttons and unzips his jeans and pulls them down a bit and fishes his penis out of his briefs and displays it for her. She's seen a lot of penises but never one this big or chocolate colored. It's thick and long and looks delicious and she'd like nothing more than to take it in her mouth and suck it but, she has the feeling that part of the game is his making her work for it.

He nods toward his lap. "I bet you'd like to taste that in the worst way, wouldn't you, baby?"

She knows he's enjoying the fact that she's never seen anything like it and can't take her eyes off it and is staring at it hungrily, but she doesn't care. "Yeah, I would."

"I know you would, baby, but you're going to have to work for it."

"Yeah, I figured."

"Hard," he adds.

She glances up at him and sees him looking at her differently now, with narrowed eyes and not even the hint of a smile. His expression looks a little menacing and now she thinks that deciding to play this game with him was a bad idea. Well, she didn't really decide. She didn't have a choice. What was she going to do? Leave? She doesn't even know how to get to Valerie's and even if she did, she's in no condition now to go anywhere. Put up a fight? Scream for help? No, she's stuck where she is, playing this game and the best thing to do is just continue to play along and hope for the best.

He sits up and slowly leans forward, resting his elbows on his thighs and clasping his hands in front of him. He stares at her and she imagines again that this is just how a mouse feels, facing a snake. Doreen comes to mind.

"Sit up straight, baby."

She slowly lifts herself up and kneels at attention with her arms at her sides and lifts her eyes from his penis to his eyes, which is where she thinks he wants her to be looking now. She can feel the muscles in her thighs twitching and it isn't from strain but fear, fear of not knowing what's coming next and the growing suspicion that it's going to be unpleasant. He furrows his brow and looks at her with concern.

"You have a lot to answer for, baby"

"Yeah? Like what?" He looks surprised by her question.

"Like three hundred years of slavery, your people treating my people like animals and property and now like second-class citizens."

She feels her body begin trembling slightly and knows he can see it. She wishes she could stop it but can't. "I didn't do any of that," she says weakly. He looks surprised by this answer too, and looks around the room and back at her.

"I don't see any other White person here to answer for it, baby. Do you?"

"No."

"Hmm. So, I guess you have to."

Her knees are hurting now from kneeling on the hard floor and she shifts uncomfortably. She sees his expression change to one of mock concern.

"Uncomfortable?"

"Yeah, I am. My knees hurt." Now she knows he's going to express feigned surprise at all her answers.

"I'll tell you what uncomfortable is. Uncomfortable is lying on your back, shackled to the deck of a ship, shoulder to shoulder with people on either side of you, being transported on a long voyage from Africa to the New World. *That's* uncomfortable. You? You're just a middle-class White girl with a big guilty conscience, who now thinks that sucking a black dick would be her way of atoning for her own racist sins and those of her kind." He cocks his head again.

"Isn't that right, baby?"

"Yeah, I guess so." Okay, she thinks, is that the point of all this? Getting her to give him a blowjob? If that's it, then what a disappointment. She can take care of that in no time and can pretty much guess what the rest of the evening would be like; he being satisfied and largely ignoring her and she being frustrated and bored.

"Can I get my drink?" she asks and sees him smile and nod. She reaches over and takes her glass, brings it to her lips and drains it and puts the empty glass back on the floor. She looks at him. His expression is a mixture of bemusement and pity.

"Seems you've acquired a new taste, baby."

"Yeah, I guess I have. I wouldn't have thought." She watches him lean closer.

"There's so much you haven't 'thought', baby. That's why I'm here. To school ya."

She notes the shift from "educate" to "school ya" and the way he's speaking now reminds her of the way poor Blacks in Newburgh sound. She thinks she knows what's coming next and braces herself for it and is happy that she's drunk as much cognac as she has. She can no longer feel her body and she's sure that's just the state she needs to be in. "Yeah? How?"

"For starters, don't look at me. Keep your eyes on the floor in front of you."

She looks down at the floor and finds a spot and tries to focus on it but isn't quite able to bring the two spots together.

"Good," she hears him say. "Now, tell me how much you want to suck my dick, baby."

"A lot," she says. She feels his palm on her cheek and he caresses it, but then she feels him tap it and then again, a little harder, and again, harder still, and the last one wasn't a tap, but a stinging slap.

No one has ever slapped her before—except her father, in his fury, when she's flagrantly disobeyed him, and for which she hates him—and she can barely contain her indignation.

"You can do better than that, baby," she hears him say. "I know you can and so do you. Lemme hear you beg."

She's never begged for anything in her life. Everything she's wanted and needed has been given to her—the necessities by her parents and principally her father—and to compensate for the lack of love she receives from her parents, the admiration she demands and—to be honest—craves from her carefully chosen friends. The idea of begging for anything seems foreign and abhorrent to her, despite which, she knows she needs to try now and do her best to sound convincing. "Please, may I suck your dick?" she asks in a whisper, with each word requiring effort to get out and feeling like its own slap in the face.

"You've never had to beg for anything in your life, have you, baby?" she hears him ask and shrugs.

"I guess not," she says, still trying to bring the two spots on the floor together.

The slap comes unexpectedly. It's more than a stinging one. It's a blow that snaps her head to the side and almost knocks her over, but she maintains her balance and straightens up and looks down and finds the spot on the floor again and tries to focus on it.

Her cheek burns and she imagines there's a red handprint on it now and that he's looking at it and admiring his handiwork. She knows it's because she's drunk that she was able to take the blow. Still, she feels proud of herself that she was able to and can take more.

She wonders if he treats all White girls this way or just her. She has the feeling just her, that she's the first to experience his naked hatred of Whites and bear the brunt of his pent-up anger, which she isn't surprised he vents against White girls. It's probably just the alcohol again, clouding her thinking, but, in a way, she thinks it's probably good for her that he's treating her this way.

She *is* proud and not in a good way. Except for Henry and Valerie, she's surrounded herself with people she feels superior to and who look up to her. Maybe she does need a lesson in humility, and if she pays for the sins of White people in the process, so much the better.

"Try again, baby," she hears him say.

"Please, may I suck your dick?" she asks. "I'll let you do anything you want to me, if you do." she says, trying her best to sound more convincing. She's ready and waiting for the blow this time but it still snaps her head to the side and almost knocks her over again. She straightens up again and he tells her again to give it another try. She does and receives another blow, and even though she's numb from the alcohol, she feels her eyes filling with tears and then the tears spilling over and running down her cheeks.

"I don't know what I'm gonna do with you, baby," she hears him say, sounding like he's speaking to a slow learning child, who's struggling to understand simple arithmetic, which is how she feels now.

She sniffs and wipes her eyes with her finger and the tears from her cheeks with her palm. "Neither do I," she says.

She feels him gather up her hair in his hands and grip it tightly with one hand at the top of her head. He pulls her head up so that she's looking at him and sees he's looking at her pretty much the way she expected he would be—smugly. She sobs uncontrollably and sniffs as she looks at him, her chest heaving. She can only imagine the way she looks. She knows her cheeks are streaked with mascara, and she can feel the snot on her upper lip.

"Please, may I have another drink?" she blubbers.

He looks at her curiously for a moment and then fills her glass and hands it to her. She gulps the cognac this time and puts the glass on the floor beside her.

"Hit me," she says, not at all pleadingly, but commanding him to. She looks at him and sees he's puzzled, and she studies his eyes as he searches hers, undoubtedly trying to determine where her desire to be hit is coming from. His confusion only lasts a long moment and this time she sees the blow coming. She straightens up and doesn't flinch and takes, while managing to hold her head still. She takes a gulp of cognac and puts the glass down.

"Again," she demands and receives another blow. She looks down art her glass and sees it's empty. She looks up and stares at him. "Put your dick in my mouth," she demands. There's that puzzled expression again and he pulls her forward by her hair. She looks hungrily at the head of his penis as it comes closer and opens her mouth and closes her eyes and savors the feel of it sliding in and filling her mouth and she sucks happily and contentedly like a baby feeding at her mother's breast.

* * *

She waits until she hears his light snoring and slowly gets out of bed and stands. She reaches down and takes the bottle and her glass from the floor and walks to the chair at his desk and sits. She tilts the bottle to refill her glass but it's empty. "Shit," she whispers. Does he have another in his closet? She hopes so.

She walks to it and opens the door and peers in but can't see anything in the darkness. Slowly her eyes adjust, and she sees two bottles on the shelf above his hanging clothes. She takes one and walks back to the chair, sits and removes the foil and the stopper from the top of the bottle. She fills her glass, sits back, takes a long sip, stares out the window at the darkness and thinks about the evening.

He was like two different people: first, the angry Black man and then, when they got into bed, the tender Black lover. He sure knows how to use that penis of his and she'd never experienced anything like it before. The feeling of having him inside her was amazing and his stamina was remarkable. She's sore from all the lovemaking and she knows she'll still be sore in the morning, but it was well worth it. She takes another long sip and thinks about what happened before the lovemaking.

She knows she should feel humiliated because of his treatment of her, but she doesn't and not just because she's drunk. Honestly, she felt she deserved it for being so proud and having surrounded herself with admiring friends, and that it was good that she humbled herself. There's a big difference between humility and humiliation. In fact, being completely honest with herself, she enjoyed it, the way she imagines penitents enjoy flogging their backs until they're bloody.

The Byron she experienced when she was kneeling on the floor in front of him was a lot like her father—harsh and controlling and demanding. Unlike her father, though, Byron was able to do more than just hurt her. He was also able to give her enormous pleasure and it was enormous in every way. There's something extremely attractive about a man like that, who can both please her and hurt her in equal measure. She's not sure she'd want a partner in life like that, but still.

She takes another long sip. Did the experience teach her anything about what it feels like to be Black? Yes, in the sense that she gained insight into how deeply affected Blacks are by their mistreatment by Whites, and how even an intelligent and mild-mannered guy like Byron can be so poisoned by anger and bitter resentment because of it that it can cause him to become verbally and physically abusive.

Well, if any girl is right for him, it's her. She knows all about verbal and physical abuse and how to take it, because of her father's explosive and uncontrollable temper. She's lost track of the number of times her father has slapped her, much harder than Byron did, and sometimes punched her, sending her to the floor. When she thinks about it, she and Byron are perfect for each other, each doing the other good, he keeping her humble and she serving as an outlet for his deep-seated anger and resentment.

She asked him, when they were finally finished making love, if he'd treated the other girls that way. She thought she knew the answer and was hoping she'd hear what she did. "No, baby, just you," he said and gave her one of those lingering "pillow" kisses of his she's come to love. She smiled when she heard it. It made her feel special. Now that she's experienced the pleasure he can give her, as far as she's concerned, he can hurt her all he wants. In fact, she's hoping he does again tomorrow evening and is looking forward to it.

She drains her glass and puts it on the desk and puts the stopper in the bottle. She's thankful to him for having introduced her to cognac. She likes the taste of it and the way it makes her feel. If he hadn't, she never would have understood her father the way she does now. She only understood him from the outside before, by observing him. Now she understands him from the inside, by feeling the way he does most of the time—drunk.

She stands and rubs her still smarting cheek, walks unsteadily to the bed, gets in under the covers and snuggles up to him.

"Thank you, baby," she says in a slurred whisper and gives his shoulder blade a kiss.

* * *

She stands beside Byron in the crowded living room, listening to him chat with his friend Marcel, a handsome kid from Queens and a classmate of Byron's who lives in the dorm. Marcel looks Hispanic to her. She remembers watching the movie *West Side Story* with her parents and thinking how strange it was that in a movie portraying Puerto Ricans, there didn't seem to be any. Well, maybe Chita Rivera, but other than her, just actors made up to look like them.

Marcel has sensuous lips and light brown eyes and a head of dark brown curly hair and a "coffee with cream" complexion. His thick eyebrows and combed back hair and cleft chin remind her of George Chakiris's character, Bernardo, in the movie and she thinks Marcel looks the way Bernardo would have, were Chakiris Puerto Rican.

She looks around the room, only just having arrived at the party, and checks, out the people, all in their late teens and early twenties. Most of them are White, but there are a good number of Blacks present and there seem to be more than a few mixed-race couples, judging from the way people are standing or sitting with their arms around each other or holding hands. She's happy to see it. It makes her feel less self-conscious about standing beside Byron with her arm around his waist and his around hers.

She touches her left cheek. It's still tender from the beating it took yesterday evening and she's hoping the makeup job she did to hide the bruise she saw this morning when she looked at herself in the bathroom mirror will keep people from noticing and asking questions.

She woke feeling woozy with a throbbing headache, the way she imagines her father does every morning, and Byron told her that the best way to cure that was to have a drink. She's heard her father use the expression "take a hair of the dog that bit you" and knows that some people do that when they wake up hung over, but she didn't think having a drink first thing in the morning was such a good idea—she's never even seen her father do that—but did so reluctantly and, sure enough, it helped settle her stomach and lessen the throbbing in her head.

It wasn't until late afternoon, when they were having a bite to eat at a deli after visiting the Museum of Modern Art, that she really felt like herself again, although she still had a lingering headache. At Byron's urging she had a beer, a pale ale, with her pastrami on rye sandwich, and found, surprisingly, that her dislike of the taste of beer had gone and by the time she finished it, what remained of the lingering headache had been replaced by a feeling of pleasant lightheadedness, which she's still feeling.

"Be right back," she hears Byron say and watches him make his way toward the kitchen. She looks at Marcel and sees he's grinning and looking at her knowingly, which she's used to by now.

"Bet you had fun last night," Marcel says.

"Yeah," she says and wonders how he could possibly know anything about what happened, since Byron's been with her all day.

"Byron sure likes to have fun," he says. "You never know what he'll get up to."

Marcel clearly admires this aspect of Byron, and it occurs to her that he does because Byron shares the details of his sexual escapades with him and will undoubtedly share with him what happened last night, probably not long after she leaves to return to Newburgh. "I guess," she says and realizes for the first time what it feels like to be involved with someone with a bad reputation and be on the receiving end of it, to be the one being used. For the first time in her life, she feels like a footnote.

She sees Byron returning with two cans of beer and he hands her one. "Thanks," she says and takes a sip.

"Anything for you, baby," Byron says.

He said it smoothly and sweetly, sounding the way he did when he talked to her during their lovemaking, and she sees him glance at Marcel and wink.

She hears Valerie's voice and turns to see her, Sandy, Vincent and Yvonne entering the living room. Valerie spots her and she and Sandy walk up to her and each give her a hug.

"Hey," Valerie says.

The two of them eye her cheek with concern. She thought she'd done a pretty good job with her makeup, but apparently not good enough to fool these two. Valerie glances at Byron and looks back at her and takes her arm and leads her a few feet away, with Sandy following.

"I'll get us a beer," Sandy says and makes her way toward the kitchen.

Colleen sips her beer and sees Valerie looking at her cheek with concern again. Valerie furrows her brow.

"What happened to you?" Valerie asks in a lowered voice.

"I hit my cheek on the open bathroom door…moving too fast…not used to the place." She sees Valerie narrow her eyes slightly and study hers.

"You expect me to believe that?"

"Yeah. It's the truth," she says and sips her beer.

"I don't buy it. I thought we were close friends and could talk to each other."

"We are...we can." She sees Valerie glance down at the can of beer in her hand and look back at her.

"And what's with the beer?" Valerie asks. "I thought you didn't like alcohol"

Colleen shrugs. "I guess I acquired the taste. It was bound to happen sooner or later. My father's a drunk, so's my uncle, and my grandfather. I guess I have the gene."

Valerie glances at Byron and looks back at Colleen. "I dunno what's goin' on with you, Colleen, but I don't like what I see. I feel responsible for you, you know? I don't want anything bad to happen to you."

"Don't worry about me," Colleen says. "I can take care of myself." Valerie looks at her wide-eyed.

"Oh yeah? You don't seem to be doin' a very good job of it from the looks of things." Valerie narrows her eyes. "Think about it, Colleen. We can talk on the bus tomorrow."

Colleen nods and takes another sip of beer and sees Valerie slowly shake her head, looking like she feels sorry for her. Colleen wants to smile. If Valerie only knew the pleasure she enjoyed with Byron yesterday evening and is looking forward to enjoying again later, she wouldn't be shaking her head and looking at her that way. She'd be happy for her, if not envious of her.

* * *

She walks with Byron and Marcel back toward the dorm after the party. The crowd in the living room was thinning and Bryon decided it was time to go. She drank two more beers, much to Valerie's chagrin, she could see, although Valerie had just as much to drink as she did, and now Colleen's feeling the way she did yesterday evening—pleasantly high and carefree.

She isn't really paying attention to Bryon and Marcel's conversation, although when she does tune in she hears it's about the tension and unrest at Columbia and where they think things are headed in the conflict between the college and its neighbors in Harlem, which she knows she should be interested in, but isn't now. What she's focused on is the image in her mind's eye of Byron's big, long chocolate-colored penis and how she can't wait to get it in her mouth and suck it and then feel it inside her as he makes glorious love to her.

She wonders if he's going to make her beg for it on her knees again and slap her. She was thinking about that part of yesterday evening's experience at the party, reliving it in her mind—being ordered to stand and face him and undress, and then kneel in front of him, and then gazing hungrily at his penis and being told to beg to suck it, and begging but not doing a very good job of it, and being slapped as a result, and crying as she looked up at him, pitifully and pleadingly.

She wouldn't have thought she had it in her but found herself longing to experience it again and she thinks she knows why. It doesn't have anything to do with her atoning for the sins of Whites against Blacks. It doesn't even matter that she's White and Byron's Black. It has to do with finally being put in her place by an intelligent young man to whom she's strongly attracted sexually, not in the way she is to Henry, which is sweetly, but like an animal.

She discovered she enjoyed being controlled and told what to do and obeying, or trying to, and being punished when she didn't well enough, in a way that she never has with her father. She felt unburdened, relieved of all responsibility for herself. She didn't have to think and make decisions, and she didn't feel ashamed about begging, because she was being ordered to do it. She didn't feel humiliated. Rather, she felt grateful to Byron for forcing her to humble herself.

She can think of much worse things he could have made her beg to do and, if he had, she would have and wouldn't have felt ashamed about it. He helped her, unknowingly and for the first time, to give expression to that part of her personality that's always felt insecure and tended toward self-loathing. He's the only person who's recognized it and exercised it and she feels a strong connection to him now that she hasn't felt with anyone else. Being with him is like being her true self in a secret life and it's thrilling.

They arrive at the dorm and walk up the stairs and down the hall toward Byron's room and she finds it curious that Marcel is still with them, but figures he must live farther down the hall and will walk on, but he stops when she and Byron do, at the door to his room, and she realizes he's going to join them inside and feels disappointed and saddened. Sitting and listening to more of their talk is not at all what she wants to do and was hoping would happen when they returned.

They enter and Marcel lounges on Vincent's bed and she sits on the side of Byron's and Byron gets the bottle from the closet and three glasses from the desk drawer. He gives one to Marcel and fills it, and then one to her and fills it, and then fills his own glass, sits beside her and puts the bottle on the floor next to him.

"Cheers," Byron says, holding up his glass and taking a sip.

"Cheers," Marcel says and does the same.

"You okay, baby?" Colleen hears Byron ask in that smooth sweet tone of voice of his. "Yeah, cheers," she says glumly and takes a long sip of her drink.

She looks at Marcel over the rim of her glass. He's lounging there, grinning at her, and the room seems very quiet now and it doesn't seem like Byron and Marcel feel like talking. She shifts uncomfortably, realizing that they obviously have something planned. She looks down at the floor and sits there holding her glass in her lap, waiting to see what it is. Several scenarios come to her mind, and she wonders which it will be or if their plan involves all of them. She has the feeling the thing to do is begin numbing herself even more than she already is and drains her glass and holds it out for Byron to refill.

"Easy, baby," he says, frowning. "There are three of us and only one more bottle."

He takes the bottle from the floor and refills her glass and puts it down again. She sees him look at Marcel and smile.

"The way this girl can drink," Byron says, "you wouldn't think she had her first taste yesterday."

"Yeah," Marcel says, nodding, "she's something." Byron looks at her and grins.

"Bet you've never done it with two guys before, have you baby?" She thinks of servicing the boys, one at a time, behind the shed.

That was different. "No," she says softly, "I haven't," and looks back down at the floor and takes another long sip to steel herself.

"Well," Byron says, "there's a first time for everything."

"I guess," she says.

"Why don't you stand and get undressed, baby," Byron says, "so Marcel can get a good look at you?"

She slowly reaches down and places her glass on the floor, then lifts herself off the bed and walks to the middle of the room and stands there, removing her clothes and tossing them aside in a pile, just as she did yesterday evening. When she's naked, she puts her arms at her sides and looks down at the floor and finds a spot and keeps her eyes on it, obediently, as she's been taught to do.

"Isn't she a fine-looking girl?" she hears Byron say admiringly.

"Hm-hmm," she hears Marcel reply and the creak of the bed as Byron stands. She listens to his footsteps as he walks toward her and stops behind her. She feels his arms around hers and his hands cupping her breasts.

"Nice big breasts," she hears Byron say and feels his fingers brushing and then squeezing and pulling her nipples. "Nice hard nipples."

She feels his hand slide down her stomach and stop between her legs and then his fingers parting her lips to expose her now tingling clit. "Nice juicy clit," she hears him say and feels his fingers move to her opening and spread it. "Nice wet pussy."

She feels his hands on her shoulders, beginning to turn her and she turns obediently by herself, keeping her eyes on the floor as she does, so that he can show off her ass to Marcel.

"Look at that gorgeous white ass, man," she hears Byron say proudly and feels him give her ass a few hard slaps. He turns her to face Marcel again and she keeps her eyes on the floor.

"And can she suck dick," she hears Byron say. "Hm-hmm. This girl's really something."

She feels him give her a nudge forward and she walks toward Marcel, still with her eyes downcast. She hears Marcel unzip his pants and she stops in front of him, lowers herself slowly to her knees, sits straight with her arms at her sides and her eyes on the floor, waiting obediently to be told what to do. She doesn't mind at all that Byron wants to share her with his friend. In fact, she's happy he does. She could hear in his voice how proud of her he is and how much he enjoys showing her off. If it makes him happy and if this is what she must do to be with him and be invited back, then she gladly will.

* * *

Colleen stares out the bus window at the houses passing by in the darkness as she and Valerie ride back toward Newburgh. They haven't said much to each other since they met at Port Authority. No sooner did they settle into their seats on the bus than Valerie opened a book and turned on the overhead reading light and began reading and she has been ever since, while Colleen's been staring out the window, thinking about her time with Byron and then with him and Marcel.

Valerie's been a little frosty with her and Colleen knows it's because she knows her story about running into the open bathroom door is a lie and a betrayal of her friendship, which has obviously hurt her deeply. Colleen can't blame her for feeling hurt and disappointed and treating her the way she is. She'd be feeling and acting the same way, if Valerie had lied to her. Maybe she'll talk with her about it. She has to give some thought to what and how much to tell her, though. There's a lot to tell and she's not sure what Valerie's reaction would be, if she shared everything with her. Valerie's open-minded and understanding, but you never know about people. Colleen's sure even Valerie has her limits.

She's faced with a dilemma: on the one hand, she doesn't want to lose Valerie as a friend, which she might, if she doesn't, at least, admit that her story is a lie and apologize; on the other, if she does, she'll have to tell her the truth, or a version of it, and there's always the possibility that if she tells her how she allowed herself to be treated, Valerie might lose all respect for her and not want to have anything more to do with her anymore. Colleen might not feel ashamed about what happened, but not everyone feels the same way she does about things. Well, there's still time to decide.

She had a pretty good idea that what happened was what was going to, that she'd suck them both and they'd take turns fucking her. She'd seen pictures of women being fucked "doggy style from behind on their hands and knees, and wondered what that experience would be like and, well, she found out. She liked it a lot, both the feel of it and the way she imagined herself looking to them, like an animal. She sucked Byron while he milked her tits and pulled her nipples and Marcel fucked her from behind, then they changed places, again and again.

What she wasn't expecting or prepared for was when Marcel positioned himself behind her for one of his turns and she felt the head of his penis pushing against her anus. When she put her hand behind her and tried to cover her opening, he pushed it away and before she knew it he was in her all the way and it hurt so much she bit down on Byron's penis and he got furious with her and took it out of her mouth and slapped her hard a few times, really hard, and shouted at her, calling her a "stupid bitch" and telling her that if she ever did it again, he'd beat the shit out of her and she believes he would. She gradually got used to the feeling of having Marcel in her ass and enjoyed being fucked there. Thankfully, Byron didn't. His penis is much too big and she can't imagine him even being able to get it in her there.

When Marcel finally left, she lay in Byron's arms in bed and he was the same tender loving guy he'd been the night before, telling her how she was his favorite girl and how good she made him feel and how special she was in that smooth, sweet tone of voice of his and she enjoyed one lingering "pillow" kiss after another as he pumped her slowly with that big, delicious chocolate-colored penis of his for the longest time. As always, it felt amazing and she wanted him to keep going all night, which he nearly did.

She turns her head and looks at Valerie in the cone of warm light, still reading her book. "I'm sorry," Colleen says, and Valerie looks up at her and raises her eyebrows.

"For what?"

Colleen studies Valerie's eyes. She knows Valerie knows perfectly well what she's apologizing for and wants to make her work to be forgiven, just as she made Valerie work to be forgiven for calling Newburgh 'hicksville'." She knows all about this aspect of human nature—withholding from people the thing they most want, to deepen their appreciation of it and gratefulness for it when they finally receive it. It's the way Byron treated her when he made her beg and the way she treats her admiring friends, when they want her attention. This is the second time this weekend she's been on the receiving end of it. "Lying to you," she finally says and watches Valerie earmark the page and close her book and put it in her lap.

"So, want to talk about it?" Valerie asks.

Colleen tells her about her first night together with Byron, about playing what she thought was a role-playing sex game and how she soon discovered it wasn't a game and that behind his smiling laid back façade is deep-seated anger and bitterness toward Whites. Valerie listens wide-eyed as she describes what happened, steering clear of the sex part and sticking to the being slapped part, and she can see by Valerie's expression that she's buying the story and decides to leave it at that. Telling her about the threesome after the party is out of the question. If she did, it would seem like lightening striking twice and she'd lose all credibility.

This is what people do, isn't it? Tell each other the version of the truth that best suits their purpose? That's been her experience in life, anyway. Her parents have played this game with each other for as long as she can remember, and she doesn't see anything wrong with it. In fact, it's kept them together. If they'd ever told each other the truth, they would have divorced long ago. Valerie finally lowers her eyebrows and narrows her eyes slightly.

"So, he physically abused you. You had sex with him, right?" Colleen nods.

"Before or after?" Valerie asks pointedly.

Colleen's uncomfortable with her line of questioning and hesitates. "After," she finally says, reluctantly. Valerie glances at the other passengers and looks back at her and leans closer.

"Did you let him," Valerie asks in a lowered voice, "or did he rape you?"

Colleen feels a twinge of panic at the mention of rape. She understands why Valerie would assume that's what happened, given her story, but she can't in good conscience accuse Byron of raping her and is fearful, if she does, of what the repercussions might be, both for him and herself. She considers the consequences of admitting the sex was consensual, what it would say about her as a person and whether Valerie would want to end their friendship. She feels trapped and angry with herself that it's a trap of her own making. "I let him," she finally says and looks down at her folded hands on her lap.

"Colleen!" she hears Valerie say, sounding incredulous and exasperated. "What's with you?"

Good question, Colleen thinks, studying her hands. She used to be so good at the game of controlling and manipulating people to get what she wants. Now that person is beginning to feel like a stranger to her.

"So, that's it, right?" she hears Valerie ask. "You're done with him."

Colleen looks at her. "Yeah, I guess so," she says as convincingly as possible and sees Valerie look at her wide-eyed again.

"You guess so? What? Are you a glutton for punishment? Did it turn you on?"

Colleen imagines what Valerie's reaction would be if she were actually to answer truthfully and say she's both. She's certain that if she did, whatever respect for her Valerie still has would be lost and their friendship would be over.

"If you see him again," Valerie says sternly, "don't use visiting me as an excuse. I'm not going to be the enabler of an abusive relationship. Understand?"

"Yeah."

"I think you have some long hard thinkin' to do about what's happenin' to you, Colleen, and the fact that you're allowin' it to happen. I told you. I don't like what I see. It's not good."

"Thanks for the advice, and your concern."

"That's what friends are for. Think about it."

* * *

Colleen leans on the sill of the open window in her darkened bedroom, smoking and staring up at the night sky. She's still thinking about what Valerie said to her and still smarting from her halfhearted hug when they said good-bye at the bus terminal in Newburgh.

She knows Valerie's right but can't get past how liberating it felt to surrender to Byron or how pleasurable it felt to make love with him. She knows it's wrong and self-destructive to feel this way but feels powerless to do anything about it.

She feels so unlike the person she was before the trip. That person was confident and proud and strong and always in control, maybe not so much with Valerie and Henry, but with everyone else in her circle of friends. How could one weekend with Byron have changed the way she feels about herself so dramatically? It doesn't seem possible.

It does make sense, though. She met someone who's masterful at discovering and preying on people's weaknesses and she played right into his hands. Valerie's right: as much as she wants to see him again, she can't do that to herself. She enjoyed the weekend, and it was a revelation but seeing him again, knowing full well what would happen—Well, that really would be humiliating and she'd lose what remains of her self-respect.

She feels drained by the weekend and still a little groggy from all the alcohol she drank and there's been a gnawing feeling in the pit of her stomach all day, as if it's craving something. She knows what it is and that she's not going to be able to fall asleep until it gets it.

She knocks off the lit end of her cigarette, compacts the filter into a ball and flicks it, sending it arcing out toward the street. She tiptoes to her bedroom door, opens it as quietly as possible and peers down the hall at her father's ajar office door. The light's on and he's in there, doing whatever it is he's doing, besides drinking. She sees the light is off downstairs, so her mother is reading in bed now with the bedroom door closed, as usual.

She tiptoes down the stairs, her pulse racing and pounding in her ears, and into the kitchen. She doesn't turn on the light. There's just enough light from the night sky coming through the kitchen window to see what she's doing. She takes a bottle from her father's supply, moving the bottle behind it forward to fill the empty space, and a glass and tiptoes out of the kitchen and back up the stairs and into her room and shuts the door. She waits a moment with her ear to the door to make sure all she hears is silence and then walks to the window.

She removes the stopper and fills the glass a quarter-full and pauses to consider the amount of whiskey, then continues pouring until the glass is half-full. She puts the glass on the windowsill and tiptoes to the closet.

She searches for a suitable hiding place for the bottle and her eyes fall on the box on the floor in the back, filled with clothes she's outgrown that were supposed to go to Good Will long ago, but are now forgotten. She buries the bottle beneath a few layers of clothes and takes the lighter and cigarette from the pack in the sock in the shoe and walks to the window.

She lights the cigarette and takes a long draw, inhaling the smoke deeply, filling her lungs, and stares up at the night sky through the elms. The night is quiet and still, unlike her mind, and the sky is clear and filled with stars. She remembers the night she imagined George Washington standing beside her, leaning against the windowsill, having a smoke with her, understanding and commiserating with her and putting a steadying hand on her shoulder, as if to say, "Everything will turn out fine." If he were here with her now, how would he feel about where she's arrived in her life and her prospects for the future? She'd like to think hopeful, but she has her doubts.

She blows out the smoke in a stream and looks down at the whiskey in the glass, the moonlight shimmering on its surface. She lifts the glass to under her nose and breaths in the aroma. It's an all too familiar smell. She's grown up with it. It's part of the atmosphere in the house. She hasn't tasted whiskey since she was a kid and her father urged her to try it that time, to amuse his friends. The alcohol part of the smell is similar to cognac and tickles the insides of her nostrils the same way, but it's different, not as mellow.

She takes a sip and holds the liquid in her mouth, savoring the taste, and slowly swallows, feeling it burn her throat on the way down. She doesn't like the taste as much as she does the taste of cognac but it's okay, she'll get used to it and she'll have a constant supply, thanks to her father. She takes a long sip and can begin to feel the alcohol's lightening effect in her head and the gnawing feeling in her stomach is subsiding too, as she knew it would. She welcomes both. Alcohol was what she needed to settle her, so she could stop thinking and sleep.

It occurs to her that Valerie never did forgive her. Well, she has more important things to worry about now, like how she's going to manage stealing bottles of whiskey from her father on a regular basis without being caught and what will happen when she inevitably is. She fills her lungs with smoke again and takes another long sip and searches the sky.

CHAPTER 8

Rocco

Colleen looks around the table in the corner store at the faces of her friends. They're chatting as they eat lunch, but she's not really listening to the conversation and gazes back out the window and returns to thinking her own thoughts. She's felt better about herself as the days have gone by, now that she's back in her familiar routine at school, surrounded by the people who are happy and grateful to be in her presence. The beginning of the week was tough going, though. On Monday she could only think about Byron and their lovemaking as she sat through one class after another and stared blankly at the teachers at the front of the room, not really hearing what they were saying or being aware of anything happening around her.

When she got home from school Monday afternoon, she sat on her bed and stared at the Princess phone, hoping it would ring and be Byron. When hours passed and it didn't, she had everything she could do to keep from calling him. She knew she shouldn't, though, and finally ended up sitting on her hands and forcing herself to stay that way. She imagined she felt the way addicts do when they're trying to kick a habit—crazed by their craving for the drug, knowing it would remove the pain and the feeling of panicked desperation.

She forced herself to wait until she was about to go to bed before having a drink and then allowed herself only a glass about a quarter-full, rationing it so that her supply of whisky on hand would last as long as possible before she'd have to steal another bottle. She's been wracking her brain, trying to think of some other way to get alcohol, but nothing's occurred to her. It's a source of constant worry for her now. Her father knows his liquor supply well and it won't be long before he realizes that bottles are missing.

Tuesday was a little better. She felt a bit more in touch and focused on things, although she spent the afternoon after school and the evening as she had the day before, sitting on the bed, staring at the phone and having a drink before going to bed. The phone did ring at one point. It startled her and she grabbed the receiver and put it to her ear and said as calmly as she could manage, "Hello? hoping to hear Byron say, "Hi, baby," in that sweet silky voice of his, but she was surprised to hear an unfamiliar male voice ask, "Colleen?" and she said, "Yeah," and was even more surprised to hear him say, "Hi! It's Rocco Napolitano."

She's never met Rocco but knows who he is: a senior at NFA with a reputation as bad as hers; his for being a hoodlum whose father owns a construction company and is rumored to be involved with the Mafia. She's seen him around school and sometimes at the corner store at lunch, always surrounded by his friends, just as she is. He looks Italian American in a way that Henry doesn't. He's big and burly with slicked-back black hair combed in a pompadour in front with a ducktail in back and sideburns. His face is square and his eyes almost black and his features babyish and his expression seems always to be one of innocence or mild surprise. He looks harmless enough, which, given his reputation, only makes him seem all the more dangerous to her and she can easily imagine him suddenly erupting into violence without any warning.

She asked him how he got her unlisted number and was surprised again to hear him say, "Your friend, Henry." She couldn't put Rocco and Henry together in her mind, couldn't imagine where they could have met or what they could possibly have in common to talk about. Sal said he ran into Henry at Phil & Neal and they got talking.

Well, that at least seemed plausible and she could sort of see it happening. Maybe Henry was there with his friends and Rocco's cousin Vito, a classmate of Henry's, was among them and Rocco stopped at the table to talk to Vito, and Vito introduced him to Henry and the two of them got talking. It was possible, although, she remembered Henry saying that Vito and Rocco's families aren't close, because of Rocco's father's reputation, and that they don't have much to do with each other, so she had her doubts that that's what had happened.

She was astonished to hear Rocco say he'd asked Henry if she had a boyfriend and that Henry had said he didn't think so, and that Rocco was wondering if she'd like to go on a date. She was speechless. His call had come out of nowhere and the idea of going on a date with him struck her as ridiculous, but she couldn't bring herself to say no. She finally told him she'd think about it and he gave her his number, which she wrote down, not thinking she'd ever actually call him, and that was that.

The experience felt bizarre and she couldn't stop thinking about Henry, sitting and talking with Rocco Napolitano, of all people. She felt hurt and offended that Henry would have handed her off to someone like Rocco and pissed that he'd given him her number. Did Henry really feel that little for her and think that little of her? She wanted to call him and tell him off but didn't and won't. What good would it do? Henry would listen patiently to her and probably apologize, but it wouldn't change anything between them. He'd still be aloof, seeing her when he feels like it, and she'd still be hoping beyond hope that, somehow, he'd wake up and see what a prize she is and fall deeply in love with her. She knows she's deluding herself, that she's a hopeless case where Henry is concerned, continuing to love him, knowing that his feelings for her won't change. She can't help loving Henry, any more than she can help thinking about Byron and how much she enjoyed being with him and misses him and, yes, wants to see him again, despite knowing that it would be a bad thing to do.

It didn't occur to her to ask Rocco, during their brief conversation, why it was he became interested in her in the first place, never having met her, but she's been wondering about it ever since. Her days of getting calls from boys who've heard the rumors about her are over. That part of her life is over and ended more than a year ago. Could it be that her reputation has lived on and Rocco heard about it and that's why he called? She wouldn't be surprised.

She looks around at the faces of her friends again. They've left her alone, as they know to do when she's gazing out the window, thinking.

She's taught them well how to recognize her moods, all but Rachel, who was only recently allowed to join her circle of admirers and is still a little green. Rachel's a Jewish girl with brown eyes and thick brown eyebrows and a hooked nose that, surprisingly, doesn't make her look unattractive, and full lips and long wavy brunette hair that falls past her shoulders. She's quiet and meek and whenever Rachel looks at her, Colleen can see in her expression her gratefulness for the privilege of being in her presence.

"Isn't Valerie joining us?" Jessica asks.

"Thought so," Colleen says. "Dunno. Maybe something came up." She sees her friends glancing at each other and knows they're wondering whether it's all right to engage her in conversation, now that Jessica's broken the ice, but Colleen lets them know by her detached tone of voice and, then, by looking past them out the window again and gazing at nothing in particular, that she still wants to be left alone with her thoughts and they return to their conversation.

She's been wondering where Valerie is. Valerie said yesterday, when they spoke briefly after school, that she'd be joining them for lunch today. Colleen always has mixed feelings when Valerie does. On the one hand, she's grateful that Valerie would want to be with her and her friends and, when she is, Colleen shows her off like a trophy; on the other, she feels uncomfortable and even a bit resentful when Valerie's present at the table, because she feels her role as the leader of the group is compromised, diminished. Valerie has a way of controlling the conversation and steering it in directions that never would have occurred to her and Colleen can see the look of respect and awe on her friends' faces as they listen carefully to what Valerie has to say. Well, she'll find out what happened when she talks with her after school.

Colleen looked for Valerie after school but couldn't find her and now she's really curious about why Valerie didn't show at lunch. Did something happen to her? Did she get sick? She picks up the receiver of her Princess phone and taps Valerie's number. She listens to the rings and, after a few, hears Valerie's mom ask, "Hello?" with that Bensonhurst accent of hers, a lazier sounding one than Valerie's.

"Hi, Missus Sansone. It's Colleen. May I speak with Valerie?"

"Yeah, hold on," Colleen hears her say and then, "Valerie! Phone! It's Colleen!" She hears the receiver being put down on the table and after a few moments Valerie pick it up and says, "Hi," and Colleen knows instantly by her tone of voice that Valerie's not happy she called and doesn't want to talk with her, and she suddenly feels weak. "Hi," Collen says cautiously.

"I'm not happy with you, Colleen," Valerie says sternly.

"Why? What did I do?"

"You didn't tell me about the rest of it, that's what you didn't do."

Colleen knows perfectly well what Valerie's referring to but instinctively feigns ignorance. "Rest of what?"

"Word gets around fast in a dorm, Colleen, the same way it does in this town. You, of all people, should have known that."

Colleen's flustered and speechless and feels herself flush. How naïve and foolish could she have been to think that Byron and Marcel wouldn't tell their friends about what happened? It's just the type of thing guys dream about doing and can't wait to boast about. She wants to apologize, even though she knows it will sound and feel insincere to Valerie. "I'm…"

"Don't apologize, Colleen. Your apologies don't mean anything. You had a bad reputation when I first met you. I heard afterward about what you did at that party, and I was willin' to overlook it. I thought you were just a girl who wanted boys to like her in the worst way and was willin' to do things like that so they would. I thought you're wantin' to be friends with me was an indication that you just hadn't found the right people to be friends with yet, that you'd surrounded yourself with people who didn't care about your reputation, or did, but wouldn't say so to your face. I thought you'd finally realized that wasn't doin' you any good. I thought you'd matured a bit and straightened yourself out, but I was wrong. To tell you the truth, I don't know who you are anymore, but whoever it is, it's not the type of person I want to be around. It would have been one thing if you'd been honest with me and told me the whole story on the bus. I could have at least understood it and maybe even accepted it and maybe I would've wanted to remain friends with you. I was worried about you, Colleen, but not anymore. You're obviously livin' your life the way you want to and don't want to change, so there's nothin' for me to worry about. Don't call me anymore, okay? And stay away from me at school."

She hears the receiver being placed in the cradle, hard, and keeps the phone to her ear, listening to the dial tone on the other end and is already thinking of the excuses she'll have to make to her friends about why Valerie isn't joining them for lunch and what will happen when one of them runs into Valerie and asks why they don't see her anymore and Valerie tells her. What will Colleen say to her friends and how will she look then? It's still early in the evening, but she needs a drink.

She hears her father, downstairs in the vestibule, arriving home late from work. She and her mother have already eaten and Colleen's sitting at the desk in her bedroom, just having finished her homework. She hears her parents—mostly her father—in the living room, discussing something heatedly in lowered voices and the hair on the back of her neck and arms begins bristling. She puts her textbooks in her book bag and then hears her father call angrily, "Colleen! Get down here!" She has the feeling she knows why she's being summoned, that he's caught on to her stealing bottles from his liquor cabinet. She's tried her best to go easy on her drinking but hasn't been able to and knew she was drinking too much to keep him from noticing.

At the bottom of the stairs, she hears her father call from the kitchen, "Get in here!" She glances at the back of her mother's head as she passes the living room. Her mother's keeping her nose in her book and shows no sign of getting up to come to her aid. She must feel confident that she's covered her tracks to Sheldon well enough, otherwise she'd already be in the kitchen, ready to defend her and intercede, if her father becomes violent.

Just as she suspected, she finds him standing in front of the liquor cabinet with the door open, loosening his necktie, his face flush with anger. He nods toward the cabinet and looks at her the way he does witnesses for the prosecution in court, letting her know by his hostile glare that whatever testimony she's about to give that doesn't agree with his understanding of the facts will be ripped to shreds.

"Explain this," he says.

It's been a while since she was last subjected to one of his angry confrontations—more than a year, in fact—and that one because her date, a boy she was with for the first time and hardly knew, kept her out long past the time she was supposed to be home, enjoying using her as a sex toy and tone deaf to her requests and, finally, pleas that he please take her home. She told her father a cock and bull story the next day about a flat tire and no spare and her date having to walk miles to the nearest gas station to get help. She's never been able to lie to her father and get away with it. He can see in her eyes when she's lying and the reason he can is because she really doesn't try very hard to hide the fact. She wants him to see it, wants to anger and infuriate him and is willing to suffer the consequences. That last episode left her lying face down on her bed, weeping and rubbing her aching cheek. For some reason, she doesn't want to lie to him now and the desire to tell him the truth feels odd. "I took them. I brought them to parties. You've got plenty. I didn't think you'd mind."

He looks at her incredulously as he unbuttons his collar. "Didn't think I'd mind? My sixteen-year-old daughter steals liquor from me to bring to underage parties and didn't think I'd mind?

As she knew he would, he cocks his head and narrows his eyes, closing in for the kill.

"Have I got that right?"

"Yeah," she says and the effect her having told him the truth—at least, the part about stealing the liquor—is having on him is curious. Rather than making him angrier, it seems to be calming him down. I fact, he seems genuinely interested in talking with her about it.

"You drink whiskey now?"

It was said more as a statement than a question, just to confirm things. She's watched him ask prosecution witnesses confirming questions in court and seen the result and knows they're among the sharpest arrows in his quiver. "Yeah, I do."

"And you like it?"

"Yeah." She watches him reach into the cabinet, take out a bottle and shut the door. He nods toward the kitchen table.

"Have a seat."

She walks to the table and sits and watches him take a glass from the cupboard and sit across from her, placing the glass on the table in front of her. She keeps her eyes on his as he opens the new bottle and fills her glass.

"Bottoms up," he says, placing the bottle on the table between them. She looks at the whiskey in the glass and then at her father and watches him unbutton his cuffs and roll up his shirts sleeves and lean forward and cross his arms on the table. She looks back at the whiskey in the glass. She knows what's about to happen.

She remembers the time when she was a little girl, five or six. Her father was sitting on the living room couch, chatting with a few of his drinking buddies, and she was sitting beside him. It was a time in her life before the time when he began to try to bend her will to his, when she looked up to him and craved his attention and affection and would ask at every opportunity if she could sit beside him and he would smile and pat the cushion, and she would gleefully scamper up and snuggle next to him. If he was sitting in a chair, then she'd sit on his lap and he'd put his arms around her. Wherever he was she wanted to be close to him and he seemed so proud of the fact and especially so when he was with his friends, as he was then. He and his friends got talking about drinking, as she learned in time they always did at some point, and she listened to her father tell them the story about when he was fifteen and began stealing sips from his father's bottle of whiskey and what happened when his father finally caught him.

Her father said his father took the bottle, which was nearly full, from his hand and told him to follow him and he did, to the kitchen. His father told him to sit at the table, got a glass and filled it to the brim and put it in front of him and told him to drink it, all of it. Her father said he kept his eyes his father's as he did, with difficulty, once past the half-way mark, never having drunk that much whiskey before so quickly. When he finished it, her father said his father refilled the glass and told him to drink that one, and so it went until he'd drunk the entire bottle too quickly for the alcohol to have taken full effect yet, as it soon would, but enough of an effect so that when his father told him to go to his room and her father pushed back his chair and stood, he promptly collapsed and his father picked him up, carried him to the bathroom and put him in the bathtub, where her father remained until he'd puked his guts out. At which point, his father turned on the shower and rinsed him off, then dragged him out of the tub onto the floor and got him out of his wet clothes, toweled him dry, carried him to his bed, put him in it and tucked him in and her father lay there for the longest time, his head spinning. Her father said he woke the next morning feeling awful and not wanting to believe that what he blurrily remembered happening really had happened, but that he knew it had when he looked out the window and saw the clothes he'd been wearing the day before hanging on the clothesline in the backyard. Her father boasted that while his father's intention had been to put him off drink, it didn't and what the experience taught him was that he could hold a lot more liquor than he'd thought.

So, here she is, sitting across the table from her father and about to endure the same ordeal he once did, being forced to, as he was. Based on his experience, she wonders if he really believes it will put her off drink or hopes that it will teach her the same thing it taught him.

She glances up at him and sees him looking at her with a bemused expression. She hasn't felt close to her father in many years, but sitting here, looking at him now, she does. He's a drunk, albeit one who's able to control his alcoholism to the point where he can go about his professional life and be successful, and she's well on her way to becoming one, although she wonders if she'll be able to do the same. She sees keen interest and even hopefulness in his expression that she'll be able to pick up the glass and drain it, as he once did, and keep on draining the glasses until the bottle is empty, proving once and for all that she's truly worthy of being his daughter. She didn't think she wanted to be, but now she does and looks at the whisky again and picks up the glass and brings it to her lips and takes a long sip, the way she did when she first discovered she liked the taste of cognac and the effect it had on her, and keeps her eyes on his over the rim of her glass as she drinks. He seems impressed, which pleases her, and she pauses only briefly before taking another long sip and sees him raise his eyebrows a little higher as she does and then the hint of a smile appear when she takes the glass from her lips and holds it out before her and shows him it's empty.

She sees now that this is the way to win her father's respect, if not his love, to descend into his world and submerge herself in it. If she were to lose herself in it, would he care? Would he come to her rescue? She doesn't think so. Drunks, she knows, like all addicts, are self-absorbed and unreliable.

Her father refills her glass. She brings it to her mouth and keeps her eyes on his as she finishes the whisky in several gulps and places the empty glass on the table in front of her. She feels the now familiar feeling of being dizzyingly high and uninhibited, but without the carefree feeling that usually accompanies it. There's a lot to be concerned about. She only has his account of what happened to him as an indication of what's about to happen to her, and she pictures herself in his place in his story as she drinks glass after refilled glass and works her way to the bottom of the bottle.

The bottle sits empty on the table between them now. She's halfway down the last glass and is having difficulty holding her head up. It and the room are spinning. Her vision is blurred and unfocused, but she can see that her father is smiling openly now and that his expression is a mixture of admiration and pride.

She drains the glass and puts it on the table. She knows what she's supposed to do and doesn't wait to be told, but pushes back her chair and stands, with difficulty, on wobbly legs. She's fully expecting to collapse, as her father did, but manages to maintain her balance, holding onto the countertop to steady herself. She looks down at him and sees him looking up at her with an expression of curiosity, slowly turning his head and body as he follows her progress. She knows he's wondering how far she'll be able to go before she gives out and hears him push back his chair. She lurches this way and that, sliding her hand against the wall to steady herself as she moves forward, and manages to make it to the foot of the stairs before she goes limp and collapses.

She feels herself being lifted up and her head lolling and knows she's in her father's arms and feels like a child again, cared for and safe from harm. He used to hold her all the time when she was a little girl. She'd run to meet him at the front door when he arrived home and he'd beam at her and put down his briefcase and spread his arms and scoop her up and dance her around the vestibule. She doesn't know why his feelings for her changed, but they did, and she remembers her growing awareness that he was becoming more distant and how painful the feeling of gradually losing his love was.

She feels herself being placed in the bathtub and, when she can manage to open her eyes a bit, sees him sitting on the toilet, leaning forward, his forearms resting on his thighs and his clasped hands held in front of him, gazing down at her. The bright lights above the mirror behind him cast his face in shadow, so when she does manage to open her eyes wider and try to focus on his face, she can see nothing in his expression that might give her an indication of his mood.

She doesn't know how long she's been lying here, drifting in and out of consciousness, but finally she feels queasy and then nauseous and her mouth begins watering and saliva begins dribbling from her mouth and mucous running from her nose and she wretches, again and again, and then vomits until her stomach is empty and her clothes are covered with greenish bile and beige chunks of undigested dinner.

She closes her eyes and turns her head from side to side, still feeling sick, but with nothing left in her stomach. She hears the water running and then feels the spray of warm water splashing against her face and then her neck and shoulders and opens her eyes a bit and peers up at him to see him kneeling beside the tub with the spray attachment in his hand, playing the water over her clothes, rinsing off the puke, washing her down.

She was a little girl the last time her father bathed her in the tub. It seems so long ago now. She used to love sitting in the tub, with him just as he is now, kneeling beside it, only then she wasn't clothed and he wasn't washing puke off her. She was naked and enjoyed the feeling of him slowly scrubbing her body all over with a washcloth, giving attention to every part of it, every inch of it. Most important, she was an innocent. Bath time with her father, she remembers, was more than a routine—it was a ritual. She'd sit naked on the toilet seat lid, knees together and hugging herself, and watch her father, kneeling beside the tub, swish the water to activate the bubble bath liquid he'd poured in. He'd swish and swish until the surface was covered with foam.

When the tub was filled, he'd turn off the faucet and say, "Now, in you go," sounding theatrically Irish. She'd step into the always just hot enough water and gingerly lower herself and settle in and he'd watch her, smiling, as he soaped the washcloth. When it was well frothed with soap, he'd say, "Let's get you sparkly clean." Not merely clean, but "sparkly clean as befitted a princess, for that's how he treated her, like his "little princess which she loved.

Her father would scrub most of her body without comment but when it came to certain parts, he'd call them by pet names he'd given them.

"Let's get those 'piggies' sparkly clean," he'd say, and she'd lift her legs out of the water and watch as he washed her feet and scrubbed between her toes, each and every one of them.

"Now 'Bunny,'" he'd say, the name he'd given to the general area between her legs because, as he explained, of the opening there and its resemblance to a burrow, a nice tight one, where any bunny would be most happy and content to live. She'd spread her legs and watch as he scrubbed "Bunny lingeringly. There was something different about how she felt when he scrubbed her there, which she didn't understand until much later. Touching her there stimulated her, even then.

"Now 'Bashful'," he'd say, referring to the general area of her behind, including between her buttocks and her anus or, as she understood that part of her anatomy to be and referred to it at the time, "where my poopies come out."

"Snow White" was one of her favorite movies and bedtime books. Her father would settle in next to her on her bed each night with several of her favorite books in hand and ask her which she would like him to read. "'Snow White'!" she'd gleefully exclaim, more often than not, and "Snow White" it would be. He dubbed her behind "Bashful" because of her initial bashfulness about presenting it to him in the bath, so that he could scrub it 'sparkly clean.' In time, she got over it and came to look forward to it and when he would say, "Now 'Bashful' like a gymnast, she would grasp her legs behind her knees and lift them out of the water and pull them back until her knees were on either side of her head and enjoy the feeling of her father scrubbing her.

When he'd finish washing her, she'd stand and turn slowly in a circle and enjoy the feeling of the water splashing against her skin as he rinsed her off using the spray attachment, just as he is now. She watches him replace it in its holder and bend over and feels him gathering up her limp body and lifting her out of the tub and laying her down on the rug and begin removing her wet clothes.

She closes her eyes and remembers how, after her bath, she would stand facing the mirror above the sink and hold her arms outstretched and watch him in the mirror as he carefully toweled her dry from head to toe, giving "Bunny" and "Bashful" special attention, and then wrap a dry towel around her head in the shape of a beehive. He'd give her a kiss on the forehead and a pat on the butt and she'd skip off happily to her bedroom, to put on her pajamas and wait impatiently for him to come read to her in bed.

How different this experience is—lying limp and barely conscious on the bathroom floor, having to have her wet clothes pulled off her and her father having to struggle to do so because she's too drunk to assist him. She feels him remove her shirt and bra and opens her eyes a bit and watches him finally get her jeans and underpants off and now she's lying naked and peers at her large breasts and realizes that the last time her father saw her naked was when she was that little undeveloped girl and wonders what he thinks of the way his little girl looks now, if he likes what he sees.

She recalls that it was when she was around twelve that her father began looking at her and acting toward her differently. Her breasts were developing. Even then they were large in proportion to her body. She didn't know if this had anything to do with the change in him or was the reason, but the way he looked at her made her uncomfortable and she was very careful never to let him see her naked. That's also when she began feeling self-conscious about her breasts.

She watches him take a clean towel from the cabinet and kneel beside her and he rolls her over on her stomach and begins toweling her dry, just the way he used to, head to toe, not missing a spot, and when he's worked his way down to her feet, he returns to her behind and makes doubly sure it's nice and dry, inside and out. She feels herself being rolled over onto her back and peers up at him as he towels her dry the same way in front, head to toe, going very slowly now, making sure her breasts are nice and dry and also that she is between her legs.

Maybe she's just imagining that he likes what he sees, that he's lingering and enjoying himself with her. Why shouldn't he? He owns her. He can do whatever he wants with her. Anyway, she's in no position to say or do anything about it and even if she were, she's not sure she would. The last time he treated her tenderly this way was when she was that little girl, and as bad as her head feels, her body feels stimulated by his toweling and she feels reconnected to him.

He gathers her up and lifts her off the rug and carries her to her bed and gets her in under the covers and tucks her in and she closes her eyes and feels his lips pressing against her forehead and then lightly on her lips. Maybe she was just imagining it, being in the drunken semi-conscious state that she is, but maybe she wasn't. Anyway, if what she thought just happened really did and if having to endure this ordeal was the price to be paid to win back her father's love, then it was well worth it.

* * *

As much as she'd hoped her father's sexual interest in her had been real and that it would effect a change in his attitude toward her, soften it and endear her to him and cause him to want to welcome her into his heart again, it didn't, and she finally decided she'd imagined it. He was his usual taciturn self at breakfast the next morning and only glanced at her once, when she sat down at the table, and then put his nose back in the case notes he'd been reading.

She dragged herself to school and through the day, still feeling awful, and when her father returned from work that evening, he lectured her sternly in the kitchen, telling her that he was now keeping close count of his liquor supply and would know immediately if a bottle were missing, and that she'd rue the day when he found one was.

She wasn't really listening to him after that as he went on. She was already searching her mind frantically for anyone she might know who was eighteen and would consent to buy liquor for her but couldn't think of anyone. Fortunately, the bottle in her closet was still three-quarters full, so she had at least a little time to try to figure something out, before she needed more. Faced with the prospect of that bottle really being her last, she did manage to ration it and made it last longer than she would have otherwise.

She finally finished it and was just over a week into life without alcohol and feeling panicked about not knowing where or how she was going to get more, when Rocco called. She hadn't been planning to call him and wasn't expecting this call, any more than she had been his first, but when she heard him say, "Hi! It's Rocco," she felt a rush of adrenaline and happy that he called.

She knew he was a senior, but not whether he was eighteen and hoped he was. She knew he was calling to ask her out and if he were eighteen, she'd agree to go out with him. She'd give him what she knew he wanted, and he'd be only too happy and willing to buy liquor for her in return. If he weren't eighteen, she'd turn him down. They chitchatted a while and he finally asked her out and she asked, as casually as she could, if he were eighteen. He said he was and asked why she'd asked. "Oh, just wondering," she said again, as casually as she could, although, with more difficulty this time because of the profound sense of relief and excitement she felt. She'd heard it clearly in her voice and hoped he hadn't. He asked if she'd like to go to the movie Saturday evening and she said sure. She didn't ask which movie. She didn't care. All she cared about was getting what she wanted. He said he'd pick her up at seven-thirty Saturday evening and she said fine, she'd be ready.

He picked her up right on time and she wasn't surprised to see him arrive in a red Olds 442 muscle car. Whatever else he might be, she thought, at least, he's punctual. When she got in the car, he said they were going to see *Murderers' Row*, starring Dean Martin, whom he said he liked a lot. About Rocco liking Dean Martin a lot, she figured it was probably because Martin and Rocco are both Italian American and the fact that Martin has mob connections through is friend Frank Sinatra.

Off they went toward downtown Newburgh, or what used to be considered downtown before the White flight, to the Ritz Theater on Broadway.

She used to see movies there all the time when she was a kid and entering the Ritz Theater seemed to her like entering a palace. It's been around a long time. She learned from her father that it's been around a long time, beginning life as an opera house at the turn of the century and then was converted to a theater in the 1930s. He said Frank Sinatra sang there in 1940, backed by Tommy Dorsey's band, and a whole bunch of other performers did too—Ella Fitzgerald, Peggy Lee and the like—but the place has been allowed to fall into disrepair and she lately heard that it's in such bad shape and ticket sales are so low that it's going to close in October. She asked Rocco why he wanted to see a movie there, of all places. He said he wasn't "afraid of niggers" and she wasn't at all surprised to hear this.

She sat impatiently through the movie, which she didn't care for, and now here they are, at Phil & Neal, making small talk. She's finished her two slices of pizza and watches as he finishes his last slice, taking his time. She's nervous and increasingly fearful that the liquor stores will close, and she'll have gone on this date with him without having gotten what she needs. Finally, he's finished and she says, "Would you do me a favor?"

"Sure. What?"

She's been thinking about how to ask him ever since their phone conversation. She'd like to be able to ask without admitting that the liquor is for her own consumption. If she were just going to ask this one time, she'd tell him that she plans to bring it to a friend's party, but she isn't going to ask just once. She's going to keep asking whenever she needs another bottle, which she knows will be often. "Would you buy a bottle of whisky for me?" She sees he's surprised and also a little disapproving and he furrows his brow slightly.

"You drink whiskey?" he asks.

She nods. "Yeah, 'Johnny Walker Black Label'." She sees his eyes widen and a smile appear, and he's clearly impressed.

"'Johnny Walker Black Label'? You have expensive taste, baby."

"That's what my father drinks. I've been stealing his, but I got caught." She watches him slowly sit back and cross his arms and cock his head and she quickly adds, "I'll pay for it." She's beginning to feel panicked that he's going to say no. He sits there studying her what seems a long time and then slowly sits forward and crosses his arms on the table and fixes his eyes on hers. She imagines this is the way all mobsters look when they carefully consider something important and finally arrive at a decision.

"Sure, baby. We better get going before the stores close."

She feels relieved and thrilled and smiles. "Thanks. Yeah, let's go."

* * *

Colleen waits in the car, staring through the plate glass window of the liquor store, watching Rocco, who's standing at the counter by the register, cradling the paper bag with her bottle in it in his arm and chatting with the owner—at least she assumes he's the owner—who Rocco obviously knows. He's taking his sweet time too, which has her feeling irritated, even though he's doing her a big favor. Finally, he and the owner finish talking and the owner waves and Rocco waves back and turns and saunters out of the store and then to the car and gets in.

"Sorry, baby," he says.

He pulls his door closed and hands her the paper bag and her twenty-dollar bill. She looks at the bill and back at him and sees him smile as he starts the car with a roar.

"My treat," he says.

She keeps her eyes on him as they pull away from the curb. "You didn't have to do that." He glances at her and smiles.

"Hey, that's the way I am. If I like a girl, I treat her nice, you know? *Real* nice."

He glances at her again and smiles.

"*Capisci?*" he asks.

She knows, having heard actors say this on TV and in movies, that it's Italian and he's asking if she understands. "Yeah. You know that guy?"

"Who, Joe? Yeah," he says, nodding slowly, "*Real* well. He's a friend of the family."

She noticed the emphasis he placed on "real" and how he drew out "real well" like it had special meaning, and also that he said "the" family and not "my" family and wonders which family he's referring to—his own or the Mafia or both. She thinks probably both. In a way, Rocco reminds her of Valerie, but only because of his accent, which sounds like hers but different.

She learned a little about his family over slices at Phil & Neal; that they're from Naples, hence the family name; that his great grandparents emigrated and settled in the Bronx; that his grandfather Nicolo moved the family to Newburgh during Prohibition and started a construction business, which his dad took over when his grandfather decided to retire; that his grandfather, whose entire life had been devoted to building and running the construction business, soon tired of sitting around all day watching TV and began coming into the office and doing this and that, making himself useful, but mostly talking the ears off the subcontractors who stopped by to pick up their paychecks, to the point where his grandfather is now driving Rocco's dad Teo and the office manager/ bookkeeper Cunzi crazy, but that his grandfather is the patriarch of the family and is owed respect and that if that's what he wants to do, then that's what he's going to do and everybody can just shut up about it.

In a way, Rocco's family sounded a lot like her own; the same respect paid to the patriarch—in her case, her paternal grandfather— and elders in general. She knew from conversations with her father about the history of Newburgh that bootleggers came up from New York City during Prohibition and established operations here, to receive shipments of illegal booze from Canada and transship them south to the city. She's pretty sure that's why Rocco's grandfather relocated the family to Newburgh, probably at the orders of the Mob. She wanted to ask Rocco if that were the case, but was reluctant to, because she didn't want to run the risk of crossing him and causing him to decide not to buy her liquor. Her curiosity finally got the better of her, though, and she did, as delicately as she could. He smiled and fixed his eyes on hers and said that his family was "well connected" and "very influential" around here and let it go at that. So, she heard what she was expecting to hear and now she knows. She's dealing with the son and grandson of mobsters.

She looks down at the paper bag in her lap. She's felt a dull ache in her stomach all week and now that a bottle of whiskey is at hand, it's become an acute pain and what she wants to do is take the bottle out of the bag and have a drink but is reluctant to because of what Rocco might think of her if she did. She glances at him and back down at the bag. Why is she worried about what he might think of her? He already knows she's an alcoholic, so what difference would it make if she had a drink? He probably knows she wants to and needs one badly.

She removes the bottle from the bag and the top from the bottle and brings the bottle to her lips and tilts it and her head back slightly and drinks. Her intention is to take a long sip, just to take the edge off the pain in her stomach and calm her jittery nerves a bit, but now that the bottle is to her lips, she's feels like she could drain the bottle. She manages to stop after drinking a couple of big mouthfuls and puts the top back on the bottle and the bottle back in the bag. She glances at Rocco and sees him looking at her with raised eyebrows, like he doesn't know quite what to make of her.

She hasn't been paying attention to where they're headed. She knew he wouldn't be taking her home from the liquor store, but first would go someplace out of the way, where they could park unnoticed and he could get what he wanted. She isn't surprised when they arrive at the entrance to what she can see by the sign is his family's construction business on the outskirts of town He pulls into the parking lot and drives to a large one-story building with an office in front. He parks behind the dump trucks and bulldozers and cranes, turns off the lights and the car, turns to face her, smiles and slowly shakes his head.

"Come on," he says.

He nods toward the bag she's clutching in her hands.

"Bring the bottle," he says.

She follows him to the building and waits as he unlocks the office door and turns on a row of overhead fluorescent lights, which, she sees peering in, gives the place and everything in it a greenish cast. She follows him through the office to a small room in back, where she sees a desk and chair and file cabinet and a neatly made single bed. She has the feeling he's the only person who uses the bed and that he's the reason it's here, so that he has a place to bring girls like her.

She places the bag on the desk and sits next to him on the bed. He puts an arm around her shoulders and she an arm around his waist and she closes her eyes as he leans toward her and feels his lips on hers and his hand on her breast. Whatever he wants to do to her or her to do to him is fine with her. She needs him, more than she's needed anyone before in her life. After a long kiss he pulls back his head and she opens her eyes and looks at him. She sees him grinning and looking at her knowingly.

"I hear you give great blowjobs."

She isn't surprised to hear this but, *is* surprised that the rumors are still lingering, although when she thinks about it, she shouldn't be. "Yeah? Who told you that?"

"Your friend, Henry."

She feels a jolt and a profound sense of betrayal and her mind and body sag. She stares blankly at Sal and remembers the dream she had a couple of nights after her phone conversation with Valerie. She was in the upstairs hall of a house, not hers but one that resembled it in an odd sort of way. The bedrooms on either side of the hall seemed to go on forever and the doors were all open.

As she walked along, she saw people standing just inside the doorways. Megan was in one and her friends were in others, but some of the people had no faces at all and were just forms. All of them shook their heads and shut the doors as she walked by. The walls of the hall began to narrow, and when she reached the last bedroom doorway, when it seemed the walls had narrowed to a point where it wouldn't be possible for her to go any further, she found Valerie standing in it, looking at her with an expression of disapproval and disappointment and, more than anything, disdain and disgust. As the others had, Valerie shook her head and stepped back and shut the door.

She saw a sliver of light at the end of the hall. At first, she thought it was the light from her father's office, but then she realized it was sunlight and saw green and it became leaves and she knew she was looking through a window in a sunlit room at the leaves of a tree outside. There was something about what she saw that made her feel that everything— her redemption, her salvation—depended on reaching that room. She continued on with a purpose, trying desperately to squeeze between the walls, but got stuck and couldn't move forward or backward, and that's when she woke and sat up in bed, feeling panic-stricken and terrified.

She understands the meaning of the dream. As a result of her steady descent into alcoholism and having slowly relinquished control over her life, she's alienated everyone close to her and has arrived at a place where she feels desperately alone, but unable to change her behavior. She's stuck, all right.

At the time, she wondered why Henry didn't appear in the dream but now understands why. She hasn't alienated him, not yet anyway, as far as she knows. Despite having been betrayed by him, she still loves him and wants him to love her. His betrayal has left her feeling empty, though, entirely without purpose and utterly lost. Nothing seems to matter anymore or make a difference.

She focuses on Rocco and sees him still smiling, waiting patiently for his reward for having bought her the bottle of whiskey. She stands and takes the bottle from the bag and the cap off the bottle and puts it to her lips. She tilts the bottle and her head back and takes a long drink, then puts the bottle on the desk and turns and kneels in front of him.

* * *

Colleen wasn't surprised to learn from Rocco that her father knows his father. Given her father's clientele, most of them shady local politicians who probably have dealings with the mob, it stands to reason that he would have met Rocco's father at some point, probably in a bar, drinking with his clients. That much made sense.

What did surprise her was the way her father reacted when she told him she'd been invited to meet Rocco's family. She saw concern and the hint of fear in his eyes, something she'd never seen before. She could tell that he didn't want her to go, but also that he wasn't going to prevent her from going. It was strange and she's still wondering what his connection to Rocco's father might be and what could have happened between them to cause her father to react the way he did.

She's never been to Orange Lake, out past the Thruway, or doesn't remember if she has. Rocco pulls onto a residential street with only a few houses on it, and down at the end she sees a very large colonial with a high brick wall around it and a closed, black wrought iron gate at the entrance to the driveway. She knows that's where they're headed.

He pulls up to the gate and she sees a speaker with a button beside it mounted on the brick wall on his side and notices a surveillance camera mounted on the side of the house and trained on the entrance to the driveway. He lowers the window and presses the button. "It's Rocco," he says, and the gate slowly swings open and they enter. She glances back and sees the gate closing behind them and has the feeling she's just entered another world, and that once in it, leaving it won't be a simple or easy matter. He pulls into the parking area at the side of the house where she sees a black Buick sedan and two black Cadillac sedans. The Cadillacs have New York plates and the Buick, she notices, has Florida plates.

The Buick, she soon learns, belongs to Rocco's older sister Nadine and her husband Frankie, who live in Miami and are visiting. One of the Cadillacs belongs to Rocco's mother and the other to one of the two middle-aged couples seated at the dining room table, who drove up from

New York City with an older man, who was introduced by Rocco, very respectfully, as Don Vecchio and who doesn't speak, but simply nods or shakes his head when asked a question. Even Rocco's grandfather treats Don Vecchio with a great deal of respect.

The conversation seems to be entirely about "the business" here in Newburgh, in New York City, in Jersey somewhere and in Miami. Whatever it is, "the business" seems to be doing well, although sometimes the talk is of "that business," and she has the feeling it's about problems "the business" either has encountered in the past and had dealt with or is currently experiencing and dealing with. It's all very circumspect and it sounds like they're talking in code, which she doesn't find surprising, given what she suspects the nature of "the business" and "that business" is—criminal activity of one sort or another.

She takes a sip of red wine, which she finds pleasant-tasting and can see by the label on the bottle is called "Chianti." Rocco tells her it's named for the region in Italy that's famous for producing it. It's not having nearly the effect on her that whiskey does and she can tell she'd have to polish off a couple of bottles or more of it to get where whiskey takes her after a couple of glassfuls.

She finishes her third glass of wine and notices people glancing at her and each other when Rocco asks if she wants another and she nods and says, "Yes, please," and he refills her glass. She doesn't care what they think about her drinking. If there's something available to drink and she's offered it, she's going to drink it. That's the way life is now and she's okay with it, although this having to rely on Rocco to buy her booze doesn't sit well with her. She doesn't like having to be beholden to him, which makes her think of her father again and what connection he might have to these people.

Rocco's mom Ellie places a large platter filled with slices of different meats and cheeses on the table in front of Don Vecchio and arranges an assortment of them on his plate until he nods. Colleen watches the platter passed around the table and Rocco tells her this first dish is called "antipasto" because it comes before the pasta dish and that the meats are prosciutto and Genoa salami and the cheeses mozzarella and provolone. She sees artichoke hearts, black olives, chick peas and roasted red peppers on the platter as well. It's delicious and she isn't surprised. She knows

Italians are famous for their food. She was too young when she visited Italy to truly appreciate it but did when she was at Regina's. She knows that every course that's served is going to be as delicious as this one.

When everyone's finished with the antipasto, Ellie removes the platter and returns with a large white bowl full of dumpling-shaped pasta and places it on the table in front of Don Veccho. She fills his plate until he nods. Colleen watches the bowl passed around the table and Rocco tells her this type of pasta is called "gnocci meaning "little lumps" in Italian.

The next course is some type of white fish smothered in tomato sauce and garnished with basil. Tasting it, Colleen recognizes it to be cod, which she's had countless times at dinner in her home, but this preparation is so much more flavorful and seems to capture the difference between Irish and Italian cuisine perfectly; the one so bland and the other so flavorful.

When everyone's finished with the fish course, Ellie removes the platter from the table and returns with a large roast beef on a platter, which she places on the table in front of Rocco's father Teo for him to carve. It's the first dish that looks familiar to Colleen, roast beef being a staple for dinner at home, although she eyes the slits in it suspiciously, wondering what's been inserted into them, as something certainly must have been, otherwise why the slits? She watches Sal's father begin studiously carving the meat as Ellie and Nadine bring bowls of potatoes and green beans from the kitchen and place them on the table in front of Don Vecchio. As usual, Ellie serves him until he nods. When Rocco's father has carved enough meat to get everyone started, Ellie takes the platter and sets it on the table in front of Don Vecchio, places two slices of meat on his plate and he nods.

Colleen's now extremely curious about Don Vecchio. He wasn't introduced as a member of the family, just as "Don Vecchio." Is everyone being so respectful of him because of his age or is there more to it? Is it also because of his position in "the business" and "the family"? She wouldn't be surprised and will ask Rocco about him later, although she won't be surprised if he doesn't tell her much. These people are *so* secretive.

She sips her wine and studies Nadine over the rim of her glass. It's uncanny how like Annette Funicello she looks; her face, her hair, her dress—everything about her, except her voice and attitude. Nadine's tough and has a thick New York accent, and when she gets talking, there's no shutting her up. Frankie, on the other hand, doesn't say much and lets Nadine do all the talking for him. It's not that he's meek, just mild-mannered and quiet. He seems like a nice guy, but Colleen can't really tell since he's barely spoken and hasn't said anything to her.

"How's your dad, Colleen?" she hears Rocco's father ask. She puts down her wine glass and looks at him. "Fine," she says. Teo glance up at her from the piece of roast beef he's cutting.

"Good," he says with a nod. "Give him my best."

He looks back down at the piece of meat and continues cutting.

"How do you know him?" she asks. Teo shrugs and keeps his eyes on the roast as he carves.

"We know some of the same people. I was able to help him out one time with a little problem he had."

Colleen's mind is racing now. Having listened to the conversation at the table and gotten a feel for how these people talk about things, she has the strong feeling that whatever this "problem" was her father had was anything but "little otherwise he wouldn't have needed Teo's help. She wants to ask him what the problem was but knows by the way he said what he did, with an air of finality, that if she did, he wouldn't tell her. Anyway, it's not the time or place to ask. Would her father tell her? She doesn't think he would either.

She glances around the table and sees everyone looking at her with knowing expressions, everyone but Don Vecchio, whose expression is blank and whose gaze is unnerving. She doesn't at all like the fact that Rocco's father and these other people know something important about her father that she doesn't, and that whatever knowledge they have gives them power over her family. She hates them for it and even more so her father for having gotten into the type of trouble that would have caused him to turn to the Mob for help.

She stares out the windshield on the ride home, her mind focused on the question of what her father's "little problem" was and how Rocco's father helped him. She wants to ask Rocco if he knows anything about the matter, but is frankly afraid to, afraid of what she might hear, if he does know and agrees to tell her. They're almost to her street and, finally, she must ask. "Do you know anything about how your dad helped my father?" He glances at her, looks back at the road and shakes his head.

"Nah. I don't hear about everything that goes on. Some things you're better off not knowin'."

Maybe he's right. Maybe she is better off not knowing, but it doesn't make her want to know any less. They turn onto her street and he pulls over to the curb, well short of her house, and turns off the lights and the engine. It's dark at the foot of her street because the trees block the light from the streetlight. She looks at him, wondering why they've stopped here, and sees that expression of his that she's come to liken to a cat's, when the cat has decided the time has come to toy with a mouse. He reaches back behind her seat and she hears the familiar rustling sound of the paper bag. He holds it up and she reaches out to take it, but he pulls it away from her and shakes his head slowly and smiles slightly.

"Not so fast, baby," he says.

He turns his body toward her and slides his butt forward and spreads his legs. How foolish. She was so preoccupied thinking about this business with her father that she completely forgot. He usually pulls in someplace out of the way and she's never had to do it here, on her street. She looks around and doesn't see anyone and quickly ducks her head and reaches for the button on the waistband of his jeans.

CHAPTER 9

Mila

Colleen still feels anxious and a bit fearful, living in the house alone with her father, now that her mother is living with Sheldon in Cornwall. Her father looks awful and has been depressed ever since her mother left. He spends almost all his time now when he's home holed up in his office, working and drinking, more heavily than usual now, late into the night.

Her relationship with him is also more tense than usual now. He hasn't come out and said as much, but she has the feeling he blames her for her mother's affair, or, at least, for having been complicit in it, which, after all, she was. She and her mother both knew it was only a matter of time before her father found out what was going on, and they both knew that when he did, it wasn't going to be a pleasant scene, but neither of them was prepared for what happened.

She was in her room, doing homework, when her father arrived home late. As usual, her mother was sitting on the couch in the living room with her nose in a book. The first sign of trouble was the sound of the front door being slammed shut and then the thud of something hitting something. Usually when her parents argued, she's kept her distance, but her father's screaming and her mother's shrieking was unlike anything she'd heard before and she felt compelled to go downstairs and see what was happening and, if need be, try to help her mother.

Halfway down the stairs, she saw her father's briefcase, lying on the floor in the vestibule, and noticed the mark on the wall and realized he'd thrown the briefcase against it in his fury. That was the cause of the thud she'd heard and not her mother's body hitting the floor, as she feared it might have been.

The scene she saw in the living room when she arrived at the bottom of the stairs froze her. Her father was grasping her mother's hair with one hand, holding her up and not letting her go, while punching her hard and repeatedly in the face with the other. Her mother looked like a life-size rag doll being beaten, and there was blood trickling from her nose and bottom lip. As terrified as Colleen was, she finally managed to move and ran into the living room, screaming at her father to stop. She grabbed the back of his suit coat and tried to pull him away, but he didn't seem to notice that she was there. Then he turned toward her and slapped her face with the back of his hand, so hard that she fell backward and hit her head on the corner of an end table. When she came to, she was lying sprawled on the living room rug, alone in the living room.

She found her mother upstairs in her parents' bedroom, hastily stuffing clothes into a suitcase. Her mother had cleaned herself up as best she could, but her lower lip was cut and her left cheek, which had borne the brunt of her father's blows, was bruised and swollen. Her mother said her father had left, telling her to be gone by the time he returned, and that Sheldon was on his way to pick her up. The idea of living in the house alone with her father terrified Colleen and she begged her mother to take her with her. Her mother stared at her and slowly, shook her head and turned her attention back to packing.

It was a painful moment of truth for Colleen. She didn't think her father would object to her going with her mother—in fact, she thought he'd welcome being rid of the both of them. Her mother simply didn't want to take her with her. Sheldon's son and daughter were living with their mother, and it was obvious to Colleen that her mother was looking forward to a life without kids in her new home. It was selfish of her mother and the realization that her mother felt so little love for her or concern for her safety hurt. Colleen thought she understood, though. She figured her mother was traumatized by what she'd just gone through with her father and could only think about herself and her own safety.

As the weeks passed, her fear gradually subsided and now she and her father have settled into an uneasy routine. They keep to themselves and avoid each other. When they do eat together, they sit across the kitchen or dining room table from each other, rarely making eye contact or speaking, and when they do speak, they say as little as possible to each other.

At least she has Mila to talk with. Her father hired her, at the suggestion of Colleen's aunt Mary, shortly after her mother left, to cook and clean during the week. Mila's from Kinsale, in County Cork, and met her husband, who was born and raised in Newburgh and works with her uncle Mick, when he was vacationing in Ireland. Mila's a young redhead with green eyes and creamy skin and freckles and a sweet lilting brogue. She's a hard worker and very respectful of Colleen's father. Still, there's something about the way Mila looks at him sometimes that makes Colleen think she recognizes something in him and not something good. She's been meaning to ask her about it.

She glances at her father and sees him put his fork on his plate and wipe his mouth and. Right on cue, Mila arrives from the kitchen to take his plate.

"Ready for dessert?" Mila asks him.

He shakes his head, pushes back his chair and stands. "None for me, thanks."

Colleen studies Mila's expression as she watches her father walk toward the stairs to head back to his office and is struck again by the feeling that Mila recognizes something in him. Now Colleen's more curious than ever about what it might be. She places her utensils on her plate and hands it to Mila.

"How about you?" Mila asks.

"I'll have some if you will. I don't like eating alone." Mila looks at her sympathetically and smiles.

"Sure. Be right back."

A few moments later, Mila returns with two plates of peach cobbler and places one in front of Colleen and the other on the table next to her and sits beside her. "Your cobbler's my favorite dessert," Colleen says.

"Enjoy!" Mila says.

Colleen puts a forkful in her mouth and savors it. "Hmm...." she says. "I love everything you make. You're a great cook."

"Thanks. I've done enough cooking in my time. I cooked for my family and there were a lot of mouths to feed. I'm the oldest of six. Four girls and two boys."

"It must be hard, living so far from home," Colleen says. "You must miss your family." Mila looks down at her plate and Colleen watches her slowly push a piece of peach cobbler back and forth with her fork as she considers her answer. Finally, Mila looks up at her.

"I couldn't leave soon enough," Mila says.

Colleen's surprised to hear this and by the bitterness in her voice. "Why? What happen?" Mila searches her eyes and seems to be considering even more carefully now what to say next.

"I know all about troubles with dad," Mila finally says. "We can talk about it, if you like."

Now Colleen's the one staring down at her plate and slowly pushing a piece of peach cobbler back and forth with her fork, considering what to say. Finally, she looks up at her. "He's a drunk, and a bully."

"Aye," Mila says, nodding slowly. "I know the type."

Colleen sees her glance over her shoulder at the staircase and then look back at her. Mila crosses her arms and leans closer.

"Has he touched you?" Mila asks in a lowered voice.

The question startles and flusters Colleen. She wants to say no, emphatically, but remembers the way her father used to bathe her and towel her dry when she was little, the same way he did recently, lingering with her breasts and between her legs. She feels herself flush and stares at Mila, not knowing what to say.

"Mine did," Mila says.

"He did?" Colleen asks, wide-eyed now.

"Aye," Mila says, nodding slowly. "The first time when I was twelve. My mum was in hospital for a month, and he said since I was acting in her place, I needed to sleep with him. He made me have sex with him, in more ways than one, shall we say."

"Did you tell anyone?"

Mila slowly shakes her head. "I was too afraid. Who would I have told? My mum? It would have killed her. The authorities? They would have thrown him in prison. My mum was too sickly to work. We would have ended up wards of the state."

"That's awful!"

"Yes, it was. Some men are animals."

Mila glances over her shoulder again and looks back at Colleen.

"My mum died when I was sixteen and he made me sleep with him whenever he felt the need. He said if I didn't, he'd make one of my sisters. I was older then, and wiser. I made the bastard *pay.*"

"You mean give you money?"

Mila smiles slightly and raises her eyebrows. "Why not? It was only fair."

"I guess," Colleen says, not sure what to make of Mila's story. "Did one of your sisters sleep with him, after you left?" Mila narrows her eyes and slowly shakes her head.

"I told my sisters what happened and told them to tell me if he approached them. I told him I'd talked with them and that if I ever heard he'd so much as a laid a finger on them, I'd tell the authorities. He knew I meant it."

"Can I ask you something?"

"Sure."

"I've noticed the way you look at my father sometimes, like there's something you recognize about him." Mila searches her eyes again and again seems to be carefully considering what to say.

"You said it yourself," Mila finally says. "I've seen enough of him to know what he's like. He's a drunk, all right, and a sullen one, just like my dad. They're all the same—angry, bitter, resentful, bottled up emotionally and ready to explode. People like that can't be trusted to behave properly. They're capable of anything."

Mila places a hand on Colleen's forearm and looks at her with concern.

"Watch yourself," Mila says.

Listening to Mila describe her own father has been like listening to herself think out loud about hers and it's filled her with a sense of foreboding and dread. "I will," Colleen says.

* * *

Colleen stares down at the paper on her desk, without focusing on it. The math problems aren't that difficult, but she's taking longer than usual to finish them because her mind is still on Mila's story and what to make of it. It's awful what happened to her, and she can only imagine how badly and deeply it affected her and continues to affect her and probably always will. It's a wonder Mila wanted to have anything to do with men after that, let alone marry one. The more she thinks about it, given the circumstances, it does seem right that Mila agreed to have sex with her father to protect her sisters. He was going to have sex with one of them, so better with her than one of her younger sisters. And it does seem only fair that she made him pay for it. Why shouldn't she have gotten something in return?

Her phone rings and her immediate thought is that it's Rocco calling to say hi, as he does around this time every evening. She puts down her pencil and picks up the receiver and puts it to her ear. "Hello?" she asks and is surprised to hear Henry say, "Hi," just as casually as you please, as if it were perfectly fine that it's been months since he last called her and perfectly fine that he gave Rocco her number and told him that she liked to give blowjobs. Who does he think he is? She feels her anger rising and wants to drown him in the reservoir of frustration and hurt he's caused her, just open the flood gates and let it pour through the phone, but she can't and sighs. The fact of the matter is that she's happy he called and to hear his voice. "Why haven't you called?" she asks, just disappointedly enough to let him know that she forgives him.

"I dunno. Just been busy. What're you up to?"

"Finishing my homework. I'm almost done," she says, just encouragingly enough to let him know that, even though it's Thursday and there's school tomorrow, she's hoping he wants to see her.

"Can I come over?"

"Sure. My father's holed up in his office, as usual. He won't bother us."

"Great. See you soon."

She smiles and places the receiver in the cradle. No sooner does she than the phone rings again and she frowns. She's certain it's Rocco calling this time and is ready with the excuse that she still has plenty of homework to do, if he wants to chat or asks to stop by. Nothing is going to keep her from Henry.

She waits at the front door, peering through the glass panel at the street. Henry seems to be taking forever but finally arrives. When he reaches the porch, she sees that smile of his she's missed so much and opens the door.

"Hey," Henry says.

She falls into his arms and presses her cheek against his and enjoys the feeling of his embrace. She only thought she knew how much she missed him. She draws her head back and brings her lips to his and kisses him long and hard. Finally, she steps back and gazes lovingly at him and he grins.

"I missed you too," he says.

"Don't tease, Henry. I should be furious with you and have every right to be." He looks around.

"You want to talk about it here?" he asks.

"No. Come on," she says and takes his hand and leads him to the living room.

"Want something to drink?"

"I'm fine," he says and grins again. "You're prettier each time I see you."

She feels herself blush. He's the same old Henry, always so sweet. The fact that he betrayed her is the farthest thing from her mind now. She just wants him to take her in his arms again and enjoy his kisses and whatever else he might want to do is perfectly fine with her. They sit together on the couch and she tucks her legs beneath her. "Did you really miss me, or did you just say that?" she asks. He puts his arm around her shoulders and draws her to him and gives her a squeeze.

"Of course, I did," he says.

He sounded so sincere. Did he really? She can't help but believe that he did. She closes her eyes and enjoys reacquainting herself with his kiss—the way he presses his lips against hers, not too hard, just hard enough; the way he gently parts her lips with his tongue and meets the tip of hers with the tip of his. This is why she loves him. Any other boy would be pawing and groping her by now, or already have her down on her knees, but not Henry. His entire being seems focused on pleasing her. His pleasure comes from giving her pleasure. It's always wonderful being with him and giving herself over to him, to do with as he pleases. He always handles her so carefully and treats her so tenderly. If only he loved her. How heavenly that would be.

How she's missed having him just like this, lying between her legs, stroking her stomach with his fingertips as he makes love to her clit with his mouth and tongue. He's the only boy who does and should someone else be where he now is someday, she can't imagine him doing it half as well and it will always be Henry's face she sees when she closes her eyes. He seems to know her body better than she does and can coax out of it pleasure greater than she ever thought possible, and when she reaches the point where the pleasure is almost unbearable, he somehow brings her past it, beyond it, until she feels her body dissolving in a thrilling cascading climax.

"Get out, you son of a bitch!" she hears her father scream, "Get out of my house!" She opens her eyes and sees her father, hovering over Henry from behind, punching the back of his head and the side of his face. "Daddy! Stop! Stop!" she screams and sits up and tries to catch his wrists, but he slaps her face hard. At least she distracted him long enough to give Henry a chance to escape and she sees him scampering toward the front door. She hears the front door close and lies back down and covers her face with her hands and begins crying and shaking uncontrollably.

She lies in bed in the dark, her face turned toward the window, staring at the leaves of the elm, silhouetted by the light from the streetlight behind them. The leaves look like the familiar school of black fish frozen in mid swirl, just like her thoughts. Her mind is focused on one thing and one thing only—her intense hatred of her father for having humiliated her the way he did and having done what he did to Henry. She was expecting to be confronted by her father after Henry left, but he just stood there, staring down at her where she was, still lying on the sofa, naked from the waist down with her blouse open and breasts exposed, paralyzed by fear. Then he turned and walked into the kitchen to get a new bottle of whiskey, which is what had brought him downstairs in the first place, and then went upstairs and into his office.

Will she ever hear from Henry again? She doesn't think so. Why would he want to call her now? If she were he, she wouldn't. Maybe she'll call him to apologize, as if that will do any good. No amount of apologizing will ever change what happened. What a nightmare it was, a real one. She's never hated her father more than she does now, never despised him or wanted him dead as much. She'd kill him herself if she could. She wouldn't think twice about doing it and would be glad to be rid of him. What type of father could make his own daughter feel this way about him? A monster, that's what. Mila probably felt the same way about her father. She must have and even more so, given what her father did to her. How could she not?

She notices the sliver of light at the bottom of her closed bedroom disappear. Her father has finally turned off the light in his office. She glances at the alarm clock on her nightstand: just past one, late even for him. He must be stinking drunk by now. She anticipates seeing the sliver of light reappear briefly as he turns on the light in his bedroom, but it doesn't and she stares at her bedroom door. She can hear his footsteps slowly approaching and feels her skin begin tingling and the hair on her arms and the back of her neck bristling. Why would he be coming? To say good night? He never does. To apologize? Not likely.

She thinks of Mila's story again and her warning. Colleen's mind begins racing. Is her father coming to satisfy his need? If the door opened and he entered her bedroom, what would she do? Scream at him to get out? That's what she should do, but would she? She's not sure. Her hatred of him has deadened her to him. She doesn't think of him as her father anymore, but as a miserable, pathetic wreck of a man, intent on making the lives of everyone around him a living hell. What difference would it make if he touched her? She wouldn't even feel it and her eyes would be closed, so he could be any man touching her. She'd make the bastard pay for it too, each and every time, just as Mila did. Maybe she'll keep a steak knife under the mattress and stick it in his neck while he's in the act.

She stares at the door, expecting it to open at any moment. She knows she should feel panic-stricken but doesn't. She feels calm and filled with a sense of purpose, prepared for whatever happens next. Finally, she hears her father's footsteps as he slowly walks back down the hall. She sees the sliver of light appear briefly at the bottom of her door as he enters his bedroom and turns on the light, and then it disappears when he shuts the door behind him. She knows what just happened will happen again, and that it's only a matter of time before her bedroom door opens.

What is she thinking? She *can't* live in this house.

CHAPTER 10

Colleen's New Family

Colleen studies her mother and Sheldon, the two of them standing next to each other in the living room, chatting happily with party guests. It's a revelation to her. This is the first time she's visited and spent time with them. The atmosphere in their home couldn't be more unlike the one in her father's house. Her father's house feels like a monster's cave now, but their home feels lively and gay and, because it's a ranch with lots of windows, open and inviting, unlike her father's old colonial, which feels claustrophobic now.

Her mother is elegantly dressed and nicely coiffed and tastefully made up, just as she always was at the parties she and her father hosted, but her spirit has been transformed. She's relaxed and obviously enjoying herself. She doesn't steal furtive and anxious glances at Sheldon, the way she did at her father, keeping a worrisome eye on him and monitoring his alcohol intake and his darkening mood as the evening wore on. She seems happy with Sheldon and Colleen's happy for her.

She'll never forget witnessing the scene in the living room and seeing how horribly her father treated her mother. In the end, the fact that her mother is his wife meant nothing to him. He had neither respect nor love for her and considered her to be a piece of personal property—just as slave owners did their slaves. She's viewed her mother differently ever since, both empathizing and sympathizing with her, and feels a bond between them, formed by their years of mutual suffering at the hands of her father. She's happy her mother escaped, which she also wants desperately to do now, and hopes it won't take having to get beaten up, like her mother was, to do it.

While she's always had a good relationship with her mother, she'd never confided in her, never unburdened herself to her, but a few days after the incident with Henry, she found herself wanting and needing to talk with her about it, both about what her father did to him and his having come to her bedroom door that night.

Her mother sounded pleasantly surprised to hear from her. They chatted a bit and Colleen was relieved to hear that the reason her mother didn't take her with her was because her father insisted she not do so and threatened her with dire consequences if his daughter wasn't there when he returned.

Colleen told her about what had happened to Henry. She smiled when she heard her say, after a pause, "That's no way to treat a young man, just because he's kissing a young woman at the top of the leg." She truly appreciated her mother's delicacy and understanding.

Then she poured out her feelings for Henry to her mother. She told her how much she loved him, although she knew he didn't feel the same way about her, and how afraid she was that she'd never hear from him again. She was surprised by how sympathetic her mother was and how genuinely concerned for her feelings she seemed to be. She was even more surprised when her mother told her to invite Henry to the party, so that she could meet him and offer her apology for her father's bad behavior.

It wasn't as easy talking with her mother about her father having come to her bedroom door. She couldn't accuse him of wanting to have sex with her. After all, nothing had happened and it was only her feeling, albeit a strong one, that something eventually would. They talked around the edges of it and she finally told her mother that she just didn't feel safe alone in the house with him and let it go at that. After a long silence, her mother said maybe she should come live with her and Sheldon and that they'd discuss it when they saw each other.

She had the feeling from the sound of her mother's voice that she wasn't all that surprised to hear about what had happened with her father, which she found curious. In any event, it felt nice being able to talk with her about things, more like friends and less like mother and daughter, and she had the feeling by the end of the conversation that their relationship had arrived at a new and better place and that they both welcomed it.

She stared at the phone a long time before mustering the courage to pick up the receiver and dial Henry's number. She could hear his reluctance to accept the invitation in his voice and she couldn't blame him. He had every reason to say no, in fact, not to have anything to do with her anymore, but he accepted, probably out of politeness, and she felt a profound sense of relief. If she could just see him again, be together with him and talk, maybe he could see past what had happened with her father and want to at least remain friends. If they could do that and see each other now and then, her hope that his feelings for her would deepen into love could remain alive.

She sips her Tom Collins, which her mother thought would be an appropriate drink for her and which Sheldon made, going easy on the gin at her mother's request, and eyes the people in the crowded living room. Some she recognizes from her parents' parties, but most are new faces. They're all White, upper middle-class professionals, just as they were at her parents' parties, and all dressed pretty much alike; the women like her mother, wearing cocktail dresses and heels, and the men like Sheldon, wearing blazers and dress shirts open at the collar and dress slacks and loafers.

She enjoyed talking with Sheldon as she helped him and her mother prepare for the party. It was the first time she really talked with him, beyond exchanging hellos, as they used to at her parents' parties. She's always liked him and knew he was a doctor, an Ob Gyn, and she was surprised to learn that he's as much a fan of modern jazz as she now is. His record collection is extensive, and it was fun going through it together and selecting their favorite albums to play during the party, then ordering them in a way they thought would match the mood of the music to that of the party as it progressed through the evening. She thinks they did a great job and is enjoying the way Oscar Peterson's *Trio Plus One* matches perfectly the spirited, bubbling sound of the voices in the living room.

She likes the fact that Sheldon is Jewish. Even though Judaism and Catholicism are rooted in the same beliefs, she's fed up with Catholicism and its rigid oppressive dogma. Judaism just seems to be a more welcoming religion and every Jew she knows is intelligent, open-minded and tolerant. Sheldon is a perfect example. Talking with him and talking with her father are like night and day. Her mother told her they plan to marry as soon as their divorces are finalized and that's fine with Colleen. She'd welcome having Sheldon as a stepdad.

She sees Barry and Sarah, Sheldon's kids, standing and talking with Vicky, a physician friend of their father who they know well and who Colleen met for the first time earlier, as she did Barry and Sarah, who grew up in Cornwall and go to school here. It didn't take long talking with them for Colleen to determine that she and they don't know any of the same people and live in separate worlds. They're both nice kids, very polite and well-mannered and smart, which doesn't surprise her, and she's happy they are since they're going to be her stepbrother and stepsister.

Barry's fourteen and a bit shy. He looks like his dad, with the same light brown curly hair, fair complexion and blue eyes. Sarah's a year older than herself, seventeen, and outgoing and talkative. Sarah must look like her mom, because she doesn't resemble her dad much. She's pretty, with large dark eyes and wing-like eyebrows, a long nicely shaped nose, gently rounded at the tip, as are her cheeks and chin, and full lips. Her narrow face is framed by long wavy black hair. She's tall and slender but her breasts are well developed, much like her own, only Sarah's aren't quite as large. She and her brother are both well dressed, Barry like his dad and Sarah wearing a sleeveless, V-neck, white silk fitted blouse that accentuates her breasts and shows off her cleavage. She's finished off her outfit with black dress slacks that flair at the bottom and black heels. She looks very elegant and there's a sensual air about her that Colleen finds intriguing.

She saw it in Sarah's eyes when she was describing the book she's currently reading, *The Garden of the Finzi-Contini.* Sarah said it was about what life was like for a wealthy Jewish family living in Ferrara, in northern Italy, before the Nazis came to power, and then their increasing isolation as anti-Jewish sentiment grew. It didn't sound like a happy story, but the way Sarah looked and her tone of voice as she described reading about the relationship between the narrator, a young man named Giorgio, and Micòl, the daughter of the family, made it seem very sexy, and Sarah was clearly enjoying that aspect of it. Colleen has the feeling there's a lot more going on beneath Sarah's poised exterior than she lets on and she's looking forward to getting to know her better.

She finishes her drink and heads to the kitchen to make herself another, a proper one this time. Her mother and Sheldon are engrossed in conversation and won't even notice. She's wondering where Henry is and keeps straining to hear the doorbell above the chatter and music. She's beginning to wonder if he changed his mind about coming. He wouldn't stand her up like that would he? She doesn't think so and hopes not.

Oscar Peterson ends and she hears Bill Evans's spare, searching, opening chords to "So What" on *Kind of Blue.* The music fills her with a bittersweet feeling. It brings Valerie to mind and everything that happened between them, first the good and then the bad. She's been missing Valerie more than ever lately. The only person Colleen's as interested in talking with is Henry and she rarely sees him. She does see Valerie at school now and then, but doesn't approach her, as she requested. Colleen's been thinking about calling her and trying to apologize again, but each time she does, she asks herself what would happen if Valerie accepted her apology and they were friends again. Colleen hasn't really changed at all. She still drinks and even though Byron blabbed to his buddies about what he and Marcel did with her and hasn't called her since that weekend, if he called tomorrow and invited her down to Columbia, she'd go. The only sex she's having these days is with Rocco, which she finds uninteresting and boring. Her one evening with Henry was a welcomed bright spot, despite the incident with her father. She wonders if Byron's forgotten about his invitation to visit him in Oak Bluffs this summer. Probably.

Finally, she hears the doorbell and walks quickly to the front door, opens it and finds Henry standing there, looking uncomfortable, which is understandable. She notices the bruise over his right eye, her father's handiwork. "Hi," she says, a little sheepishly. "Thanks for coming. I really appreciate it."

"Yeah, no problem."

She wants to put her arms around him and kiss him, but only if he makes the first move, which he doesn't seem in the mood to do, so she takes him by the hand and leads him in. "Can I get you a drink?"

"Sure."

"I just made myself a Tom Collins. Want one?"

"Sure."

They take their drinks and she leads him to the living room and up to her mother, who notices them approaching and turns toward them and smiles at Henry. "This is Henry," Colleen says.

"So nice to finally meet you," her mother says warmly.

Her mother leads them to a corner of the room, where they can talk a bit more privately. Shem notices the bruise over Henry's right eye and looks at him sympathetically. She sighs and shakes her head slowly.

"I'm so sorry for what happened," her mother says. "Colleen's father can be brutish when he's drinking, but there's no excuse for his behavior. Please accept my apologies."

"Sure," Henry says, shrugging slightly, "no problem."

"Perhaps when the two of you want to…"

Her mother hesitates and glances at her and then looks back at Henry and raises her eyebrows slightly.

"Spend time together," her mother says delicately, "you could see each other here."

"Thanks," Henry says.

"Well," her mother says, smiling, "Nice meeting you. Enjoy yourselves."

Colleen watches her walk off to rejoin Sheldon and looks back hopefully at Henry.

"You living here now?" he asks and sips his drink.

She sees him glance over her shoulder in Sarah's direction. She doesn't even have to look to know that he's looking at her and she can see in his eyes that he likes what he sees. "No, not yet," she says. "I hope to. We're going to talk about it."

"So, how's it going with Rocco?"

Hearing this, her heart sinks. Why did he have to bring him up? Rocco's the last person she wants to talk about. "Okay," she says, and she can hear how unconvincing she sounds. "He's nice. He spoils me. He's constantly buying me things." She glances down at the ring with the single small diamond setting she's wearing, Rocco's latest gift, which he said was an engagement ring, if she wanted it to be, which she doesn't, but said she'd think about. She looks at Henry and sees him looking at it. "He wants to get engaged. I don't. I consider him a friend." She can tell by the way Henry's looking at her that he feels sorry for her, but not really. Why should he? She's the one who got involved with Rocco as a matter of convenience and she has no one to blame but herself for the situation she's in with him.

"Right," Henry says.

She sees him glance over her shoulder again in Sarah's direction.

"So, who's she?" he asks, nodding toward Sarah.

Colleen glances over her shoulder in time to see Sarah looking at him and quickly turn her head away. She looks back at Henry. "Sarah, my mom's boyfriend's daughter. I just met her earlier. She's nice. I'll introduce you."

She stares at Sarah and sips her drink and tries to keep a polite smile on her face as she listens to her and Henry chatting about their favorite books and movies. What an unbelievably brazen flirt Sarah turns out to be! What she wants to do is take Henry by the hand and lead him away. He's eating it up, though, and delighting in Sarah's attention. He's as big a flirt in his own way as Sarah is and has turned on the charm, which Sarah's clearly enjoying. She finishes her drink and goes to the kitchen to make another and returns to find them just as she left them, smiling warmly at each other and chatting away. "What's your last name?" she hears Henry ask Sarah as she arrives at his side.

"Rothstein," Sarah says, "on Hudson Street."

"I'll give you a call."

"Do! I'd like that!"

"Nice talking with you."

"It was! I enjoyed it!"

Colleen tries not to let her jealousy and the fact that she wants to strangle Sarah show when Henry looks at her.

"I've got to get going," he says.

She's surprised and disappointed. He's only been here a little over an hour and has spent most of it talking with Sarah. She was hoping he'd want to spend some time with her. "Why?"

"I'm meeting friends at Phil and Neal."

She searches his eyes. Is that really what he has planned? She wouldn't be surprised if he's off to meet some girl. She really is a hopeless case where Henry is concerned and doesn't think she'll ever learn. "Okay," she says disappointedly.

They walk slowly in silence toward his car, parked on the street at the end of a long line of cars because he arrived late, and now she has the strong feeling that this might be the last time she sees him, that he won't call her and that if she calls him, he'll say he's too busy to see her.

She's been meaning to ask him about his conversation with Rocco and, more important, how he feels about her and if he sees any future for the two of them but hasn't had the courage to. Now she does because, more than ever, she feels she doesn't have anything to lose. "Why did you give Rocco my number?" she finally asks and sees Henry shrug.

"Your home phone is listed. He would have gotten in touch with you, one way or another."

"Why did you say what you did about me?" she asks and sees him shrug again.

"You said you weren't ashamed of it, right?"

Yes, she did, but still—"Do you even care about me, Henry?" He stops walking and she stops and they turn toward each other and he sighs.

"Of course, I care about you, Colleen. We just feel differently about each other. You want me all to yourself. That's not who I am."

"You could see other people. I mean I'm seeing Rocco, right? Not that I really want to." There's that look again, of being sorry for her, but not really. He shakes his head. She can see he knows as well as she does just how much of a hopeless case she really is. She feels her eyes begin filling with tears and throws her arms around his neck and clings to him and the tears begin streaming down her cheeks. "My life's a mess, Henry," she blubbers. "You see what my father's like, what I have to deal with! That's not the half of it!" She's happy to feel his arms around her waist and takes some comfort in it but, knows he's only being friendly and trying to console her.

"Maybe you should talk with someone about it," he says. "Sheldon's a doctor, right? I'm sure he can recommend someone."

She unwraps herself from him and takes a step back and sniffs and wipes the tears from her eyes. "You think I need a *shrink*?"

He shrugs. "Maybe. It can't hurt. Anyway, what's wrong with getting help? Lots of people do. What do you care what people think?"

She stares at him, dumbfounded and unable to speak. What does she care what people think? Who's the crazy one here? She cares a lot. All her life that's what she's cared about most, and the idea of people finding out that she's so damaged and vulnerable and helpless that she needs therapy—Well, it seems unthinkable!

"Give it some thought, Colleen. You need to take care of yourself," he says.

He steps forward and takes her in his arms, gives her a kiss, draws his head back and looks in her eyes and smiles.

"I'll call you," he says.

She watches him turn and walk toward his car until she can barely make him out in the darkness. She's left alone with her feeling of profound hopelessness. Maybe he's right. It can't hurt. As for what people think of her, they think little enough of her as it is, so what difference would it make. Anyway, Henry and Valerie are the two most important people in her life and they've both, in their own way, expressed their concern for her well-being and counseled her to seek help. She tells herself she values what they think, so maybe she should take their advice.

She turns and walks back toward the house. The light above the front door is on and the windows are aglow, and warm light is pooled on the ground below them. She can hear the sounds of the party growing louder, the voices raised in spirited conversation, punctuated by laughter, and bubbling in the background, "Blue Rondo `a la Turk" by the Dave Brubeck Quartet. Everyone sounds so happy, engaged in life and celebrating it. For herself, she feels removed from life and isolated. She wants to view the house as her new home, the place where she can make a new beginning, but she's exhausted and dispirited and just wants to crawl into bed and pull the covers over her head. To think that she was once so proud. She's not that person anymore, and not sure who she is now. She remembers the dream of being stuck in the hallway. She's stuck, all right, in limbo. She needs another drink.

CHAPTER 11

Ellie

Colleen sits across from Rocco's mom Ellie at the kitchen table, sipping a glass of Chianti and watching her snap the stems off beans and toss the beans into the colander in front of her on the table. Colleen hates visiting Rocco's family now, and does so only because she has to, to remain in the relationship, so that he'll continue to buy her booze. She's getting to the point where her hatred of these visits and her relationship with Sal is becoming greater than her fear of having her supply of liquor cut off. She's being irrational, of course, because she has no idea where or how she would get it, if she ended the relationship.

The visits are always the same. She and Rocco arrive on Saturday or Sunday, depending on when the Yankees are playing, and she sits with him and his father in the living room. Rocco and his father make small talk until the game begins, and then the only talk between them is about the game. She's uninterested in baseball and is thoroughly bored and eventually excuses herself and goes to sit with Ellie, who's inevitably in the kitchen, preparing food for dinner after the game.

She feels suffocated, trapped, and has to endure being here until they've finished eating and Rocco finally takes her home. At least she's living at her mother and Sheldon's now and the nightmare of living at her father's is over. During the last couple of weeks, she was still living with him before moving to Cornwall, he came to her closed bedroom door, which she'd taken to locking, late at night on several occasions. She's still uncertain why he did. Whatever his intentions were, the situation was creepy beyond belief, and she felt enormously relieved to finally be out of his house. She was surprised that her father let her go without a fight. He almost seemed relieved to be rid of her. Something happened to change him. She's not sure what, but something did.

She's given a lot of thought to what Henry said that evening in the driveway, about seeing a shrink. She's thinking about talking with her mother and Sheldon about it and even about her drinking, which she's managed to conceal from them as she did, for the most part, from her father, when she was living at his house. She knows it's the right thing to do but hasn't been able to bring herself to do it. She will, though, she must.

Now, she walks around in a daze. Her thinking is fuzzy and her grades are suffering. Her life is out of control and she has to do something about it, but the idea is scary. It will be hard and probably painful. She remembers how she felt after she ran out of liquor and before Sal began buying it for her. The constant wrenching feeling in her stomach was awful, and she's not looking forward to experiencing that again.

She sips her wine and studies Ellie as she methodically snaps off stems and tosses beans in the colander. Ellie's around her own mother's age but already looks old. With her floral print housedress, white apron, black hair worn back in a bun, dark complexion and dull, sad black eyes, she looks like a peasant. Rocco's father obviously does well and they have money, but the only indication of it in Ellie's appearance is the gaudy diamond ring on the ring finger of her right hand. She seems to live in the kitchen and all Colleen's ever seen her do is either prepare food for dinner or serve it. Is Ellie happy? She doesn't look it. She looks resigned and weary. Colleen can only imagine what a life like Ellie's is like—pure drudgery, day in and day out. Well, her own life isn't fun and games either at the moment, so she can sympathize with her. She has no intention of staying with Rocco, let alone getting engaged to him, but she's certain that if she did and they married, her existence would be just like Ellie's. It's too awful to contemplate.

"Rocco and his dad have been talkin'," Ellie says, without looking up.

Colleen mentally shakes her head. It's so typical of Rocco's mother. Whenever she has something to say, which isn't often, this is the way she begins, sounding ominous, like she's about to reveal a deep dark secret.

"Yeah? What about?"

"Buildin' a house."

"That's nice," Colleen says, wondering why Ellie's even mentioning it. She knows Rocco's father invests in real estate, owns a lot of property and occasionally builds houses for sale, so what's the big deal? She sees Ellie glance up at her and then at the ring Rocco gave her, then look back down and take another bean from the pile next to her on the table.

"Here, on the property," Ellie says, snapping off the stem and tossing the bean on the pile in the colander.

It sounds significant but strikes Colleen as a bit odd. Why do they need another house? This house is too big as it is. Now she has the feeling she's missing something, something obvious and important, and also that she is because her thinking has gotten so fuzzy and she's angry with herself.

* * *

Colleen brings a piece of veal to her mouth and chews it slowly, keeping her eyes on her plate. She knows the food is delicious—everything Ellie prepares is—but she has no appetite and can barely taste it and is just going through the motions of eating the meal. She picks up her wine glass, washes the veal down and glances around the table. Always the same arrangement; Rocco's father sitting at one end of the table to her left and his grandfather at the opposite end and his mother across from her and Rocco.

As usual, very little is said and she says nothing unless asked a question, which, thankfully, she hasn't been so far and she's hoping to make it through the rest of the meal and the visit without having to say a word. She just wants out of here and can't leave soon enough. At least, there's the wine. She drains her glass and puts it on the table. She sees Rocco reach out, pick up the wine bottle and refill her glass half-full. He doesn't even ask any more if she'd like more. He just refills her glass whenever it's empty and it always draws the same judgmental glances from his family. She's not just imagining it, because she glances up and notices their glances and looks back down at what's left of the wine in her glass. "So," she hears Rocco's father say and knows he addressing her. She looks up and sees him looking at her with raised eyebrows as he picks up his wine glass.

"Rocco says you wanna be a lawyer, defend poor people."

"Yeah," Colleen says.

"Those people have the government to defend them," Rocco's grandfather says disdainfully, without looking up from his plate. "Bunch of freeloading deadbeats. Don't waste your time."

She looks back at Rocco's father and sees him shrug.

"Pop's right," Teo says. "Anyway, the family has plenty of lawyers. Keepin' house is a full-time job. Just ask Ellie," he says, nodding toward her.

Colleen looks at Ellie and sees her nod, her expression looking even more resigned and weary. It finally dawns on her that Rocco's family is under the impression that she and he are engaged, and she feels the blood drain from her face and her stomach clench. She looks down at her plate and keeps her eyes on it. Why did he tell them that? She said she'd think about it and even he should know just how ridiculous she thinks the idea of getting engaged to him is. Why has he been deluding himself?

"We're thinking about building another house," Teo says.

She glances up at him and nods and looks back down at her plate. "Yeah, I heard."

"On the far end of the property, by the lake. Very private."

"Sounds nice," she says, glancing up at him again and looking back down at her plate. She feels panic-stricken and in desperate need of more wine, but doesn't dare reach for her glass, because she knows if she did, her hand would begin shaking and she'd spill it.

Colleen stares blankly out the windshield with her hands folded in her lap as they head toward Cornwall on 9W. It felt like the meal would never end. No one said the words "engaged" and "married." They didn't have to. She's furious with herself and Rocco and wants to confront him but hasn't been able to muster the courage, and neither of them has said a word since they left his parents'. Living with her father was a nightmare toward the end and she thought it was over, but this feels a lot like it. She has to end the relationship, and she has to do it now. It doesn't matter that her liquor supply will be cut off. She'll think of something. She has no idea how he'll react. In all the time she's known him, she's yet to see him angry, but her suspicion that he has a bad temper and that his anger could become violent has always been there. At least, he's driving and they're on the highway. What could he do?

"Why'd you tell your family we're engaged," she finally manages to ask and receives a slap in the face so forceful that her head bounces off the passenger-side window. She's stunned and the left side of her face hurts badly. She covers her head with her arm to protect her face and presses herself against the door, getting as far away from him as possible. She feels her eyes filling with tears and wants to cry but fights to keep from doing so. She doesn't want to give him the satisfaction of seeing her cry, not even of hearing her sniff. "What?" she hears him ask and doesn't have to look at him to know he's sneering at her. "I'm not good enough for you? My family's not good enough? Look at me, you stupid bitch!" She slowly lowers her arm and cautiously turns to look at him and sees him pointing at her the same way her father does, like his index finger is the barrel of a gun.

"You're a drunk! You're pathetic!" he says. "I'm the best thing that ever happened to you and don't ever forget it!"

"Sal, listen…." she says, and sees him ready to hit her again. She flinches and covers her head, cowering against the door.

"No, you listen! We're officially engaged, as of now! Got it? You too good for me. What a joke."

She slowly lowers her arm again and keeps her face turned away from him, watching the trees rush by in a blur, just as her thoughts are. The only one that really matters now is that they're almost to her exit and she'll be home soon and rid of him for good. "My dad told me about what happened with your father," she hears him say and feels a shock. She can hear his sneer again and looks at him. "What happened?" she asks.

"That's *our* little secret. Let's just say I don't think you want it to get out."

"What are you talking about?" she asks and sees him slowly shake his head.

"Welcome to the real world, baby. We play hardball. You just be a good girl and do as you're told and everything's gonna be fine."

She gets out of the car shuts the door and walks to the house without looking back as he drives off. She heads straight to the bathroom and brushes her teeth to get the taste of him out of her mouth. She stares at herself in the mirror as she brushes. She looks ashen and feels shaken, and her emotions are a mixture of anger and fear; anger with him and fear of him for hitting her and making her blow him before letting her out of the car, and his family for whatever it is they know about her father. Most of all she's angry with herself, for having gotten herself into this situation and fear because there doesn't seem to be anything she can do to get herself out of it, and the prospect of actually having to marry him to protect her father's reputation? As ridiculous as it seems, it's still terrifying.

She rinses out her mouth, wipes it with a towel and joins her mother on the living room couch. Her mother has her nose in a book, as usual, and looks up at her as she sits.

"What on earth is the matter with you?" her mother asks, putting the book face down in her lap. "You look awful."

"I feel awful."

"Are you ill?" her mother asks.

She shakes her head. "No, well, sort of. I feel sick." She stares helplessly at her mother, not knowing what to say or where to begin. She feels herself begin shaking and her eyes filling with tears and can see her mother's concern turn to alarm.

"Colleen!" her mother says, waving her toward her. "Come here!"

She scoots toward her mother and lays her head on her lap, curls up and lets the tears flow. She can't remember the last time her mother held her in her arms like this, but it feels good and makes her feel a bit less panic-stricken. She wishes she could stay like this forever, safe in her mother's arms, with her mother stroking her hair, trying to soothe her, and that the business with Rocco and his family and what they know about her father would just go away, but she knows she can't and it won't and that she has to tell her mother everything, including about her drinking and the fact that she feels her life is spinning out of control. When she's cried herself out, she sits up and the words flow out of her like a rushing stream. Her mother stares at her in disbelief as she listens. When she tells her mother about Rocco's father having helped her father out with a "little problem," she asks her mother, "Do you know what happened?" Her mother looks haunted now and slowly shakes her head.

"No," her mother says, "only that something did, an accident of some kind, involving someone named Tiffany. Your father came home late one evening, very agitated. I'd never seen him so distraught. He went straight to his office and spoke with someone on the phone and raised his voice at one point. That's when I heard him mention an accident with Tiffany. He wouldn't talk about it with me. I found out from the phone bill that he'd called the Napolitanos."

Colleen's afraid to ask but has to. "What do you think happened?" Her mother narrows her eyes a bit.

"I don't know, and I don't want to know. Whatever did, I'm sure it was sordid, at the very least. It's none of my business now."

"But it's mine. I need to know. I'm not going to be blackmailed into marrying Rocco Napolitano. It's crazy!" Her mother looks at her sympathetically and slowly shakes her head.

"You've gotten yourself into quite a fix, haven't you? Talk with your father. Maybe he can help." Her mother narrows her eyes again. "This drinking business has to stop," her mother says. "You have your father's gene."

"Yeah, I know," Colleen says weakly.

* * *

Colleen sits at the desk in her bedroom and stares at the Princess phone, trying to muster the courage to call her father. The situation is crazy, all right. The more she thinks about it, what good is talking with him going to do? Even if he does tell her what happened, which she doesn't think he will, she'd still have the threat of Rocco's father revealing the secret hanging over her head. There's always the possibility that what happened wasn't really all that bad and that her father doesn't care if Rocco's father tells. Anyway, maybe her mother is right. Maybe her father can help her somehow. Once again, she's left with the feeling that she has nothing left to lose and picks up the receiver and dials her father's number. She listens to the rings and glances at the alarm clock on the nightstand. Just past nine-thirty. He'll be well along in his drinking by now. "Hello?" she hears him say, with his familiar late evening slur. "Hi, Daddy, how're you?"

"Waddya want?"

His mood is familiar too, just as Mila described it—angry and bitter and resentful. "I need your help," she says and explains her predicament with Rocco. "What does his father know?" she asks and listens to the long hissing silence on her father's end. Not hearing anything from him, she asks, "Who's Tiffany? What was the accident? What happened to her?" She listens to more hissing silence.

"It's none of your business," he finally says.

She's alarmed by the change in his tone of voice. It's flat and weak and she can barely hear him. Still, it's clear that he's not going to tell her anything about it. "It is now!" she says. "Whatever it is, Rocco's using it to blackmail me into marrying him! Can you talk with his dad?" She listens to still more hissing silence and strains to hear his answer, when and if it comes, but hears only the click of the call being terminated on his end. She places the receiver in the cradle and stares at the phone. She's left feeling certain that whatever happened was bad, *really* bad, and that her father is powerless to help her, that and a sense of dread.

* * *

Colleen thinks about her brief conversation with her father as she chews another spoonful of cereal. The slow steady crunching sound in her ears makes her think of the plodding footsteps of a hopeless soul, walking toward doom, perhaps a convict being led to the gallows or death chamber. She's filled with an eerie sense of foreboding and stares blankly at her mother and Sheldon at the kitchen table, both with their coffee cups in hand and their noses in different sections of yesterday's *Newburgh Beacon News*, which, she's learned since living here, they always read the next morning, one of several rituals she's noticed they've developed, like kissing each other good-bye before getting in their cars and heading off to their offices, something her mother and father never did.

She's nervous and on edge and starts at the sound of the ringing phone on the kitchen wall behind her. Her mother glances at her curiously as she gets up, walks to the phone and answers it. "Hello?" she hears her mother ask and then say, "Yes, this is she," and then ask in disbelief, "What?" Colleen turns and sees her mother standing there with the phone to her ear, staring at her with a shocked expression.

"Yes," her mother says, "okay. Thank you."

She watches her mother hang up the phone, slowly walk back to her chair and lower herself into it, sitting with her hands folded in her lap and staring into the distance with that same shocked expression.

"Who was that?" Sheldon asks with concern.

"Jim's housekeeper," her mother says. "He's in the hospital."

"What happened?" Sheldon asks with alarm.

"She found him a while ago in bed. He had his gun in his hand but hadn't shot himself. He'd vomited and she couldn't feel a pulse. She thought he was dead. She called the police and they arrived with the paramedics. He wasn't dead, but close to it. Apparently, he'd taken sleeping pills."

"Jesus," Sheldon says, shaking his head.

The way her mother is looking at her now, Colleen can see that understanding they have between them about her father, an understanding that only the two of them can have, having lived with him.

"Did you speak with your father last night?" She nods.

"How did he sound?"

"Drunk, as usual." Her mother glances at Sheldon and looks back at her.

"Did you ask him about what we talked about?" She nods again.

"What did he say?"

She narrows her eyes. "It's none of my business." Her mother sighs and slowly shakes her head.

"Given everything that's going on in your life," her mother says, "I think it's time we changed your situation."

"Meaning?" she asks.

"Boarding school. I know just the one for you."

"Where?"

"Our Lady of Mercy in Purchase. It has an excellent academic rating and they, ah, have counseling for, ah, kids…."

She sees her mother glance uncomfortably at Sheldon and it dawns on her that her mother hasn't told him anything about what's going on with her and is embarrassed to talk about it. Colleen sits back, crosses her arms, raises her eyebrows and tilts her head slightly. "With a drinking problem?" she asks. Her mother can't keep her eyes on hers and looks down at her folded hands and nods. Colleen looks at Sheldon, who's looking at her mother with concern now, and waits for him to look at her to see what his reaction will be. Finally, he does and raises his eyebrows and shrugs, as if to say, "What's the big deal? You have a drinking problem. You need help."

The more she's gotten to know Sheldon, the more she likes him. She can't help wondering how different she'd be as a person and how different her life would be in general if Sheldon had been her father, instead of her father. Well, what's done is done and she is who she is and her life is a mess and her mother's right about her situation needing to change. Continuing to live here would be a disaster and the sooner she puts distance between herself and Rocco, the better. She has no one to blame but herself for having gotten involved with him in the first place, but enough is enough, and if she doesn't get free of him, she won't be able to live with herself.

As far as what Rocco's family knows about her father is concerned, it isn't her concern any longer. If her father was stupid enough to do something so bad that he'd rather kill himself than have people know about it, then that's *his* problem. For all she cares now, Rocco's father can tell the world about it, and she's going to make damn sure that when she leaves, no one knows where she's going. This is her chance to regain control of her life and no one, least of all a low life like Rocco, is going to stand in her way.

* * *

"Hey, Colleen!" she hears Valerie call. "Wait up!" It's the first time she's heard her voice since their last phone conversation. As Valerie requested, she's given her a wide berth at school and only occasionally runs into her and when she does, it's an awkward moment and she quickly moves on.

She stops on the sidewalk, turns and sees her walking quickly toward her with a concerned expression. Why does Valerie suddenly want to talk? Nothing's changed between them as far as she can tell. They haven't had anything to do with each other, so how could anything have changed? It's curious. Valerie stops in front of her and looks at her sympathetically.

"I heard about your dad," Valerie says. "I'm so sorry. How is he? Is he okay?"

So, that's it. Her father! How did Valerie find out? She hasn't said a word about it to any of her friends. Then it occurs to her. Of course, Jeanine must have told her. Jeanine's mother's a charge nurse at St. Luke's and must have told Jeanine that her father was admitted and the reason why and Jeanine promptly told Valerie. It's pathetic how Jeanine sucks up to Valerie now. All of her friends seem to have distanced themselves from her and only Megan still looks up to her. So much for friendship and loyalty. Well, it's not important. She'll soon be leaving them behind. She looks Valerie in the eyes. "To tell you the truth, I don't know and I don't care." She sees Valerie's taken aback.

"Jeez," Valerie says, "I knew you didn't have the greatest relationship with your dad, but I didn't think it was that bad."

Colleen studies her. She remembers the way she felt about Valerie when they first met. She looked up to her and admired her and wanted in the worst way to be her friend. She's never forgotten the way it felt when Valerie shut her out of her life, and she's never forgiven her for doing it.

She can tell by Valerie's demeanor, a bit nervous, and her expression, a bit hopeful, that she wants to make amends. Should she? Does she want Valerie back in her life, after what she said to her on the phone?

She remembers the feeling of having power over people, of being able to bend them to her will, the way her father does, or used to, anyway. She knows now that she's stronger than he is. He's lying flat on his back in the hospital, having tried to kill himself, and she's standing here tightening the screws on someone she once thought was superior to her.

She knows it's wrong to be treating Valerie this way, toying with her, but she feels her confidence stirring. She hasn't felt confident in herself in a long time and it feels good. She can feel herself gaining strength, which is also good. She's going to need all the strength she can muster to deal with Rococo and her drinking. She raises her eyebrows slightly. "Well, now you do," she says and waits to see if Valerie has anything more to say. Valerie searches her eyes a moment and Colleen can see she's looking for forgiveness.

"Listen," Valerie says, "I'm sorry I went off on you like that. I guess I overreacted."

Colleen keeps her eyes fixed on Valerie's and makes her face a mask of indifference. She sees it has the desired effect. Valerie's searching her eyes desperately now and looks exasperated.

"Okay!" Valerie says, throwing up her hands. "I apologize!"

"Sure," Colleen says, and Valerie looks relieved and smiles and she savors the moment. She has everything she can do to keep from smiling triumphantly. Valerie steps forward and hugs her and Colleen waits a few moments before hugging her back, not as half-heartedly as Valerie's last hug at the bus terminal, but also not as tightly as Valerie's hugging her now. Just tightly enough so she feels forgiven.

She *does* forgive her, and they *are* back to being close friends, but things will never be the same between them again, at least not as far as she's concerned. She feels they're on equal footing now and, if anything, that she has the upper hand in the relationship. Valerie steps back and beams at her.

"Jeanine said you're livin' in Cornwall now and have your own car," Valerie says.

Jeanine again. That girl can't keep her mouth shut. "Yeah," Colleen says.

"That's great! No more takin' the bus!"

Colleen's always found Valerie's "Benzinhoist" accent amusing and was always careful never to let it show, but she feels emboldened now and hearing her pronounce bus "buzz," as she always does, she smiles.

"Wanna get a soda before you head home?" Valerie asks hopefully.

"Sure," Colleen says.

* * *

Colleen slowly blows out a stream of smoke and studies Valerie, sitting across the table from her, hunched over with her arms folded around her glass of Coke, sucking on a straw and looking thoughtfully at Rocco's engagement ring. Valerie looks up at her with a puzzled expression and removes her mouth from the straw.

"So, what's with you and Rocco Napolitano, of all people?"

Colleen shrugs and begins slowly swishing the foot of her crossed leg, like an angry cat's tail.

"I don't know him," Valerie says, "but I know about him. He doesn't strike me as your type, you know? I mean, he has a bad rep."

Colleen draws on her cigarette and inhales deeply. How close does she want to let Valerie get to her now? How much does she want to share with her about what's been going on in her life, the parts that even Jeanine doesn't know about and couldn't have shared with her? She's not sure what she wants her relationship with Valerie to be just yet. She trusted her completely once and her trust was broken. Should she trust her again? Valerie was the only person she enjoyed talking with, other than Henry, and she's felt her absence from her life. It's good to have someone to talk with, to confide in. She blows out the smoke in a slow steady stream, taps the ash off her cigarette into the ashtray and fixes her eyes on Valerie's. "So do I," she says. "That's why he called me." Valerie looks at her sympathetically and understandingly, which Colleen appreciates. Good. They're off to a good start.

"What type of guy is he?"

"A jerk, controlling and abusive." Valerie looks puzzled. "What?" Colleen asks.

"What is it with you and abusive guys?"

Valerie's question catches her off guard and she stares at her, not knowing what to say. It's a good question and she knows the answer is complex and has everything to do with her relationship with her father. She's not prepared to discuss that now and Valerie can see it.

"So, why're ya goin' out with him?" Valerie asks.

"He buys me booze." Now Valerie's the one who's caught off guard and Colleen watches her as she tries to decide whether talking about her drinking would be wise. She's pleased to see it. Valerie should always be this respectful of her and give careful consideration to every personal question she asks, just as she should always feel grateful if she chooses to share the details of her personal life with her. Colleen feels herself brimming with confidence now.

"So, you're still drinkin'," Valerie says cautiously.

"Yeah, but I'm quitting, *and* ending the relationship with Rocco." She sees doubt in Valerie's expression and fixes her eyes on hers.

"Good!" Valerie says, "That's good!"

"I'm leaving at the end of the month," she says and anticipates Valerie's surprise.

"Leavin'? Where ya goin'?"

"Boarding school."

"Yeah? Where?"

"I'd rather not say." Valerie looks hurt. "I don't want anyone to know where I am, and especially Rocco."

"Jeez, Colleen, I thought we were friends. Don't you trust me?"

She takes a sip of her Coke and savors the moment as she studies Valerie's worried expression. It's time to unburden herself and let Valerie know exactly how she feels about what happened between them and put her on notice that if it happens again, it will be the end of their friendship—forever. "I did once, Valerie. Friends don't do what you did to me, turn your back on me like that. Friends stand by each other through thick and thin." She watches Valerie squirm in her seat.

"I said I was sorry, Colleen."

"I know. Just so you know. Anyway, I don't know why you were so offended by what happened between Byron and me. It was none of your business."

"Well, it was, kind of," Valerie says. "It didn't reflect well on me, you know?"

She looks sadly at Valerie and slowly shakes her head. "I can't believe that after everything you and Sandy have been through, you give a shit about what anyone thinks about you. Who cares what people think? I don't. I like sex, Valerie, and I don't think there's anything wrong with that. I enjoyed what happened with Byron and I'm looking forward to seeing him again this summer."

Colleen's as surprised to hear this as Valerie appears to be. She hasn't thought about Byron much lately, or his invitation to visit him, and it just came out. Thinking about it, though, the idea does sound nice. She's been on the fence about whether she should take him up on it and was uncertain whether she'd be able to make it happen, but that was before her circumstances changed and she's sure her mother will let her go. She's pleased to see Valerie giving the same careful consideration to discussing the subject of Byron as she did her drinking, and she's having a hard time not gloating openly.

"You know he's not good for you," Valerie says.

She shrugs and stubs her cigarette out in the ashtray. "I know what I'm doing. He's a plaything, just for fun." Valerie smiles and slowly and shakes her head. "What?" Colleen asks.

"You," Valerie says. "You're a piece of work."

"I'll take that as a compliment."

"It was meant as one. How's things with Henry? See much of him?"

She shakes her head. "Nothing's changed. We see each other once in a while. He calls me when he feels like it." She sighs. "The only consolation is that I know he's not serious about anyone else. I know the sex isn't as good with any of them, that's for sure. How's Sandy?"

"Good! She asks after you all the time."

"I think about her too. Give her my best. Regina and Connie?"

"They're good too. They ask after you too. They really enjoyed meeting you, Colleen."

"Yeah. I enjoyed meeting them. Give them my best."

"I will."

"I'm glad we reconnected, Valerie."

"So am I. Maybe the next time Miles is at the Village Gate, you can come down, huh?"

"Yeah, that would be nice."

"I understand you don't what to tell me where this boarding school is, but it's not that far away, right?"

She shakes her head.

"Good! So, now that you have a car, you won't have to take the bus into the city."

She smiles and looks at Valerie fondly.

"What?" Valerie asks.

"You and that 'Benzinhoist' accent. It cracks me up." She sees Valerie's shoulders relax and her eyes brighten and a toothy smile appear. For the first time, she looks genuinely relieved and happy that they're friends again.

"Hey," Valerie says, "that's what friends are for, right?"

* * *

Colleen stares down at the chicken cacciatore on her plate as she cuts off a small piece. She pushes her fork into it and keeps her eyes on it as she crosses her fork and brings the food to her mouth and puts it in and forces herself to chew it. Her stomach muscles are tense and she feels slightly nauseous, she thinks probably because of the adrenaline that's flooding her body because of her anxiety and apprehension. She tries to avoid eye contact with Ellie across the dining table and doesn't look at Teo or Rocco's grandfather or Rocco when he says something to her or asks her a question. She's withdrawn into herself and when she does take her eyes off the food on her plate, so as not to draw attention to herself, she glances around the dining room; at the dark, heavy dining room furniture and gaudy decorations; at the sideboard to her left, behind Teo, on which are proudly displayed two cherished heirlooms, a cut crystal punchbowl and a china soup tureen; through the glass doors of the shelves above it, filled with dinnerware and who knows how many different sets of dishes, all, she's sure, decorated with floral patterns, as the dishes on the table are; at the by now familiar bad artwork on the wall facing her, flanking the window behind Ellie, the oil painting on the left in a mahogany frame of a street scene in some Italian village, the one on the right in a similar frame of the Bay of Naples with a smoking Vesuvius in the background; at the white valence, with its gold patterned border; at the parted gold and silver brocade drapes, held back by thick gold tasseled cord.

Her only consolation in this situation is knowing that when she leaves Rocco's this evening after dinner, it will be for the last time and she'll never see this room or the rest of the house his family again. Ever. She'll probably see him at school before she leaves for boarding school, but she won't have anything to do with him, which she intends to make perfectly clear to him when they talk later and she gives back the ring.

Out of the corners of her eyes she notices Teo looking at her. She's never asked Rocco why his father's nickname is "Skull," which she finds creepy, and after this evening she'll no longer care. She glances at the old photographs of the man and woman in the gilt frames on the wall to her right, behind Sal's grandfather, to avoid making eye contact with him. She'll no longer care who the man and woman are who stare down at her either. The photographs look like they were taken around the turn of the century, and the man and woman look like peasants, uncomfortable and posed stiffly in their black clothes. They're probably Rocco's great great grandparents but she's never inquired about them and he's never bothered to tell her who they are. No matter. When she leaves here this evening, she'll never see them again, either. Ever.

"Did Rocco show you the site?" Teo asks.

She feels a twinge in her stomach and glances at him. "No, no he didn't." Teo looks pleased with himself and smiles.

"It's almost cleared. We excavate the foundation next week."

"That's nice," she says, trying her best to sound interested, but not doing a very good job. She picks up her water glass and sips, keeping her eyes downcast. She hasn't had a drink of whiskey in almost a week, ever since she finished the last bottle, and while her hand is trembling slightly, it's a lot steadier than it was earlier in the week and she's thankful for that.

"Awful thing about your dad," Teo says. "How's he doing? He's out of the hospital, right?"

She puts down her glass and looks at him and nods. "Yeah, he is. I guess he's okay. I haven't seen him or spoken with him. My mom keeps me posted."

"Your family's not close?" Teo asks.

She hears the concern and displeasure in his voice and feels her anger rising. She wants to tell him to go fuck himself and mind his own damn business but instead glances at him again and shakes her head. Teo leans forward and puts his elbows on the table, clasps his hands and fixes his eyes on hers.

"That's too bad. Well, as you know, we're a close family, and anyone who's invited into it is expected to respect that and fit in. *Capisci?*"

"Yeah," she says softly. She understands perfectly well and can't wait to escape this nightmare. She takes one last long look at him. She wants always to remember the way he looks right now, with his eyebrows raised and that air of malice about him, and the way he just sounded, threatening while offering her "friendly advice." She wants the memory always to serve as a reminder to never again relinquish control of her life.

"Good," Teo says, picking up his wine glass. "Just so you understand."

* * *

Colleen stares through the silhouetted trees at the moonlight reflected on the surface of the lake as she and Rocco walk to his car. She knew this moment had to come, but she's been dreading it. Having experienced one of his violent outbursts, she's fully expecting another one now and is resigned to it. She just has to endure it and it will be for the last time. What's causing her pulse to race and pound in her ears is her certainty that he'll be even more violent this time. She really didn't say or do anything the last time to provoke him, but this time is different and she can only imagine how he'll react to what she has to say.

She gets in the car and stares out the windshield at the shimmering moonlight and steels herself. "We need to talk," she says, before he can start the car. She can feel his eyes on her but keeps hers on the shimmering moonlight.

"Yeah? What about?"

"Us." She hears him settle back in his seat.

"What about *us*?"

She takes a deep breath and tenses. "I'm ending the relationship." She's prepared for the blow, but it doesn't come, and she stares out the windshield and waits. A long moment of silence passes.

"Oh!" he says, "So, *you're* ending the relationship! Well, howdy-doo! Who the *fuck* do you think *you* are, telling *me you're* ending the relationship?"

She glances down at the ring and begins working it off her finger.

"What are you doing?" he asks menacingly.

"Giving you back the ring," she says and finally manages to remove it. She holds it out to him without looking at him, but he doesn't take it and she waits.

"I can't fucking *believe* you!" he says. "What are you, *retarded?* You see what my father's doing? He's building us a house!"

"I didn't ask him to," she says. "I never said I wanted to be engaged. I said I'd think about it, so I've thought about it and I don't want to be. I never should have taken the ring in the first place. I'm sorry." She looks at him and sees him staring at her angrily. "Go on," she says, "Take it. I don't want it." She sees his expression slowly go blank and has no idea what he'll do next. She's surprised and a bit relieved that he hasn't hit her yet and doesn't seem about to. His calm is unnerving, though. Finally, he reaches out, keeping his eyes on hers, takes the ring and tosses it in the console between them. A long moment passes and he slowly turns his head and looks down at the key as he puts it in the ignition and starts the car. He looks like he's in a trance and she turns her head and stares out the windshield again at the shimmering moonlight. Could it be that he's not going to become violent? That's he's actually going to be reasonable? She can't believe it and resists feeling that it could possibly be this easy to break things off with him.

They ride in silence and she's beginning to think that maybe, just maybe, that's all there was to it, but she feels a jolt as her body is flooded with adrenaline when, instead of continuing on to 9W to take her back to Cornwall, he turns onto the street that leads to his father's company. "Rocco," she says, trying to sound as calm and polite as possible, "please take me home." He stares straight ahead and shows no sign that he even heard her. "Rocco," she says, pleading now, "I don't want to go there. Please take me home." It's clear to her that he's not going to, not yet, anyway, not until he's used her, hopefully, for the last time. Well, how bad could it be this time? No worse than any of the others, and if that's what she must do to finally be rid of him, then so be it and it will have been worth it.

He parks the car reaches behind her seat and she hears the familiar rustle of the paper bag. "Rocco," she says, hoping he'll finally talk to her and be reasonable, but she sees he's not going to or be and gets out of the car before he drags her out.

She follows him to the room in the office and he takes the bottle out of the bag and puts it on the desk next to the water glass he keeps there for her to use. He sits on the bed and stares blankly at her.

"Get undressed," he says.

There's no point in saying anything more and she pulls off her clothes and stands there, staring down at him and waiting for instruction. He nods toward the bottle.

"Pour yourself a drink," he says.

"Rocco, I'm going to quit. I don't want to." He stares at her blankly a moment and then slowly raises his eyebrows.

"Pour yourself a drink before I beat the shit out of you. Understand?"

She sighs and takes the cap off the bottle, fills the glass and puts the bottle back on the desk. She stares at the amber liquid in the glass. The ordeal with her father is vivid in her mind. Does Rocco have the same thing in mind? Is he going to make her drink the whole bottle, or just enough to get drunk? Probably just enough to get drunk. She won't be much fun for him, if she's passed out. She picks up the glass, brings it to her lips and takes a long sip, keeping her eyes on his. She works her way to the bottom of the glass and, when it's empty, he nods toward the bottle and she refills the glass, brings it to her lips and drinks.

It hasn't been that long since she was last drunk, but long enough that her body had rid itself of alcohol and her head had finally cleared and now it feels like she and her body are reacquainting themselves with an old friend. By the time she's finished her third glass, she's arrived at that familiar place where she's drunk but can still function. Her legs are wobbly and it's an effort to keep her head from lolling forward and to the sides and he must realize that she's had enough, because he looks at the glass in her hand and then at her and nods toward the desk.

"Put it down and get over here," he says.

She puts the glass on the desk and carefully walks the few steps over to him, stumbling and catching herself once. She stands in front of him, swaying and looking down at the two of him she now sees, one drifting slightly above the other.

"Get on your knees," he says, "where you belong."

She lowers herself carefully to her knees and puts her hands on the floor on either side of her to steady herself. She stares at the two lines of "Napolitano Construction Co." on the front of his tee shirt, one drifting slightly above the other. She looks down and watches him unbutton and unzip his jeans lift his butt off the bed and pull them and his underpants down around his ankles. Judging from his erection, watching her standing here naked, getting drunk, must have been a real turn on for him.

"You like sucking cock, baby?" he asks.

Before she can answer he grabs her hair at the top of her head and pulls her toward him and she puts her hands on his thighs to steady herself. She opens her mouth and feels his penis slide in, and he pushes her head down on it until it's poking against her glottis and she gags.

"That's all you're good for, you worthless piece of shit," she hears him say, "sucking cock."

She doesn't feel ashamed or embarrassed or humiliated or even angry with him, just drunk. The alcohol has dulled her senses, but hasn't affected her reflexes and his penis, poking against her glottis, makes her gag again and now her stomach heaves. "Humph!" is all she manages to get out and tries to pull back, but he keeps pushing her head down on his penis. She gags and heaves again and now she's afraid that if he keeps this up, she'll vomit.

"Don't you dare puke!" she hears him say and feels him pushing her head down harder. "You'll be one sorry bitch if you do!"

Her nose begins running and the tears that have been welling in her eyes begin spilling over and running down her cheeks. She gags and heaves again and this time her stomach contracts forcefully and she feels its contents rising in her throat. "Humph! Humph!" she exclaims again and struggles to pull back, but he tightens his grip on her hair and pushes her head down even harder.

"Suck, you fucking slut!" she hears him say.

Maybe he wants her to puke, even though he's telling her not to and threatening her if she does. Maybe he thinks that would be the ultimate degradation. Who knows? All she knows is that she's about to, unless he lets her head up. She feels him press down harder still and now the head of his penis isn't poking against her glottis, it's past it and she gags and her stomach heaves and this time its contents don't stop in her throat but come spewing out of her mouth and nostrils.

"Jesus!" she hears him scream. "You stupid bitch!"

He yanks her head up and she glimpses his face and sees he's enraged. A second later she feels his fist smash into her cheek and her head snaps back and after that—nothing.

* * *

She's feels movement—every now and then a gentle swaying—but has no idea what's causing it. She slowly becomes aware that she's sitting slumped against something and opens her eyes slightly, or tries to, and finds her left eye won't open. She peers with her right eye at the bright lights and realizes it's an oncoming car and that she's in Rocco's car and remembers what happened and figures he must be driving her home.

The left side of her face aches and she puts a hand to her eye and feels its puffiness and figures it's swollen shut. She feels her cheek, which is also swollen, and just touching it sends a shock of pain through her body. Is her cheekbone fractured or broken? She wouldn't be surprised. He really hit her hard and probably not just that one time.

Now she's aware that her left side aches and touches her ribs gingerly and the pain increases. Why would her ribs ache? Did he punch her there too? That doesn't seem likely, and it dawns on her that she probably collapsed when he punched her and was lying unconscious on the floor and he must have kicked her in the ribs. The left side of her pelvis and left buttock hurt too. Yes, that's what he must have done, kicked her. Jesus!

It occurs to her that when she felt her ribs, she touched skin and looks down and sees that she's still naked and her clothes are heaped on her lap. He didn't even bother to get her dressed! He must have carried her to the car and got her in and thrown her clothes in afterward. She knew he was crude and a thug, but punching her in the face and kicking her while she was lying on the floor unconscious and then driving her home naked, treating her like a piece of meat? Well, she has no one to blame but herself, and what a fool she was to have thought that ending the relationship would have been that easy. There's a price to be paid for every bad decision in life and she's paid dearly for having decided to become involved with him.

The car slows and stops, and she assumes they've arrived at her house but she's too drunk and hurt to look around or move and peers with her one good eye out the windshield at the trees illuminated by the headlights. She hears him get out of the car and sees him pass in front of the headlights as he walks around the front of the car to her side. Her door opens and she begins falling out, but he grabs her by the hair and drags her out and down onto the asphalt.

She lies there on her side, curled up and clutching her clothes, waiting to see what happens next. Nothing does for a long moment and just when she thinks he's going to walk away and get in his car and drive off, she feels hot liquid on the side of her face and shoulder and arm and the smell of urine fills her nose. At this point, she's not surprised that he's pissing on her. In fact, it makes perfect sense to her. Given the fact that he's an ignorant asshole, this is the only way he can express his contempt and disgust.

The stream slows to a trickle and she's hoping that's the end of it when she feels a hard kick in her ass and then another and another. She clenches her buttocks and teeth, expecting to receive yet another blow, but hears her car door shut and then his footsteps walking away and then his car door shut and the screech of tires as he speeds off.

She feels cold now and begins shivering. With great difficulty she gets to her feet and turns and peers with her good eye at the house at the bottom of the driveway. The light is on above the front door and the windows are aglow and warm light is pooled on the ground below them. She remembers looking at the house the evening of the party, after Henry left, and listening to the happy sounds of the people inside and how lost and empty she felt. She doesn't feel that way now, though, as beaten up and hurt as she is. She feels relieved and thankful and happy to be rid of Rocco and hopeful about her future without him. She just needs to reach the house to begin it.

She makes her way, teetering and stumbling, down the driveway, hugging her clothes. She drops a shoe and squats, rather than bends over, to pick it up. She knows if she bends over, she'll fall flat on her face. She raises herself up, stands unsteadily, takes a tentative step and continues slowly down the driveway toward the house, keeping her good eye trained on the front door.

She can imagine what her mother's and Sheldon's reactions will be when they see her like this. Her mother will want to call the police and have Rocco arrested, but Colleen will insist that she not. She doesn't want to press charges. She figures Rocco did what he did because he knows his father isn't going to tell anyone about whatever it is her father did, and this was his way of getting back at her for breaking up with him. She's fine with it.

She finally makes it to the low concrete slab in front of the front door and lifts her foot to step on it, but stubs her toe and falls forward, banging her head against the door on her way down. She's only lying there a moment or two when the door opens and she hears Sheldon cry in alarm, "Colleen!" and then back into the house, "Kathleen! Come here!"

She feels Sheldon working to get his arms around her, so that he can lift her up and she's reminded of religious paintings she's seen of Jesus, being taken down from the cross and carried into the tomb, limp and naked except for his loincloth. She imagines her body looks just like that with a jumble of clothes covering her instead of a loincloth. She's never believed that Jesus rose from the dead. She's always believed his disciples made up that part of the story to convert people to their new religion. It's understandable. Believers need a god to believe in so his disciples turned Jesus into one, just as envious people need someone to envy and she was that person in her circle of friends, until her drinking got the better of her and her reputation caught up with her.

"Oh, my God!" she hears her mother cry.

Colleen feels Sheldon lifting her up and it does feel like she's being resurrected. She's felt dead for so long, ever since she began drinking, and her craving for alcohol replaced her self-confidence and her addiction sapped her energy and undermined her resolve and her life began spiraling out of control. As drunk as she is now, she knows she just has to sleep it off and that as bad as she'll feel tomorrow, it will be a new day and her life will once again be filled with hope and promise. All she has to do to achieve her dreams is get sober and stay sober.

CHAPTER 12

Stephanie

Colleen stands in the line of girls, waiting her turn to use the pay phone on the wall in the hallway of her dorm. Most of the girls, like herself, have their hair in curlers and are in their bathrobes and wearing bathroom slippers. She leans against the wall, her legs crossed and an arm hugging her waist, reading *On the Road,* which she's been meaning to finish ever since she read the first two chapters of "Part One" at Valerie's.

She wasn't surprised that she couldn't find the book in the school library, when she looked for it shortly after arriving at Our Lady of Mercy. She got to know the librarian Missus McCarthy well in her first few weeks at the school and discovered that she's also a fan of the Beat writers and thinks it's wrong that schools ban their books and also thinks they should be required reading in American Lit classes. Colleen asked, if she gave her the money, would she buy a paperback copy for her and Missus McCarthy said she would and brought it in today, discreetly took it out of her bag and put it in Colleen's and handed her the change with a knowing nod and wink.

She glances at her wristwatch. A minute to go and then there'll only be three girls ahead of her. She quickly learned the rule about using the payphone: when someone else is waiting to use it, you're limited to five minutes of talk time.

She leans forward slightly and looks to her left at Candice, a pudgy, but pretty, junior who's on the phone, standing with her back to the line of waiting girls, to try to enjoy some semblance of privacy. It's a long line this evening and all the girls are waiting to talk with their boyfriends, as Candice is talking with hers now, and all for the same reason: to make absolutely certain they'll be here tomorrow for the Spring Formal, really the junior prom, as all the girls refer to it; that nothing's "come up" at the last minute and that they're all set with the rented tux and the corsage and boutonnière and won't forget to bring them.

She glances to her right and sees the expressions on the faces of the girls, waiting behind her, and they all look the same: nervous and worried. They have good reason to be. While she's been standing in line, waiting her turn, she's overheard two girls' reactions to hearing that their boyfriends are bailing on them. Both girls were incredulous at first, asking their boyfriends how they could do this to them, and then became furious, telling them to go to hell. Both slammed the receiver down as hard as they could, and both cried inconsolably while the other girls near them put their arms around them and talked soothingly to them.

She must admit that she's nervous and worried too. When she called to invite Henry, she honestly didn't think he'd want to come, both because of the way she feels about him and what her father did to him. She was overjoyed when he said sure, he'd be happy to. It's been hard, but she's only called him two or three times in the weeks since to remind him and make sure he's still coming. She hasn't wanted to seem to be pestering him about it. She knows him well and that he wouldn't appreciate her doing that. She told him she'd call him this evening, just to double-check, and he said sure, that would be fine and he'd be expecting her call. Still, like the other girls, she can't help feeling nervous and can't help worrying that she's going to hear something's "come up" at the last minute. She doesn't believe Henry would bail on her. He's not that type of person. Still, you never know.

As much as she didn't think he would come, she thought about what would happen if he said he would. Of course, she'd have to tell him where she is and wondered if she could trust him with that information. After all, he gave Rocco her unlisted number. The more she thought about it, though, she had to agree that Henry was right when he said

Rocco could have called her home phone or just walked up to her at school. He was also right when he reminded her that she was the one who told him her enjoyment of sex was part of who she is and that she enjoyed giving blowjobs, because of the power she felt it gave her over boys, which is why he didn't think twice about telling Rocco what he did. It wasn't Henry's fault she got involved with Rocco, but her own. She explained to Henry what happened with him and asked that he not tell anyone where she is and he said he understood and wouldn't and she believes and trusts him. Loving him the way she does, she can't do otherwise.

She's also trying not to get her hopes up that Henry's feelings for her have changed. She knows they haven't. She can hear it in his voice. Still, she can't help hoping.

She leans back against the wall, glances down at the book in her hand and thinks about her experience with it so far.

She reread the end of chapter two, to reacquaint herself with the story, and had the same feeling she did when she read it at Valerie's. She felt as disappointed as Sal, the narrator, about how badly he bungled his first attempt to travel west, following that "one long red line" on the roadmap called Route 6 that led from Cape Cod to Ely, Nevada. Sal hitched rides north to the Bear Mountain Bridge, where he got caught in a downpour and met a couple who pulled into a filling station there. The man told him, "There's no traffic passes through 6. If you want to go to Chicago, you'd do better going across the Holland Tunnel in New York and head for Pittsburgh." The couple gave Sal a ride to Newburgh, where he stayed overnight and took a bus filled with chattering schoolteachers, who'd been visiting Bear Mountain, back to New York the next day.

She knew the book was going to be filled with destinations and reminds herself that it isn't going to be about them, but about Sal's and his friends' adventures, traveling to them and staying in them for a time, before traveling on. Still, she can't help feeling sad, as she did the first time she read about Sal's misadventure, trying to take Route 6 west, that the city where she's spent her entire life so far received only two mentions, one when Sal accepted the ride from the couple and the other when he arrived and observed, "In Newburgh it had stopped raining." She's pretty sure those will be the *only* mentions it will receive.

She remembers taking the bus with Valerie down to New York, watching the houses pass by, wondering who lives in them and what life is like for them, thinking that it's too much to contemplate and that's the way it is on a grand scale with cities, when you're just passing through. She smiles when she considers Sal's mention of the rain having stopped in Newburgh another way. It *has* stopped—raining *piss* on her head. She's free of Rocco and sober and Henry will be here tomorrow, or so she hopes.

"Good evening, girls," Sister Francis Xavier says with a nod as she walks down the line of waiting girls, her black habit flowing and the silver crucifix on the black beaded rosary hanging from her belt swing.

Colleen holds the book at her side, hiding the cover. "Good evening, Mother Superior," she murmurs respectfully, along with the others. She watches her sweep past and walk down the hall and remembers their meeting in her office when she first arrived at Our Lady of Mercy.

Sister was polite as she welcomed her and described what life at the school is like and firm about what would be expected of her. Colleen should fit in and make friends, study hard and obey the rules. Sister said she could see from Colleen's transcript that she's a good student and that her grades suffered a bit as a result of her "problem," but that now that she's here, she'd soon be back in form. Sister noted that Colleen was several chapters behind in her Latin studies, which was to be expected, coming from a public school, but said she was sure that if she applied herself, she'd soon catch up with her class. Sister told her that, while there is "counseling" for students with "problems," her door is always open and she's always available to talk, as her schedule permits. The school's approach to dealing with addiction, she said, is primarily to make it impossible to procure alcohol or any illegal substance or unprescribed drug.

Colleen knew exactly what Sister meant. As she saw when she arrived, Our Lady of Mercy is located on the outskirts of Purchase and the cluster of large, gothic brick buildings sits in the middle of an expanse of land surrounded by a high fence and the only road in and out is gated and attended. The girls are allowed to go into Purchase each Saturday, to shop or just walk around. They travel in groups by bus and each group is chaperoned by a Sister. To her thinking, it's not so much a school as a reform school for girls disguised as one. She's okay with it, though. This is where she wants to be, far from Rocco and her bad reputation in Newburgh and, for all intents and purposes, cut off from the outside world, most importantly, from alcohol.

At last, it's her turn. She picks up the sweat-covered receiver drops coins into the slot, dials Henry's number, turns her back to the waiting girls, leans against the wall and holds the receiver to her ear, listening to the rings.

"Hello?" she hears Henry's mom say. "Hi, Missus Chiaromonte. It's Colleen. May I speak with Henry?"

"Hi, Colleen!" she hears her says brightly. "How are you? I haven't seen you in ages! How's your new school?"

That's Henry's mom, always so interested in her and how she's doing. "Fine and thanks for asking. I'm still adjusting."

"Well, that's only natural. You will. I know what it's like, having to get used to new surroundings."

That's Henry's mom, always so encouraging and supportive. It's a wonder to her how she can always be so positive and upbeat and especially having lost her husband recently. Henry's mom is such a strong independent woman and Colleen has always admired and respected her and never more so than now.

She'd talked with his mom about her about her feelings for Henry the last time they saw each other, at Christmastime. Henry called and asked her if she'd like to come over for some "Christmas cheer," as if he had to ask, and she arrived to find his mom home alone and Henry still out doing an errand. She and his mom talked while they waited for him to return, sitting at the dining room table, smoking and enjoying a glass of red wine. His mom listened patiently and sympathetically as she described her plight and when she was finished, his mom said, "Well, I understand the way you feel, honey, but that's Henry. He's a lone wolf." It was the first time Colleen heard the expression "lone wolf," and she thought it described Henry perfectly. She also agreed with his mom when she said that she didn't think it was something Henry had chosen to be but, rather, that it was in his nature to be the way he is. His mom is so wise. How wonderful it would be to have her as a mother-in-law, to always have her there to confide in and counsel her. The girl that does will be very fortunate, but as much as she wishes and hopes it will be her, she knows it won't. She just knows it.

"Nice talking with you, dear," Henry's mom says. "You take care. I'll get Henry."

"Thanks, I will," Colleen says. As nice as Henry's mom is to her, she knows she's the same way with all of Henry's female friends. Still, having shared with her the way she feels about Henry, she fancies she occupies a special place in her heart. It's nice to think so, anyway.

"Hi," she hears Henry say and smiles.

"Hi," she says. "So, all set for tomorrow?" she asks and closes her eyes and holds her breath.

"All set," Henry says. "Okay if I arrive around five?"

She exhales and beams. "Yeah, that's fine! The dance isn't until seven. That'll give us time to catch up and I can show you around."

"Sounds great. Looking forward to it. See you tomorrow."

"Yeah, so am I!" she says excitedly. "Good night!"

"Good night."

She hears the click on his end, puts the receiver back in the cradle, turns and sees the nervous and worried expressions of the girls, waiting their turn. She feels for them. Well, she's all set and that's all that matters. "Good luck," she says cheerily and hears several girls say worriedly, "Yeah, thanks," as she walks down the hall toward her room.

She arrives outside the open doorway and hears the loud pop of Stephanie's gum, coming from inside. Colleen rolls her eyes and smiles and shakes her head. The hardest thing to get used to when she first arrived at Our Lady of Mercy was her roommate and what she considered at the time her annoying habits. In addition to Stephanie's constant gum chewing and popping, she spends hours sitting on her bed, filing and painting her fingernails and toenails, or sitting at her desk, gazing at herself in her travel mirror, brushing her shoulder-length brunette hair, or tweezing her eyebrows and the hair on her upper lip, or rubbing crèmes on her face.

Colleen couldn't figure out why Stephanie was so preoccupied with her appearance. She's a pretty girl, Greek American, with a high forehead, aquiline nose, sculpted cheekbones and sharp chin. Colleen learned later from Stephanie that her preoccupation is the result of her parents having told her, when she reached puberty and began developing pronounced facial hair, that she wasn't a "natural beauty," as some girls are, and that if she wanted to look attractive and be noticed by boys, she'd need to improve on the looks God gave her. Apparently, they kept nagging her about her appearance as the years went by. Colleen's since learned a lot more about Stephanie's parents and it's a wonder she has anything to do with them.

She enters the room and isn't surprised to find Stephanie in her bathrobe, with her hair in curlers, sitting on her bed with a leg up, painting her toenails. Stephanie pops her gum and looks up at her and raises her eyebrows, holding the brush poised above the toenail she's painting.

"He's coming, right?" Stephanie asks.

"Yeah," Colleen says, walks to her bed and sits on it.

Stephanie nods. "Good," she says, pops her gum, looks down at her toenail and continues painting it. "Can't wait to meet him."

Colleen smiles and shakes her head again. How wrong we can be about people sometimes. Her understanding and estimation of Stephanie and feelings for her have changed completely since they first met.

Her first impression of Stephanie was that she was a pampered princess and Colleen soon learned that the other girls viewed her the same way, and also that Stephanie kept to herself and didn't say much and wasn't very close with her former roommate, who transferred to another school, not because of Stephanie, but because her roommate's family moved and wanted her closer to them. Sister Francis Xavier informed Colleen, during their meeting, that Stephanie's roommate's departure was the reason she was here, because it opened up a spot in the dorm. Having only spent a week or so with Stephanie, she thought that it was just her bad luck that it had to be Stephanie's roommate who left.

Maybe it was because she'd begun feeling more of her old self-confidence and exuding more of her old air of superiority that, as the days passed, Stephanie began looking at her differently and answering more than "Yeah" or "Sure" or "Okay" when she asked a question. That led to their actually talking about things, albeit briefly, and one evening, when they were sitting on their beds in their pajamas, Stephanie opened up and told her story and it changed everything between them.

Stephanie's from Westchester and her dad owns a chain of furniture stores. He's done very well for himself. According to her, he's a millionaire many times over and they live in a mansion. Her dad belongs to an exclusive country club and spends all his free time there, playing golf and drinking with his friends. Her mom loves to travel, and her dad sends her and her best friend, who's been her best friend since they were kids growing up together in Scarsdale, on expensive trips several times a year to wherever they want to go. According to Stephanie, he does this just to get her mom out of the house for extended periods of time.

Stephanie's their only child and she's been indulged all her life. Everything she's ever wanted she's gotten, except for two things and not wanting to attend Our Lady of Mercy is one of them.

She said the reason she's here is to keep her away from her boyfriend, Eddie. As Colleen listened to Stephanie describe Eddie and their feelings for each other and what happened between them that caused her parents to send her to boarding school, she was reminded of every story she's ever heard about star-crossed lovers.

Eddie also lives in Westchester and he and Stephanie have been sweethearts since elementary school. His family is middle class. His dad's an accountant and his mom's a housewife and with six kids in the house, her work is never-ending, and the family just gets by on what his dad earns. They're lucky if they're able to vacation once a year and, when they are, they usually go to the Jersey shore for a week.

As good as Stephanie had it at home, living in the lap of luxury, she felt much closer to Eddie's family than her own. Her parents have never shown her much love and affection and they don't love each other at all, at least, they don't act like they do, and she wonders if they ever really did. They've slept in separate bedrooms as long as she can remember and it's an open secret that her dad's having an affair with his secretary that's been going on for years. Her mom never says a word about it. She's perfectly content to look the other way and enjoy living a selfish and self-indulgent life.

Stephanie spent as much time at Eddie's as she could; doing homework together, hers from the local private school she was attending and his from public school; talking with his mom as she helped her with housework.

Eddie's on the fence about whether he wants to attend college after high school or enlist in the Army or Navy and have the government pay for college, either of which would be fine with her. What she wants is to get married, settle down and have kids and be like his parents, who love each other dearly and are always very affectionate with each other.

Of course, her parents looked down their noses at Eddie and his family and wanted her to have nothing to do with him. They couldn't prevent her from seeing him and spending time with him but tried their best to discourage her from doing so. Her dad even changed the terms of her inheritance, which she'll receive when she marries, making receipt of it contingent on his approval of her spouse. It was cruel and heartless of him, but she doesn't care. Her parents might not know what love is, but she and Eddie do, and *true* love is what they feel for each other.

Then came the heartbreaking part of the story. As careful as Stephanie thought she was being with contraception, she got pregnant. She felt awful about having messed up and was reluctant to tell Eddie, but, of course, had to and when she did, he was surprised but smiled and hugged her and said he was the happiest man in the world, and they'd just get married sooner. She knew that's what he'd say and felt relieved and happy and wanted more than anything to get married and have the baby. As it happened, that's the second thing in life she wanted, but didn't get.

Her parents were anything but happy about the news. Her dad told her in no uncertain terms that she was going to have an abortion and reminded her that she was a minor and didn't have any say in the matter. His doctor would handle all the arrangements, and she'd get the best medical treatment money could buy.

She told Eddie what her parents had planned and said she was ready to pack up and leave, if that's what he wanted to do, but he said they were in no position to do that and, of course, she knew he was right. He said that, as sad as it was, the best thing to do would be to have the abortion and that once she was of age and they got married, they'd have all the kids they wanted.

So, her dad took her to a posh clinic and she had the abortion. She knows he paid through the nose for it, but he sure didn't get his money's worth. After the procedure, she lay in her bed in her private room, curled up in the fetal position, just as her baby had been when it was sucked out of her, and cried uncontrollably. After a time, her doctor came into her room and pulled a chair up beside her bed and sat in it and began by saying that he was very sorry to have to tell her this but, unfortunately, there had been "complications" during the procedure and, as a result, she would no longer be able to conceive. That news devastated her. Until then, she'd been resentful of her parents meddling in her life, but now their intrusiveness had damaged her irreversibly and changed her life forever and she hated them. She was severely depressed and stayed home from school and slowly recuperated. When she felt well enough to get out of bed and bathe and dress herself, her parents packed her off to Our Lady of Mercy.

When Stephanie finished her story, they sat on their beds, gazing tearfully at each other. Colleen got up and walked over and sat beside her, put her arms around her and hugged her and Stephanie hugged her back and pressed her cheek against Colleen's chest. Colleen heard her sniffing and then sobbing and felt her begin shaking. She held her tight and stroked her hair until she cried herself out and was calm again. When she was, she straightened up and gazed at Colleen and Colleen gazed back. Finally, Stephanie smiled a little smile and wiped the tears from her eyes and said it was the first time she'd cried since the abortion and Colleen hugged her again and Stephanie hugged her back and they stayed in each other's arms a long time.

From that moment on, there's been a strong bond between them and Colleen has shared everything with Stephanie, about her bad reputation and hopeless love for Henry and disastrous relationship with Rocco. Colleen loves her like a sister and knows Stephanie feels the same way about her.

Colleen studies her: hunched over, carefully painting her toenail, her jaw in constant motion, like a cow's, chewing cud. As close as they are now, Stephanie's gum popping still drives her crazy. She'll never get used to it and laughs when Stephanie pops her gum again, more loudly than usual. Stephanie looks up at her and raises her eyebrows and holds the brush poised above her toe.

"What?" Stephanie asks.

"You," she says, shaking her head. "You're too much."

"Huh," Stephanie says, looking puzzled. "Eddie's always telling me that and now you."

She grins. "We have our reasons."

"I guess," Stephanie says, pops her gum again and returns to painting her toenail.

Colleen looks at her tenderly. The girl with the "problem" in the bathroom at the Village Gate comes to mind, as she did when Colleen first heard Stephanie's story. She wonders again what happened to her. She'll never forget her and will always wish her well. It's funny how people become a part of our lives, sometimes complete strangers and without their ever knowing it and sometimes people who put us off at first, until we get to know them better. That's the way she feels about Stephanie and knows Stephanie feels the same way about her. They haven't said as much to each other and don't have to, but having begun their relationship with so much distance between them, and then unburdened themselves to each other and accepted each other completely and unconditionally, they both know theirs is a very special friendship and the bond between them is extremely strong. Colleen knows their friendship will last forever. She can feel it.

Stephanie glances up at her and Colleen realizes how sappy her expression must look. It certainly feels that way. Stephanie raises her eyebrows and holds the brush poised above her toenail.

"What?" Stephanie asks.

"You. You're too much," she says, smiling and shaking her head. Stephanie looks at her a moment longer with that puzzled expression of hers.

"Whatever," she says with a shrug, pops her gum, looks down and returns to carefully applying polish to her toenail.

He was so well-behaved and what a pleasant change he was from all the other boys she'd dated. The way he treated her at the drive-in and at Phil and Neal

* * *

Colleen and Stephanie sit side by side in the crowd of girls on the steps outside the Administration Building, waiting for Henry and Eddie to arrive, smoking and watching the cars on the road in front of the school slow and come through the gate and be directed by the security guard and his assistant, both hired for the event, to parking spaces at the end of the several rows that have formed on the front lawn. The rows remind Colleen of her first date with Henry at the Middle Hope Drive-In, to see *Dr. Strangelove,* and she remembers it fondly.

He was so well-behaved and what a pleasant change he was from all the other boys she'd dated. The way he treated her at the drive-in and at Phil and Neal afterward, so respectfully, made her want to give herself to him all the more, and the way he treated her in Moira's basement, so gently and tenderly and lovingly, opened her eyes to the way she viewed boys and how she was treating them, and she wanted nothing more to do with them after that, but only to be with Henry.

She tells herself again that she was wrong to want to blame Henry for telling Rocco what he did and reminds herself again that she has no one to blame but herself for getting involved with Rocco. She's come to understand that what she really wanted to blame Henry for is not feeling the same way about her that she does about him. How silly, really, and immature, when she thinks about it. She has so much to be thankful to Henry for. He's been such a good friend and the only boy who's always been open and honest with her. If anything, Henry should be the one blaming her for not wanting what's best for him and he'd have every right to.

Will she ever stop hoping that he'll have a change of heart? There was a time when she didn't think so, but she's changed. Her experiences with alcohol addiction and Rocco laid her low, so low it frightened her to the point of truly wanting to change and regain control of her life, and frightened enough so that she was able to find the courage and strength to do it and rid herself of both. She grew as a person in the process. Her feelings about Henry have changed, from wanting him all to herself to wanting him always to be a part of her life. It's a subtle change, but to her it feels profound. It's a change she welcomes, but also one she knows is going to take some getting used to and she tells herself that if her feeling of possessiveness rears its ugly head during the evening, she'll just do her best to beat it back down. What more can she do? You can't help the way you feel.

One by one the boys emerge from their cars and their girlfriends stand and bounce up and down excitedly on the balls of their feet, clapping like gleeful kids, then make their way down the steps through the crowd of waiting girls. They run up to their boyfriends, throw their arms around them and kiss and then lead their boyfriends by the hand to some remote spot on the grounds, to spend time together alone, before having to get ready for the dance. It's a sweet scene and the public display of affection between the girls and boys stands in stark contrast in Colleen's mind to the day-to-day, cloistered all-girls life at the school. It's been so long since she's felt Henry's arms around her and hers around him. Being in Rocco's arms the few times she was felt nothing like being in Henry's. She glances at her wristwatch. Henry should be here any time now.

"Eddie's here!" Stephanie says gleefully, clapping her hands and leaping to her feet.

Colleen sees a low-slung black sedan with rear fender skirts, making its way slowly along the road in front of the school. It's old but looks brand new. "What kind of car is that? I've seen them before."

"Hudson Hornet," Stephanie says proudly. "It's a '53. It was a real piece of junk when Eddie's uncle gave it to him. The backseat is *really* big and comfy."

Colleen looks up at Stephanie and can tell by her smile and the dreamy way she said this that she and Eddie have spent a lot of time on it and not sitting and chatting. She smiles. "I bet it is."

"Come on," Stephanie says, waving her up. "I'll introduce you."

Colleen stands and sees Henry's mom's blue Chevy Impala station wagon coming along the road. "Perfect timing!" she says happily. "Henry's here!"

She can't take her eye off Henry as they stroll hand in hand across the lawn, toward a far corner of grounds, by the fence. Being in his arms and kissing him when he arrived felt every bit as wonderful as she knew it would and she's still having a hard time believing he's actually here.

"They're nice," Henry says.

"Yeah. I didn't like Stephanie at first, but I got to know her. She's been through a lot." Henry looks at her and smiles.

"Your life hasn't exactly been a bed of roses lately."

She shrugs. "I'm rid of him and I'm sober. That's all that matters."

They find a spot and sit side by side on the grass. She takes out a cigarette and so does Henry and he lights them both and they smoke and enjoy the warmth of the sun on their faces. She lets a few long moments pass and then places a hand on Henry's and looks at him. "I really appreciate your coming. I didn't think you would." Henry looks at her and raises his eyebrows.

"Why wouldn't I?"

"Because of what happened with my father, and the way I feel about you. I know it makes you uncomfortable." He shakes his head and looks at her sadly, as if to say, "What am I going to do with you," and her eyes go from his eyes to his lips. She watches them coming closer and closes her eyes and feels them pressing against hers and it's one of his sweet tender kisses that she loves. As lovely as Byron's "pillow" kisses are, they're not nearly as heartfelt as Henry's and she's going to miss them dearly.

She knows what the future holds in store. He's been accepted at Emerson College in Boston, where he'll begin studying in the fall. He plans to major in creative writing and stay in Boston during the summers and work. He'll meet plenty of girls and undoubtedly enjoy being with them and won't miss her in the least. Maybe he'll think about her now and then and maybe they'll see each other when he comes home to visit his mom. She hopes so, anyway. She draws back her head and searches his eyes and sighs. She knows she can search them forever but will never see what she's hoping to—a change of heart.

* * *

Colleen sits beside Henry at the table in the gym and gazes at him as he chats with Stephanie and Eddie. As he always does with people he's only just met, he quickly made them feel like they're the best of friends and they opened up to him and are telling him their story and Henry's listening raptly, as he always does, every now and then making an observation or asking a disarming question in that charming way of his that encourages them to share more about themselves. It's a talent of his and she can easily imagine him being a psychiatrist or a politician but knows that studying creative writing is exactly what he should do. Writing is his true love. He's fascinated by people and enjoys getting to know them and loves hearing their stories. She imagines every word that Stephanie and Eddie are saying to him is being recorded in his mind and she's sure that someday he'll remember and reflect on what they've shared with him and that it will appear, in some way, shape or form, in one of his stories.

This is what she loves most about him, his interest in people, in everything, really, his intellectual curiosity and imagination and ability to articulate his thoughts in a way that she always finds interesting. Ever since they first met, she's imagined how wonderful life with Henry would be. She knows it isn't going to happen, and it just isn't fair because he's ruined her for all other boys and men too, and that it only remains for her to find that out.

Henry's handsome in his tux. Eddie is too, but he looks a bit uncomfortable and stiff in his, as most of the boys at the dance do. Not Henry. He looks perfectly at ease in his and his movements are as languid as ever, when he puts his cigarette to his lips and takes it away or gesticulates when he speaks.

She sees Stephanie glance at her every now and then with a concerned expression, which is understandable. Colleen isn't really participating much in the conversation, and she knows Stephanie knows that while she's happy to be sitting here with Henry, she's also profoundly sad and now that Stephanie's met him and seen him in action, Colleen also knows that Stephanie understands perfectly well why.

The four of them take their turn to have their pictures taken, standing in front of the white trellis decorated with multi-color paper flowers, first Stephanie and Eddie with an arm around each other's waist, smiling at the camera, and then Colleen and Henry, and then the four of them together, with Colleen and Stephanie in the middle and Henry and Eddie flanking them. Colleen wishes these photographs really could stop time, freeze the moment, keep her and Henry together like this forever, but she knows they can't and that whenever she looks at the photographs in the future, she'll see her big smile and happy expression and remember that her heart was breaking because the dance was almost over and Henry would soon have to leave, and that what she was thinking, as she smiled at the camera, was that when he leaves, her foolish dream of being with him forever will be over.

They make their way slowly out of the gym with the rest of the couples, all walking hand in hand and all looking a bit sad that their time together is coming to an end, the girls more than the boys, Colleen notices, which is understandable. The boys will get in their cars and return to normal life, where they're free to come and go as they please and do whatever they please, but it will be back to regulated and monitored cloistered life for the girls.

She glances at Henry. He doesn't look happy to be leaving, but doesn't look sad either, which is also understandable and not surprising. She isn't the only girl in his life, and she knows that while he enjoyed being here with her, he was really doing her a favor by coming. She's not concerned or worried about the girls he'll be seeing in Boston. There's only one girl she's concerned or worried about—Sarah. She knows, without having to ask, that he's kept in touch with her and is going to see her during the summer. She can only imagine what sex between those two is like and it hurts to think about it. She knows he'd tell her about it, if she asked, but she isn't going to. Hearing about it would just be too painful.

They arrive at Henry's car and stand beside it. She wants nothing more than to get in the back of the car with him, but they can't. The rule is that the girls can hug and kiss their boyfriends good-bye, but it's to be done outside the vehicles and the security guard and his assistant are enforcing it by patrolling the rows of cars with flashlights in hand. She watches the assistant walk past with the beam of his flashlight trained on the lawn in front of him and turns to face Henry. She sighs and puts her arms around his waist and presses the side of her face against his shoulder and feels him put his arms around her. She can't imagine letting him go with just a good-bye kiss.

Okay, so they can't get in the car. She lifts her head and looks around at the other couples, standing in the dark by their cars, and sees they're all engrossed in hugging and kissing and petting. She looks in Henry's eyes and sees by the way he's looking at her, with his eyebrows slightly raised and smiling that bemused smile of his that asks, "Really?" that he knows what she has in mind.

She brings her lips to his and tightens her hold on him and turns him so that her back is to the car and leans against it and plants her feet wide. She thrills as she feels his hand on her breast and moves her hand to the bulge in his pants and gives it a squeeze and feels him pressing against her hand. Good.

She gathers up her dress in front and takes his hand and places it between her legs and unzips his pants and places her hand on his briefs and feels his erection. Good.

She pulls down his briefs and takes out him out and pulls him toward her and he lowers himself slightly. She lets go of him and pulls her underpants aside and he enters her and begins slowly pumping inside her. Good.

Her mouth is by his ear, and she gasps and whispers, "Don't worry, it's okay."

She bites her lip and clasps her hands at the back of his neck, rocking back her hips and standing on tiptoes, enjoying the feeling of him slowly pumping inside her. It might not be the last time they'll ever make love, but that's what it feels like and she wants to savor every moment of it.

"I've missed this," she whispers, "missed it so much, so, so much." This is the way she wants to be made love to for the rest of her life and the thought that it's not going to happen makes the moment bittersweet. She bites her lip again and meets his strokes and the movement of their bodies and their timing seem perfectly matched to her, as they always do when they make love. They're like dancers who know each other's every move and anticipate them. God, how she loves making love with him and how she's going to miss it!

She feels him quicken his pace and she quickens hers, meeting his strokes perfectly. Are any of the other girls he knows as good a partner as she is? Is Sarah? Maybe, but none of them appreciates him as much as she does, that's for sure. She tightens her grip on his neck and feels him thrusting harder. "Come," she whispers urgently in his ear, "please come, come inside me." She hears him breathing hard and feels his body jerk as he comes inside her. She presses against him, feeling grateful for his gift and wishing this perfect moment could last forever, but it ends and he withdraws and steps back and arranges himself and she does the same.

She sees the assistant glance at them as he heads back between the now thinning rows of cars. Did he see anything? She hopes not, but if he did, she can't do anything about it now. She looks back at Henry.

"Thanks for coming," she says. He smiles and steps forward, gives her a kiss and draws back his head and looks in her eyes.

"I had fun," he says. "I enjoyed meeting Stephanie and Eddie."

"Yeah, I know they enjoyed meeting you too. See you this summer?" she asks hopefully. Henry opens the door and gets in, shuts it, rolls down the window and looks up at her and smiles.

"Sure," he says, "I'd like that."

He starts the car and she grips the door and leans down so her eyes are level with his. "You know how I feel about you and what I want," she says. "I can't help the way I feel, but I want you to know that I know I can't have you and I'm okay with it. I just want you in my life, Henry, always." They hold each other's gaze a long moment and his expression of surprise at her seriousness and frankness changes to one of admiration and he smiles.

"Love you," he finally says.

"You know I love you," she says and thinks hopelessly. He leans forward and she gives him a last lingering kiss, then steps back, crosses her arms and stands looking down at him, trying not to let her sadness show, the night air feeling chill against her bare skin now. "Drive carefully."

"Thanks. I will. Take care."

She watches him back out and waves when he stops and changes gear and he waves back out the window and slowly drives off toward the gate. She knew the evening had to end and they did make love, which felt wonderful, as usual, but as she watches him drive slowly through the gate and pull onto the road and turn and drive off, accelerating, she feels her sadness settling on her like a heavy weight and when the car's taillights disappear, she turns and walks slowly across the lawn toward the dorm with her head bowed and her arms crossed, rubbing her bare arms with her hands.

"Colleen!" she hears Stephanie call. She stops and turns and sees Stephanie walking quickly toward her. When she reaches her, Colleen turns and they walk side by side toward the dorm, both with their arms folded and their heads bowed.

"He's really nice," Stephanie says.

"Yeah, so's Eddie." They walk in silence a few moments and Colleen glances at Stephanie and sees her looking at her sympathetically.

"You never know about people," Stephanie says. "He might come around. You just have to wait and see," she says and looks down again.

Colleen's appreciative of Stephanie's words of encouragement, but they don't lift her spirits in the least. If anything, they make the sadness feel heavier and the night air seem colder because she knows Stephanie knows as well as she does that it's not going to happen with Henry. She looks at Stephanie and thinks about how deeply she and Eddie are in love and how much the two of them are looking forward to their life together. Yes, Stephanie suffered and what her parents did to her was unforgivable, but Eddie was there for her and will always be. Stephanie notices her looking and looks up at her.

"What?" Stephanie asks.

"You're one lucky girl." Stephanie nods and looks down again.

"I know."

CHAPTER 13

Byron's Family

It's been a journey filled with interruptions and long periods of setting the book aside, but finally Colleen arrives at the end of *On the Road* and stares down at the last five words: "…I think of Dean Moriarity."

It's a powerful ending, given everything that's happened between Sal and Dean in the book, and she has mixed feelings about it.

It's taken her so long to read the book that when she neared the end, she deliberately slowed her pace to savor the car trip to Mexico City, reading wide-eyed about Sal and Dean and Stan, arriving in Gregorio and meeting Victor, who lived there, and buying marijuana from him.

And then Victor rolling a cigar-size joint for them and the three of them smoking it and getting unbelievably high, while Victor's brothers stood around the car and studied them with amusement.

And then Victor taking Sal and Dean and Stan to the local whorehouse, and the three of them dancing the mambo with the prostitutes as the townspeople watched from the windows, dancing and dancing and now and then taking the girls to the little rooms in back to have sex with them, and then change girls and dance with them and take them to the rooms again.

And then Sal and Dean and Stan's encounters with the natives in the towns and on the road to Mexico City and finally arriving there and finding it to be the "great and final wild uninhibited Fellahin-childlike city that we knew we would find at the end of the road."

And then Dean abandoning Sal there, when Sal was sick, and Sal returning to New York City and meeting Laura, the "girl with the pure and innocent dear eyes" that he'd always searched for and for so long and finally found by accident.

And then Dean, traveling across the country on boxcars from San Francisco to New York City to marry Inez, his third wife, having secured a divorce in Mexico City from Camille, his second wife, but also to see Sal and his "sweet girl."

And then Sal and Laura sitting in the back of Sal's friend Remi's Cadillac, about to be driven with Remi and his girl by Remi's bookie to a Duke Ellington concert at the Metropolitan Opera, and Dean standing there beside the car with his suitcase, wearing an overcoat against the cold winter evening, asking Sal if he could get a ride to Fortieth Street and Remi saying no because he liked Sal, but not any of his friends.

And then Sal, waving at Dean as they pulled away and seeing him for the last time walk around the corner at Seventh Avenue, headed to Penn Station to catch the train and begin the long journey back to San Francisco.

She stares out the window of the bus at the New England landscape, gliding by as she heads to Woods Hole and the ferry to Martha's Vineyard, and then looks back down at the last paragraph and now she wants to re-read it, slowly, not only because she's reluctant to be done with the book, but also because she's curious to see if the paragraph is grammatically correct, which she's not sure it is, as she's not sure so much of Kerouac's prose is, being so unlike anything she's read before:

> "So in America when the sun goes down and I sit on the old broken-down river pier watching the long, long skies over New Jersey and sense all that raw land that rolls in one unbelievable huge bulge over to the West Coast, and all that road going, and all the people dreaming in the immensity of it, and in Iowa I know by now the children must be crying in the land where they let the children cry, and tonight

the stars'll be out, and don't you know that God is Pooh Bear? the evening star must be drooping and shedding her sparkler dims on the prairie, which is just before the coming of complete night that blesses the earth, darkens all the rivers, cups the peaks and folds the final shore in, and nobody, nobody knows what's going to happen to anybody besides the forlorn rags of growing old, I think of Dean Moriarty, I even think of Old Dean Moriarty the father we never found, I think of Dean Moriarty."

She closes the book and puts it on her lap, clasps her hands on it and stares out the window again. What is it about Dean, a self-centered ex reform school kid who puts his own interests above everyone else's and mistreats women and takes advantage of his friends and especially Sal, that Sal finds so endearing? Certainly, Dean is like a force of nature and had a profound effect on Sal, but does Sal think of him fondly? She imagines he does, but also sadly. Her sense is that by the end of the story, Dean is a changed man, bowed by life and resigned to never truly connecting with anyone. As strong as Dean's desire was to experience life to the fullest and as frenzied as his pursuit of new experiences was, he was never satisfied, was always restless and always uncomfortable in his own skin. Maybe what was missing in his life was his mother's love, which nothing can replace. Her mother might not have been as affectionate as Colleen would have liked, but her mother does love her and it's deeply felt and appreciated.

She also has the strong feeling that Dean is a real person, that his name isn't Dean Moriarity, but that he's real and that the things that he said and did in the book are based on things that really happened. He just doesn't strike her as the type of character you make up, as Holden Caulfield in *Catcher in the Rye* didn't. She suspects there's a lot of J.D. Salinger in Holden. Dean's neither a hero nor a villain, just an oversized irresponsible kid, if a brainy one, and a hell-raiser and she wonders, if he is real, what his life is like now and what the future holds in store for him, if he's even alive.

As to whether Kerouac's prose is grammatically correct, in the end it doesn't matter. It's as much English as Shakespeare's, only different, just as Miles's music is as much music as Beethoven's, only different. Thinking about Kerouac and Miles now, she's struck again by how similar they are, both artists with distinct and unique voices, giving freeform expression to their thoughts and feelings. It's a time of change in American society and Kerouac and Miles are at the forefront creatively, leading the charge. She wonders if they've ever met and are friends. It seems to her they would be, being kindred spirits of a sort. Even if they haven't met, they certainly know each other's work and she wonders what they think about it. It seems to her they'd like it.

* * *

Colleen stands outside on the deck and gazes at Martha's Vineyard in the distance as it draws nearer. She's relieved and happy to be here, just a short ferry ride from Vineyard Haven, where Byron is waiting for her.

Sister Francis Xavier's prediction that she would soon be back in form proved correct. Having been weaned cold turkey off her craving for alcohol and with a clear head, her grades improved dramatically and at the end of the semester she was once again an honors student. She'd even anaged to catch up with her class in Latin.

She knows she isn't cured of her addiction to alcohol, though, and that she never will be. Once an addict, always an addict. No one told her as much, but she knows it intuitively and can feel it in her bones. All it will take is one drink and she'll fall off the wagon, so the best thing to do is avoid having one. She thinks she's regained the self-respect and strength to do it.

When school ended and she and Stephanie were saying their good-byes, Colleen hugged her and didn't want to let her go. She confided to Stephanie that she viewed the prospect of having to return to Cornwall for the summer with a sense of dread, because it meant being near Rocco, even though he lives miles away on the other side of Newburgh. Being in the same state with him feels too close for her. Stephanie commiserated with her and told her she could always come visit her and stay for as long as she likes. Colleen thanked her and said that she just might take her up on the offer before the summer ends. The good news is that the two of them are going to be roommates again in the fall. Sister Francis Xavier was only too happy to accommodate their request.

She really didn't have an opinion of Sister when she was new at the school, other than that she's a friendly, but direct, person and a strong believer in following the rules. Colleen never did understand why some of the girls badmouthed and mimicked Sister, other than that it's typical behavior for some teenage girls and boys to make fun of their school principal and teachers. Sister is fair and even-handed and took a personal interest in her from the first day she arrived at the school and always stopped when they passed in the hall to ask how things were going and if there's anything she could do for her. Granting her and Stephanie's request to room together next year was only the latest kindness Sister showed her and her respect for Sister grew enormously.

Rocco comes to mind again and she wonders if he's really done with her, if what he did to her that last night together satisfied his desire for revenge for her ending the relationship. She wants to believe it did, but is still fearful of running into him somewhere, so she laid low in Cornwall and didn't go out much, which made for a boring existence, although she did have *On the Road* and a couple of other books she was reading to occupy her time. Still, she could only read for so long each day and had no interest in watching the daytime soaps, which are melodramatic pap.

She did see Henry once. They went to see *You Only Live Twice*, the new James Bond film, at the Middle Hope Drive-In. Henry suggested it, saying that it would be fun, and she said sure. She would have agreed to anything he suggested, just to be with him. For all the action on the screen, though, her mind wasn't on the movie, but on what they would hopefully do afterward. When the movie was over and he suggested they get a bite to eat at Phil & Neal, she said she wasn't really hungry, which was true, and also felt uneasy about going to the restaurant, for fear Rocco would show up. Henry said he understood and that he wasn't all that hungry, either. "Why don't we just go somewhere we can be alone?" she asked and he smiled and said, "Yeah, let's." She stared out the windshield as they rode along 9W back toward Newburgh. She purposefully didn't ask Henry about the other girls she knew he was seeing, particularly about Sarah, but her curiosity got the better of her. "So, what's she like?"

she asked, a little reluctantly, knowing that Henry would give her an honest answer, as he always does about anything she asks him.

"Who?"

She looked at him. "You know who. Sarah." Henry shrugged and glanced at her.

"She's nice. Intelligent and well-read. Very bright."

"I know that. You know what I mean." He glanced at her again.

"You mean sex?"

"Yeah." She watched him as he stared out the windshield at the road ahead and carefully considered his answer, as he always does when the question is important.

"She's self-conscious about her body, which I find surprising. I wouldn't have expected that, given the fact that she's so sensuous."

"I bet you're curing her of that," she said and regretted having said it as soon as she did. She didn't mean to sound bitchy or hurt but could hear a bit of both in her voice. Henry glanced at her again and then looked back at the road. "I'm sorry," she said. "I shouldn't have said that. It's really none of my business."

"No problem."

"As long as we're on the subject of sex, though, can I ask you something?" Henry glanced at her again.

"You can ask me anything. You know that."

"Why do you see me, knowing the way I feel about you? Is it just the sex?" Henry looked at her long enough for her to be concerned that his eyes were off the road that long.

"That's pretty insulting, Colleen. I can't believe you actually believe that."

"No, I don't. I shouldn't have said that, either. I'm sorry. Well, since I've already made an ass of myself, one more question, okay?"

"Sure."

"Do you enjoy sex with anyone else as much as you do with me?" Henry glanced at her and smiled.

"No, I don't." "Why?"

"No one else feels about me the way you do, that's why."

"Are you toying with me, Henry?"

"I can't believe you actually believe that, either."

She finally took her eyes off Henry's face and stared out the windshield. "No, I don't. You know you're driving me crazy, though, don't you? I can't understand why you wouldn't want to have me all to yourself all the time." Out of the corners of her eyes she saw him look at her and shake his head. He should be shaking his head and has every right to, she thought. She'll always be a hopeless case where he's concerned.

It was a typical summer evening in the Hudson Valley—hot and humid, the air thick with mosquitoes. They parked in the dark on a road at the back of a field with the windows up and the car idling with the AC on. They climbed in the back of the station wagon and lay together in each other's arms and made glorious love, as they always do.

Afterward, as they rode toward Cornwall, she stared out the windshield and found herself thinking the unthinkable, that maybe she's addicted to Henry the way she is to alcohol, and it would be better for her not to see him anymore. It seemed crazy to think that, but the more she thought about it the more sense it made. She told him about her upcoming trip to visit Byron and he listened with interest and nodded and said he hoped she has a great time, as she knew he would. Henry's just so damned understanding and reasonable about things, whereas she's hopelessly in love with him and can't help feeling hurt because he sees other girls. Continuing to see him isn't doing her self-esteem any good, that's for sure.

Later, when she was lying in bed and feeling sleep approaching, she considered her relationship with him differently. Maybe he isn't an addiction. Maybe he's an example. Maybe he's in her life to help get her past the idea that loving someone necessarily means wanting or needing to possess him. Henry forces her to examine herself and question her beliefs. He's like a mirror held up to her. She knows he isn't going to change. Maybe she's the one who should.

It seemed today would never arrive and by the time she boarded the bus to Boston early this morning, she felt stir-crazy. She's feeling better now, having put so much distance between her and home, and she's looking forward to enjoying her weeklong stay with Byron and his family.

Byron said they'd just hang out on the island, spend the days taking bike trips, or at the beach, or sailing in the family's Laser, which he said is a lot of fun, and maybe in their bigger boat, a 40-foot Hinckley named *Freedom Bound*. She's never sailed on a boat of any kind, but Bryon assured her he'd teach her to crew and that she'd learn in no time and do just fine.

It felt good talking with him on the phone after such a long time. She enjoyed hearing the sound of his voice again and he seemed genuinely happy about the fact that she was able to come visit and really looking forward to seeing her. There wasn't a hint of the menacing and manipulative Byron she'd experienced during her weekend stay with him at Columbia and she's hoping she doesn't encounter that aspect of his personality during her stay. She's pretty sure she won't because of the circumstances, being with his family, and that he'll be on his best behavior. She'll have the guest room to herself, but she's also pretty sure he'll be tiptoeing into her room at night to spend time with her and hopes he does. She's looking forward to reacquainting herself with that marvelous part of his anatomy.

It's curious to her how she can feel so differently about Byron and Henry. She enjoys sex with them both, but with Byron it's just that, well, sex, and the fact that he has sex with other girls doesn't bother her at all. As she told Valerie, Byron's just for fun. If only she could feel that way about Henry, not the just for fun part—she could never think of him that way—but the part about not feeling hurt because he has sex with other girls. She's thought a lot about it since they were last together and she's sure now that's the lesson she needs to learn from him, that if you truly love someone, then just love them and don't try to change them. She's sure that's it and that it isn't going to be an easy lesson to learn, but that she will, eventually.

The ferry is close enough now that she can make out people standing by the railing at the ferry dock. They're still just specks but she spots a bright red polo and can see that the person wearing it is one of only a few blacks there and she knows it's Byron. Even at this distance she can see that he's leaning on the railing with his arms crossed and has a foot up on the bottom of it.

She wonders what he's thinking as he watches the ferry approach. Can he see her standing here on the deck, watching him? She waves and sees him wave back. Does he truly enjoy humiliating and hurting white women? Is it possible that he uses the pose of the wronged Black man who makes white girls pay for the sins their kind has committed against his just to satisfy himself sexually? She wouldn't be surprised and that seems more likely the case. Well, despite the pose, she considers him a decent person and likes him. He's still young, after all, and has a lot to learn about life, as she does.

She's looking forward to meeting his parents and sister, but especially his dad. Byron says he knows all the leaders of the Civil Rights movement and that while his dad doesn't agree with them all about how they're trying to achieve equality and economic opportunity for blacks, he does respect them for what they're doing. His dad's opinion is that they're all putting their lives on the line by standing up to the White power structure and trying to change the status quo, and that Whites have a lot at stake and will stop at nothing, including murder, to prevent that from happening. Look at what happened to Medgar Evers and the three Freedom Riders, Chaney, Goodman and Schwerner in Mississippi. It doesn't matter if you're Black or White, as Goodman and Schwerner were. If you threaten the White power structure, you do so knowing that you could be killed. Everyone in the Civil Rights movement knows this, especially the leaders, and Byron said the reason his dad has so much respect for Martin Luther King, Jr. is that King used to keep a shotgun in the house and have armed guards to protect him and his family, until Bayard Rustin convinced him that non-violence is a more effective way to combat aggression, which Rustin had learned from Gandhi and his followers in India. Colleen's heard Rustin's name mentioned on TV and read it in the paper but knows little about him. This is the reason she's looking forward to talking with Byron's dad. She senses there's so much he can teach her that she needs to know about the Civil Rights movement to understand it and how she can be most effective in helping to achieve its goals.

* * *

Colleen wades out of the water, walks to the large beach towel, plops down and begins drying her legs off with a bath towel. Just as they were when she left them on the beach to go for a swim and cool off, Byron and Jeffrey are still making small talk, as are Byron's sister Jasmine and Jeffrey's sister Dawna and their friend Harriet. Jeffrey and Dawna are from Washington, D.C., like Byron and Jasmine. Their two families have known each other a long time and they vacation together on Martha's Vineyard each summer, renting the same houses next to each other in Oak Bluffs. Harriet is from Chicago. She met the others vacationing with her family here in Oak Bluffs a few years ago and they've been back every summer since. Jeffrey is Byron's age and attending Howard University. Dawna's seventeen and a junior in high school, just as Colleen and Jasmine are. Harriet's eighteen and a senior in high school. Jeffrey and Dawna's dad is a surgeon and Harriet's dad is a college history professor.

Colleen towels herself dry, puts the towel aside, picks up the sunscreen, squirts some on her palm and begins smoothing it on her legs. With such fair skin, she needs to make sure she's covered with the stuff and applies a new coat to her body each time she returns from a swim. She's sunburned badly in the past and it hurt like hell, so she's diligent about taking care of her skin.

She's midway through her weeklong vacation and, so far, things have gone pretty much the way she thought they would. Just as Byron said they would, they've hung out at the beach and gone for bike rides and sailed in the Laser, which is great fun, although they haven't taken out the bigger boat yet, so she hasn't learned to crew. Byron doesn't need any help sailing the Laser, it being such a small boat, and he's taught her to take the helm, which she enjoys doing.

His parents are nice and made her feel right at home. She talked with Byron's dad a bit at dinner the first night about her desire to practice law and her interest in representing people whose civil rights have been infringed. He seemed impressed and encouraged her to do both. She'd like to talk with him more about the Civil Rights Movement, but didn't want to monopolize the conversation at dinner. She's hoping the opportunity arises before she leaves.

Just as she thought he would, Byron comes to her room each night and they make love. It's an effort to keep quiet and especially when she's climaxing, but she bites her lip and, so far, they haven't brought attention to what's going on in her room each night. If his parents are aware of what is, they don't seem to mind or are willing to tolerate it.

When she and Byron are in bed together, he's as sweet as can be, treating her very gently and only being forceful and rough when she wants him to be. There hasn't been any of the game playing that went on when they were together at Columbia and she's happy about that. It's probably because his parents are in the house and they need to be quiet, but whatever the reason, she's happy he's behaving himself.

The only unpleasant thing about the vacation, so far, is dealing with Jasmine's attitude toward her. Jasmine hasn't come out and said as much, but Colleen can tell she resents her being here and does so because she's White. In fact, Colleen has the feeling Jasmine resents all White people and possibly even hates them.

When Colleen arrived, Jasmine was in her bedroom and didn't bother to come out and meet her. When they finally did meet at the dinner table and Bryon's mom introduced Colleen to her, Jasmine looked at her with that same sullen expression she saw in the photograph on Byron's desk at Columbia, and Jasmine mumbled, "Nice to meet you," and seemed to have a hard time managing to say even that.

Colleen's gone out of her way to avoid Jasmine and tries not to make eye contact with her. She doesn't want a confrontation with her, although she is curious why Jasmine feels the way she does. Colleen broached the subject delicately with Byron the next day, when they were out riding bikes, and he just shrugged and smiled and said, "She's a Black separatist." He shrugged again and added, "And an impressionable kid," and Colleen got the feeling Byron thinks his sister's radicalism is just a phase she's going through.

Colleen squirts more sunscreen on her palm and smooths it on her chest and neck and shoulders. The way Jasmine eyes her body makes her self-conscious and she wishes now that she'd packed her one-piece bathing suit as well as her bikini. She would have worn it, so she wouldn't show so much white skin. Not that she really believes it would have made a difference with Jasmine.

What's puzzling her about Jasmine's attitude toward Whites is that, like Byron, she's living in the lap of luxury, as are Jeffrey and Dawna and Harriet, whose parents are also well-off. Jasmine doesn't have a thing in the world to worry about and, in fact, her parents have done very well for themselves in a White dominated society. Colleen understands why

Jasmine would be angry and bitter about the treatment of Blacks by Whites, as she knows Byron is and suspects the other kids are too, and their parents, but they all seem to be much better able to deal with it than Jasmine, and they treat Colleen with courtesy and respect.

She squirts more sunscreen on her palm and reaches around, twisting her torso to try to apply it to her back. "I'll do that for you, baby," she hears Byron say and he takes the bottle from her. "Thanks," she says as he begins rubbing it on her back. She glances at Jasmine, who's sitting between Dawna and Harriet on their large beach towel, and sees her scowling at her. Colleen quickly looks away and keeps her eyes on the waves rolling in as Byron rubs her back. What is it with that girl? And what's with the white tee shirt with the big black fist on the front, held up in a "Black Power" salute. It's all she ever wears! It's like her uniform!

It occurs to Colleen that since she's been here, she's yet to see Jasmine smile. Jasmine always has that sullen expression on her face or, as she does now, a scowl. Her attitude is in stark contrast to the other kids'. They seem like typical teenagers, happy to be here on vacation and clearly enjoying themselves, and if you didn't know they were Black and heard a recording of their conversations, you'd never know it. Well, you would by the way they emphasize the "Blackness" in their speech now and then, for effect. Still, they talk about the same things that intelligent, well-educated White teenagers from affluent families do. There hasn't been any talk of racial politics or the Civil Rights movement, except for that one time.

The afternoon after Colleen arrived, when she was with Byron and Jasmine and the other kids at the beach for the first time, she asked Byron what the latest was with the situation at Columbia and he filled her in, which led to a brief conversation about it. Everyone took part in the conversation except Jasmine, who held back with that sullen expression until the very end, when she looked directly at Colleen and scowled and said bitterly, "The sooner Blacks are done with Whites, the better." There was an awkward silence afterward and Colleen could tell by the glances she received from Jeffrey and Dawna and Harriet that they were embarrassed by Jasmine's comment. Byron took it in stride and simply looked at his sister and said calmly, but firmly, "Give it a rest." What is it with that girl?

Byron finishes with Colleen's back, wipes his hand on the beach towel and takes a beer from the cooler. That's one thing that's gone very well, so far, on the trip—not falling off the wagon. When Byron's mom asked her at the first dinner if she would care to have a glass of wine with her meal, as everyone else was, she politely declined. She told Byron afterward about her struggle with alcohol, that she doesn't drink anymore and has been sober for months. He was impressed and said he was sorry he'd gotten her so drunk the weekend they were together. She told him there was no reason for him to be sorry, that she loved the taste of cognac and that no one was forcing her to drink it, that she'd done so willingly. "Don't get me wrong," she told him, "I'd like nothing more than to be able to drink, but I can't control it. I'm an alcoholic, like my father, and always will be." Byron nodded and said he understood and that he had a lot of respect for her. She was glad they had the conversation, because his attitude toward her seemed to change after that. He was still very sweet to her, but she could tell he considered her less an inexperienced seventeen-year-old plaything and more a mature self-aware person and an intellectual equal. Since then, their conversations about things have been much more interesting and wide ranging, like the one they had about the relationship between love and marriage, as they strolled hand in hand along the shore at sunset.

Byron said he thought the reason a lot of marriages fail is because people don't understand that love is an emotion and marriage a religious and social institution and legal agreement and the two don't necessarily have anything to do with each other. People fall in love, and they've been taught to associate that with getting married and buying a house and having a family. It doesn't take married couples long to discover the truth of the proverb "Familiarity breeds contempt." They feel betrayed when they discover that what they were taught to believe—that one person can satisfy all their intellectual, emotional and sexual needs—is unrealistic, a fantasy. Some couples make an uneasy and unhappy peace, believing it's better to remain together for the sake of the family, but, increasingly, people are realizing that it's healthier to deal with the situation and try to change it for the better, and if they can't, to divorce. Byron said he understands why monogamy and then marriage came about, as part of the socialization of human beings, to enable them to live together peacefully and productively, but that he can easily see a time when marriage, as we know it, will be a thing of the past and people will come together to have and raise children and then go their separate ways, as they probably did for hundreds of thousands of years.

Colleen found what Byron had to say very interesting and thought provoking. She shared with him her parents' experience in their marriage, which seemed to fit his description to a tee. She also told him about her relationship with Henry and her strong feelings for him, and how she used to feel that because she loved him so deeply, he should naturally want to be with her in an exclusive relationship, but that he doesn't, and she thinks she's learned now that loving someone means just loving him and not trying to change him. She'll never forget the way Byron looked at her as she said this, studying her eyes and smiling slightly.

"That's a valuable lesson to learn, baby," he said. "You're way ahead of the game."

"Do you even want to get married?" she asked. He shrugged and looked out at the horizon.

"I dunno. Other than the tax advantages, I can't see the benefit.

"Don't you want to have kids someday?"

"You don't have to be married to have kids. There are lots of kids whose parents aren't married. The kids don't care. Maybe other folks do, but the kids don't. Anyway, if I do get married, it's going to be to someone who feels the same way I do about it."

"Which is?" He looked at her and fixed his eyes on hers.

"Relationships should be open."

"Wow! So, you want a wife who doesn't mind you seeing other women?" He nodded.

"Just as I wouldn't mind her seeing other men," he said.

"You actually think you'll find someone like that?" He shrugged and looked back out at the horizon.

"Maybe, maybe not. We'll see. Anyway, marriage is a long way off, if it's going to happen at all."

She's thought about that conversation a lot ever since. Could she be with a man who felt the way Byron does? Does she have it within herself to be that strong and self-confident, that unselfish and understanding that it would be perfectly fine with her if her husband saw other woman?

She's not sure. If she'd never met Henry, she knows she couldn't be that person, but now it seems at least within the realm of possibility. It still seems a stretch, though.

On the other hand, look at what happened with her parents. They vowed to love, honor and cherish each other till death parted them and began married life with every intention of being faithful to one another, but her mom had an affair with Sheldon and while Colleen doesn't know what happened between her father and Tiffany, she's pretty sure he was having sex with her and that Tiffany wasn't the only one. Maybe Byron's take on things is better. She's just not sure, but it sure is interesting to think about.

* * *

Colleen stands by the window in the guest bedroom in her bathrobe, drying her hair with a towel as she gazes out the window at another beautiful day. There are only a couple left before she leaves and she's really looking forward to this one because they'll finally be taking the Hinckley out for a sail. The only thing she's not looking forward to is being in such close proximity to Jasmine. The boat is big but not that big.

She hears a sharp rap on the bedroom door, walks to it and opens it to find Jasmine standing there in her bathrobe with her arms crossed, scowling at her. "Hey, what's up?" Colleen asks. Jasmine raises her eyebrows and cocks her head.

"What's up?" she asks. "I'll tell you what's up. You're a pig, that's what's up."

Colleen's not sure if Jasmine is insulting her about her personal hygiene or accusing her of being a "White racist pig, which she knows some radical Blacks call Whites. Whatever the case, she's flabbergasted and stares wide-eyed at Jasmine. "Excuse me?" she asks.

"What kind of people raised you?" Jasmine asks. "Weren't you taught to clean up after yourself in the bathroom?"

"I did," Colleen says angrily. "I always leave the bathroom clean."

"Well," Jasmine huffs, "there's blonde hair in the bathtub drain, so we know whose it is," she says smugly, "don't we?"

"Look, I don't know what you've got against me, but you've treated me like shit ever since I arrived. I tried to be nice to you and when that didn't work, I avoided you. What is it with you, the fact that I'm White? You don't even know me." Colleen's startled when Jasmine pushes her in the chest with the flat of her hand, shoving her backward and nearly sending her to the floor. She regains her balance and Jasmine steps into the room, closes the door and stands glowering at her.

"Oh, I know *all* about you," Jasmine says accusingly. "Just another privileged White chick whose head is filled with racial stereotypes about Blacks, in your case mostly about Black male genitalia. I know *exactly* why you're interested in my brother. He's had dozens of girls like you. He can't go through them fast enough, although why he keeps you hanging around is beyond me."

Colleen can't deny the truth in what Jasmine said. She does have stereotypical ideas about Blacks and she does associate the fact that Byron is well-endowed with his being Black. Still, she's offended. "That's not fair!" she protests.

"What's not fair?" Jasmine snaps.

"What you said about why I like your brother!"

"Oh, right. It's his charming personality you're interested in."

Jasmine takes a step closer and looks menacingly at Colleen, who wonders if things are about to get physical and braces herself.

"*I'll* tell *you* what's not fair," Jasmine says. "The way Blacks in this country have suffered at the hands of Whites. The fact that they're still treated like second-class citizens, that Blacks risk their lives in this country when they make their voices heard in the fight for civil rights. That Whites enjoy *all* the bounty this country has to offer, while Blacks get scraps from the table. The fact that you can come waltzing into our family and have a nice vacation and then be on your merry way back to whatever White racist community you came from. *That's* what's not fair."

Colleen's not surprised by what Jasmine said. It's pretty much the type of thing she expected to hear. Still, the fact that Jasmine assumes she's a racist rankles her. She knows that nothing she can say will change Jasmine's opinion of her, but she can't let the accusation go unchallenged. She unclenches her teeth and takes a deep breath. "I'll be honest with you, she says. My father's a racist and my mom grew up in a racist family and worked hard to rise above it. I give her a lot of credit. Before I met your brother, I had very little experience with Blacks, none, really. Was my head filled with stereotypical ideas about Blacks and Black males? Sure, it was. That's only natural. Ignorance is a void that must be filled by something. I enjoy having sex with your brother, he's a great lover, but that's not all I enjoy about him. He *is* charming and I love that about him. I also love the fact that he's intelligent and articulate and thoughtful, and I enjoy talking with him as much as he does talking with me. I know you don't believe it, but not all Whites are racist and I'm not." Jasmine studies her eyes a moment and Colleen sees a smug smile appear on her face.

"That's the problem with people like you," Jasmine says. "You're racist and don't have the good sense God gave you to see it. You're more dangerous than the Klan. At least they know who they are, but you? You're just a typical privileged White chick who thinks she's so high minded and who'll probably end up in a position of power someday, and when push comes to shove will do what the rest of your kind does—protect your own. You make me sick."

Jasmine lingers long enough for Colleen to get a good look at her disgusted expression and then turns and stomps out of the room, leaving the door open behind her. Colleen stares blankly at the empty doorway. The confrontation has left her shaken and she takes a few deep breaths, trying to calm herself down. As much as she'd hoped she could avoid the type of thing that just happened with Jasmine, she realizes now that it was bound to happen and that Jasmine was just biding her time, until she felt she had a good, if flimsy, excuse—blond hair in the bathtub drain. She probably felt time was running out and had to make her move. What is it with that girl?

She dresses and finds Byron standing in the kitchen, drinking a glass of orange juice.

"Hey, good morning," he says.

"Morning," she says glumly and continues walking through the kitchen toward the front door. "Where're you going?" she hears him ask. She stops at the door and turns. "For a walk on the beach," she says. He places the glass on the counter.

"I'll come with you."

"I need some time alone." He walks toward her, looking concerned. "Hey, what happened? What's wrong?"

"I don't want to talk about it right now. Maybe later." He places a hand on her shoulder and studies her eyes.

"You sure?"

"Yeah," she says, nodding. He lingers on her eyes a moment and then smiles and chucks her under the chin with a finger.

"Cheer up! Whatever it is can't be all that bad."

"Yeah. I'll be back." She turns and opens the door and hears Byron say, "You might run into my dad. He's out beachcombing."

Walking across the sand toward the shore, she sees Dawna and Harriet in their bathing suits, lying next to each other on their stomachs on a beach towel, both with books open in front of them. Dawna glances up and notices her approaching.

"Hey," Dawna says.

"Hey," Colleen says, but doesn't stop to chat. She knows the two girls are looking at each other and then her, walking away, and wondering what's going on with her, but she doesn't care. She's not in the mood to talk with anyone now, with the exception of Byron's dad, if she runs into him, which she hopes she will.

She's been walking for about fifteen minutes and finally spots him in the distance. He's dressed in his usual outfit, khaki shorts and polo shirt, a bright blue one today, and has his canvas bag in his hand. He's walking very slowly toward her in the wet sand with his head down, searching for shells and rocks that look particularly interesting to him, and also beach glass.

He loves beachcombing and does it every morning. He says it gives him an opportunity to be by himself and think about things, or not, and just enjoy the morning air. She thought about asking him if she could accompany him on one of his walks but thought better of it. She didn't want to intrude. She's hoping he won't mind talking with her now and doesn't think he will.

She sees him stop, bend over and pick up something that caught his eye. He inspects it closely, lets it fall back on the sand and straightens up. Whatever it was obviously wasn't all that interesting to him. He's very particular about what he brings back to the house to add to the collection in the rock garden in the backyard.

She's spent enough time with Byron's dad and heard enough of what he has to say about things to know that he's a very intelligent and thoughtful person, very open and welcoming. He strikes her as a person who genuinely likes people, no matter the color of their skin, or social status, or religious or political beliefs. Byron's mom is much the same way, but his dad is even more so. It's baffling to Colleen how Jasmine could have developed into the bigoted hateful person she is toward Whites with parents like them. She's hoping maybe Byron's dad can enlighten her. If anyone can, she thinks, he can. He looks up as she approaches and smiles. "Hi, Mister Sheffield," she says.

"Good morning, Colleen!" he says brightly. "How are you?"

She stops in front of him. "Okay, thanks." She hesitates a moment and adds, "Well, not really," and he looks at her with concern.

"Something wrong?"

She looks down at the wet sand, sparkling in the sunlight. "I had a run in with Jasmine."

"I'm sorry to hear that."

"She said I left hair in the bathtub drain, but I didn't. She made it up."

"I see," he says sympathetically.

She looks up at him, cocks her head and squints her right eye slightly. "Why does she feel the way she does about White people? I don't get it, and especially with parents like you and Missus Sheffield. You're both so open-minded about things." He sighs and looks out at the horizon.

"She didn't always feel the way she does now."

"Did something happen to her?" He looks at her and studies her eyes and she can tell he's giving his answer careful consideration. Finally, he smiles slightly.

"You strike me as an intelligent young woman with a thirst for knowledge and a desire to understand people. That's good. They're admirable qualities. I'll tell you what happened, if you promise me that it will remain between us. Hmm?"

She nods. "I promise."

"Good. Let's talk as we walk back."

They walk slowly, side by side, and Colleen can see by his slightly furrowed brow that what he's about to share with her is an unpleasant and probably still painful memory. Finally, he glances at her, purses his lips and looks down at the wet sand.

"Jasmine had a White boyfriend," he finally says. "They were together for two years. He seemed like a nice enough young man, and I never heard any complaints from her about him, so I assumed everything was fine between them. It was only later that I learned that sex was a real bone of contention between them."

She sees him glance at her and seems uncomfortable with what he's about to say.

"Apparently, he kept pressing her to have intercourse and she kept telling him that she didn't want to, that she felt they were too young. You know as well as I there are plenty of teenagers, some of them young teenagers, who have intercourse. She just wasn't one of them. I knew the way she felt about it and I respected her for it. Apparently, her boyfriend didn't."

He didn't say this in a way that leads Colleen to believe he knows Byron steals into her bedroom each night and they have sex, although she wouldn't be surprised if he does. Anyway, she has a pretty good idea now where this story is going and already the pieces of the puzzle that is Jasmine are falling into place.

"Last winter, she and her boyfriend and a few of their friends went on a ski trip to Vermont. She was really looking forward to it. She'd never been on skis, but her boyfriend, or I should say former boyfriend, is from New England and skis well. She was looking forward to him teaching her. Of course, there was drinking going and, apparently, one evening her boyfriend got really drunk and raped her when they were alone in their bedroom. Apparently, he also called her ugly names while he did, all racial slurs."

"That's awful." He looks at her.

"Yes, it is."

"What happened to him?" He raises his eyebrows.

"Nothing."

After a long pause, he looks down at the wet sand and she can see the anger and frustration in his expression.

"She didn't call the police or call us to tell us what had happened. She waited until she got home. I spoke with the local authorities in Vermont, but already knew they wouldn't do anything. They viewed it as a matter of 'he said, she said' between two minors who'd had too much to drink and let things get out of hand."

"Wow! So much for justice." He looks at her.

"By the way, the fact that they didn't pursue the matter had nothing to do with the fact that she's Black. I didn't mention it to them, because it really had no bearing on the matter from a legal standpoint."

"I understand," she says. He nods and looks down at the wet sand and shrugs.

"Obviously, she was deeply affected by what happened and it changed her attitude entirely toward Whites. She channeled all the anger and bitterness and frustration and resentment she felt toward him into her political thinking, and it radicalized her."

"Yeah, I can see that." He looks at her.

"It's important not to jump to conclusions. You don't have to be raped by your White boyfriend to believe what she does, that the sooner Blacks are done with Whites, the better. There are plenty of Blacks who feel just as she does. The chasm in the Black leadership between those who think as Martin does and those who think as Stokely does is ever-widening."

"Byron told me you know all the Black leaders." He nods and looks down at the wet sand.

"I do. They're all fine people and all putting their lives on the line in the struggle for civil rights. They just happen to disagree about their goals and how to achieve them. While I disagree with some of them, they all have my admiration and respect."

"What would you like to see happen? What do you think will?" He looks at her and smiles warmly, then gazes at the horizon.

"Martin and I used to have long conversations about this when we were at Boston University Law School. We both want to see Blacks afforded the same rights and opportunities that Whites enjoy and envision a time when the color of a person's skin will have no bearing on how he or she is treated in American society or, for that matter, any society. We both agree that we'll probably be dead and gone long before that happens, but that there's no nobler cause to dedicate our lives to than helping to hasten that day's arrival."

She can tell by his expression that he's been enjoying talking about his old friend, but now it's as if he's looking at a dark cloud that's obscuring the sun.

"We try to remain positive and optimistic that our people will reach the Promised Land," he says, "but it's difficult sometimes. Our fear is that before we do, White society will reap the whirlwind because of its mistreatment of Blacks and that Blacks will suffer horribly as a result. We pray it doesn't happen."

His expression softens and he looks at her and smiles.

"So, you seem determined to become involved in civil rights."

"Yeah, I am."

"If you'd like, I'll ask Martin the next time I talk with him if he can put you to good use in his organization, maybe work for him next summer."

She's thrilled and stares at him wide-eyed. "Really? You'd do that?"

"Of course."

"Were you with him when he gave the 'I Have a Dream' speech? I bet you were!" She watches his smile widen until almost all his teeth are showing and he nods forcefully.

"I was!" he says excitedly. "Not on the Memorial steps, but on the mall with the family."

"I'll bet that was *really* something!"

"It was a *glorious* day!"

He looks at her and she can see he's enjoying her expression of amazement and awe.

"I'd be happy to have you intern at my law firm when the time comes. Let's keep in touch."

"Wow! That is *so* kind and generous of you! I can't thank you enough for the offer!"

"My pleasure. I'm only too happy to help bright young people like you get ahead in their careers. Let's head back, shall we? We want to get a good day of sailing in."

They pick up their pace and she beams at him. "You bet!"

* * *

Colleen eyes *Freedom Bound,* moored in the harbor, as she walks toward the beach to say goodbye to Jasmine and Dawna and Harriet. She knows that Jasmine could care less if she says goodbye to her and it was just like her to head to the beach without saying a word to Colleen, knowing that she's leaving today. Well, Colleen's thinking about Jasmine changed because of the conversation with her dad. She continued to give Jasmine a wide berth, though, not wanting another confrontation with her, and decided to wait until the last moment before speaking to her. She's not sure it will do any good, or change Jasmine's thinking about her, but she's determined to give it a try.

What fun sailing was! She had a fantastic time! As it happened, she didn't have to worry about being in close quarters with Jasmine because Jasmine begged off, saying that sailing was a "White bourgeois thing," and she didn't want to waste her time. Colleen must admit: Jasmine is nothing if not consistent in her condemnation of all things "White." Hypocritical, yes, but consistent.

She learned how to crew, all right, dutifully hauling in and letting out the line to the mainsail on her side of the boat and securing it around the cleat each time Byron's dad tacked. She received high marks from him for being such a quick learner. It was a little scary at first when he would put the boat on the edge of the wind and it would heel over and she would rise up and have to hold on tight to the rail, staring almost straight down at the water. It was scary but also exhilarating. She nearly got hit in the head a few times by the boom, when Byron's dad tacked and it swung from one side of the boat to the other, even though his dad always yelled, "Helm's alee!" before he did each time. She felt foolish about it, but he said it happens all the time to people who are new to sailing.

The most amazing part was when Bryon's dad let her take the wheel. She did so reluctantly and was afraid of doing something wrong that might damage the boat, but Byron's dad was right beside her, instructing her, and told her not to worry about it. She was a timid skipper at first, content to keep the boat off the wind and just enjoy the feeling of steering something that big through the water, but Byron's dad kept encouraging her to point the boat further up into the wind and she finally mustered enough courage to do it, and as the boat caught the wind and heeled and picked up speed, it took her breath away. "That's it!" Byron's dad kept shouting, "Now you've got it! Now you're *sailing*!" It took all her strength to keep the boat on the edge of the wind, but with her hands clutching the wheel tightly she began to be able to feel the boat's movements through it and anticipate when the boat was about to fall off the wind and bring it back up into it. It was like nothing she'd ever experienced, and the figure of speech "ship of state" came to mind.

The first time she heard it she understood the metaphor—that a country is like a ship that needs to be steered forward—but she never fully appreciated it until that moment. She fancied that what she was doing was what the President of the United States does on a much grander scale, only the current he has to deal with is political in nature and the wind the "wind of change" and that just as the current and wind she was dealing with were fickle and sometimes unpredictable and always changing, so are the ones he has to deal with. It made her think that if she could steer this 40-foot sailboat through the water and keep it on the edge of the wind the way she was, then maybe she could steer the country someday, if not as President, then as a Congresswoman or Senator and it rekindled her interest in pursuing a career in politics.

She finds Jasmine and Dawna and Harriet in their usual spot on the beach, sitting cross-legged and facing the water with their backs to her, talking. She walks up to them. "Hey," she says. They turn their heads and look up at her.

"Hey," Dawna and Harriett say.

Jasmine, of course, says nothing and scowls up at Colleen. "I'm off to catch the ferry," Colleen says. "Just wanted to say bye and that it was nice meeting you. I had a lot of fun."

"Nice meeting you too," Dawna says, shading her eyes from the sun with her hand.

"Yeah," Harriett says, squinting, "Have a safe trip home."

"Thanks," Colleen says and looks at Jasmine. "Can I talk with you moment?" Jasmine glances at Dawna and Harriett and Colleen sees that her request has caught her off guard.

"Why?" Jasmine asks.

"Just for a moment." Jasmine slowly stands and Colleen turns and walks away from Dawna and Harriett with Jasmine following. When they're out of earshot, Colleen stops and turns to face Jasmine, who stops in front of her.

"What do you want?" Jasmine asks brusquely.

Colleen fixes her eyes on Jasmine's. "To apologize for the hair in the bathtub drain." Colleen can see her apology has caught Jasmine off guard and she watches her struggling to decide what, if anything, to say in response.

"Fine," Jasmine finally says.

Colleen reaches into the pocket of her shorts and removes the folded piece of paper and holds it out to Jasmine. "Here," she says. Jasmine stares down at it and then looks up at Colleen.

"What's this?" Jasmine asks.

"My mailing address and my phone number at home and at school. Take it." Colleen sees Jasmine's eyes narrow.

"Why should I?" Jasmine asks suspiciously.

"So we can keep in touch," Colleen says.

"Why would I want to keep in touch with *you?*" Jasmine asks disdainfully.

"That's what friends do."

"We're *not* friends," Jasmine snaps.

Colleen shrugs. "Maybe not now, but you never know. Things might change. Take it." Jasmine looks down at the folded piece of paper and glances up at Colleen.

"Go on," Colleen says. "Take it." She keeps her eyes on Jasmine's as Jasmine slowly reaches out and takes it. Colleen smiles. "Good," she says and steps forward and wraps her arms around Jasmine and hugs her. She doesn't wait for Jasmine to hug her back. She knows it isn't going to happen. Hugging her is enough. She unwraps her arms and steps back. "Hope to hear from you," she says. She can see her hug caught Jasmine off guard yet again and that she's having a hard time controlling her emotions. She glances down at the folded paper in Jasmine's hand and sees that it and her hand are trembling. She looks Jasmine in the eyes again and sees they're moist now. "Take care," Colleen says and turns and walks away.

Byron's dad's comment comes to mind about his and Dr. King's fear that White society will reap the whirlwind because of its mistreatment of

Blacks and that they both pray it doesn't happen. So does she, and while she knows her offer of friendship to Jasmine means nothing in the great scheme of race relations, she feels good that she extended it and knows it was the right thing to do. She could see it broke through Jasmine's defenses, and if it made her question her hatred of Whites even for a moment, then it was worth it.

She looks back over her shoulder and sees Jasmine still standing there, looking down at the now unfolded piece of paper. Jasmine glances up at her and Colleen smiles and waves and sees her slowly bringing her hand up to wave back, but hesitate and lower it. Good, she thinks. Even that slight gesture on Jasmine's part is a victory, if not in the war, then in their little battle.

* * *

Colleen stares up at Roberta, who's standing behind the lectern on the stage, delivering the valedictory address to the auditorium filled with soon-to-be-graduated seniors, their family and friends and the faculty. She thinks Roberta looks as funny in her cap and gown as all the other girls, herself included. She's only half-listening to Roberta's farewell speech. She hears phrases expressing optimistic sentiment, such as "a bright and exciting future filled with promise" and "dedicate our lives to the betterment of humanity," but doesn't feel at all optimistic or inspired by them. She's filled with the same anxiety and doubt and pessimism about the future that she has been ever since Martin Luther King, Jr. was assassinated, and then Robert Kennedy just two months later.

Her eyes drift from Roberta back to Kathy, the girl who's seated directly in front of her, and settle again on the tassel on Kathy's mortarboard. Again, the memory of staring at the tassels on the dining room drapes behind Ellie comes to mind and again she replaces it with the memory of steering *Freedom Bound* and thinking of the powerful socio-political crosscurrents in the country that are rocking the ship of state. Her eyes glaze and she continues her musing.

She was twelve when President Kennedy was assassinated. Like the rest of the country, she kept vigil with her parents in front of the TV, staring at the screen with disbelief as the tragic and bizarre events in Dallas unfolded, and then with sadness as President Kennedy's flag-draped coffin was carried on a horse-drawn caisson to the Capitol to lie in state, and then to Arlington National Cemetery to be buried. She was old enough to understand and appreciate the enormity of what had happened and to be filled with a feeling of dread about what tragedy might befall the country next. She remembers feeling that way for some time, and that the feeling gradually subsided when no new tragedy occurred, and the country moved on and normalcy returned.

Dr. King's assassination affected her differently, more deeply, perhaps because she was older and certainly because she knows Byron's dad, who was a friend of his. She felt like she'd lost a friend too.

When she heard the news that Dr. King had been assassinated and that the alleged assassin was a White man named James Earl Ray, her immediate thought was that she'd lost Jasmine as a friend too.

A long time passed after she left Oak Bluffs before a letter from Jasmine arrived at school. In it, Jasmine apologized for the way she'd treated her and even shared with her what had happened with her boyfriend. Colleen didn't know for sure, but didn't think Jasmine had written to her because of her dad's urging. In any event, they began corresponding and then talking occasionally on the phone and by the time Dr. King was assassinated, they'd become good friends.

She was worried sick that the actions of a White racist would end their friendship and as she dialed Jasmine's number, shortly after she learned of Dr. King's assassination, her pulse was racing and her heart pounding and the hand holding the receiver to her ear was shaking. She didn't know what she was going to say to Jasmine. Saying that she was sorry didn't seem appropriate. The way she felt about it was that Dr. King's loss was everyone's loss and just as much hers as Jasmine's.

No, apologizing on behalf of Whites wouldn't do. But if not that, then what? She couldn't think of anything else to say, other than that she was sorry, and when Jasmine picked up the phone and said, "Hello," she said, "Hi. It's Colleen," and the two of them didn't say anything more for the longest time but just listened to the emptiness of the phone line. Finally, Colleen couldn't take it anymore and said softly, "I'm sorry." After a long pause, she heard Jasmine say, "There's no need to apologize. I know you feel his loss as deeply as I do." The sense of relief Colleen felt was overwhelming and, to her thinking, that moment marked the cementing of their friendship. She no longer felt she needed to be careful talking with Jasmine about anything and especially race relations and the Civil Rights Movement.

The change in their relationship truly was remarkable. Just a week before Dr. King's assassination, she and Jasmine talked on the phone about the student protest at Columbia. Byron had been keeping them both abreast of developments, as Valerie, who was in her first year at Barnard, had been Colleen. It was clear from everything Colleen heard that student anger about the university's affiliation with the Institute for Defense Analyses, a weapons think-tank affiliated with the U.S. Department of Defense, and its plan to build the Morningside Park gymnasium had grown to the point where, as Vincent had predicted, things were going to explode.

Jasmine might have softened, but she could still be blunt in sharing her opinion about things, and when she said she could care less about Columbia's affiliation with the IDA and described Vietnam as a White man's war in which Blacks do the dying. Colleen wanted to point out that Blacks weren't the only people dying, but bit her lip.

Then, a couple of weeks after Dr. King's assassination, when the activists in Columbia's Students for a Democratic Society and Student Afro Society held a second confrontational demonstration, she and Jasmine talked about it on the phone and Jasmine's tone was different. Colleen said she gave the student activists credit for having the courage to march to the gymnasium site to attempt to stop construction and then scuffle with the New York City Police officers who were guarding the site—one student was arrested—and then occupy the university's administrative offices. Jasmine said she did too, and didn't sound grudging when she did, but sincere, and Colleen knew it was Dr. King's death that had caused the change in her attitude. It was testimony to how profoundly his death had affected people that it could have changed Jasmine the way it did. Colleen wouldn't have thought it possible before Dr. King's death.

Byron continued to keep her and Jasmine informed about what was happening as best he could. He steered clear of the protest, as did Vincent, not surprisingly. Valerie was active in the protest, more because of her opposition to the gym than Columbia's ties to Defense, and she also kept Colleen informed and Colleen shared the information with Jasmine. Valerie wasn't among the students occupying the administrative offices, but she was right in the thick of things and her firsthand account of events as they unfolded was thrilling to Colleen.

She was particularly interested in Valerie's description of Mark Rudd, the leader of SDS, who led the march to the administrative offices and acted as the spokesperson for the protesting students. According to Valerie, Rudd is rabidly anti-war and a pro-communist who's fighting American imperialism. Apparently, he and some of the other leaders of SDS were invited to Cuba to meet with Cuban, Soviet and North Vietnamese delegates, which strikes Colleen as traitorous, since the U.S. is engaged in a war with the North Vietnamese, who are backed by the communist Chinese and the Soviets. Valerie said Rudd considers life in Cuba to be "extremely "humanistic," which Colleen knows is propaganda. She's read and heard enough about Cuba to know that it's a police state and that, except for the powerful elite, Cubans live a life of deprivation and are unable to leave the country, just like people in every other communist country.

The war in Vietnam is becoming an increasingly confusing issue, though, ever since Walter Cronkite returned from visiting South Vietnam. Based on what he learned from talking with the soldiers and generals fighting the war, he's convinced it can never be won and thinks we should negotiate peace with the North Vietnamese and bring the troops home. He isn't afraid to say so on the evening news, either, and he's no traitor. He's a real patriot.

She can sense the mood of the country changing about the war. People seem to be dividing into two camps—pro-war and anti-war—and the rhetoric on both sides of the issue is getting louder and more acrimonious all the time. People aren't so much discussing the war as they are shouting at each other about it and not listening to what the other side is saying, which Buffalo Springfield captured well in their song "For What It's Worth."

It's also interesting that just as with the issue of slavery and segregation, the Northern and Southern states seem to be dividing in their position on the war, with the North becoming increasingly anti-war and the South increasingly pro-war. She never would have thought it possible, but she's begun to entertain the idea that Walter Cronkite might be right, that the war is unwinnable. It seems un-American to think that, but she does.

Dr. King was an outspoken critic of the war long before Walter Cronkite, much to the chagrin of many leaders in the Civil Rights Movement, who felt it distracted from the main issue they were fighting for—equal rights for Blacks. President Johnson considered Dr. King's opposition to his administration's policies in Vietnam to be a personal betrayal, especially since Johnson had worked so hard to get the Civil Rights Act of 1964 passed.

She read the transcript of the speech Dr. King gave at the Riverside Church in New York City, eerily a year to the day before he was assassinated. The speech was titled "Beyond Vietnam: A Time to Break Silence" and in it he argued that the U.S. was in Vietnam "to occupy it as an American colony" and called the U.S. government "the greatest purveyor of violence in the world today." Reading the text of the speech made her uncomfortable, because she has so much respect for Dr. King and hearing these things from him forced her to view the country she loves in a different light and at least consider the possibility that he might be right.

Even Robert Kennedy came to believe the war is unwinnable. As a Senator from New York, he proposed a three-point plan to help end the war, which included suspension of the U.S. bombing of North Vietnam and the gradual withdrawal of U.S. and North Vietnamese troops from South Vietnam, with replacement by an international force. When he campaigned for the Democratic nomination for the Presidency, he ran on a platform that included non-aggression in U.S. foreign policy, as well as economic justice, decentralization of power and social improvement. He engaged young people in dialogue about the war and challenged those who supported the war while benefiting from draft deferments.

She was energized by Robert Kennedy's youthful vitality and idealism and the fact that he was steadfast and unflinching in his defense of the programs for social improvement he was proposing. She read that Kennedy had addressed the students at the Indiana University Medical School and took questions afterward and was asked where the country is going to get the money to pay for all the new programs he was proposing and that he replied, "From you." She thought that took a lot of courage and admired him for his honesty, which she's come to learn is a rare quality in politicians.

Just as she was when she heard the news that Dr. King had been assassinated, she was shocked when she heard that Robert Kennedy had been too, only more so because it came so soon after Dr. King's assassination. It really did seem to her that the country was under siege by some unknown evil force, bent on silencing every voice raised in support of civil rights and social progress and against the Vietnam War. The fact that Kennedy was assassinated by a Palestinian bus boy named Sirhan Sirhan at the Ambassador Hotel in Los Angeles, where Kennedy had just given his victory speech, having won the California primary, because, according to Sirhan, he felt betrayed by Kennedy's support of Israel during the Six-Day War, which, again, eerily, had begun exactly one year before the assassination, didn't diminish her feeling that someone or something was orchestrating events behind the scenes and that Sirhan and James Earl Ray were just pawns in a deadly game.

She doesn't believe that Richard Nixon, the front-runner for the Republican nomination at the time, had anything to do with Kennedy's assassination, although she knows there are people who wished him dead, just as they did Dr. King. Part of the reason she was so enamored of Kennedy is her dislike and distrust of Nixon and the fact that she felt Kennedy stood a good chance of defeating him, if they faced each other in the Presidential election. She doesn't know what it is exactly about Nixon that she dislikes and distrusts, but she still feels the same way about him, even though he's the President now. There's just something about him that seems creepy and sneaky. Maybe it's those beady eyes of his and that forced smile.

The day after Kennedy was assassinated, she received a call from Jasmine. Colleen answered the phone and heard her say, "Hi. It's Jasmine," and the same thing happened that happened in their conversation after Dr. King's death. Neither one of them said anything for what seemed a long time. As Colleen listened to the emptiness of the phone line, she knew that Jasmine was feeling the same way she had about Dr. King's death and was thinking the same thing—that Kennedy's loss was everyone's loss and just as much hers as Colleen's—and that saying she was sorry wouldn't be appropriate. Colleen wasn't surprised to finally hear her say, "I'm sorry," and she said the same thing to Jasmine that Jasmine had to her: "There's no need to apologize. I know you feel his loss as much as I do."

As uncertain and worried about the future of the country as she is, the fact that she and Jasmine were able to break down the barriers between them and establish a close friendship gives her hope that the rest of the country can do what they've done. It's a faint hope but hope all the same.

She looks up at Roberta and focuses on her, listening to what she's saying and is relieved to hear her say, "In conclusion…." She glances over her shoulder at her mother and Sheldon and her father, Sheldon sitting beside her mother and her father in the row behind them and a few seats away. She looks back at the tassel on Kathy's mortarboard and resumes her musing.

Her mother and Sheldon were looking forward to attending her graduation and are happy to be here, but she knows her father came grudgingly and from the moment he arrived he's seemed disgruntled. She knows her father knows she knew about her mother's affair with Sheldon and that he holds it against her, and also holds her partly responsible for her mother's leaving him. It's bullshit, of course, but typical of him to blame her and everyone else, rather than accepting the fact that it was his abusive behavior that drove her mother into Sheldon's arms and ended the marriage.

She hasn't set foot in her father's house since she moved out and doesn't see him and rarely speaks with him on the phone, and then only briefly. Mila still cooks and cleans for him and Colleen calls her occasionally to find out how her father's doing, more out of curiosity than concern and to chat with Mila about what's going on in her life. Mila's a good person to bounce things off and her reports about her father confirm what Colleen already knows.

Her father's never really been the same since his attempted suicide. He's still successful in his practice and is probably still able to browbeat witnesses and intimidate members of the jury into seeing things his way, but the old bravado is gone. He's like two people now, the one he pretends to be professionally and the deflated and depressed man he is in his private life, sitting in his office at home until late in the evening, working his way through the bottles in his liquor cabinet, or sitting here in the auditorium, brooding behind her mother and Sheldon.

She's lately found herself wondering just how much longer her father has to live. He's only forty-five, but he punishes his body and longevity doesn't run in his family. They're all alcoholics. His grandparents died in their sixties, his mother died at sixty-five and his father is sixty-six and in poor health and probably won't last much longer. Her Uncle Mick's in poor health too, but at least he has a wife who looks after him, or tries to. It's a testimony to just how alienated from her father Colleen's become that when she wonders about this, she finds herself thinking he'd be doing everyone, himself included, a favor by dropping dead like his mother did and the sooner the better. She knows it's shameful to think that but doesn't feel at all ashamed. It's the truth.

She looks up at Roberta and listens to the remaining idealistic goals Roberta is challenging her classmates to achieve in life. This is the first valedictory address Colleen's heard and the phrase "laid on with a trowel" comes to mind, which she knows is from *As You Like It,* having studied it this year in English Lit. She suspects they're all like this, to one extent or another, filled with high-mindedness and idealism and optimism. The next time she'll hear one will probably be four years from now when she graduates from Barnard, unless she attends Valerie's graduation and hears that one.

She wonders where the country will be four years from now. Will race relations have improved? Will we still be fighting in Vietnam, or will we have given up and negotiated a peace and left the country? Will President Nixon be re-elected, or will a Democratic challenger like Robert Kennedy emerge, one with vitality and vision, and unseat him? She wishes she and her classmates could achieve even a fraction of the goals Roberta has challenged them to, but she's still filled with doubt and uncertainty about the future.

She looks down at the cover of the burgundy, faux leather pebble-grained folder on her lap, with "Our Lady of Mercy" stamped in gold foil and beneath it "Class of 1969" and thinks of what she's been through the last four years to earn the diploma inside. It's taken a lot of hard and sometimes painful work, both academically and personally, and at times she wasn't sure she could find the strength to do it, but she did. She graduated Magna Cum Laude and managed to get rid of Rocco and put a lot of distance between herself and her bad reputation back home. Most important, she managed to quit drinking and stay sober. She's just like the country, she thinks. If *she* was able to get through the last four years, the country will be able to get through the next four. They'll both endure.

Her mother looks tenderly at her, steps forward, puts her arms around her and gives her a hug.

"Congratulation, honey. We're so proud of you."

Her mother steps back and takes her hands and beams at her. "Thanks," Colleen says. She sees Sheldon beaming at her too, and that he's eager to give her a congratulatory hug, which he does and she glances at her father, who's standing at a distance from her mother, and sees he isn't smiling and doesn't seem at all eager to hug her or congratulate her. He looks as brooding as ever and as if he can't wait to be on his way back to his house and office upstairs and a glass of whiskey. She wouldn't be surprised if he has a bottle in the car or at least nips for the drive home.

Sheldon steps back and she looks at her father and studies his eyes, waiting to see what he's going to do. He couldn't not say anything and just turn and walk away, could he? Finally, he reluctantly steps forward and puts his arms around her, but lightly. "Congratulations," she hears him grumble and it sounds insincere. She feels a single light tap of his hand on her back, but it's not a tap that conveys congratulations for a job well done. There's a feel of finality to it, of judgment having been passed, and she can well imagine what her father is thinking: So, after everything I've done for you, you betray me.

He steps back and gives her a final accusatory look and, without looking at her mother or Sheldon or saying anything more, turns and walks away through the crowd of celebrating students and parents and faculty toward his car.

Colleen watches him go until he disappears in the crowd. She wonders why he even bothered to come. Yes, she thinks, he should drop dead and the sooner the better.

CHAPTER 14

Everett

"**Y**ou okay back there?" Colleen hears Valerie ask for the umpteenth time. She opens her eyes just enough to see Valerie studying her in the rearview mirror from the driver's seat and Sandy looking over her shoulder at her with concern from the front passenger seat. "Yeah, fine," she mumbles and wraps the sleeping bag tighter around herself as Sandy glances at Valerie and they both look back at the road ahead.

Colleen peers at the hair on the back of Sandy's head, which Sandy has let grow longer than usual without being cut, long enough to look as if she's slept on a hillside for the past four days. Is it her imagination or is Sandy's head covered with tiny, slowly writhing serpents? Her imagination, she tells herself and realizes she's experiencing her first "flashback." Before taking acid at the festival, she knew from her reading that the term, in the context of psychoactive drug use, means to re-experience a hallucinogenic moment from a past "trip." Never having "tripped" or hallucinated, she had a hard time then imagining what the experience might be like. Not now. Her gaze drifts down to the back of Sandy's seat, a quiet and calming field of putty gray vinyl. She stares at it until her eyes glaze, relieved not to see Everett's "Day-Glo raspberry fishnet" pattern appear on it, then closes them and lets her mind roam.

She's not at all fine, as Valerie and Sandy know, which is why they keep asking her how she's doing. She's mentally and physically exhausted from having slept so little over the past four days and her head is still spinning and her stomach queasy from all the pot and the LSD, even though she came down hours ago. So much for "3 Days of Peace & Music." There was plenty of music, all right, but precious little peace, that's for sure. Well, it was an incredible experience, literally a mind-blowing one and one she doesn't regret, despite how lousy she feels now. And to think she almost didn't come.

She'd heard about the big music festival that was going to be held in Bethel in August with all these big name bands—Creedence Clearwater Revival and Jefferson Airplane and Sly & the Family Stone and The Who and Jimi Hendrix—scheduled to perform, but she wasn't planning on going, not because of the price of the ticket, although eighteen dollars was steep, but because the prospect of being out in the open for three days surrounded by God knows how many thousands of people didn't seem very appealing.

Then Valerie called and said she and Sandy were going and were about to buy tickets and would get one for her if she wanted to go. Valerie said she was borrowing her grandmother's car, and they'd pick her up in Cornwall on the way up. "Come on!" Valerie urged her. "It'll be fun! Besides, what else have you got planned?" Colleen had to admit not much. It struck her as odd, though, that Valerie, being such a city girl and prone to car sickness, was willing to drive all the way upstate and rough it for three days to listen to rock music, which isn't her favorite. Valerie said she was more interested in the event, itself, than the music. She had the feeling it was going to be "something really big, a once in a lifetime experience." How right she turned out to be.

Valerie and Sandy picked her up early Thursday morning, the day before the festival—it was Valerie's idea to arrive a day early and it's a good thing they did, as they soon found out—and off they went up the Thruway to Bethel, all three of them with backpacks filled with clothes and sleeping bags—Valerie and Colleen each had to buy one. Sandy had hers from her summer camp days in the hinterlands of Long Island. Sandy had the idea to bring a couple of plastic tarps, in case the weather turned bad and it rained, and that idea turned out to be a brilliant one and a lifesaver. That's Sandy, always thinking ahead about how to protect everyone, a real guardian angel. Sandy can't wait to get to

Fort MacClellan and begin Officer Candidate School. She says she can taste it now that she's in college, although it's still three years away.

The three of them have yet to go to the Apollo to see James Brown, but, as it happened, Colleen got to see Sandy in action. They'd sat through a day and a half of music without Sandy ever getting up to dance, but something happened to her when Sly & the Family Stone performed in the wee hours of Sunday morning. Colleen noticed a blissful smile appear on Sandy's face and she began bobbing her head with her eyes closed and jerking her upper body and swaying her shoulders to the beat. Her movements became more and more exaggerated until the band began playing "Dance to the Music" and Sandy leapt to her feet and began dancing with abandon, like a wild woman, twisting and shimmying, beautifully and gracefully and powerfully. It was as if Pallas Athene had wanted to party and inhabited Sandy to do it! Colleen stared up at her wide-eyed. Sandy had had a few beers but, as usual, hadn't smoked pot or done any other drugs. It was the music that seemed to have transported her to a world of her own. When Colleen finally managed to take her eyes off Sandy and looked around, she saw that everyone around them was staring, transfixed, not at Sly & the Family Stone but at Sandy and here and there people began clapping in time to the music and whistling and shouting encouragement at her. Valerie wasn't kidding. That girl can get down!

She's jerked forward as Valerie brakes hard. "Shit!" she hears Valerie scream and opens her eyes just enough to see the brake lights glowing red on the car in front of them. It must have slowed or stopped suddenly.

"I nearly ran into that asshole!" Valerie screams, banging the steering wheel with her fist. "That's all I need! To wreck Nonna's car!"

Sandy puts a calming hand on Valerie's shoulder. "Take it easy, baby," she says soothingly. "Keep more distance between you and this guy. It's gonna be stop and go like this."

Colleen turns her head and peers at the cars in the lane next to theirs, crawling along as they are. At least they're making better time now than they did getting to the Thruway from Bethel. What a nightmare that was. She leans back and closes her eyes again.

The trip north on the Thruway to the festival seems like ages ago now. So much has happened since. She'd seen photographs and news footage of hippies—there are kids walking around Cornwall and

Newburgh who try to look like them, but aren't really—and knew about their lifestyle and the closer they got to the Bethel exit, she found herself being more and more surrounded by them. She'd never seen so many VW Buses and Bugs, most of them decorated with flower and peace sign stickers and crazy painted designs and every one filled with young men and women with long hair, wearing tee shirts, a lot of them tie-dyed, and denim shirts and those with glasses wearing wire rims.

People were passing around joints and pipes in a lot of the cars and as they were crawling along toward the Bethel exit, a smiling girl with long frizzy light brown hair and glazed eyes in the backseat of the car next to theirs leaned out the open widow and held out a joint to Colleen. She took it and said, "Thanks," and the girl's smile widened. "Peace!" the girl said and made the peace sign. Valerie brought pot, but not taking the joint from the girl didn't seem the right thing to do. She was quickly learning that sharing is an important part of hippie culture. She was glad later that she took it.

It was slow going getting to the concert site. She stared at the farmland bordering the road leading to it and thought the event should have been called "An Agrarian Music and Arts Festival" rather than an "Aquarian" one. Judging from the line of cars parked on the sides of the road and stretching out of sight, it was clear that they should have come a day earlier.

The walk to the concert site seemed endless. By the time they arrived, the field was filled with people halfway up the hill in front of the stage. They settled in and were soon joined by three boys who looked to Colleen to be around twenty, one taller and lankier than the other two. The boys settled in next to them on the right with the tall lanky one sitting next to her. He introduced himself as Everett and she said her name was Colleen and they said it was nice meeting each other and she and Everett turned toward their respective friends and began talking among themselves.

Her first impression of Everett was that he was soft-spoken and polite and a little shy, which she could see in his blue eyes. He had a hard time keeping them on hers whenever their eyes met. His sandy hair fell over his ears and was neatly trimmed and parted on the side, unlike most of the men's hair, which was long and parted in the middle, if at all. A lot of men were sporting long, bushy, frizzy hair that looked like it had never seen a comb or brush, the way Jimi Hendricks and his two bandmates' hair looks on the *Are You Experienced* album cover. It made her think of dark dandelions.

Everett was wearing a light blue and green plaid shirt, blue jeans and white tennis shoes. With his longish styled hair and outfit, his look struck her as kind of "hippie-preppie" and she could tell he identified with both cultures. She noticed him glance at her from time to time and she had the feeling he wanted to begin a conversation, but couldn't muster the courage to break the ice, which she found sweet. She figured that since they were going to be spending so much time together, the sooner she engaged him in conversation the better and kept her eye on him, waiting for an opening. It finally came when she overheard him mention to his friends that he was going to use the facilities. As it happened, she needed to as well and when he stood, she did too and it startled him. "Mind if I go with you?" she asked and he said, "No, not at all," and off they went, making their way slowly through the crowd toward the Porta Potties.

They chatted as they waited in line, which was a long one, so they had plenty of time to talk and she learned a lot about him. He said he's attending Beloit College in Wisconsin and majoring in Anthropology. She'd never heard of the school and listened with keen interest to his description of it; a small liberal arts college with a small student body, only around thirteen hundred students; highly ranked academically and offering a year-round curriculum, called the "Beloit Plan" which comprises three full terms and a "field term" of off-campus study. Apparently, the college has a reputation for having a high percentage of graduates go on to earn a Ph.D. and is focused on students putting their education to work after graduation.

"Where is it in Wisconsin?" she asked.

"Beloit. It's a small rural town on the Wisconsin-Illinois border. The town's nickname is 'The Gateway to Wisconsin'."

"What's campus life like? What are the people like?" she asked, and he grinned.

"Party animals. Beloit has a well-earned reputation for being a party school and everyone's into drugs."

* * *

"What type of drugs?"

"Anything they can get their hands on but mostly pot and psychedelics."

His mention of psychedelics piqued her curiosity. "So, you've taken them? Psychedelics?" He nodded slowly.

"Yeah, I have. You?"

She shook her head. "I've wondered about them, though. What's the experience like? From what I've read, it seems kind of crazy and random."

"You've got that right. 'Crazy and random' is a good way to describe it, but there's logic to it. It's hard to see sometimes, but there is. You should try acid."

She widened her eyes. "You have some?" she asked and, still grinning, he narrowed his eyes slightly and nodded.

"Owsley's 'White Lighting' formula," he said. "I've tripped a couple of times on it. It's awesome."

Hearing this thrilled her. Her curiosity about the counterculture had grown to the point where she read Tom Wolfe's *The Electric Kool-Aid Acid Test,* so she knew Owsley Stanley is a legendary producer of chemically pure LSD and a friend of Ken Kesey and The Grateful Dead. She also discovered that her suspicion that Dean Moriarty in *On the Road* was based on a real person was well-founded. His name was Neal Cassady and he was one of Kesey's Merry Pranksters and the driver of Further, their bus, and she wasn't surprised to read that after he left the Merry Pranksters, he was found unconscious outside a small town in Mexico, lying beside railroad tracks, and died soon after from the barbiturates he'd taken and the heavy drinking he'd done on top of them.

"You're welcome to try it," Everett said.

"Thanks," she said, "maybe I will. Have you ever had a bad trip?" He looked off in the distance and nodded.

"Yeah, once. There's bad acid out there. Why anyone would make it and sell it is beyond me, but people do. Some people have no professional ethics. They're just interested in the money."

He looked back at her and smiled reassuringly.

"This stuff is pure," he said.

"Yeah, I bet," she said and felt her apprehension about trying acid dissolving. She knew then and there she was going to try it and that it was only a matter of when.

They were finally able to use the Porta Potties and decided to take a walk around and check out the people and the goings-on, which were everywhere. It seemed to her that a tribe had descended on Bethel from the four points of the compass, a tribe yet unnamed, whose members had known it existed but had never before assembled and were at last together and celebrating that fact. Here and there were groups of people, sitting cross-legged in circles, playing guitars and banging on makeshift instruments while people danced around them. The movements of some of the dancing people seemed to have nothing to do with the music being played. They stood, swaying their bodies and waving their arms, like trees in the breeze or anemones in an ocean current as they slowly turned round and round.

Many of the young women were bare breasted and seemed more than unconcerned about it—they seemed happy and proud to be! There were couples, lying together, making out, and their attitude seemed the same as the bare-breasted young women's. It seemed to her that the rules of behavior laid down by her parent's generation had been suspended here and people were free to do as they pleased. She wondered if they'd behave like this after the festival or if they'd go back to living life as they had before. Having experienced this type of freedom, she didn't think it would be possible for them to ever go back to the way things were, not entirely. She sensed that the young people here were changing society and that it would never be the same again afterward. That's why Valerie was so interested in coming, because she had the feeling that's what the event was going to be about.

Thinking of Valerie and Sandy, that was the one thing she found curious and a bit odd as she and Everett walked around and studied the people. She saw only a relatively few openly homosexual couples. Given the number of people here, she knew a lot more of them had to be and she thought it sad that even here, where freedom seemed to reign, they were still unable or unwilling to express their sexual identity. Some prejudices are more deeply rooted and harder to overcome than others, she thought. It's sad, but there it is, although change seems to be in the wind and, she hopes, is inevitable.

On the ride up from Cornwall, Valerie talked excitedly about the riots at the Stonewall Inn in Greenwich Village, just a month and a half ago. Colleen hadn't heard anything about the riots, which Valerie said wasn't surprising. Only the New York City papers covered them and not very favorably. Even *The Village Voice,* a supposedly liberal paper, described the events as "Sunday fag follies" and the rioters as "forces of faggotry" and "limp wrists."

According to Valerie, the Stonewall Inn is run by the Mob and was one of the only places where gays—mostly men, but also women—could meet in the city and socialize. The police routinely raided the place, as they do every other bar catering to homosexuals, but the cops were on the take and always tipped off the bar ahead of time. Not this night.

There were just over two hundred people in the bar, some in drag. Female police officers took customers wearing women's clothes to the bathroom to verify their sex and arrest any that were men, which, Valerie assured her, is what routinely happens during these raids. Female customers were required to be wearing three pieces of women's clothing and if they weren't, they'd be arrested. Valerie said that for years "gays," as she calls them, have put up with this type of harassment and have allowed themselves to be arrested and have gone meekly to the police station, but this raid didn't go as planned.

Men dressed as women refused to go with the police officers and customers began refusing to show the police their identification. A scuffle broke out—apparently a drag queen hit a cop over the head with his handbag—and the police were outnumbered. The scuffle spilled out into the street, where the customers from the bar were joined by gays from the neighborhood, and a crowd grew to ten times the number of police and people began taunting them. Valerie said the drag queens formed a kick line and sang a song they made up to the theme of the "Howdy Doody Show." Colleen could only imagine what that must have been like, a line of police confronted by a kick line of singing drag queens. Valerie said people began throwing things at the police and that, for the first time, gays were fighting back, fighting for their right to be openly who they are. She said someone shouted, "Gay power!" and someone else began singing "We Shall Overcome." The fight continued until early Saturday morning and, in the end, thirteen people were arrested.

The gays assembled the next night in front of the bar and battled again with the police and Valerie said there were, as one paper described it, "surprising displays of homosexual affection" in the streets. "Good!" she said. "It's about fucking time we stood up for ourselves and lived our lives like human beings!"

It wasn't the first time Colleen equated the struggle of gays for their civil rights with that of Blacks, but the similarity between the two came into sharp focus as she listened to Valerie. Rights are rights and people denied them will only allow it to go on for so long. Looking around at the sea of people on the hillside, she wondered if they would support gays in their struggle as they do Blacks in theirs. It seemed to her that these freedom-loving people would, and she hopes they do.

She and Everett chatted as they made their way down toward the stage and the pond behind it. "Where are you from?" she asked and saw him glance at her and grin mischievously.

"Everett," he said.

She knew he was having fun with her, but didn't get the joke. "Sorry?"

"Everett. That's where I'm from. It's near Boston."

She grinned. "'Everett from Everett'!" she said gleefully. "That's what I'll call you from now on!"

"Fine with me," he said.

"Did your parents name you after the place?"

"Sort of. My family goes way back. I'm related to Edward Everett. He was a prominent politician in the Nineteenth Century, a Representative and Senator from Massachusetts, the Ambassador to England, U.S. Secretary of State, President of Harvard. He was an interesting and controversial character. The town's named after him."

She remembered the joint the girl had given her. They'd passed so many people smoking pot that she figured why not smoke it now with him. She fished it out of the pocket of her shorts and held it up and grinned again. "A girl gave me this. Want to smoke it, Everett from Everett?" His eyes lit up and he grinned.

"All right!" he said.

The way he looked at her and said this suggested to her that he wasn't so much surprised that she'd produced a joint as he was that she smoked pot at all. "What?" she asked, meeting his surprise with her own. "You thought I was Little Goody Two-Shoes? Is that what you thought,

Everett from Everett?" He looked at her knowingly and his grin had almost a smug quality to it now.

"Let's just say that, in my experience, people aren't always who they seem to be."

She'd had the same experience with people but wanted to keep the conversation focused entirely on the two of them and searched her mind frantically for something to say, finally settling on, "Well, you know what they say about judging a book by its cover." As soon as she'd said it, she realized it didn't sound at all worldly-wise, as she'd hoped, but thoroughly sophomoric. She couldn't decide if his expression now was one of compassion or pity and was relieved when he smiled and nodded in the direction of the pond, and they moved on.

They sat on the grass by the pond and he took a lighter from the pocket of his jeans and lit the joint for her and they handed it back and forth as they smoked. They watched the people in the pond, some standing in the water, talking, others splashing each other and laughing, others embracing and kissing. Not surprisingly by now, some of the young women were completely nude. Colleen gazed at them. She'd only had a few hits of the pot but already could tell that it was more powerful than any she'd smoked before. Just as she had the first time she smoked with Valerie in the alley in Greenwich Village and the few times she had with her since, she felt a tingling between her legs and a growing sense of horniness, but she'd never felt as horny or as high as this stuff was making her feel. Everett held up the joint and eyed it discerningly.

"This is good shit," he said.

He sounded like he knew what he was talking about. "Yeah?" she asked. "You can tell?" He nodded and handed her the joint.

"Acapulco Gold," he said.

Valerie had mentioned Acapulco Gold and how good it supposedly was and how she was looking forward to trying it. Colleen inhaled deeply and handed the joint to Everett and held her breath as she debated whether to tell Valerie that's what the joint the girl had given her turned out to be. She slowly exhaled and decided it would probably be better not to. Why disappoint her unnecessarily. "You sure know your pot, 'Everett from Everett'."

"I should," he said. "I've smoked enough of it."

She felt the intensity of the tingling between her legs growing and her gaze settled on a couple in the water, embracing and kissing passionately. She squirmed as she watched them and the only thought in her head was that she wanted to be doing that and more with Everett right now. So what if they just met and hardly knew each other? They knew each other well enough and no one would care or even notice. They'd just be part of the tribal celebration going on around them.

They smoked the joint down to almost the end and Everett fished a roach clip out of his pocket and they smoked what was left of it. The feeling between her legs had grown in intensity to the point where she felt like an animal in heat that needed to scratch itself against something. She looked at Everett and he looked at her. "Come on, 'Everett from Everett'," she said, "let's take a walk."

"Sure." he said.

They stood and she looked around and saw the line of trees in the distance. She took his hand and led him toward it. She would have been perfectly happy to make love with him by the pond, but in deference to him, knowing that he's a bit shy, she thought it best to have some degree of privacy. They didn't say a word as they walked toward the trees. She was pretty sure he knew what she had in mind, and he was coming willingly, so she assumed he wanted the same thing she did.

They reached the trees and she led him deeper into them. She could see groups of people and couples here and there, off to the sides but, far enough away, she thought, and when they reached a spot that seemed most private, she stopped and he did too. She turned and faced him and looked in his eyes and put her arms around his neck and pressed her body against his. "Kiss me, Everett from Everett," she said dreamily and closed her eyes and pursed her lips and expected to feel his on hers. When a moment passed and she didn't, she opened her eyes and saw him searching them with his nervously and a little fearfully. "What's the matter?" she asked. "Don't you like me?" He looked away.

"It's not you," he said. "It's me. I have trust issues."

She slowly unwrapped her arms from around his neck and stood with her hands at her sides looking up at him, puzzled. "'Trust issues'?"

"I don't let people get close to me."

"Why not?" she asked and he shrugged. She was more puzzled now. It was clear she wasn't going to satisfy her desire to have sex with him, at least not until she listened to what he had to say and maybe not then, either. There was a chance she would, though, if she could get him to talk with her and she took his hand and sat on the ground and drew him down next to her as she did. "Why not?" she asked. She watched him as he searched her eyes again and understood now that what he was trying to decide was if he could trust *her*. "Did someone do something to you?" she asked. His searching became more frantic and after a long moment, he stopped and fixed his eyes on hers and his expression changed. He no longer looked nervous and fearful but—there was no mistaking it—evil and she felt her skin tingle and the hair on her arms and the back of her neck bristle.

"Yeah," he finally said. "Mister Black."

His voice had changed too. It was flatter and a little deeper. "Mister Black?" she asked cautiously. "Who's he?"

"He's in my head. He speaks to me."

She tried to remain calm and not to let her alarm show but felt the beginnings of panic. Was Everett crazy, she wondered? He seemed perfectly normal until just a few moments ago. She glanced around and was reassured by the fact that the people she could see were within calling distance in case she needed help. She looked at Everett and saw that he hadn't taken his eyes off hers and she found the way he was staring at her now unnerving. It was like he was trying to bore into her head through her eyes to see what she was thinking. She'd never experienced someone with mental problems and didn't know whether the best thing to do would be to continue talking with him or get up and walk away. It seemed to her that either decision could be equally wrong, so she decided to stay put and continue talking. "What does he tell you?" she asked. She watched him consider his answer and saw his head tick slightly as he did.

"Not to trust people," he finally said.

She hesitated to ask but did. "Is he telling you not to trust me?" She was relieved to see him grin, albeit a little devilishly.

"Not yet," he said.

"Good," she said and took a breath. "How long has he been speaking to you?"

"A year or so."

She was encouraged enough by the fact that he was still grinning to continue asking questions. "Did he just begin speaking to you one day? Did something happen to make him?" His grin faded and he was back to boring into her eyes with his and she shifted uncomfortably and waited for his reply.

"My bad trip," he finally said.

"Are you getting help?" she asked and saw him nod, once and abruptly.

"I take Thorazine. It's an antipsychotic. My doc at the Naval Hospital in Chelsea prescribed it. I see him once a week."

"Was your dad in the Navy?" she asked and saw him nod.

"Still is," he said. "My parents divorced when I was a kid, but I'm still a military dependent."

"Well, that's good," she said, "I mean, that you're getting help." He nodded again. "So, why do you still take acid, if it's done this to you?" Now he was the one who looked puzzled.

"Done what?"

"Put Mister Black in your head."

"Acid didn't put him in my head," he said with conviction. "I did. I let a bad trip make me paranoid and I opened the door to my mind and let him in. He's there because of my weakness."

Everett was becoming increasingly emboldened, and she stared at him wide-eyed and resolved to say nothing and just listen.

"Acid's helped me learn a lot about myself. You can't hide from yourself when you're tripping. You come face to face with yourself and have to confront your true self. Some people can do it and learn from the experience and others can't and end up curled up in a ball in the corner, cowering."

He paused and while his eyes were still on hers, they looked a bit unfocused, like he was looking right through her.

"People have used psychedelics for ages. The American Indians consider them a sacrament and experience being in the presence of the Great Spirit when they take them. I know how they feel. I'm not a religious person, but I am a spiritual one. When I trip, I experience life free of all the bullshit society dumps on our heads. Well, except for that one time, when I couldn't escape my own bullshit."

He paused again and slowly focused his eyes on hers again. "Meeting with my doc is a waste of time. The only reason I do is for the Thorazine. It helps settle me. My doc is clueless. He thinks Mister Black is a figment of my imagination, the result of my latent resentment of my father for having abandoned my mom and me. It's bullshit. My father was a prick, an abusive drunk, and my mom was happy to see him go. So was I."

She waited a moment to make sure Everett was finished. "Do you think Mister Black will go away sometime?" she asked hopefully. He shrugged.

"Dunno. Some things linger. The first time I tripped I remember staring at the floor to ceiling curtains in the room. They began rippling and then they were covered with a bright raspberry fishnet pattern."

He stopped and searched her eyes, as if waiting to see what her reaction to this last piece of information might be. Seeing none, he shrugged, as if to say, who knows where these things come from?

"Anyway, to this day, if I stare at curtains when I'm not tripping, they begin slowly rippling and sometimes the pattern appears on them."

She was at a loss for anything more to say about Mister Black, or Everett's trust issues and didn't want to talk about them anymore. She was still horny and decided to take a different approach to see if she could satisfy her desire to have sex with him. She looked at him tenderly. "Well, *I* trust *you*, 'Everett from Everett', and *I* want *you* to get close to *me.*" She stood and glanced around and, not seeing anyone watching them, pulled off her tee shirt and removed her bra and tossed them aside. She looked down at him and raised her eyebrows. "Like what you see, 'Everett from Everett'?" He admired her breasts and nodded, once and abruptly.

"Very nice," he said.

"I'm glad you like them," she said. "You don't think they're too big?" she asked worriedly. He studied her breasts and slowly shook his head and smiled.

"No. They're perfect."

"Good!" she said. "Now we're getting somewhere!" She quickly removed her shorts and underpants and tossed them on the other clothes. Sat facing him with her legs to the side and reached out and took his hand. "Touch them," she whispered. She tried to guide his hand to her breast but felt him resist and pouted. "Please, 'Everett from Everett'? I want you to touch them. Don't you want to? Wouldn't you enjoy doing that? Hmm?" He kept his eyes on hers and showed no sign of touching her breasts and she sighed and let his hand go and watched him place it on his thigh. She put her hand on his and glanced at his crotch and thought why not at least give it a try? She moved her hand along the inside of his thigh and placed it over the bulge in his jeans and gave it a gentle squeeze. She was startled, but not really surprised, when he immediately grabbed her wrist and moved her hand away.

"I have a daughter," he said.

She stared wide-eyed at him. "You do?" she asked and he nodded, once and abruptly. "Wow," she said softly. He let go of her wrist and placed his hand on his thigh again and she placed her hand on his. She felt her horniness diminish, replaced by curiosity and concern. She wanted to ask him how he came to be a father and if he was married, although she didn't think he was, but wasn't sure he wanted to say anything more about it and just stared at him and waited.

"My girlfriend lied to me," he finally said. "My *ex*-girlfriend," he added bitterly. "She told me she was on the pill. She wasn't and got pregnant and her parents wouldn't let her get an abortion. They're Boston Irish, strict Catholics. She had the baby and they forced her to give it up for adoption through the Church."

She waited a moment to see if he had anything more to say, and when she saw he didn't, asked, "Did you want to keep it? Did you want to get married?" He slowly shook his head again.

"She lied to me," he finally said. "Anyway, I'm in no position to take care of a kid. I barely get by on the allowance my mom gives me each month and what I earn working in the cafeteria at school."

She gave his hand a gentle squeeze. "Just so you know, 'Everett from Everett', I'm on the pill and I wouldn't lie to you." He studied her eyes more intently than ever and his head twitched slightly as he did. She noticed a vein in his forehead bulging now and had the feeling he was thinking so hard about whether to trust her that his head was about to explode.

"Let's go," he finally said.

All the way back she thought about the issue of women and their right, or lack of it, to make decisions about their own bodies. She thought about the young woman with the problem in the ladies' room at the Village Gate and wondered what happened to her. She thought about Valerie and Sandy's friend Nadine, who tried to induce an abortion by sticking plastic tubes in her cervix and blowing into them and hemorrhaged so badly she died trying. She thought about Stephanie and how her parents forced her to have an abortion, and now Everett's girlfriend and how her parents forced her to have the baby and then give her up for adoption. It seemed supremely unfair and wrong that women should be controlled and manipulated the way they are by their parents and a patriarchal society. Women might not be a minority, but they suffer just as much inequality and persecution and repression as Blacks and gays, although most women won't admit it to themselves. She knows that's beginning to change, though.

Shortly after she arrived home from school for summer vacation, she was searching among her mother's books for something to read and came across *The Feminine Mystique* and was soon absorbed in Betty Friedan's depiction of the roles of women in industrial societies, especially the "full-time homemaker" role, which Friedan deemed "stifling." She read about housewives, who'd been brainwashed by society into believing they were somehow not as intelligent and capable as men and had no business being outside the home and felt trapped. She read about Friedan's own experience, of being a depressed suburban housewife who dropped out of college at the age of nineteen to get married and raise four children, of her "terror" at being alone and of her never once in her life having seen a positive female role model who worked outside the home and also maintained a family.

Nothing she read was a startling revelation—she only had to look at her friends' mothers, most of them housewives, to see the proof of what Friedan was talking about—but it helped her to gain a deeper understanding of where the relegation of women to secondary roles in society is coming from and Friedan's outspokenness about what she calls "The Problem That Has No Name" filled her with indignation and outrage at the mistreatment of women. It also made her determined to become involved in the feminist movement and advocate for women's rights. She feels she owes it to women to do so and, first and foremost, to herself.

Friedan's book also caused her to view her mother differently and helped her to gain a deeper appreciation of what she's accomplished in life, attending college and then law school and then going into practice as a lawyer and maintaining her practice, while being a wife and mother. She also gained a deeper appreciation of the fact that, unlike most women in a bad marriage, her mother freed herself from hers. Not many women would have had the courage to stand up to an abusive alcoholic husband and leave him the way her mother did. She admires her mother now for having done it and understands better why she was reluctant at first to take her with her into her new life with Sheldon. Her mother wanted to be free of her father and everything associated with him and knew that Colleen could fend for herself, so her mother didn't really abandon her and was there for her when she needed her, which is all that matters.

She discussed Friedan's book with her mother, as she was reading it, and not long after finishing it, her mother handed her an issue of *New York Magazine* and suggested she read Gloria Steinem's article, titled "After Black Power—Women's Liberation." Colleen was struck by the irony of Steinem's article, appearing in an issue of the magazine whose feature article by Jimmy Breslin is titled "Namath All Night Long." She didn't read Breslin's article, but assumed it's about Joe Namath's exploits as a playboy, since the cover features Namath's face, with those bedroom eyes and easy smile of his, on a poster, cut into four squares that are being held together by gorgeous young women in loungewear. It couldn't be more stereotypically sexist and she had the feeling, having read Friedan's book and before reading Steinem's article, that she was staring at the problem women face in this country. Women are here to serve and please men, however men wish, whether it's doing equal work as men for less pay or keeping their mouth shut at home and making sure the house is clean and meals are on the table, or being at Joe Namath's beck and call, whenever he's feeling frisky and wants to play.

She found Steinem's article to be a good account of the current state of the nascent and growing Women's Liberation Movement and the various groups that have formed, and how they're taking action to advance the cause of women's rights. She wasn't surprised to read that most of the women who are active in the movement are "White, serious, well-educated young women just like herself. She knew about the Barnard girls who held a student sleep-in in the men's dorm at Columbia, to protest the absence of co-ed dorms that are springing up at other universities, and how it resulted in a course being offered about "women as an oppressed class." Valerie had told her about that. What was a revelation was the number of different groups that have formed and the fact that they don't speak with one voice but have different and sometimes competing and conflicting agendas. In thinking about it, though, she realized she shouldn't have been surprised. What's happening in the Women's Liberation Movement is exactly what's happening in the Civil Rights Movement, and it seems inevitable that it should be. Not all women are alike, just as not all Blacks are alike.

"How you doin'?" she hears Sandy ask and opens her eyes just enough to see her looking over her shoulder at her with concern. "Fine," she mumbles and turns her head just enough to the side to see that traffic is moving faster now. She has no idea where they are or how much longer it will be before she gets home, but she knows the first thing she's going to do when she does—pull off her mud-caked clothes and soak in a nice hot bath for an hour and then curl up in her comfortable bed and sleep as long as her body needs her to.

She's not big on camping and is uncomfortable sleeping on the ground. In all, she probably didn't get ten hours of sleep in the four days they were there and what sleep she did get was fitful. The tarps that Sandy brought helped, but eventually everyone was soaked by the rain and caked with mud and she was miserable, despite being high on pot. At one point she and Valerie and Sandy debated whether they should pack up and leave early and decided to tough it out and she's glad they did. If they'd left, she wouldn't have tripped with Everett and it would have been very sad, indeed, if she'd missed that experience. It was the most incredible one she's ever had and she's still trying to make sense of it. This much she does know—it changed her life. She might not know how yet and maybe never will completely, but she knows it did, knows it and feels it. She settles back in the seat and wraps the sleeping bag tighter around herself and closes her eyes.

She and Valerie and Sandy spent a lot of time with Everett and his two friends on that hillside, listening to music and enduring the rain, talking and sharing food and smoking pot—Sandy passed on the pot, of course—and by the time Sandy was up and dancing to Sly & the Family Stone's music, they'd become a clan, like the many that had formed in the large tribe assembled at the festival, like brothers and sisters, watching out and doing things for each other and walking around together during lulls in the performance schedule. At first, they travelled as a group, all six of them together, but then Valerie and Sandy began going off with Everett's friends. No one said as much, but she knew that as she and Everett drew closer together, the others wanted to give them their space, such as it was in a sea of people. No one seemed to mind the fact that she and Everett had become close, sitting close together with an arm around each other and going off hand in hand to take walks. No one gave any indication of feeling neglected by the two of them. They were just being courteous and respectful.

After the conversation in the woods about Everett's trust issues, she made no further mention of it and didn't think the subject would come up again. She was surprised when the next day, a propos of nothing they were talking about at the time, Everett fixed his eyes on hers and said that other than his doc, she was the only person who knew about Mister Black, and that other than his mom, she was the only person he'd told about having a daughter. His two friends found out about his daughter without his having to tell them, because they live in the neighborhood in Everett, and everyone knows everything about everybody there.

Hearing this filled Colleen with joy. It seemed that after struggling hard with the question of whether or not he could trust her, he'd decided he could, and she felt happy and honored. Her feelings for him changed and deepened. Interestingly, despite her being in an almost constant state of horniness because of the pot, she didn't want to find out whether his trusting her meant that he was ready to have sex with her. She didn't want to test that boundary, only to be rebuffed again, and decided that if he wanted to have sex, he'd let her know. As time went on, it didn't seem that he did, which was fine with her.

Since he'd shared with her what he did about himself and decided he could trust her, she told him about the bad reputation she hoped she'd outlived and what had happened with her father and her relationships with Henry, Rocco and Byron. He just listened and nodded and asked the occasional question, but didn't comment about anything and never criticized or judged her, for which she was grateful. He seemed willing to accept her for who she is, flaws and all, and it filled her with a sense of well-being.

They were sitting close together with an arm around each other, listening to Sly & the Family Stone and watching Sandy dance. They'd smoked a joint at the beginning of the band's set and Colleen was flying. She didn't know if she felt so high because of the cumulative effect of all the marijuana in her system, or if it was this particular type of pot, but she began experiencing the music in a new way. She had the sensation that the sounds of the different instruments were resonating in different parts of her body; the guitar between her legs; the bass guitar in her stomach; the drums in her chest; the trumpet in her breasts and particularly in her nipples, which tingled each time the trumpet sounded; and the organ and voices in her head.

She became aware of Everett looking at her and looked at him and saw that he was smiling with his eyebrows raised slightly and holding up a tiny pill between his thumb and forefinger. She knew it was acid. He'd told her earlier that he was going to take it before The Who came on. He'd said he was a huge fan of The Who and was pretty sure they were going to play a lot of songs from *Tommy*, which he loves, and wanted to experience it tripping. He hadn't asked her if she wanted to drop acid with him, but knew she was curious about the experience and now here he was holding it up and looking at her questioningly and she just stared at the pill.

He'd shared more with her about his acid trips, and she knew that the experience could be an ecstatic or hair-raising one and sometimes both and she thought hard about whether she wanted to risk having a bad trip and especially here, exposed on a hillside in a sea of people. What if she freaked out and began acting crazily, spinning in circles and pulling her hair and screaming at the top of her lungs? What would Valerie and Sandy think if that happened? Still, she was determined to experience tripping. If she didn't, she'd always regret it and wonder what she'd missed.

Finally, she looked up at his eyes and then back at the pill and reached out and took it, put it in her mouth and swallowed it with a gulp. Everett had another pill in his hand did the same with it, then leaned toward her and she toward him and they kissed and it felt to her that with that kiss, her fate was sealed. She felt Everett give her an encouraging squeeze and pulled back her head slightly and looked at him and tried to put on as brave a face as possible. The truth was that while she was excited by the prospect of finding out what tripping was like and looking forward to finally experiencing it, she was also fearful. What was done was done, though, and there was no turning back. She'd just have to deal with whatever was going to happen.

Blind Faith's song *Sea of Joy* came to mind. She'd spoken with Henry on the phone a week or so ago, the first time in a long time, and he recommended the band's just released debut album, and she bought it and listened to it and liked it. *Sea of Joy*, with its mysterious feel, stood out and its lyrics proved haunting. They came to mind often and now she felt she understood for the first time the meaning of the lyric, "Waiting in our boats to set sail, sea of joy." That's exactly how she felt, like she and Everett were waiting in their boats to set sail, hopefully, on a sea of joy.

By the time Sly & the Family Stone were playing *Stand* she had a taste in her mouth like aluminum foil and she was aware of the pot high being replaced by a new and different sensation and a change occurring in her perception of things. The members of the band now looked like puppets and moved like them too. She saw strings attached to their heads and shoulders and elbows and hands and feet that led up into the sky and she looked up expecting to see puppeteers, hovering above the stage and manipulating the strings, but didn't. What she did see was a star-filled sky, which was odd because the sky had been overcast, and that the stars were much brighter than usual and not all white, but also red and blue and green and that some of them looked like Fourth of July sparklers. She looked back at the stage and now Sly Stone was a black bird, wearing sunglasses, flapping his long feathery wings and jumping up and down and she expected him to take flight at any moment, but he didn't.

The first frightening moment came when the band had finished their set and the stage was being readied for The Who. She and Everett had their faces close together with their foreheads almost touching. They were talking urgently in hushed voices, sharing with each other what they were experiencing, and the features of his face began changing, morphing into one face after another. She told him with alarm what she was seeing, and he said not to worry about it, that it was a "common hallucination." The idea struck her as absurdly oxymoronic. She thought he must know what he's talking about, though, having done so much acid. It put her at ease a bit, but it was still weird and unsettling. She was frightened again when his face began to sag and the skin looked like it was going to melt. She told him about that too and again he said not to worry about it, that it was also a common hallucination.

The Who began their set and, just as with Sly & the Family Stone, they looked and moved like puppets. She saw the same strings attached to them and, just as with Sly Stone, Roger Daltrey turned into a bird, this one a white one with long outstretched wings.

She looked up at the sky and was amazed to see the stars arranged to spell the word "HEAVEN," but only for a moment and then they raced back to their original positions. She closed her eyes and concentrated on listening to the music. Snatches of lyrics appeared, like purple neon signs, on the insides of her eyelids: "ETERNAL LIFE" and "NEVER DIE." They lingered a moment and then slowly faded away.

She opened her eyes and looked up at the sky again and the stars began slowly coming closer and she realized it wasn't the stars that were moving, but Earth, that it had begun moving toward them and was picking up speed. Another lyric from *Sea of Joy* came to mind: "Once the door swings open into space and I'm already waiting in disguise, or is it just a thorn between my eyes?" There *is* a door that opens into space, she thought, and her outward appearance *is* a disguise, skin stretched over bone, masking her true self, who's a stranger to her, and her nose *is* just like a thorn between her eyes, sticking out and always in her field of vision, looking as big as a rhinoceros's horn, as it does to her now. These things were perfectly obvious to her, and it seemed odd that she hadn't been aware of them until now.

She closed her eyes again and saw a path, stretching before her as far as she could see. She looked up and saw a blue sky filled with puffy white clouds and people in white robes, cinched with gold cords, gathered at the clouds' edges, looking down at her. She looked down and saw beneath the path on either side a fiery landscape filled with naked people, whose skin was seared black from the flames. They looked hopeless and wailed as they shuffled along slowly and wandered aimlessly.

She began walking and saw a person appear on the path in the distance, walking toward her. Even at a distance, she could make him out. He was an older man, dressed in a shimmering silver robe, wearing sandals and carrying a staff. The top of his head was bald and the long golden hair at the sides of his head draped around his shoulders, and his long golden beard flowed almost to the ground. A raven sat on one of his shoulders and a chimpanzee on the other.

She knew he was a sage and that there was an important question she needed to ask him, and she began reviewing her life from that moment, moving backward in time. She considered every thought and action, every decision and its consequences. By the time she neared him she'd arrived at the moment of her birth and was wondering what the point of it all was. They both stopped and stood facing each other and the sage looked down at her knowingly. "Why?" she asked. She searched his eyes hopefully as he studied hers impassively.

"I can't explain," he finally said.

Hearing this she felt profoundly disappointed. All her life she'd been asking herself that question and the thought that not even this wise man could answer it, that there might not be an answer, filled her with despair. He looked down at the path beside her and she looked where he was looking and saw a child of three or four years old, with curly blonde hair and wearing only white underpants, standing beside her. The child could have been a boy or a girl and she had the strong sense that it was herself at that age and then she heard the sage say, "It's a boy," as if he were reading her mind and wanted to set her straight, "a son." Yes, she thought, the sage would know. The child must be her son and his name is Tommy. She looked at the sage and he narrowed his eyes.

"What about the boy?" he asked. "He saw it all."

Yes, she knew the sage was right. Somehow Tommy had seen it all, had witnessed every moment of her life, had watched her time and again get on her knees and open her mouth and make herself a receptacle for boy's sperm. The thought of it filled her with disgust and shame. What kind of mother would subject her son to that, even unknowingly? What kind of person?

She looked down at Tommy and he looked up at her. "You didn't see it," she insisted. Even as she said it, she knew it was futile and wrong to try to convince him of that and she took another tack. "Never tell a soul what you know is the truth," she said. He stared at her blankly and she watched as his eyes became opaque and unfocused and unblinking. She looked up at the sage and saw him looking down at Tommy, studying him. Finally, the sage looked at her accusingly.

"Deaf, dumb and blind boy," he said.

She knew it was true, and that Tommy had become so because the knowledge of what she'd done was too much for him to bear. She'd been so concerned about her bad reputation and so hoped that it had been forgotten, as if *it* were the problem. No, the problem was what she'd done, and she knew the reason why lay at the heart of who she is, at the core of her being. She wouldn't bother to ask the sage why. She knew his answer would be, "I can't explain."

She looked down at Tommy and knew it was pointless to ask but did anyway. "Tommy, can you hear me?" she asked, and then again, louder, and again, shouting, as if that would make a difference. She looked at the sage and he turned and began walking in the direction he came from, and she knew to follow him and took Tommy by the hand.

They weren't walking long before the sage stopped and stepped aside, and she and Tommy stopped and she saw a gypsy caravan in the middle of the path. The sage swept his staff toward it and she and Tommy walked on and climbed up the steps into the back of it.

The space inside was dark, except for the light from a few flickering candles and a brightly glowing crystal ball on the floor in front of a woman, seated behind it on a cushion. The woman had long, jet black curly hair and a red silk scarf tied around her head. She wore a red robe decorated with odd-looking white symbols that were constantly rearranging themselves to form new patterns. Colleen knew the symbols had meaning and that each new pattern had a different one, but she had no idea what. The woman gazed at her serenely and then looked at Tommy and smiled salaciously. After a long moment, the woman looked back at Colleen and her smile faded and her stare turned icy.

"I'm the Gypsy," the woman said, "the Acid Queen."

The woman stood and reached out her hand. Colleen put Tommy's hand into it and the woman led him to the rear of the space. She parted a curtain hanging there and the two of them disappeared behind it. Colleen watched the curtain fall back and no sooner had it settled, than the space on the other side of the curtain was suddenly illuminated by bright light and the curtain became transparent. She saw the woman and Tommy standing, facing each other. She watched as the woman lowered herself and knelt in front of him and slowly pulled his underpants down around his ankles. The woman glanced up at him and put the flat of her hands on his chest and slowly brought them down to his penis. She put it in her mouth and moved her hands to his buttocks and drew him to her. Tommy just stood there, staring straight ahead. Colleen knew that, as Tommy's mother, she shouldn't be allowing the woman to do what she was to him, but she also knew it would cure him and that was more important. She knew too, that the woman wanted her to watch and that watching would be beneficial to her. She didn't understand how or why, but she knew it would be, and she did.

She glanced down at the crystal ball and saw herself on her knees in front of one of the many boys she'd serviced. She couldn't recognize him and it wasn't important. She lowered herself to the floor and sat staring at the scene in the crystal ball. She watched as boy after boy stood in front of her and she serviced them robotically. Who is that girl, she wondered, and why is she doing what she is? Is she trying to prove something to herself or perhaps to someone else? Why did she begin in the first place? Did something happen to cause her to? Something must have, but what?

The scene in the crystal ball changed. She saw a little girl around Tommy's age, sitting on the couch beside a man old enough to be her father. The resemblances between the little girl and herself at that age and the man and her father when he was younger were strong, but they were different people. The little girl was snuggled against the man and gazed up at him adoringly and he gazed down at her tenderly. The man's hands were in his lap and Colleen watched as he unzipped his pants, keeping his eyes on the little girl. He fished out his penis and reached over and took the little girl's hand and drew it to it. The little girl glanced down at the man's penis and then looked back up at him apprehensively. The man smiled reassuringly and wrapped her little hand around his penis and the little girl began stroking it, keeping her eyes on the man's. The little girl's expression was a questioning one now. She was searching the man's eyes and clearly seeking his approval and reassurance that what she was doing was good. Finally, the man smiled and nodded and the little girl smiled and looked relieved and pleased with herself. The little girl stroked the man's penis until it was erect and then he put his hand on the back of her head and gently guided her mouth to it. The little girl opened her mouth and wrapped her lips around the head of his penis and closed her eyes and sucked happily and contentedly.

What was happening between the little girl and the man seemed like a ritual. Colleen had the feeling they'd done these many times and always in the same way. She'd never done this with her father. If she had she certainly would have remembered it, wouldn't she? Did she want to, though, and did he? When she was the little girl's age, she wanted to please her father in every way possible. Had he wanted her to do what the little girl was doing, she gladly would have. That's how much she loved and admired him. Is that why she began doing what she did with boys? Was she using them as surrogates for her father? Did she treat them disrespectfully because she was punishing her father for not allowing her to please him in that way? Where would she have gotten the idea to do it? A girl that age isn't aware of such things.

The scene in the crystal ball changed again. She was standing in the upstairs hall in her parent's house, in front of their bedroom door. The door was closed, but slowly swung open, as some of the doors in the house do, if not shut tightly. There was her mother in her business clothes, on her knees with her face in her father's lap and her hands on his thighs. He was sitting on the side of the bed with his legs spread wide. Colleen could only see his legs, but his underwear and pants were down around his ankles and he had on his shoes. Her father pointed toward the doorway and her mother lifted her head from his lap and as she did, Colleen saw her father's penis emerge from her mouth. Her mother looked at her, leaned back and closed the door, but not before Colleen got a good look at her father's erect penis and saw her own reflection in her parents' full-length mirror. She only saw it for an instant but got enough of a look to see that she was wearing the pajamas she used to wear when she was the little girl's age. Did this really happen? Wouldn't she have remembered a scene like that? Had she repressed the memory, the way Tommy had his memory of her, on her knees, servicing boys?

The crystal ball flew away and began bouncing around the room, off the walls and ceiling and floor, just like a pinball. She looked toward the woman and Tommy and saw the woman was now sitting in front of her, just where she'd been when they arrived, only it wasn't the Gypsy, the Acid Queen, but her mother, gazing at her with that serene expression of hers and dressed just as she was in the bedroom.

Colleen looked past her mother and saw not Tommy, but her four- or five-year-old self, wearing the same pajamas. Her young self stood stiffly erect, facing her, staring blankly into space with her arms held at her sides. Moira and Jeanine and Kathy and Jessica appeared and stood flanking her, dressed in white robes, looking like disciples. They stared accusingly at Colleen, and she looked back at her mother. She *was* in competition with her mother for her father's love and her mother *knew* it, which is why her mother treated her so coolly. Colleen resented her both because she withheld her love from her and because her mother was able to do things with her father that she couldn't.

She was aware that the music had stopped and heard a man shout into the microphone, "I think this is a pile of shit! While John Sinclair rots in prison—!" She opened her eyes and saw Pete Townsend, holding his guitar like a weapon, and a man tumbling off the stage to the applause and cheers of the crowd. She turned to Everett and saw him staring wide-eyed at the stage and grinning. "What happened?" she asked.

"Pete Townsend just knocked Abby Hoffman off the stage. Serves him right for being a loudmouth." He looked at her. "Where've you been?" he asked. "How're you doing?"

Where had she been? How was she doing? She didn't even know where to begin and just stared at him with a blank expression.

She feels the car slowing and opens her eyes just enough to see they're approaching the Vails Gate exit on the Thruway. Good. She'll be home soon and soaking in that nice hot bath. Sandy looks over her shoulder at her.

"Almost there," Sandy says. "Howya doin'?"

"Fine," Colleen mumbles and closes her eyes again.

Pete Townsend was really pissed off about the incident and told the crowd, "The next fucking person who walks across this stage is gonna get killed! All right?" He looked and sounded like he meant it too. The incident and Townsend's anger changed Colleen's mood completely. It was like she'd been gliding along the surface of an ice-covered pond and suddenly the ice broke and she fell in frigid water. She began trembling and then shaking. Was she freaking out? Was that what was happening? Everett put his arm around her shoulder and held her tight and she pressed her forehead against his chest. "I'm frightened," she said. "I don't know why, but I am."

"Let's go," he said.

He drew her to her feet and turned and she wrapped her arms around his waist and pressed her forehead against his back between his shoulder blades and closed her eyes. She heard Valerie call, "Colleen! You alright?" but didn't turn and answer. She didn't want to see anybody or anything. She just wanted Everett to lead her out of there, anywhere. She didn't care where. She just knew that wherever he took her would be better than where she was.

She shuffled along after him, trusting him to lead her safely out of the sea of people. She had no idea how long it took them to finally reach the edge of the crowd but when they did, he put his hands on hers and took them from around his waist and turned and put his arms around her and kissed her. His kiss felt electric and she put her arms around his waist and held him as tightly as she could. She had no intention of stopping kissing him—ever. She wanted to stay just as they were and enjoy the feeling of the electricity flowing from his lips into hers and throughout her body. The longer they kissed, the more she felt the electricity was her lifeblood and that if she stopped kissing him, she'd die. She was surprised that she didn't when he finally took his lips away, and that she now felt perfectly calm and warm and glowing. He smiled down at her and took her hand and led her toward the pond.

As they approached it, she saw the surface of the water was churning and thought it must be because the pond is stocked with bass. She remembered her father telling her on a fishing trip when she was a kid that they feed at night. The closer she and Everett got, though, the less she thought the type of turbulence she was seeing was caused by fish the size of bass and when they arrived at the edge of the pond, she saw the backs of creatures the size of dolphins breaking the surface of the shimmering water. The pond was teeming with them and she stood looking at them as they writhed in the water. They looked like eels, but she knew they weren't. They were much too big and had iridescent spearhead-shaped scales on their backs. They were serpents of some sort and they transfixed her. "What do you see?" she heard Everett ask and looked up at him. "Serpents," she said. "Don't you see them?" He smiled at her and began unbuttoning his shirt. "What are you doing?" she asked with alarm.

"Getting undressed. Let's go for a swim."

She looked at him incredulously and then back at the creatures. "In there? With them?" she asked and looked up at him.

"Don't worry," he said knowingly. "They're harmless."

He looked and sounded so confident. She wanted to believe him but was hesitant. She was surprised that he was speaking in another language now. It was the oddest thing. What he said sounded something like, "Doan twere. Dare hahmless," but she understood him perfectly.

"You'll see," he said in that curious language of his and pulled off his shirt.

They got out of their clothes, Colleen reluctantly, and stood naked, facing each other, gazing at each other's eyes. Everything about Everett had changed. He was not at all shy or distrustful of her. He seemed bold and courageous. He took her hand and led her into the water, which was surprisingly warm. As they waded in, she kept her eyes on the writhing serpents, now a little farther out in the center of the pond. When she was in up to her chest, she felt something smooth slide between her legs, rubbing against the insides of her thighs and her crotch. It startled but thrilled her and the pleasure she felt was enormous and no sooner had whatever it was slid through, than she felt another just like it slide between her legs. When that one slid through, she parted her legs more, welcoming the creatures to come and please her and they did, time and again.

Everett positioned himself behind her and she felt his body press against hers, in particular his hard penis, which was much warmer than the water and felt fantastic nestled between her buttocks. She felt his hands cup her breasts and the feeling of him caressing them, as he nuzzled the back of her ear and his penis pressed harder and deeper between her buttocks and the creatures slid between her legs, was blissful.

"Come on," she heard him murmur in that curious language of his and he stood beside her and dived into the water. She dove after him and touched his back and felt her way along it to his shoulders and put her hands around his neck and lay stretched out on his back and now he was carrying her along, breaking the surface of the water and diving beneath it, just like the creatures swimming around them.

How long were they swimming? An instant? Eternity? She had no idea. Time seemed suspended, or non-existent. It didn't matter. Everett flipped her and himself over and faced her. He lay on top of her, and she felt herself and him being lifted up on the back of one of the creatures. She put her arms around his neck and he put his around her waist and they kissed and she parted her legs and he entered her and she wrapped her legs tightly around him.

Round and round they went on the back of the creature, breaking the surface of the water and slipping beneath it again. Each time they slipped beneath the surface, she closed her eyes and held her breath and each time they surfaced, she opened them and took a breath. She could just make out Everett's features in the darkness, gazing at her as he thrust inside her. They slipped beneath the surface and surfaced again, and she was startled to see not Everett's face but her father's, not as he looks now but, as he did when he was Everett's age, looking just as he does in his college photos. She felt panic-stricken and her body went rigid.

Why is this happening? She doesn't want to have sex with her father. The idea disgusts her. She tried to will her father's image away but couldn't. It came and went. They'd surface and there it would be. They'd surface again and there would be Everett. Then it occurred to her. It isn't because she wants to have sex with her father. It's because she knows he wants to have sex with her. As much as she liked to believe she was rid of him and that he no longer had power over her, she realized she'd been kidding herself. She escaped his house, but not his presence in her head. Even now, tripping with Everett and making love with him, her father can muscle in and have his way with her. She wished him dead but despaired that even dead he'd still be in her head. She wished herself dead. At least then she'd finally be rid of him or hoped she would be. Who knew? She wished she'd never been born or could be reborn as a new person.

They surfaced again and now the face she saw was neither Everett's nor her father's, but the one she visualized when she was on her knees, servicing some boy—Jesus's. It took her breath away, but she understood why he'd appeared. If she were to be reborn as a new person, with no memory of her past, it would be miraculous and who better to perform the miracle than Jesus? He'd do it through Everett, just as God impregnated Mary through the Holy Spirit. He'd plant the seed of her new person in Everett and Everett would plant it in her and she would nurture it and it would grow and slowly inhabit her body, forcing out all the bad memories from her past and especially the ones lurking deep in her subconscious until not a trace of them remained, most important, of her father.

They submerged and resurfaced and now Jesus was gone and Everett was back. She felt the creature beneath her slowing and the feel of it changing. Its back had felt supple and rounded but now it felt hard and flat. Everett took her hands from around his neck and spread her arms wide and she felt her hands attach to something, also hard and flat. He took her legs from around his waist and spread them wide and she felt her feet attach to the same hard flat thing. They'd stopped moving now and whatever it was she was attached to began tilting slowly forward until she was upright, waist-deep in the water. She pictured Jesus on the cross and felt like she was about to be crucified too, although she imagined that whatever she was attached to wasn't shaped like a cross but an X. Yes, she *was* about to be crucified, crucified for all the sins her old self had committed, so that she could die and be reborn a new person, innocent and pure.

Everett looked different now and was looking at her differently. He looked like an incubus about to ravage her, although she wasn't sleeping. At least she didn't think she was. Still, she knew he was doing Jesus's bidding. She's no stranger to the sacred and profane comingling. That's what happened every time she serviced a boy, was on her knees, imagining it was Jesus she was worshipping.

Everett wrapped his hands around her wrists and she closed her eyes, and with each thrust reviewed another of her sins. One by one she worked her way through them and as she did, was filled with an overwhelming sense of humiliation and sorrow and shame. She couldn't help the person she was in the past. She did the things she did deliberately and willfully. She might not understand why she was who she was then and acted the way she did, but she was ready to repent and atone for her sins.

Everett began grunting and growling and pushing harder against her and deeper inside her and she felt him flowing into her and when he finally came to rest and withdrew, she felt the seed of her new self inside.

She feels the car break and slow and opens her eyes just enough to see that they're at her exit on 9W in Cornwall. Her last evening with Rocco comes to mind and she closes her eyes and forces the memory away by picking up where she left off in her recollection of the trip.

The first thing she was aware of in her new life was that loud music was playing, but it didn't sound familiar. She was listening to it but not listening. It was just there—a presence. She was aware of lying on her back and opened her eyes and saw a gray overcast sky, which was surprising, since she and Everett had just been in the pond in the dark. She stared at the sky like a newborn, seeing it for the first time and finding everything about it fascinating, but comprehending nothing about what she was seeing. It was like watching a movie filmed entirely in gray tones, in which random cloud shapes became objects or bodies or faces. The images all seemed interrelated and as each new one appeared, the story continued to unfold in her mind. The story had no plot, no meaning, no message or moral. The point of the story seemed to be simply that it kept unfolding.

Two cawing crows flew overhead, their caws sounding much louder to her than the loud background noise. Their cries and passage seemed to mark the beginning of a new scene in the movie. In this one, a prancing pig, a saltshaker, a dog's head, a coat button and a mermaid appeared. She didn't question the story unfolding in her mind. She simply watched the movie and accepted it. The story was baffling to her, but she trusted it made sense, just as she trusted the happenings in her own life made sense, although there was much about them that didn't seem to sometimes. In fact, there seemed to be just as much point to the story in the clouds as there was to her life, which was unfolding according to its own logic and seemed to have direction. Whether or not she understood the point of it all, or where she was headed was unimportant. The important thing was that she'd been reborn. Her soul was still blemished, but at least she hadn't sinned in her new life. That was important.

At some point, she became aware of Valerie's and Sandy's faces coming into view and looking down at her with concern and then disappearing. Sometimes both of their faces appeared, and she could see they were talking about her. It wasn't important. She kept her eyes on the sky and watched the movie and followed the story unfolding in her mind. She knew that was what she was supposed to do and that it was of utmost importance that she did, that everything that happened in her life from this point forward—every word spoken, every action taken, every decision made—depended on it.

Finally, she watched the movie slowly fade to black, just as she imagined she'd watch whatever room she might be in at the end of her life slowly fade to black as she passed out of this life. After that, there was nothing.

When she opened her eyes, she realized her mind and body had simply been too exhausted to remain awake and she'd crashed. She didn't know how long she'd been sleeping, but probably a long time. Glancing at herself, she thought it curious that she was dressed just as she'd been when she and Everett left and went to the pond. She had no recollection of having gotten dressed after what happened there and none of walking back to the hillside. Had they even left? Did she just imagine it all? Was it all just a hallucination?

When she finally came around enough to sit up, her head spinning and her stomach queasy, she looked at Everett and saw him sitting with his knees up and his arms wrapped around his legs, dressed just as he'd been when they left, staring blankly toward the stage. She studied his profile and couldn't see a trace of the person he'd become at the pond. Then she noticed his shaking.

She stands in the driveway, hugging her sleeping bag, and watches Valerie and Sandy slowly pull away. She sees Valerie wave out the open driver's side window and returns the wave, then turns and walks down the driveway and into the house and finds that no one is home. Her mother's car is in the driveway, so she and Sheldon must be off doing something for the afternoon. It's just as well. She doesn't feel like talking to anyone now.

She stands in front of the washer in the laundry room, pulling off her mud-caked clothes and throwing them in as the washer fills with water. When they're all in, she closes the lid and walks to her bathroom and begins filling the tub with water. As it fills, she stands in front of the mirror and studies herself. The word that comes to her mind is "frightful," but it's followed by another that she feels best describes the person she sees: "haunted." She looks exhausted and weary. The experience at the festival was an ordeal and enduring it seems to have aged her. She's most struck by her eyes, which stare back at her like those of a person who's seen a vision and is now haunted by it and probably always will be.

The tub filled, she turns off the faucet and climbs in and lowers herself gingerly into the just-shy-of-too-hot-water and stretches out, settling back with the water up to her chin and her eyes closed.

She didn't enjoy the festival very much after coming down. The acid took its toll on her. Her head felt like it was filled with dense fog that wouldn't lift and her queasiness persisted. Shortly after she woke, Joe Cocker and the Grease Band performed and when they finished their set, the rain came and lasted for hours. Valerie and Sandy sat huddled together under one of Sandy's tarps and Colleen and Everett under the other. His two friends sat with their sleeping bags over their heads and the bags got soaked and never did dry out, which made sleeping in them uncomfortable that night and they ended up sleeping on them.

Her time spent under the tarp with Everett was a bizarre experience. He was silent for a long time and seemed very withdrawn and it finally dawned on her that perhaps he'd taken more acid and was tripping again. As it happened, she was right. When she finally asked if he was okay, he put a finger to his lips and shushed her and said he was listening to Mister Black. Judging from his expression, intense and concerned, and the twitching of his head, which was more frequent and pronounced than it had been in the woods, it seemed to her that whatever Mister Black was saying to him was disturbing. From time to time, Everett's eyes would widen and the vein in his forehead would bulge and she honestly thought he was about to begin shrieking like a mad person, but he didn't.

He'd just begin breathing heavily and rapidly and that seemed to calm him down to the point where he could get himself back under control. As fantastic as her experience was on acid, she wondered what Everett's experience was like. Whatever it was, she didn't think it was worth the anguish the drug caused him or that he was doing himself any good by taking so much of it.

Much later, after Everett had crashed and slept and Crosby, Stills, Nash & Young were performing in the wee hours of Monday morning, she asked him what he remembered about the trip they'd taken together and if he remembered going to the pond. He looked at her and raised his eyebrows slightly.

"Why?" he asked, just loud enough to be heard over the music. "Do you?"

She shrugged. "I think I do," she said, "but I'm not sure if it really happened or if I just imagined it." He smiled impishly.

"Reality's tricky," he said. "Anyway, what does it matter? You experienced what you experienced. That's all that matters."

He took a joint from his shirt pocket, which seemed to hold an endless supply, and lit it and offered it to her. She really wasn't in the mood to get high but thought that maybe it would clear her head and settle her stomach. She took the joint and inhaled deeply and handed it back to him.

As they smoked and passed the joint back and forth, she thought about Everett's answer, and it fed the sense that had grown in her during the festival that society was being cut loose from its moorings. It no longer mattered what other people thought. All that mattered was what *you* thought, what *you* experienced. Even reality, itself, didn't matter anymore. If *you* thought something was real, then it was.

All this talk about peace and love didn't seem to square with the philosophy that Everett was espousing, which seemed self-absorbed and self-indulgent—just plain selfish. Was that where the country was headed? A society filled with people like that? She wondered what such a society would be like? Enlightened? No, more likely dysfunctional and hostile. How could it not be? Her only consolation was that the pot did clear her head and settle her stomach. It didn't make her feel horny, though, and she thought it was because her body was just too worn out to feel that way.

Valerie and Sandy wanted to leave during Jimi Hendrix's performance and Colleen had had enough of the festival and was ready to go. She and Everett exchanged telephone numbers and mailing addresses and asked each other to get in touch. She was doubtful that she'd ever hear from him again and she could tell he felt the same way about her. Would they contact each other? Well, she thought, time would tell.

They said their good-byes and hugged, and she and Valerie and Sandy began the long walk to the car as Jimi Hendrix began playing *The Star-Spangled Banner,* or his version of it, anyway, which sounded angry and mocking. He would play a few notes of the song and then use his guitar to make sounds like bombs falling through the air and exploding, then play a few more notes and make more bombs-falling-and-exploding sounds. He was clearly commenting musically on the war in Vietnam and proclaiming his opposition to it. Beyond that, she wasn't sure what message he was trying to convey. That America is belligerent and warmongering or just the Nixon Administration? She'd read that Hendrix served in the military and was a paratrooper and hated the experience. Did he just have a gripe with the Army?

Whatever his message was, it came as no surprise to her that Hendrix was against the war in Vietnam. Everyone at the festival was, as far as she could tell, although where the young men were concerned, she wasn't sure if they were against it on principle or because they didn't want to be drafted and sent to fight in it. She was struck by the fact that Hendrix followed his politically charged version of the national anthem with *Purple Haze* and it caused her to think again about Everett's use of psychedelics and his drug-induced philosophy and the fact that so many people seem to be where he is. Life is all about *them* and how *they* view it and what *they* want.

She hears her mother and Sheldon arriving home and glances at the closed bathroom door. They're chatting happily, as they always do and in a way that her mother and father never did. She sighs and closes her eyes.

Well, she thinks, that's the type of decade it's been, filled with conflict and struggle, with people fighting for their rights, fighting to change society for the better, or so they believe. Living in the U.S. is becoming like swimming in a swift-flowing river filled with powerful currents, pushing and pulling her this way and that. To get where she wants to go, she's going to have to learn to negotiate them. And where she wants to go is into the law and possibly politics, to fight for civil rights and the right of women to be treated equally and fairly in society and be allowed to make their own decisions about their bodies.

She smiles as she remembers what Valerie and Sandy told her about what happened when she was tripping. The three of them were walking to the car with the sound of Jimi Hendrix fading in the distance. She was reluctant to broach the subject, for fear of hearing something she'd rather not hear, although she had no idea what that might be, but her curiosity was just too great and she finally asked, "Did Everett and I leave during The Who?"

"Leave?" Valerie asked, her eyebrows knitted and clearly puzzled.

Colleen told them she thought she and Everett had gone to the pond and Valerie and Sandy looked at each other and laughed and then looked back at her with big grins.

"Gone to the pond?" Valerie said dismissively, as if it were the most absurd thing she'd ever heard. "You didn't go *anywhere.*"

Sandy shook her head and smiled at her.

"You kept trying to take off your clothes," Sandy said. "I had everything I could do to keep them on you. You were all over Everett. You wanted to fuck him in the worst way. He was pretty out of it. I don't think he was even aware of what was happening."

* * *

Finally home, she lies in the hot bath, enjoying the feel of it. She's been thinking about taking this bath for days now, to wash off the mud, but more important to purify and rejuvenate herself. She takes a deep breath and holds it, slides down the tub until her entire body is submerged.

She'll be off to Barnard in the fall and plans to attend Columbia law school after that. She doesn't know what the future holds in store, for herself or the country, hopefully, great things, but she's filled with a sense of purpose and determination and is ready to face whatever comes next, and to hell with her father and her bad reputation. She holds her breath until she can't any longer and sits up and takes what feels like the deepest breath she's ever taken and the first breath of her new life.

Dave Gioia

A Girl with a Bad Reputation